PRAISE FOR *IN MY DREAMS I HOLD A KNIFE*

"Tense, twisty, and packed with shocks, Ashley Winstead's assured debut dares to ask how much we can trust those we know best—including ourselves. A terrific read!"

—Riley Sager, *New York Times* bestselling author of *Home Before Dark*

"Deeply drawn characters and masterful storytelling come together to create an addictive and riveting psychological thriller. Put this one at the very top of your 2021 reading list."

—Liv Constantine, international bestselling author of *The Last Mrs. Parrish*

"Fans of *The Secret History*, Ruth Ware, and Andrea Bartz will devour this dark academic thriller with an addictive locked-room mystery at its core. Ten years after an unsolved campus murder, the victim's best friends reunite, knowing one might be a monster—but is anyone innocent? Over the course of a single shocking night, Ashley Winstead peels back lie after lie, exposing the poisoned roots of ambition, friendship, and belonging itself. An astonishingly sure-footed debut, *In My Dreams I Hold a Knife* is the definition of compulsive reading. The last page will give you nightmares."

—Amy Gentry, bestselling author of *Good as Gone*, *Last Woman Standing*, and *Bad Habits*

"Beautiful writing, juicy secrets, complex female characters, and drumbeat suspense—what more could you want from a debut thriller? I'm Ashley Winstead's new biggest fan. If you liked Marisha Pessl's *Neverworld Wake* or Laurie Elizabeth Flynn's *The Girls Are All So Nice Here*, trust me—you will love this."

—Andrea Bartz, bestselling author of *The Lost Night* and *The Herd*

"With its compelling puzzle box structure and delightfully ruthless cast of characters, this twisty dark academia thriller will have you flipping pages like you're pulling an all-nighter to cram for a final. *In My Dreams I Hold a Knife* is required reading for fans of Donna Tartt's *The Secret History* and Amy Gentry's *Bad Habits.*"

—Layne Fargo, author of *They Never Learn*

"Nostalgic and sinister, *In My Dreams I Hold a Knife* whisks the reader back to college. Glory days, unbreakable friendships, all-night parties, and a belief that the best in life is ahead of you. But ten years after the murder of one of the East House Seven, the unbreakable bonds may be hiding fractured secrets of a group bound not by loyalty but by fear. Twisty and compulsively readable, *In My Dreams I Hold a Knife* will have you turning pages late into the night, not just to figure out who murdered beloved Heather Shelby but to see whether friendships forged under fire can ever be resurrected again."

—Julie Clark, *New York Times* bestselling author of *The Last Flight*

"An unsolved murder, dark secrets, and dysfunctional college days, all wrapped up in a twisty plot that will keep you flipping pages."

—Darby Kane, #1 international bestselling author
of *Pretty Little Wife*

IN MY DREAMS
I HOLD
A KNIFE

A novel

ASHLEY WINSTEAD

CONTENT WARNING: CONTAINS PHYSICAL AND SEXUAL VIOLENCE

Published by Sourcebooks Landmark, an imprint of Sourcebooks
P.O. Box 4410, Naperville, Illinois 60567-4410
(630) 961-3900
sourcebooks.com

Library of Congress Cataloging-in-Publication Data is on file with the publisher.

Printed and bound in the United States of America.
LSC 10 9 8 7 6 5 4 3 2 1

For Don and Linda Tannenbaum, whose kindness changed my life.

CHAPTER 1
NOW

Your body has a knowing. Like an antenna, attuned to tremors in the air, or a dowsing rod, tracing things so deeply buried you have no language for them yet. The Saturday it arrived, I woke taut as a guitar string. All day I felt a hum of something straightening my spine, something I didn't recognize as anticipation until the moment my key slid into the mailbox, turned the lock, and there it was. With all the pomp and circumstance you could count on Duquette University to deliver: a thick, creamy envelope, stamped with the blood-red emblem of Blackwell Tower in wax along the seam. The moment I pulled it out, my hands began to tremble. I'd waited a long time, and it was finally here.

As if in a dream, I crossed the marble floor of my building and entered the elevator, faintly aware of other people, stops on other floors, until finally we reached eighteen. Inside my apartment, I locked the door, kicked my shoes to the corner, and tossed my keys on the counter. Against my rules, I dropped onto my ivory couch in workout clothes, my spandex tights still damp with sweat.

I slid my finger under the flap and tugged, slitting the envelope, ignoring the small bite of the paper against my skin. The heavy invitation sprang out, the words bold and raised. *You are formally invited to Duquette University Homecoming, October 5–7.* A sketch of Blackwell Tower in red ink, so tall the top of the spire nearly broke into the words. *We look forward to welcoming you back for reunion weekend, a beloved Duquette tradition. Enclosed please find your invitation to the Class of 2009 ten-year reunion party. Come relive your Duquette days and celebrate your many successes—and those of your classmates—since leaving Crimson Campus.*

A small red invitation slid out of the envelope when I shook it. I laid it next to the larger one in a line on the coffee table, smoothing my fingers over the embossed letters, tapping the sharp right angles of each corner. My breath hitched, lungs working like I was back on the stationary bike. *Duquette Homecoming.* I couldn't pinpoint when it had become an obsession—gradually, perhaps, as my plan grew, solidified into a richly detailed vision.

I looked at the banner hanging over my dining table, spelling out C-O-N-G-R-A-T-U-L-A-T-I-O-N-S-! I'd left it there since my party two weeks ago, celebrating my promotion—the youngest woman ever named partner at consulting giant Coldwell & Company New York. There'd even been a short write-up about it in the *Daily News*, taking a feminist angle about young female corporate climbers. I had the piece hanging on my fridge—removed when friends came over—and six more copies stuffed into my desk drawer. The seventh I'd mailed to my mother in Virginia.

That victory, perfectly timed ahead of this. I sprang from the couch to the bathroom, leaving the curtains open to look over the city. I was an Upper East Side girl now; I had been an East House girl in college. I liked the continuity of it, how my life was still connected to who I'd been back then. *Come relive your Duquette days,* the invitation said. As I stood

2

in front of the bathroom mirror, the words acted like a spell. I closed my eyes and remembered.

Walking across campus, under soaring Gothic towers, the dramatic architecture softened by magnolia trees, their thick curved branches, waxy leaves, and white blooms so dizzyingly perfumed they could pull you in, close enough to touch, before you blinked and realized you'd wandered off the sidewalk. College: a freedom so profound the joy of it didn't wear off the entire four years.

The brick walls of East House, still the picture in my head when I thought of home, though I'd lived there only a year. And the Phi Delt house at midnight, music thundering behind closed doors, strobe lights flashing through the windows, students dressed for one of the theme parties Mint was always dreaming up. The spark in my stomach every time I walked up the stone steps, eyes rimmed in black liner, arm laced through Caro's. The whole of it intoxicating, even before the red cups came out.

Four years of living life like it was some kind of fauvist painting, days soaked in vivid colors, emotions thick as gesso. Like it was some kind of play, the highs dramatic cliff tops, the lows dark valleys. Our ensemble cast as stars, ever since the fall of freshman year, when we'd won our notoriety and our nickname. The East House Seven. Mint, Caro, Frankie, Coop, Heather, Jack, and me.

The people responsible for the best days of my life, and the worst.

But even at our worst, no one could have predicted that one of us would never make it out of college. Another, accused of murdering her. The rest of us, spun adrift. East House Seven no longer an honor but an accusation, splashed across headlines.

I opened my eyes to the bathroom mirror. For a second, eighteen-year-old Jessica Miller looked back at me, virgin hair undyed and in need of the kind of haircut that didn't exist in Norfolk, Virginia. Bony-elbowed with the skinniness of a teenager, wearing one of those pleated skirts, painted nails. Desperate to be seen.

A flash, and then she was gone. In her place stood thirty-two-year-old Jessica, red-faced and sweaty, yes, but polished in every way a New York consultant's salary could manage: blonder, whiter-teethed, smoother-skinned, leaner and more muscled.

I studied myself the way I'd done my whole life, searching for what others saw when they looked at me.

I wanted them to see perfection. I ached for it in the deep, dark core of me: to be so good I left other people in the dust. It wasn't an endearing thing to admit, so I'd never told anyone, save a therapist, once. She'd asked if I thought it was possible to be perfect, and I'd amended that I didn't need to be perfect, per se, as long as I was the best.

An even less endearing confession: sometimes—rarely, but *sometimes*—I felt I was perfect, or at least close.

Sometimes I stood in front of the bathroom mirror, like now, slowly brushing my hair, examining the straight line of my nose, the pronounced curves of my cheekbones, thinking: *You are beautiful, Jessica Miller.* Sometimes, when I thought of myself like a spreadsheet, all my assets tallied, I was filled with pride at how objectively good I'd become. At thirty-two, career on the rise, summa cum laude degree from Duquette, Kappa sorority alum, salutatorian of Lake Granville High. An enviable list of past boyfriends, student loans *finally* paid off, my own apartment in the most prestigious city in the world, a full closet and a fuller passport, high SAT scores. Any way you sliced it, I was *good.* Top percentile of human beings, you could say, in terms of success.

But no matter how much I tried to cling to the shining jewels of my accomplishments, it never took long before my shadow list surfaced. Everything I'd ever failed at, every second place, every rejection, *mounting, mounting, mounting,* until the suspicion became unbearable, and the hairbrush clattered to the sink. In the mirror, a new vision. The blond hair and white teeth and expensive cycling tights, all pathetic attempts to cover the truth: that I, Jessica Miller, was utterly mediocre and had been my entire life.

No matter how I tried to deny it, the shadow list would whisper: *You only became a consultant out of desperation, when the path you wanted was ripped away. Kappa, salutatorian? Always second best. Your SAT scores, not as high as you were hoping.* It said I was as ordinary and unoriginal as my name promised: *Jessica*, the most common girl's name the year I was born; *Miller*, one of the most common surnames in America for the last hundred years. The whole world awash in Jessica Millers, a dime a dozen.

I never could tell which story was right—Exceptional Jessica, or Mediocre Jessica. My life was a narrative I couldn't parse, full of conflicting evidence.

I picked the brush out of the sink and placed it carefully on the bathroom counter, then thought better, picking it up and ripping a nest of blond hair from the bristles. I balled the hair in my fingers, feeling the strands tear.

This was why Homecoming was so important. No part of my life looked like I'd imagined during college. Every dream, every plan, had been crushed. In the ten years since I'd graduated, I'd worked tirelessly to recover: to be beautiful, successful, fascinating. To create the version of myself I'd always wanted people to see. Had it worked? If I could go back to Duquette and reveal myself to the people whose opinions mattered most, I would read the truth in their eyes. And then I'd know, once and for all, who I really was.

I would go to Homecoming, and walk the familiar halls, talk to the familiar people, insert New Jessica into Old Jessica's story, and see how things changed.

I closed my eyes and called up the vision, by now so familiar it was like I'd already lived it. Walking into the Class of 2009 party, everyone gathered in cocktail finery. All eyes turning to me, conversations halting, music cutting out, champagne flutes lowering to get a better look. Parting the sea of former students, hearing them whisper: *Is that Jessica Miller? She looks incredible. Now that I think about it, I guess she always was the most beautiful girl in school*, and *Did you know she's the youngest-ever female partner at Coldwell New York? I heard she's being featured in* Forbes. *I guess she always was a genius. Wonder why I never paid attention.*

And finally, arriving at my destination: where I always gravitated, no matter the miles or the years. The people who pulled me into their orbit. Mint, Caro, Frankie, Coop. Except this time, no Heather or Jack. This time, Courtney would be there, since she'd reinserted herself so unavoidably. But it would be okay, because this time, I would be the star. Caro would gasp when she saw me, and Frankie would say that even though he ran with models, I was still the prettiest girl he'd ever seen. Courtney would turn green with envy, too embarrassed by how successful I was, how much money I made, to talk about her ridiculous career as a fitness influencer. Mint would drop Courtney's hand like it was on fire, unable to take his eyes off me, and Coop…Coop…

That's where I lost the thread every time.

It was a ridiculous vision. I knew that, but it didn't stop me from wanting it. And thirty-two-year-old Jessica Miller lived by a lesson college Jessica had only started to learn: if you wanted something bad enough, you did anything to get it. Yes, I'd go back and relive my Duquette days, like the invitation said, but this time, I'd do it better. I would be Exceptional Jessica. Show them they'd been wrong not to see it before. Homecoming would be my triumph.

I released the ball of hair into the trash. Even tangled, the highlights were pretty against the Q-tips and wads of white tissue paper.

But in a flash, a vision of torn blond hair, sticky and red, matted against white sheets. I shook my head, pushing away the glitch.

I would show them all. And then I would finally rid myself of that dark suspicion, that insidious whisper—the one that said I'd done it all wrong, made the worst possible mistakes, ever since the day East House first loomed into view through my parents' cracked windshield.

At long last, I was going back.

CHAPTER 2
NOW

The night before I left for Homecoming, I met Jack for a drink. In the weeks since the invite arrived, my excitement had been tempered with guilt, knowing Jack had gotten one, too, but couldn't go back, not in a million years. Traveling across the city to his favorite bar—a quiet, unpretentious dive—was small penance for all the things I'd never be able to atone for. Chief among them, the fact that my whole life hadn't come crashing down around me when I was twenty-two, like his.

I slid into the booth across from him. He tipped his whiskey and smiled. "Hello, friend. I take it you're Duquette-bound?"

We never talked about college. I took a deep breath and folded my hands on the table. "I fly out tomorrow."

"You know…" Jack smiled down at his glass. "I really miss that place. All the gargoyles, and the stained glass, and the flying buttresses." He lifted his eyes back to me. "So pretentious, especially for North Carolina, but so beautiful, you know?"

I studied him. Out of all of us, Jack wasn't the most changed—that was probably Frankie, maybe Mint—but he'd certainly aged more than ten years warranted. He wore his hair long, tucked behind his ears, and he'd covered his baby face with a beard, like a mask. There were premature wrinkles in the corners of his eyes. He was still handsome, but not in the way of the past, that clean-cut handsomeness you'd expect out of a youth-group leader, the boy in the neighborhood you wouldn't think twice about letting babysit.

"I wonder how campus has changed." Jack wore a dreamy smile. "You think the Frothy Monkey coffee shop is still there?"

"I don't know." The affection in his voice slayed me. My gaze dropped to my hands.

"Hey." Jack's tone changed, and I looked up, catching his eyes. Brown, long-lashed, and as earnest as always. How he'd managed to preserve that, I'd never know. "I hope you're not feeling weird on my account. I want you to have fun. I'll be waiting to hear about it as soon as you get back. Do me a favor and check on the Monkey, okay? Heather and I used to go there every Sun—" He cut himself off, but at least his voice didn't catch like it used to. He was getting better. It had been years since he'd called me in the middle of one of his panic attacks, his voice high as a child's, telling me over and over, *I can't stop seeing her body.*

"Of course I'll go." One of the bar's two waitresses, the extra-surly one, slid a glass of wine in front of me and left without comment. "Thanks," I called to her back, sipping and doing my best not to wince while Jack was watching. My usual order was the bar's most expensive glass of red, but that wasn't saying much.

I forced myself to swallow. "What else should I report back on?"

He straightened, excited, and for a second, he looked eighteen again. "Oh man, what do I want to know? Okay, first, I want all the details about Caro and Coop—how did he pop the question, when's the date, what's she wearing?" Jack barreled on, neatly sidestepping the fact that he wasn't invited to the wedding. "Do you think they hooked up in college and kept it a secret from the rest of us? *Ask* her. I want the dirt. Who would've pictured the two of them together? It's so unexpected."

I tipped my glass back and lifted my finger for another, though I knew the waitress hated when I did that. "Mm-hmm," I said, swallowing. "Sure."

Jack grinned. "I need the *full* report on what Coop looks like now. I need to know how many tattoos he has, if he's still rocking that *Outsiders* vibe, if he cut his hair." He tugged a strand of his own hair. "What do you think... Did I get close to the way Coop used to wear it?"

Death by a million paper cuts. "It's very *zero fucks* meets Ponyboy. Classic Coop. Um, what about Caro, anything?"

His gaze turned thoughtful. "I guess I just want to know she's happy. I don't know... Caro never really changes. You talk about her the most, anyway."

He was right. Caro looked and acted exactly the same now as she did then. She still texted me regularly, albeit not every five minutes, like in college. In fact, the only thing that had really changed about Caro was the addition of Coop.

"You have to tell me if Mint still looks like a movie star," Jack said, "or if his hairline is finally receding like his dad's. God, I don't know whether I want you to say he's even more handsome, or his hair is falling out, 'cause that would serve him right. I can't believe he left law school to rescue the family business. There was always something off about his family, right? His dad, or was it his mom? I remember that one time senior year, when Mint lost it—" Jack stopped midsentence, eyes widening. "Oh *crap*, I'm sorry. I'm an idiot."

And there it was. Pity, even from Jack. Because I'd lost Mint, the person who used to make me valuable just by association. And even though no one had been there to witness the breakup, to see how deep the blow had struck, it seemed everyone could sense it anyway.

"First of all," I said, trading the waitress my empty glass for a full one, "that was a long time ago, and I literally could not care less. I'm actually looking forward to seeing Mint. And Courtney. I'm sure they're very happy together." I blinked away a vision of my laptop, shattered against the wall, screen still stuttering on a picture of their wedding. "Second, *crap*? I find it adorable you still don't curse. Once a Boy Scout, always a Boy Scout. Hey," I continued, "did you know Frankie just bought one of Mint's houses?"

Knife, twist. Tit for tat.

"Really?" Jack shrugged, playing nonchalant, but his Adam's apple rose and fell as he swallowed hard. "Good for him. I guess he's getting everything he wanted." He tossed his hair, another stolen Coopism. "Whatever… Everyone in the world sees Frankie every Sunday. Not hard to tell how he's doing. What I really want is for you to come back and tell me Courtney's into new age crystals and meditation, or she does physical therapy with retired racehorses. Something charitable and unexpected."

I almost snorted my wine. "*Courtney?* If she's even one iota less a mean girl, I will consider that immense personal growth."

Jack rolled his eyes. "I said it was my *hope*, not my expectation, Miss Literally-Could-Not-Care-Less."

"Ha."

"You know, I always felt bad for her. Underneath the designer clothes and bitchiness, Courtney seemed like an insecure little girl, desperate to be liked." He gasped, lifting a hand to his chest. "Will you look at that… I *cursed*. Soak it in, 'cause it's not happening again. The Baptist guilt hangover is already setting in."

I shook my head, trying to keep the smile on my face, but inside my heart was breaking.

"Jess." Jack laid his hand over mine. "I really do want you to have fun. For both of us."

Fun. I was going back for so much more than that. I cleared my throat.

"After I give you my report on everyone, my reward is that I finally get to meet Will."

Jack withdrew his hand. "Maybe. You know I like to keep things... separate."

Jack had never introduced me to his boyfriend. Not once in the years since we'd been friends again, which was itself a strange story. When Jack was accused of murdering Heather our senior year, in the few months before he left campus for good, the other students crossed the street wherever he walked, sure down to their bones they were looking at a killer. If he entered a room, everyone stiffened and fled.

But not me. My limbs had remained relaxed, limber, fluid around him—no escalating heartbeat, no tremor in the hands—despite the police's nearly airtight case.

It wasn't a logical reaction. Jack was Heather's boyfriend, the person most likely to kill her, according to statistics. The scissors crusted with Heather's blood—used to stab her, over and over—were found in his dorm room. Witnesses saw Jack and Heather screaming at each other hours before her body was found. The evidence was damning.

But in the end, the police weren't able to convict Jack. In some ways, it didn't matter. He was a murderer in everyone's eyes.

Everyone except for me.

Slowly, inch by inch, my body's knowing filtered into my brain. One night, a year or so after I moved to New York City, I woke in a cold sweat, sitting up rigid as a board in my tiny rented bedroom, filled to the brim with a single conviction: Jack was innocent.

It took me another three months to reach out to him. He was also living in the city, trying to disappear. I'd told him I thought he was innocent, and from that day forward, I'd been one of his few friends. I was his only friend from college, where, until Heather died, he'd been popular. Student body president. Phi Delt treasurer. Duquette University Volunteer of the Year.

To this day, I hadn't told anyone I still saw Jack. He was my secret. One of them, at least.

Looking at him now, radiating kindness, filled me with anger. Jack was undeniably *good*, so easy to read. The fact that so many believed he was capable of brutal violence was baffling. I'd met dangerous people—*truly* dangerous people—and seen the violence in their eyes, heard it brimming in their voices. Jack wasn't like that.

So I understood why he wanted to shield the new people in his life from his past, the horror of the accusation that remained unresolved, despite the dropped charges. It's not like he could ever truly hide it from someone, not with the internet, or the fact that his whole life, he was doomed to menial jobs that wouldn't fire him after a startling Google search. *Or* the fact that he barely spoke to his family anymore. Though, to be fair, that was because of more than Heather, because of their southernness, their Baptistness, their rigidness…

I understood why Jack would want to draw a solid, impenetrable line between *now* and *then*. But still, it was hard to wrap my mind around, because the past was still so much with me. I lived with the constant unfolding of memories, past scenes still rolling, still playing out. I heard my friends' voices in my head, kept our conversations alive, even if for years now it had just been me talking, one-sided, saying, *Just you wait.*

A thrill lifted the small hairs on my arms. Tomorrow, there'd be no more waiting.

Jack sighed. "Thanks for coming to see me before you left. You know, I'm glad you never changed. Seriously. Ten years, and same old Jess."

I nearly dropped my glass. "What are you talking about?" I waved at myself. "This dress is Rodarte. Look at this hair, these nails. I've been in *Page Six*. I've been to Europe, like, *eight times*. I'm totally different now."

Jack laughed as if I was joking and rose from his seat, leaning forward to kiss my forehead. "Never stop being a sweetheart, okay? You're one of the good ones."

I didn't want to be a sweetheart. How uninteresting, how pathetic. But I did want to be one of the good ones, which sounded like an exclusive club. I didn't know how to respond. At least Jack had given me what I'd come here looking for, besides the penance: his blessing. Now I could go to Duquette guilt-free. For that, I held my tongue as he tugged his coat over his shoulders.

He stepped away from the table, then turned back, and there was something in his eyes—worry? Fear? I couldn't quite pin it. "One more thing. I've been getting these letters—"

"Please don't tell me it's the Jesus freaks again, saying you're going to burn in hell for all eternity."

Jack winced. "No. Kind of the opposite." He looked down at me, at my raised brows. "You know what, it's not important. It might not mean anything in the end." He squared his shoulders. "Put your wine on my tab. Clara never makes me pay."

He squeezed my shoulder and took off, winding around the bar's motley collection of chairs. He paused by the door and looked over his shoulder. "Just... When you get to Duquette, say hi to Eric Shelby for me." Then he was out the door, on the sidewalk, carried away by a sea of people.

This time, I actually did spit out my wine. *Eric Shelby*—Heather's younger brother? Eric had been a freshman when we were seniors. I'd never forget the look on his face when he came flying around the corner the day they found Heather, saw the crowd gathered outside our dorm room, scanned it for his sister's face, didn't find her...

The last time I'd seen Eric and Jack in the same place, it was outside the library ten years ago. A crowd had gathered around them. Eric was screaming at Jack that he was a murderer, that he was going to pay for what he'd done to his sister, that even though the cops had let him go, Eric wouldn't stop until he found out the truth. Jack's face had gone white as a ghost's, but he hadn't walked away. He'd stood there taking it with fists clenched as Eric screamed, his friends trying to hold him back by his scrawny, flailing arms. If there was anyone alive who hated Jack Carroll more than Eric Shelby, I didn't know them.

So why the hell would Jack tell me to say hi to him?

CHAPTER 3
AUGUST, FRESHMAN YEAR

The day I moved into Duquette, all I could think about was the fourth grade. We'd moved to Norfolk from Bedford over the summer, so I'd entered fourth grade at a new school, desperately shy. I barely talked to anyone, kept my eyes on my feet and the linoleum floor. Miraculously, my teacher saw something in me and suggested I take the gifted test. I scored high enough to get in, and all of a sudden, everything changed. I was given books to read at the ninth-grade level. Math test after math test came back with big, fat 100s scrawled in red marker. I felt as if a radioactive spider had bitten me and infused me with boldness, like a superpower. I started looking up from the floor to people's faces when they spoke to me, because for the first time, I felt I might be worth the attention.

Fourth grade promised to be the best year of my life. I loved my teacher, Mrs. Rush, a short, blustery woman who swept around the classroom, calling out compliments and ruffling students' hair. The day of our big field trip to the tide pools, I'd gotten permission to go to the bathroom to change into galoshes before we lined up for the bus. I'd studied the animals that lived in tide pools every day after school and had begged my mother to buy me galoshes so I could wade in and show everyone what I'd learned. Like an expert. A gifted student.

But when I arrived back at the classroom, it was empty. The class had left without me. After thirty minutes of waiting for them to realize their mistake, I made my way to the front office. There I sat, for the rest of the day, in an uncomfortable plastic chair. Trying—and failing—to keep myself from crying. For hours, my throat ached.

Mrs. Rush finally appeared in the office near the end of the day. She walked straight to the receptionist and said, "I counted my kids and you're right, I only have thirty-one. But I've racked my brain and can't for the life of me think who I forgot."

The words cleaved me in half. Mrs. Rush, my favorite teacher—the one I felt surely saw me, recognized I was special—couldn't remember I existed. The receptionist gave a small nod in my direction, whispering, "Jessica Miller has been waiting here for hours." Mrs. Rush spun and pressed her hands to her face. "Of course—*Jessica M.* There are just so many Jessicas to keep track of. I'm very sorry."

I let her hug me, ruffle my hair, but I never forgot it. I never forgave her. Most of all, I never absolved myself of the sin of being so utterly forgettable.

It was this tide-pool memory that haunted me on Freshman Move-In Day. Move-In was supposed to be thrilling, a Big Moment marking the transition from childhood to adult life. But all I could think about was that empty classroom, the excitement spiraling into disbelief, then pain. My stomach was a pit of butterflies—and underneath, a thread of something darker.

What was I so afraid of?

The four-and-a-half-hour drive from Norfolk to Winston-Salem felt like a week, thanks to my dad's desire to turn off the radio and talk a mile a minute. First about college and then about anything and everything that popped into his head. This was something new I was still getting used to—a version of my dad who participated. Hell, who spoke. When I was younger, I would've given anything to have a conversation with him, have him take interest in me. But by now, through all our ups and downs, it just felt wrong, like an imposter living inside my dad's skin. The energy with which he pointed out the window and twisted in his seat to ask me questions was too much. Unsustainable. There was no way this upswing could last.

By the time we finally circled downtown Winston-Salem and made our way to the outskirts, where Duquette University sat tucked away like a secret, my mother's knuckles were white against the steering wheel. She'd stopped trying to turn on the radio hours ago and instead drove silently, letting my dad talk and talk.

We took a left, and finally, there it was: the larger-than-life stone arch marking the entrance to Duquette. Just like in the brochures. The butterflies beat their wings. I clutched my stomach in the back seat.

"Well, that does impart a sense of grandeur, doesn't it," said my dad approvingly. Even my mom took her eyes off the road long enough to shoot me an impressed look.

We glided under the arch and onto campus, driving slowly. Duquette was more than grand. Blackwell Tower, home to the chancellor's office, was modeled after the Notre-Dame cathedral in Paris, single spire piercing the sky in a lethal spike, buttresses creeping out the sides like spindly spider legs. In the blazing glory of late August, rows of red crepe myrtles formed a sea of crimson everywhere, the ocean of color interrupted only by gnarled magnolia trees, twisted arms reaching out with scattered white blooms, clinging late into their season. Crimson and white. Blood and spirit, like the Duquette motto: *Mutantur nos et vos, corpus et animam meam. We will change you, body and soul.*

I was ready to be changed.

I shifted to see past the large crack in the windshield, left over from Dad's incident. It had been months now, but we still didn't have the money to replace the windshield, so we'd all learned to lean a little to the left.

"There it is," I breathed. "East House."

Although Blackwell Tower and the Dupont Observatory were the most iconic buildings on campus, I'd fallen hard and fast for East House. It was a modest-sized dormitory nearly covered, root to roof, with thick, green ivy. Though it was one of six halls reserved for freshmen, it was the only one that looked like a castle from a storybook, or a house out of *The Secret Garden*. Carved above the front door were the words "The sun rises in the east."

This beautiful building—this imposing campus—was *my* life now. I'd earned Duquette, been selected out of thousands competing to go to *U.S. News & World Report*'s sixteenth-best college in the country. It may not have been what I'd originally longed for, or what my father expected—it was no Harvard—but it could be the start of something good. A new life. I could be a different person, starting now.

It wasn't until my mom parked that I fully registered the circus of people around us. The dark thread of worry resurfaced.

"Well," said my dad, unbuckling, "guess this is it. Time to see how knockoff Crimson Campus stands up to the real deal." He reached for the door.

"Wait—" All I could think about was what he'd insisted on wearing: his Harvard alumni shirt. For the first time in my life, seeing it brought shame instead of desire. What would all these people—these Duquette students—think? Surely, they would understand the message my father was sending, not just to me anymore, but to all of them.

My mother gave me a sharp look, as always, finely attuned to conflict. "What's wrong?"

I looked back and forth between them. My parents. Both here, though neither wanted to be, for vastly different reasons. It would only take two days, and then they'd strap themselves back into this car and make the return pilgrimage to Norfolk, to do who knows what in their empty house. I could stand it.

"Nothing," I said, leaning back in my seat. "Let's start with the trunk."

My parents ended up leaving earlier than expected, but not before my mother got choked up during a tour of campus—*It was just so expensive; didn't I realize what I was getting myself into?*—and my dad declared the campus pretty, but nowhere near as impressive as Cambridge. And oh, here's an idea, what if I waited a semester and applied again to Harvard as a transfer student? I would never have to tell anyone I'd spent a semester in North Carolina.

After all that, and the hard work of cramming my stuff into the small, cinder-block dorm room, I thought I'd be relieved to see them go. But as soon as I was alone, I bawled like a baby. With a roommate—especially mine, Rachel, who was eerily silent and shot me anxious looks every time I breathed too loud—I had to lie under my comforter to hide my sobs.

College was not what I'd expected. All the other freshmen seemed to become best friends instantly. They were having the time of their lives. In the afternoons I walked down the hall with my head ducked, listening to conversations in doorways about all-night frat parties and hangovers so bad they had to skip 8:00 a.m. classes. In a flash, I was nine years old again, walking into that classroom and finding no one. It was like being invisible. Nothing had changed.

One night I woke at 3:00 a.m. and shuffled to the bathroom, catching two girls stumbling back to their room, actually crying with laughter. They were clearly drunk, but they were also glamorous, in miniskirts and bright lipstick. I'd noticed them before. They were both blond, and one was the most beautiful girl I'd ever seen. Her hair was so glossy. Ever since I'd first spotted her, I'd spent nights wondering what shampoo she used, or if it was just genetics. It was a strange feeling to admire her so intensely from afar, like being half in love.

The other girl was pretty, if you were being generous, but more importantly she seemed wholly at ease in her own skin. She looked people in the eyes and spoke in a loud voice and acted like the universe revolved around her. Which, by the way the beautiful girl clung to her arm, it might. As I watched them together, the ache inside me sharpened to a knifepoint.

The next day was the freshman honor code ceremony, where we all had to sign our names on a contract pledging not to plagiarize. Everyone in our hall, even my roommate, who never opened her mouth to say anything, complained about having to go. It *was* a bit annoying to put on heels and a dress, but I was secretly grateful to be doing something with the whole freshman class, like we all belonged equally. It felt nice to move in a herd from the dorms to Eliot Lawn.

On the way back from the ceremony, the first hints of dusk darkened the summer sky. Someone bumped my elbow, and I turned, apologizing.

"Hey," said the girl, dark eyes lighting up. "You're in my dorm, right? East House, fourth floor?"

"I am." I almost reached out for a handshake, then thought better of it. *Too formal. Too weird.* "Jessica Miller."

"Caroline Rodriguez." She shook out her long, brown hair, which I noticed was almost as glossy as the mystery blond's. "You live with that mute girl, huh?"

The laugh cracked out of me before I could help it. "She's not actually mute, but yeah. Rachel. She pretty much never talks. Or leaves the room."

Caroline rolled her eyes. "That's a nightmare. I have an über-nerd roommate too. Don't tell her I said that if you meet her. Her name is literally Eustice. I don't know how Duquette's algorithm matched us."

"It's a pretty simple algorithm, actually." I was enjoying walking side by side with Caroline and wanted to stretch it out as long as possible. "I researched it, and it's just a bunch of weights assigned to different answers and plugged into a formula. Not very sophisticated."

Caroline stopped walking. "What are you, good at math?" The way she said it sounded like an accusation.

I stopped too. "I guess. I mean, I'm not a savant or anything. Just regular good. I mean, *probably* good. Normal." The truth was, I'd taken hours of extra math classes at the community college back home, trying to build a résumé that would get me accepted into Harvard's economics program, like my father before me. But I had an instinct revealing this tidbit might convince Caroline to stop talking to me.

"Well, even with my roommate, I'm glad I got put in East House and not Donahue, or Chapman Hall." Caroline's nose wrinkled. "I heard people steal your laundry right out of the dryer in Chapman."

She laughed at my scandalized expression. Caroline was small and olive-skinned and pretty, and she laughed with her whole body. She pointed to one of the wrought-iron picnic benches in the middle of the quad. Groups of students sat there every night, hanging out and smoking weed you could smell with your window open. "Want to chill for a sec? I'm not dying to get back to Eustice. She says she wants to give me a Klingon name so we can be Klingon warrior sisters, whatever that means."

"You don't know *Star Trek*?"

Caroline gave me a blank look.

"The TV show?"

We walked to the table and sat on the bench, still warm from a day's worth of sunshine. Other freshmen walking past gave us interested looks. I tried to imagine what they saw: two pretty girls in sundresses, best friends maybe, waiting for the rest of our friends to arrive. I sat up straighter and smoothed my hem.

"This is going to make me sound weird," Caroline said, "but my parents didn't let me watch TV or movies growing up." She reached for the necklace resting on her collarbone—a delicate gold cross—and rolled it between her fingers. "Our pastor said it was a bad influence. Of course, that didn't stop my mom from inhaling telenovelas. Only *I* had to suffer. I swear, the first night after my parents left Duquette, I binged the entire first season of *Dawson's Creek*. Just ate it up. I wanted to watch that show so bad when I was twelve."

"And? Verdict?"

"Not worth the six years I spent pining." We laughed; then something caught her attention, and she waved over my shoulder. "Heather! Over here!"

I spun, trying to keep my face neutral so no one could see how disappointed I was that Caroline was already moving on to someone else. Then I spotted who she was waving at. The confident blond from my floor stomped through the grass in our direction.

"Caro! Was that a snoozefest, or what? God only knows why we had to sign that in person instead of through email, like we're actually living in the twenty-first century." This close, I could see a light dusting of freckles across the girl's nose, and I realized her forehead was several sizes too big. It was what threw off the symmetry of her face, kept her from being truly pretty. But her navy dress—it was dense material, beautifully tailored. It screamed money. I longed to reach out and touch it.

The girl turned to me and stuck out her hand. "I don't know you yet. I'm Heather Shelby."

"Jessica Miller." Her handshake was very firm.

"How do you know Caro?"

Caro. The nickname rolled off her tongue, easy and intimate. "We just met. We live in the same dorm."

Heather blinked. Then she surprised me by dropping onto the bench. "Shit. That means you're in East House, too."

I nodded and tried hard not to care that Heather had passed me in the hallway a hundred times before, yet clearly I hadn't registered. *It's because you don't stand out*, whispered that insidious voice.

"Ohhh," Heather said, something dawning on her. "Wait, you're roommates with that, like, nun who took a vow of silence, right?"

How had Rachel made more of an impression than me?

Caro leaned in, and Heather and I instinctively drew closer. "Don't look now," she whispered, "but there's this guy in our dorm who is, like, the *epitome* of everything my mother warned me about, and he's walking by right now. I said, *Don't look*," she hissed as both Heather and I turned.

It was easy to tell who she was talking about. He was the one person in a sea of skirts and blazers who hadn't dressed up. Instead, he wore black boots and a T-shirt with the collar hanging loose, a colorful tattoo half-hidden by his sleeve. He was tall and lanky, with a shock of dark hair so thick it made him taller. There was something about his face— the cut of his jaw, the fullness of his lips. I shivered.

"My mom would take one look at him and faint," Caro said.

As if he could feel us staring, the boy turned sharply, his eyes landing on me. My mouth turned dry. His eyes were a light color, though I couldn't tell which at this distance. A small smile curled his lips.

"He's hot," Heather said, speaking at an alarmingly normal volume. "In a one-time, get-the-bad-boy-out-of-your-system kind of way. I've moved on to nice boys. But every girl has to go through it. Rite of passage."

"Am I crazy, or is he walking over here?" I whispered, heart hammering.

"He is definitely coming closer," Caro confirmed.

The boy came over and stopped, resting one of his black boots on the bench. "Hi," he said, turning a little to include Caro and Heather. As soon as his eyes left my face, I felt a rush of relief, mingled with disappointment. "You guys feeling honorable, after swearing your oaths and everything?"

"Not particularly," Heather said.

"Excellent." He dropped into a seat on the other side of the table and pulled something out of his pocket. "In that case, want to smoke?"

He held out a joint.

I almost toppled off the bench. "Out in the *open*?"

He grinned at me, and I had the sudden feeling this was what he'd walked over for, to bait me into talking to him. I made the mistake of looking at his eyes, which I could now see were green as summer grass.

"What, you don't take risks?" He was still grinning in that way that made it seem like he was responding to a second, secret conversation, one I couldn't yet follow.

"I'll take the risk," Heather said. "As long as it's good weed. Nothing skunky, please—life's too short."

"None for me," Caro said, fingering her cross.

The boy stuck the joint in his mouth, pulled out a lighter, and flicked up a flame, sucking in a breath. Effortless. He ran a hand through his hair, and it remained lifted high on his head, long after his hand dropped back to the table. He took another drag and passed the joint to me.

I shook my head, the movement slight. He smiled a small, knowing smile and held the joint out to Heather, who took it immediately.

His eyes found me again. "Brandon Cooper. East House, floor three."

"Jessica Miller." I pressed sweaty hands against my dress. "On four."

"I know." He reached into his pocket, digging for something. When he pulled his hand out, he held a small piece of paper.

"I got this for you."

25

It was a fortune from a fortune cookie. I picked it up and gaped at him. "What? Why?"

"I've seen you around. I got this and thought of you. I was going to tape it to your door, but here you are."

My blank stare was broken by a loud voice calling from across the lawn. "Coop, dude, are you smoking in the middle of the quad again?"

The four of us turned in unison, like windup toys. Three boys ambled in our direction, led by the one in the middle, who was grinning like he'd stumbled on the funniest thing in the world.

It was hard to keep my mouth from dropping open. All three boys were attractive, but the leader in the middle was easily the most beautiful boy I'd ever seen. He was golden—there was no other way to describe it. His skin, light gold, his hair, dark gold, his eyes so crystal-blue they were startling. His teeth were perfectly straight and white—unreal teeth, the kind no human actually possessed. He wore a navy blazer with a crest sewn into it and matching navy slacks.

Caro leaned in close and whispered, "I think we just fell into an Abercrombie catalog."

The three boys stood in front of us, brimming with good humor.

"You've got brass balls, Cooper," said the massive guy standing to the prince's left. He had a shaved head and bronze skin, tall and broad, his chest and shoulders thick with muscle, stuffed into an ill-fitting jacket. He held his body stiffly, in a way that screamed *athlete*. He darted a glance to the prince after he spoke, seeking approval.

Coop shrugged. "If I get kicked out, that's one less bill to worry about." He took the joint back and held it up. "Interested?"

Inside, panic swelled. I'd never heard anyone talk openly about bills, as if not having money was simply a fact of life. As if there wasn't shame in it, and you weren't broadcasting to everyone that you were a small and unimportant person. I felt a sudden, irrational terror they'd turn to me next, make me talk about my family's bills.

"You kidding?" The big guy crossed his arms and shook his head. "I'm on the football team. My dad would kill me if he knew I was standing this close to you."

"Speaking of which," Coop said, smiling slyly around the joint, "I heard your dad yelling at you during Move-In. Man's scary-invested in your college football career. I'm worried he's going to come back in the middle of the night, cut your face off, and wear it around campus, pretending to be you."

"Fuck off."

"Give it here," said the prince, waving at the joint. "Roommates ought to rise and fall together." He dropped next to Coop and took the joint, tilting his head back to the sky.

"My name's Jack Carroll," the last boy said politely, holding out his hand. If Coop would've had Caro's mother reaching for the holy water, Jack was the boy she would have chosen out of a catalog. His hair was brushed neatly to the side, cardigan perfectly pressed, tie straight as a pin. He looked like an eighteen-year-old Mr. Rogers.

We each shook Jack's hand, and he folded himself onto the bench, carefully brushing his slacks.

"Jack's an Eagle Scout," the prince said. "If you couldn't tell just by looking at him."

"And Mint's heir to a real estate empire," Jack countered, loosening his tie with one hand. "If you couldn't tell by his sense of entitlement."

"Mark Minter," the prince said, once he'd blown a ring of smoke. He nodded in the direction of the big guy. "And that's Francis Kekoa, Duquette's newest football star. Pride of Oahu, according to his dad."

"*Frankie*," the boy said quickly, heaving himself onto the bench next to Mint. "No one calls me Francis except my mom."

"Frankie lets me, though." Mint sucked deeply, then passed the joint back to Coop. "Because he loves me."

Frankie rolled his eyes, then nodded in Caro's direction. "I like your necklace. Got one just like it." He dug under the collar of his shirt and drew out a thick gold chain, carrying a heavy cross. "Us Catholics gotta represent."

"Just because I'm Colombian doesn't automatically make me a Catholic," Caro snapped, dropping her necklace and folding her hands. "I'm Presbyterian."

Coop laughed, coughing on smoke. "Good one, Frankie."

"Sorry," Frankie said. "I got excited to share my Catholic guilt with someone."

"Where in Colombia?" Mint asked Caro.

"I have family in Bogotá." The word rolled crisply off her tongue, with a punch at the end. "My parents and I are from Miami."

He nodded. "I've visited Colombia a bunch. Lots of people summering in Cartagena lately."

"*Summering.*" The word withered in Coop's mouth.

"If we're jumping into families and religion," Jack said, "then *my* parents are at that really fun stage of Southern Baptism where they've ceased being human beings and have transformed into walking, talking bibles. So it was fun showing them around campus and stumbling on Greek row." He took the joint and squinted at Mint. "Let me guess: Methodist. That's what rich kids always are."

Mint snorted. "The only religion my parents worship is money."

We laughed. Dusk deepened, the sun a rich orange-rose, sinking through the branches of the trees. A warm breeze kissed my skin. I pictured it circling the picnic table, touching all of us, drawing us closer.

"What about you, Coop?" Mint asked. "We haven't even had the family conversation yet."

Coop looked down at the table. "My family is one person. And she's an atheist. We don't believe in believing."

Frankie snorted. "How metal." He nodded at Heather. "What's your deal?"

With all eyes on her, Heather smiled like the cat that ate the canary.

"My parents worship the one true god." She spoke slowly, basking in our attention. "*Me*." Her eyes lingered on Jack. "You should try it sometime."

Jack turned bright red as the whole table burst into amazed laughter. Frankie and Mint shared an incredulous look, and then suddenly Mint turned across the table and grinned at *me*. I sucked in a breath. The world's most beautiful boy, a foot away, and he was smiling at me, sharing a joke. The miraculousness of it did something to me. Confidence sang through my blood.

"Now *there's* a pair of brass balls," I said, and the whole table rocked with laughter, even Heather. Mint gave me an appreciative look.

I was addicted. This was all I wanted—to make these people laugh and have Mint look at me just like that, his skin glowing in the setting sun.

"Your turn." Caro elbowed me. "How'd you grow up?"

My smile dimmed. My parents weren't religious, but they each had their devotions. My dad's life was a shrine built to everything I'd struggled with. He'd never said it out loud, but I knew what he believed: if you couldn't be the best, be the winner, life wasn't worth living, and you had to find some way to escape. He'd found a very effective way, once life started disappointing him. My mom, on the other hand, was simple. She devoted herself to anything my dad thought wasn't worth our time. She worshipped settling, he would say. A constant tension.

How could I possibly explain that?

I cleared my throat. "Why are we spending a Friday night talking about religion like a bunch of nerd theology majors? Here's what I want to know: where are we going tonight?"

"Hell yeah." Frankie pounded the table. "Phi Delt Anything-But-Clothes party." He gestured between himself, Jack, and Mint. "We got invites from one of the brothers."

The table broke out into a heated discussion about how to fashion clothes out of trash bags and how early we should start drinking in East

House before walking to frat row. I leaned back and watched. All around us, fireflies dotted the air, sparks of light, here and gone. Tree branches swayed and stalks of grass lifted with the breeze, in time to some secret song. I could feel it, humming and weaving around us, the lawn and the trees and the brilliant dying sun. Knitting us together.

It was magic. Each of them a star on earth, pulling me in with the force of their gravity. I was theirs. In that moment, I gave myself over completely. I worshipped them. I died and started new, right there in the grass, in the center of the lawn.

The next day, rolling awake in bed, trash-bag dress sticking to my legs, I finally opened Coop's fortune. Seven strange words: *Today, something starts that will never end.*

I taped the fortune to my door. I thought I knew what it meant. But I was young, and so naive. I had no idea what was barreling toward us, just around the corner.

CHAPTER 4
NOW

At night Duquette was a dark kingdom, lit by old-fashioned lamps that cast circular glows, like halos in a Byzantine painting. The cab dropped me at the edge of campus, outside the Founder's Arch. As I walked under the imposing white stone, carved with the school promise—*We will change you, body and soul*—I thought of how it had impressed even my father, on his first and only trip to campus.

When I passed to the other side, the air changed. I could hear, distantly, the sound of music and voices. I took off down the path, listening for it against the *clack-clack* of my heels on the stone, the *thump-thump* of my heart.

My flight had arrived late, giving me only enough time to rush to my hotel room and presenting me with the perfect excuse to beg off on Caro's invitation to get ready together. I knew I'd have to see her—there was no getting around it, she was my best friend. But tonight I would talk to as many people as possible, dance away, flit to different crowds. I had a plan, and it had many purposes.

In front of me, in the center of Eliot Lawn, rose the white tent. I could see them now, hundreds of my classmates in dress clothes, the tent spilling over with dark suit jackets and black cocktail dresses. Music swelled from a string quartet in the corner. I took a deep breath, smoothed my dress over my hips, and walked in.

At first, no one noticed me as I wove toward the bar. But then, the first head turned, caught by the plunge of my neckline, the delicate snow-white straps over my shoulders that gave way to nothing but the smooth plane of my back. I'd spent two months' mortgage on this dress, and it was worth it. More heads followed the first, and then they were turning everywhere I walked, the girl in white cutting through a sea of black. They whispered, scanning me head to foot. But it didn't matter what they said, only that they were talking. The adrenaline had me buzzing, making my hands tremble as I finally touched the bar.

It was working.

Just as I lifted a glass of wine to my mouth, Caro materialized at my side. "Jessica!"

I almost spilled wine down my dress. "*Christ!*"

She wrapped herself around me, hugging tight. How had she found me so fast? I supposed my dress had turned me into something of a beacon.

She pulled back, examining me at arm's length. "Look at you. I love this so much. You're like a sexpot angel or something." Out of habit, she reached for the cross around her neck, though she hadn't worn it in ten years.

Caro. My truest friend. The one who'd never left my side, who loved me as much today as the day we graduated. The guilt threatened to overwhelm me.

"I'm so happy to see you," I said, swallowing my feelings. "You look great, as always." She hadn't aged a day since we'd met. Like everyone else, she wore a tasteful black dress, but since she was Caro, small and dark and beautiful, she pulled it off better. The sameness of her made it hard to avoid the only thing that had changed—the sparkling diamond on her hand. I cut my eyes to the crowd.

"Who's here?"

"Oh, everyone," she said dreamily.

Not Heather, whispered a voice, but I cut it off. Searching for Heather's face in a crowd was a habit I'd put to rest years ago. I couldn't start again now.

"I'm so happy with the turnout," Caro said. "This whole weekend was Eric's vision, you know."

I froze. "Eric?"

"Eric Shelby. Remember? He works at Duquette now. We were on the Homecoming planning committee together." Vaguely, I recalled something about Caro volunteering to send reminder emails to the Class of '09. It must have been from one of her many text messages, half of which I'd deleted without opening, out of sheer fear she'd tell me she and Coop were pregnant, or they'd gone ahead and eloped. "Eric grew into such a sweetheart." Before I could say anything else, Caro grabbed my arm and started to pull. "Come on, we should find the rest of the gang."

No, no, no.

I dug my heels in. "Is that Elizabeth Barley and Vanessa Reed?" I waved with feigned excitement at the girls, standing a few yards away. It seemed to work, because they rushed over.

"Oh my god," Elizabeth gushed, hugging me. "You're blond now? You never dressed like this in college. You're so *pretty*."

"Thanks." I hugged her back, collecting and savoring each of her words. Elizabeth and Vanessa belonged to one of the lower-tier sororities, rungs below Caro and me on Duquette's social ladder. You were supposed to act like you weren't aware of those sorts of things. But even now, ten years later, I could feel us slipping into our old places, obeying the order.

"Aren't you a consultant in New York? I swear my cousin sent me some society paper a year ago with you in it. You were dating some big shot." Vanessa spoke casually, but I could hear the edge of longing in her voice, a recognition that I had something she didn't. "You're, like, absolutely killing it."

I preened. "You're too nice. Yes, I'm a partner at Coldwell."

"Youngest female partner *ever* in the New York branch," Caro said helpfully, and Elizabeth and Vanessa *oohed*.

This was my apotheosis. Everything was going exactly to plan.

"And Caro," Elizabeth said, turning from me. "Let's see the ring!"

My stomach dropped. Caro laughed and held up her hand, wiggling her fingers.

"It's so pretty," Vanessa said, examining the gem. "I still can't believe you're marrying *Brandon Cooper*. I would have put money on him never marrying."

"Totally," Elizabeth agreed. "Every girl in school was in love with him. It's that bad boy thing, you know? He was, like, such a James Dean. With his motorcycle and his leather jacket."

"*James Dean?*" Vanessa squealed. "What are you, ninety?"

Elizabeth laughed. "All I know is I had the biggest crush on him. There were always those rumors he was dating a million girls, but I never actually saw him with anyone. You're lucky, Caroline."

"Actually—" Vanessa's voice lowered. "I think those rumors got started because of what he did, remember? He was always in and out of people's rooms 'cause he sold—"

"Hey!" I said quickly, watching Caro's frown grow. "Remember that girl whose sex tape leaked? What's she doing now?"

Caro's eyes widened at me, disbelieving. Again, I swatted away guilt, satisfied at the distraction.

Vanessa looked puzzled. "The one a year below us who transferred? I heard she's a kindergarten teach—"

"Oh my god," Elizabeth breathed, her gaze catching on something across the room. "Look, it's Courtney Kennedy."

Whether it was natural human instinct or the power of her name, I didn't know, but we all spun to follow Elizabeth's gaze. Sure enough, there she was, standing in the corner of the tent surrounded by other Chi Os. Seeing her in real life after so long was like spotting a celebrity in the wild—a little shock to the system.

Courtney wore a tight, blood-red dress, dark eyeliner, and bright lips. The memory flashed back: freshman year, before I had any friends, watching her stumble back to her room, clinging to Heather's arm and laughing hysterically. The most beautiful girl I'd ever seen—still, to this day. Always the belle of the ball.

"Courtney *Minter*," Vanessa corrected, then snapped "What?" when Elizabeth elbowed her. Vanessa realized and looked at me in horror. "Oh god, I'm sorry. I spaced. This must be so weird for you."

A tidal wave of emotions—pain at seeing Courtney, still so perfect, and fury that Vanessa's and Elizabeth's delicious envy was quickly turning to pity. I downed my wine. "Don't apologize. Mint and I broke up years ago. Seriously. I'm over it."

No one said anything for a second, and then Elizabeth spoke in a rush. "It's just that he's so perfect and you guys dated all through college. I mean, you were a Duquette staple. It was so inspiring to see the two of you together. It gave the rest of us hope, you know? That unlikely pairings can happen. Now he's with Courtney and it's just so...*obvious*."

My stomach dropped. Gave the rest of us hope?

I could feel rage welling, an urge to knock the vodka tonic from Elizabeth's hand.

"Jess and Courtney are actually really good friends," Caro said in a bright singsong voice, lacing her arm through mine. "We're going to talk to her now, in fact. Have a good night!" She walked away quickly, tugging me after her.

Elizabeth's comment sent me straight back to high school. Freshman year, when we were all obsessed with rankings, making lists of teachers, movies, sports teams, and finally, the boys had the nerve to rank the girls. For days, we heard whispers about who was the hottest. We speculated at lunch, voicing support for every girl publicly and making our own more cutthroat calculations privately. I knew I wouldn't be ranked first, though I longed to be. At fourteen, I'd already learned you rarely got your exact heart's desire. But I figured I'd be in the top five, maybe top three. I was tall, true, which wasn't yet a virtue, but when I slid my eyes around the classroom, taking measure, I felt sure: *I am one of the best-looking girls here.*

The list was passed around near the end of biology, when poor Mrs. Sikes was engaged in the Sisyphean effort of trying to teach us cellular mitosis. Michael, the leader of the boys, slipped Madison a single piece of folded paper. Madison pretended not to care, but finally looked. A wide smile curved her mouth, and my heart plummeted. *She was number one.* I'd suspected it might be her—Madison and her dumb, perfect corkscrew curls. Apparently, for all my talk about being satisfied with second or third place, I'd still harbored secret hopes.

The note wound its way around the tables until finally it reached me. With trembling fingers, I unfolded it and read. Madison was first, Whitney second? My heart beat faster. Renata third—*Renata?* I pored down the rest of the list, scanning only for my name. My heart skipped at number twelve, but it was only Jessica C. Where was I? I came to the bottom of the list, where poor Marybeth was number twenty-five, a horrible cruelty because of her acne. Then the horrifying truth hit me. *I wasn't even on the list.* Forget one of the top girls—I didn't even merit mention.

I really was a nobody. Nothing but background noise, filler, and I'd been blind to it. That day, I swore: *never again.*

But Elizabeth's comment made me feel like I'd been a nobody all four years of college and hadn't realized. Is that what people truly thought of me?

"What trolls," Caro muttered, when we were past hearing range. "Sharks, hunting for blood."

Something about Caro's face, so serious and angry, spilled sunlight through the dark places in my mind. I wrapped my arm around her and squeezed. "You really are the greatest friend."

"Well, keep that in mind, because I actually *am* walking us over to Courtney."

"What? No!" I tried to disentangle.

"Too bad, we're here—this will be good for you. Hi, Courtney!" Caro plastered a giant smile over her face. I glanced around. We really were here: in the tenth circle of hell, with the Chi Os.

Courtney stopped talking to the girl beside her, eyes laser-focusing on me. A satisfied smile stretched her mouth. With her ridiculous chest-to-waist ratio and glossy hair, she looked like a living, breathing Barbie doll. Who'd just been handed the one thing she wanted most in the world.

"Caro! And *Jessica*—so good to see you. It's been so long since the wedding." She kissed Caro's cheek, then mine, while I stood stiff. The Chi Os gave us a wide berth.

"Speaking of, sorry I had to leave early," I said through gritted teeth. "I'm not sure if Mint told you, but I had to catch a plane to Paris with my boyfriend at the time. Chris Beshear of the Manhattan Beshears—you might know him."

Courtney tilted her head. "I heard you're single again. What a shame. Paris is the perfect place to get engaged. Sorry it didn't work out for you."

Caro looked like she was trying desperately to figure out some way to cut in, but her mind couldn't work fast enough.

"Oh," I said, with faux surprise. "You like Paris? I assumed your taste was a little more down to earth. Like, you know, American fast-food chains. You and Mint did first hook up in a Wendy's bathroom, right?"

A Chi O next to us gasped. Courtney reddened. It was one of my trump cards, and I wished I hadn't used it so early, but she was just too much in person, not a flaw on her, not a slip in her delivery. I knew a few of her dirty secrets, though, including where she and Mint first hooked up, wasted after a night out. I knew because Mint had confessed it to me in person, tears in his eyes.

Just as Courtney opened her mouth, someone walked into my line of sight. I turned and found the source of everything.

Mark Minter. The man *I* was supposed to marry.

"Jess." He gave me the same appraising look he always did, the one that made me stand at attention, wanting to measure up right. He leaned in and put a cool hand on my naked back, pressing me into a hug. My skin tingled with goose bumps.

"Mint, you asshole, took you long enough to show up." Caro grinned at him.

"Hi, Tiny." He gripped her in a hug. "Good to see you, too." I watched them embrace, using the excuse to study him. He'd aged. He was still the most handsome boy—man, I supposed—in the room, but the chiseled lines of his face had softened with age. It was a little less of a shock to look at him.

A booming voice cut in. "Is that *Caroline Rodriguez* and *Jessica Miller*? No, it can't be, because they would have searched the whole party for me the instant they got here, desperate to see their best friend Frankie."

Frankie strode up from the bar with two whiskeys and handed one to Mint, then grabbed Caro in a bear hug. Of course—wherever Mint was, Frankie was no more than a step behind. He still wore his hair shaved like in college, but now his suits fit perfectly, even though his shoulders had somehow grown broader. The suits had gotten a lot nicer, too.

Frankie dropped Caro and hugged me. "Look at you. *Damn*, Miller, bringing the heat. Minty, aren't you sad you—" Frankie stopped and swallowed. Courtney's eyebrows were currently located north of her hairline. "Sorry, old habits. Anyway, look at this reunion! God, it's good to see you guys."

One of the Chi Os lingering at the edge of our conversation giggled. "Frankie, I promised my husband I'd get a picture with you. He's a huge Saints fan. Is that okay?" Her eyes dropped demurely, like simply holding his gaze was an honor.

Frankie shoved his drink at Caro, who accepted it automatically, and rushed over. "I'd never leave a fan hanging. Want to make it a video? What's the lucky guy's name?"

I rolled my eyes and caught Mint's gaze halfway through. Out of habit, we grinned at each other. "Something tells me being an NFL star has gone to Frankie's head," he said.

"Really? I was thinking, wow, Frankie hasn't changed since college."

Mint laughed. Courtney slid her arm through his and side-eyed me.

"What I want to know," Caro said, "is what Frankie's dad is up to. Remember how that man lived and breathed Frankie's football career? He must be living his best life."

Mint groaned. "Everything you're thinking, triple it. Frankie's dad moved from Hawaii to live in his pool house. He pretty much follows Frankie everywhere, even on the road. It's not living vicariously—he's *literally* living Frankie's life."

"Well, that's because Frankie got the life his dad always wanted, right? Way back when his dad was a football star, before he got injured?" Caro shook her head. "Parents, man. They can be so unintentionally creepy."

"It's like Freud said," a dark voice cut in. "You have to kill your father before you're free." A pause. "Or was that a rap song?"

I froze. The voice triggered every nerve in my body, sparking them to life. I turned slowly, fighting a pull as irresistible as gravity. Maybe, just maybe, if I didn't look, I could remain safe. Safety had to be better than what lay at the end of this turn, nothing but him, flesh and blood, and the short distance between us.

I stopped turning. And looked.

They all thought I mourned Mint. That the sight of him and Courtney together would set me off. Yes, Mint had hurt me, but he wasn't the person who'd cut me so deeply the wound would never heal. Mint wasn't the face I saw at night when I tossed and turned. Mint wasn't the person I'd betrayed so profoundly that the weight of it had seeped into everything—my dreams, the words I spoke, the very cadence of my steps, as if I walked everywhere carrying an extra heaviness. Mint wasn't the cause of what I now realized was a decade-long panic attack, unfolding in excruciatingly slow motion.

No. That man stood in front of me now, looking at me with wild abandon, grass-green eyes dangerous as ever.

Coop.

CHAPTER 5
OCTOBER, FRESHMAN YEAR

We stood in the abandoned field behind grad student housing—in the hiding place we'd thought was secret—and stared at the wreckage. There were no clues to whisper what happened. There was nothing but twenty students gripped by silence, even the squirrels frozen in the trees, even the dry, dead leaves muted underfoot.

We were a single day out from the Homecoming parade, and our pride and joy—the float we'd spent weeks building—was crushed. Decimated. Themed *Duquette Royalty* in what Courtney assured us was a playful but not arrogant reference to East House's five-year winning streak in the Battle of the Freshmen Halls, the float was an elaborate, fourteen-foot replica of East House, styled as a castle, complete with real, intricately woven vines.

Or it had been. Now the entire structure was caved in, as if it had been hit with a wrecking ball. The coup de grâce was supposed to be a short round of fireworks we'd planned to set off from each of the turrets, the ammunition generously paid for by Mint's parents and currently stowed in his backpack, ready to be tested. But the turrets were smashed, hanging at odd angles like broken limbs.

We were supposed to dazzle the Homecoming crowd into handing East House its sixth first-place win, and cement our place in campus history. I'd worked for weeks drawing the entire thing, from the castle to each flower that surrounded it, directing others where and how to paint.

All of our work, for nothing.

What the hell happened?

I searched my friends' faces, seeing my panic mirrored. We'd worked with other people from the dorm, sure, but this competition had been ours. *Our* stroke of genius, our leadership. Our excuse to see each other every day, on top of every night. In such a short time, we'd become the kind of friends who were less separate, distinct people and more limbs you couldn't live without. This attack felt like a personal affront.

Mint, standing near the head of the float, dropped his backpack full of fireworks. It hit the ground with a heavy thud, causing Frankie, hovering behind him like a shadow, to shift out of the way, eyeing it warily. Beside me, Caro braced her hands over her face, shielding her eyes from view.

Coop stepped close to me and lowered his voice. "That float was a piece of art."

I dropped my eyes, feeling the loss of my work more sharply now that someone had named it. "It was just a little painting. Not important."

Jack picked up a piece of limp, broken vine and cradled it. "What in the world could have done this? It's like the float was hit by a bulldozer."

"Wrong question. You mean *who* could have done this." In the crowd of stunned faces, Heather's alone was mercenary. Heads turned in her direction.

Courtney put her hands on her hips, her slim elbows making razor-sharp angles, even under the bulk of her coat. "We all know exactly who did it. It was those freaks from Chapman Hall. Led by twin weasels

Trevor Daly and Charles Smith. They want to win so badly they decided to take out the competition."

There was a murmur of agreement. Trevor and Charles were loud-mouths and well known for pulling pranks only they thought were funny. Like stealing girls' underwear out of the laundry room and stringing it up on tree branches.

"Hey, now," Mint said, shoving his hands in the pockets of his peacoat. "Trevor and Charles are rushing Phi Delt." He offered this like it was a talisman of protection against accusations, an endorsement that couldn't be argued with. Phi Delt was, after all, the best frat on campus. It was where everyone knew Mint would end up. They were rushing Frankie and Jack, too, but that was mostly because they came with Mint, like a package deal.

"How did Trevor and Charles even know where to find our float?" It had been my idea to hide it behind the grad student apartments, tucked on the edge of campus, where undergrads rarely ventured—an idea I'd been proud of until this moment.

Frankie rubbed a hand across his reddening face. "I might have… mentioned something during beer pong…about blowing things up and grad students yelling at us…"

A chorus of groans and *What the fuck, Frankie*s echoed around our small group. And that was definitive proof the situation was dire, because normally the whole dorm loved our resident football star.

"Frankie, you and your big mouth." Jack blew out a frustrated breath. "*One secret*, man. I dare you to keep *one* secret in your whole entire life. Do it, and I'll die of shock."

"Do you see?" Heather was transitioning into her favorite mode: high theatrics. I could picture her striding across a stage, lifting a sword, bellowing *Now we are at war* to a rapt audience. "They *knew* we were the dorm to beat, and they knew where to find our float. This is sabotage."

One of the guys who lived a few doors down from Mint and Coop had drifted to the back of the float. Now he started laughing, pointing at the crumpled castle wall. "Mint, you gotta see this. They left you a message."

We moved en masse to look. Drawn across the back of the float in lurid red paint, lines marred by drip marks, was a stick-figure boy cradled in the lap of a stick-figure woman. They were surrounded by crude dollar signs. The boy had a dialogue bubble protruding from his mouth: *My mommy bought me this float.* Underneath the stick figure, in ragged letters, were the words *and all my friends*, followed by *East House cheats. Love, Chapman.*

"How do we know that's supposed to be Mint?" Caro whispered.

"Please," Heather scoffed. "Of course it's Mint."

I chanced a look at him. Even though we were friends now, looking at him hadn't stopped feeling dangerous, like each time I was skimming too close to the sun. But he wasn't looking anywhere except at the painting, even with Courtney standing so close behind him, her shoulder brushing his every time he moved. It seemed Mint and Courtney were an inevitable pairing—like to like—so I tried to ignore the way their closeness rubbed at me, stirring old, bitter feelings.

But something was wrong with Mint. In the two months I'd spent watching him, I'd never seen his face look like this, with tracks of scarlet blooming down his cheeks and neck. His skin looked painful, hot to the touch. His eyes darted around, taking in the snickers and soft laughter.

Coop rested a hand on Mint's shoulder. "You've been immortalized. And here I thought it'd be your name on a building or something." His mouth quirked. "The likeness is chilling, you have to admit. I told you to double down on leg days. Those calves are looking a little thin, man."

Mint wrenched his shoulder away. "Get the *fuck* off me."

His anger was a lightning strike, completely unexpected. Coop took a half step back and raised both hands in surrender. "Okay, easy."

Behind Mint's back, he found my eyes, and a smile tugged at the corners of his mouth.

It was a message for me alone, a look to make a private space between us. He was always doing that. It didn't matter if we were at a party, packed wall to wall; or if I was leaving a lecture hall, adrift in a sea of people, only to spot him reading on a bench; or if we were having lunch and he was the last to arrive, setting his tray at the opposite end of the table. He always found me, and for that first, single moment when our eyes met, we existed in a separate place. A private room he'd built to tell me something I could never parse before the moment was over.

"It's not funny," Mint said sharply. I looked away from Coop, drawn to Mint's hands, which he'd clenched into fists. "It's a lie."

"Obviously," said Frankie, ever loyal.

"Fucking *losers*." Mint kicked the float, right in the center of the painting, and it cracked, wood splintering. "*Liars*." A hush fell over the group as he kicked again, still red-faced. And then Frankie was kicking, too, until the side of the castle gave away completely and the painting turned into a gaping hole.

For a few seconds the only sound was Mint's hard breathing. Then Jack said, "I guess we're not salvaging the float."

One of the girls from my floor sighed. "I can't believe I wasted so much time on this. What a disaster." She tossed her hair, turning to walk away.

"Where are you going?" asked Caro, her face the portrait of betrayal.

The girl gave her an incredulous look. "It's the night before *Homecoming*, Caro. I'm not missing parties just to cobble together some pitiful makeup float and lose tomorrow anyway."

"Me either," someone else said, and that was the death knell, the curtain falling. There was murmuring, and then everyone was shifting, adjusting backpacks over their shoulders. In twos and threes they walked away, muttering about Chapman Hall and dick-swinging contests and pranks gone too far.

It left only the eight of us, doing our best not to look at the hole in the float.

"Can you believe them?" Caro asked. "One setback and they jump ship. Where's their *loyalty*?"

Jack sighed and sank to the ground, perching among the dead leaves. "I hate to be the one to say it, but I think we're screwed."

Heather dropped beside him and leaned in close. Jack's cheeks turned rosy, and he glanced around to see if we were watching. After two months of being friends, I knew that particular shade of pink meant Jack was happy with Heather's affection but would melt if anyone mentioned it. Heather called this shyness *Jack disentangling from years of repression*, a line she'd cribbed from one of her Intro to Psychology books. At night when she and Caro and I sat around talking, waiting for our face masks to dry or watching mindless TV, Heather told us secrets Jack had told her, like that he'd never been kissed, never been allowed to have a girl-friend. But she was patient; she made the first move with him, over and over, fresh each day. Heather was like that. She was a girl who did things I'd never known were an option.

"Come on, there has to be *something* we can do to fix the float. Or at least a plan to get back at Chapman." Heather dropped her head on Jack's shoulder. He sat straight as a rod.

"Let's just burn Chapman to the ground and be done with Homecoming," Coop said. "Shit's lame."

"Coop's right. I still can't believe I let you talk me into this." Courtney turned to Heather, her red-painted mouth pulling into a frown. "I told you from the beginning that winning a glorified arts-and-crafts contest wasn't going to put us on top of Chi O's list. And now we're not even going to win. It's humiliating."

Like Phi Delt, Chi Omega was the best on campus. The sorority boasted a perfect rush record. Every year, each girl they offered a spot took it, gratefully, knowing a place in Chi O meant four years breathing rarefied air. It was rumored none of the other sororities came close to their record, not even the second-best, Kappa.

I'd learned quickly that social life at Duquette revolved around two things: football and Greek life. Winning a football championship was life or death, the stakes only outmatched by getting in to the right house. In some ways, it was antiquated—the football and Greek life like something out of *Pleasantville*—but in another way it was timeless: these were just more ways of being sorted. And as every student who'd fought or sunk their way to Duquette knew, life was nothing if not a constant cycle of *compete, rank, sort*. Hierarchy, that was normal. What was strange was how deeply you could come to need it; how eventually, over enough time, you would long for someone to come and put you in your place.

"Courtney," Frankie snapped, "can you shut up for *one* second and let us think?"

Courtney's eyes flew open. No one talked to her like that.

I slipped away to where Mint stood, arms folded tight over his chest, and—taking a quick, steeling breath—brushed a hand over his shoulder. "Hey. You okay?"

He didn't pull away from the touch, but he didn't look at me, either. "I overreacted. It's just that Charles's family knows my family, and I thought—"

My heart drummed.

"You know they're just jealous, right?" I decided to chance it, leaving my hand on his shoulder, my eyes on his face.

He turned to me, the movement sharp. "Jealous?"

I was caught. Warmth bloomed through me like sunlight. "Obviously."

He smiled.

"Jessica." Courtney's icy voice broke through. "I know you've got to take your best shot at Mint while he's down, but now is really *not* the time for flirting."

It was like she'd reached across the grass and slapped me. Or worse—like she'd wrenched my top off, leaving me exposed, my intentions and desires naked for everyone to see. I recoiled, pulling my hand from Mint's shoulder, eyes stinging with hot humiliation. But before I could draw one shaking breath—to say what, I didn't know—Heather cut in.

"Courtney, stop being such a bitch."

Maybe I shouldn't have been surprised. Heather was dogmatic about right and wrong, saw the world divided up smoothly into *good* and *bad*. I'd attributed this to the fact that her life had been uncomplicated, devoid of obstacles, for eighteen years. The easy sailing had allowed her to believe the world was black and white, no gray. Heather could afford to think this way because she didn't need to claw, constantly, for what she deserved, or live her life in the gray just to understand the people she loved. It was yet another luxury, like her beautiful clothes and her purses.

Still, Heather and Courtney were a pair—best friends, roommates. That's where her loyalties should lie.

"Are you serious?" Courtney looked as stunned as I was. A kick of wind blew her glossy, magazine hair around her shoulders. "You're choosing *her*?"

There it was, a line in the sand. I could do nothing but blink at both of them.

Heather was quiet for a beat, then said: "Yes. Stop punching down."
She'd chosen me.

Courtney's mouth fell open. She searched the circle of faces, looking for an ally, some measure of sympathy. Her gaze lingered on Mint. But whatever she saw had her swallowing hard, then rolling her eyes. "Fine, whatever. I'm bored. Have fun wasting your time on lost causes." She glanced at Heather. "I guess I'll see you later, or something." It sounded more like a question: *Will I?* In that moment, Courtney looked young and unsure.

Heather nodded curtly. "See you at home." But when Courtney walked away, she found my eyes and smiled.

I filled with light. Forget Mint; *this* was like looking into the sun. Heather had defended me. Picked me. Who had ever done that?

"*You guys.*" Jack's eyes were wide with excitement. "I just got an idea. A way to get back at Chapman *and* reenter the Battle. The only problem is, it's slightly illegal."

And just like that, the last half hour was washed away, the slate wiped clean. We grinned at each other.

"Spill," Frankie said.

Jack winced at Caro. "Okay. You know how Charles is obsessed with Caro?"

Mint cracked a laugh. "Oh, this is going to be good."

"Whatever you're thinking, *no*," Caro said.

"Hear me out. What if, since Chapman destroyed our float, we stole theirs?"

"Silly Jack," Coop said. "You had me at illegal."

I tried to smile at Coop, but he wouldn't look my way.

"We know Chapman's hiding their float behind Bishop." Bishop Hall was a dorm for seniors, so one of the Chapman freshmen must have had an upperclassman connection. "All we need is for Caro to get into Charles's room and take the keys to their float. Then tonight we steal it, turn it into the East House float, and tomorrow we ride it to victory."

"Brilliant," Frankie breathed. "We can even use the fireworks."

I rolled my eyes. "So the whole plan hinges on Caro being James Bond for a night. No pressure."

"Yeah, forget it," Heather said. "Caro can't prostitute herself. She hates Charles. He's a lacrosse douchebag."

"A *Phi Delt* lacrosse douchebag," Coop corrected. "Which means it's okay."

"No, wait a second." Caro took a deep breath. "I'll do it. For you guys."

I squinted. "You sure?" Sometimes I worried about the depths of Caro's loyalty.

Frankie clapped. "We're going to be *legends*."

"One small hiccup," Mint said. "I'm pretty sure I remember Trevor saying the Chapman float theme is *Duquette in Paradise*."

"Meaning?" Heather asked.

"Meaning it's a rolling beach, palm trees, sand, and everything. They were planning to ride it in bathing suits."

"It's *October*," I said.

"Yeah, well, clearly they'll do anything to win. Point is, we'll look pretty stupid riding in sweaters."

"Shit. Well. Thank God we've been working out all semester." Frankie looked around at us and frowned. "What? Why are you all looking at me like that?"

Coop patted Frankie's shoulder. "It's sweet how your mind works."

"As soon as they realize their float's missing, Chapman will know we took it," Jack said. "We need to hide it somewhere they won't find it before the parade starts. Let them panic, waste their time searching."

"They won't dream we had the balls to enter it," Heather said. "But we should get to the stadium early anyway. Be out in the middle of the parade before they even realize."

Coop bit his lip. "I know a place we can hide it. Old abandoned field a few blocks away. Pretty shady, but they won't think of it. I can guarantee."

Caro snorted. "How can you do that?"

He only shrugged. "I know which Duquette students know about it, and which don't."

"Whatever. Coop's creepy field works for me," Heather said.

"Okay, then." Jack slung an arm over Caro's shoulder. "Text us when you have the goods and we'll put this plan into action."

We skidded into the near-empty parking lot outside the basketball sta-dium as soon as the cheerleaders moved aside the orange cones, signal-ing the parade was moments from starting and floats should line up.

Heather scanned the parking lot as we bumped along. "Excellent. No Chapman Hall spies." A smile curved her lips. "Probably still pulling their hair out, running around campus."

We were early enough that there was only the grand marshal's float ahead of us, which by tradition was always first, and always filled with rowdy football players. After a few minutes of tense waiting, watching every float that drove into the parking lot behind us, music swelled from the other side of the stadium. A voice boomed over the loudspeakers, saying something I couldn't quite make out, but it sounded rousing. Suddenly the cop directing parade traffic straightened to attention. He pointed at the grand marshal's float, then looked at us and waved us forward.

It was too late to turn back now. Before today, I'd never imagined committing grand theft auto, then flaunting it for the world to see. Now here I stood atop a stolen float, shivering in—of all things—a black bikini, about to reveal myself to the entire student body and the alumni. And all I could think about was whether the cops serving as parade orga-nizers would be gentle when the jig was up, and they wrestled me down.

What price, glory?

Mint nodded at Jack in the driver's seat, who gave him a thumbs-up, and then we were puttering forward, out from behind the cover of the basketball stadium and onto the parade route.

Caro squeezed my hand. "This better be worth it."

I glanced at her. Caro had sacrificed more than anyone. "How long did it take you to get the keys from Charles? I tried waiting up for you, but I fell asleep. How'd you end up doing it?"

Caro's cheeks flamed. "It took a long time," she mumbled. "And never mind how."

Strange—

"Wave, idiots!" Heather, who looked completely at home in her bright-yellow bikini, glared at us, waving enthusiastically at the crowd.

The crowd. Hundreds of people, lining both sides of the street as far as I could see. From the moment we rolled into view, I could see them pointing and laughing at us, the ridiculous college students dressed for the beach in the middle of a North Carolina fall.

"Do you hear that shouting?" Frankie flexed for the crowd. "They love us!"

And actually, he wasn't wrong. Everyone I waved to grinned and waved back. Kids were cheering on Mint as he pretended to swim through the waves. The Chapman students had cleverly packed the back of the float with red and white confetti, and now Coop was tossing it, raining it down on everyone we passed, letting kids fight over handfuls. I'd even stopped feeling cold. The adrenaline heated my blood, making me forget the chill in the air as we zoomed down the street. Blackwell Tower, the end of the parade route, couldn't be too far ahead.

We were actually pulling this off.

"Trouble!" Heather yelled, pointing ahead.

It was the Chapman students, rushing to the side of the road.

"Thieves!" yelled Trevor—who, to Courtney's credit, actually did look like a weasel, small and furrow-faced. "Those assholes stole our float!"

"No shit we did!" Frankie pointed to the banner we'd left hanging up front, crossing out *Chapman Hall Champions* and writing *East House Seven.*

"You destroyed ours first!" Heather shouted.

"Caroline!" That shout came from Charles, who stood on the sidelines in a red-and-white lacrosse jersey, blinking up at her. "I trusted you!"

"Uh-oh," Caro said, ducking behind me.

"We won't let you use our float to win!" One of the Chapman students broke through the parade barrier and ran into the street, directly in our path, followed quickly by more. They were trying to block us from reaching the finish line at Blackwell. If they stopped us, we'd hold up all the floats in line behind us. The entire parade would come grinding to a halt.

Jack leaned over, shouting from the driver's seat. "What do we do?"

"Just hit one," Coop yelled, still throwing confetti in wild handfuls, the red and white paper everywhere, but mostly strung like tinsel through his hair. "The rest will learn!"

In a flash of desperation, a thought seized me. It was crazy and might lead to nothing but trouble, but there was something about being surrounded by Coop and Frankie, Mint and Heather and Caro, that made me feel like nothing bad could really happen.

"The fireworks," I said. "Shoot the fireworks to scare them."

Frankie didn't ask questions; he simply ran to where we'd hidden them behind the palm trees.

"Aim *up*," Mint called. "And be careful, you don't want to—"

How it happened, none of us would ever figure out, no matter how many times we replayed it. One minute, Frankie was fumbling with the Roman candle; the next, his bathing suit was smoking, the firework was whistling upward, we were all shouting, and Frankie was doing what he later swore was the only thing he could think of: yanking his burning bathing suit off his body. He kicked it away right as the Roman candle exploded in the air, cracking like gunfire. The crowd gasped; the Chapman students ran, fleeing the street.

"Someone cover Frankie!" Mint yelled. Frankie was wide-eyed, frozen in shock, hands cupping his middle. For once, Coop was obedient, tearing a giant leaf off a palm tree and shoving it at him. For a second, Frankie just looked at the leaf. Then, slowly, he shook his head.

"Let's hear it for the *Crimson*," Frankie yelled, darting forward around the perimeter of the float, hands high in the air, while Coop chased him with the leaf. The crowd lost it when Frankie turned his back to them.

"Show-off!" Jack yelled from the driver's seat. He put his foot to the gas, and the float lurched forward.

It was utter chaos.

"More fireworks!" Heather called. I whipped around, pulled by the laughter in her voice, and sure enough, she was beaming, looking out over the running Chapman Hall students and the shrieking crowd like this had all been perfectly executed.

"Are you crazy? We'll burn down the float!"

Ignoring me, she lit a Roman candle. It sailed into the air in a perfect arc, cracking open into a sparkling flower. She shrugged. "I shoot fireworks with my dad every Fourth of July."

Of course. Father-daughter time, that mysterious thing.

We turned the corner, revealing Blackwell Tower—and, in front of it, the massive stage where the chancellor gave his Homecoming address. We were so close.

Coop stepped to my side, his face wreathed in a halo of confetti.

"You look like a maniac," I told him. "A school-spirit angel."

He handed me a lighter. "Come on, we both know you want to." When he glanced at me, the look was back, and it was just the two of us, the rest of the cheering, laughing, exploding world fading into the background. It was the return of that look, more than anything, that had me flicking the lighter, touching flame to the firework.

"Jessica the *rebel*," Coop shouted, as the Roman candle shot up.

I watched through my fingers as it crested and opened, raining light like glittering gemstones.

The float neared the stage. And, for the first time, we came face-to-face with the chancellor, standing in the center of it, gripping a tall microphone. Even from here, I could see his face was purple.

"Will *all students*," he bellowed, "who wish to remain enrolled in this university kindly *cease fire*."

We were heroes. Not to the administration, of course, who'd escorted us straight into the chancellor's office in Blackwell, where we'd had to wait an hour just to be yelled at about *indecent exposure, illicit fireworks, complaints from irate Chapman Hall students*. The chancellor kept questioning Coop, the only one of us who'd refused to put on a shirt, like he was the dark mastermind behind the whole thing. But there was still Mint, with his family's clout, and Frankie, the football star, to contend with. So in the end he gave us two months' community service and a stern warning to stay out of trouble for the next three years.

No, the administration hated us. But the *students*...

We walked into the Phi Delt Homecoming party that night, the seven of us together, arms laced, and stopped dead in our tracks. Hanging from the staircase in the foyer was the banner from our float, the one where we'd crossed out *Chapman Hall Champions* and painted *East House Seven.*

"Holy shit," Heather breathed. "They saved it."

The frat house was madness, filled with more people than usual, regular students plus alumni, the latter mostly slick, polished lawyers and bank managers in dad jeans. A guy standing at the top of the staircase near the banner spotted us and pointed with his beer. "*East House Seven!*"

Everyone in the foyer turned, their eyes like spotlights swinging in our direction. "It's those streakers from the parade!" someone shouted. "The ones who tried to shoot down the chancellor!"

Cheers and whistles exploded across the room. "You shoulda won the Battle!" someone yelled from the back.

A Phi Delt senior rushed forward, grabbing Frankie. "Man, you guys have balls of steel." He slung an arm over Jack's shoulders, then winked at Heather and me. "But seriously, what'd the Chance say? You're not kicked out, are you? 'Cause you clowns were born to be Phi Delt." He punched Mint's shoulder. "And *you*. Fucking troublemaker, who knew? I love it."

The brother dragged the boys away in the direction of the bar. I raised my eyebrows at their backs. If Frankie and Jack weren't being rushed on their own merits before, they certainly were now.

"Come on," Caro said, tugging my hand. "Dance floor!"

I turned, realizing I hadn't seen Coop since we walked in—where had he disappeared to, and so fast?—but Caro was already pulling me.

It turned out it wasn't only the boys who were famous. When we stepped onto the dance floor, the crowd parted, dancers turning to tell us they loved our float, our bikinis, that we were a breath of fresh air, subversives taking on the administration and skewering Homecoming traditions. We laughed at their compliments, but we didn't correct them, didn't say, *We were only out for revenge; everything else was an accident.* We just smiled and drank what they handed us.

Only Courtney wasn't impressed. She glared at us from the corner of the dance floor, surrounded by her usual coterie of girls who were dressed like knockoff versions of her. They whispered, pressing close, wanting her shine to rub off on them. I almost felt sorry for her, but then again, I could afford to now. It could have been the East House Eight, but she'd bet wrong. Now we had the glory, and she was cut out. I could already feel the divide growing between us, invisible but solid.

Heather paid no attention to Courtney, spinning on the dance floor with her arms outstretched. We'd switched dresses tonight: she was wearing my pink dress that tied in the back, and I wore a black dress I'd coveted since the day I saw her buy it at the mall, though I blanched even remembering the price tag. When we were getting ready, she'd asked, *Want to borrow?* And it hadn't even been a question. Immediately I'd turned to her closet, looking right where this dress hung, fabric whisper-thin and shimmery. But I couldn't admit I wanted it until she'd said, *I'll wear one of yours. An even trade.* Then it had been okay. She'd pulled my pink dress on, and said, *Perfect fit*, with a little smile. And then, to her reflection, tugging on the bow, *Charmingly down-market.*

It was that word—*down-market*—that made something click when it hadn't before. Made me remember what she'd said to Courtney when she defended me yesterday: *Stop punching down.* Meaning I was Heather's friend, yes, but that's how she saw me: beneath her.

I wore her black dress anyway. So maybe I was.

The song changed to something Frankie liked to play on repeat in his room, and Jack came swinging around the corner, clutching a bottle of whiskey, his perfectly combed Mr. Rogers hair mussed over his forehead like he'd been roughhousing.

"It's my *song*," Frankie said, skidding onto the dance floor behind Jack, losing his balance so fast Jack had to grip him to keep him upright. Without losing a beat, Frankie whirled to Caro and lifted her by the waist. "Has anyone told you you're *tiny*?"

"But mighty," Mint said, stepping up behind them with another bottle of whiskey, his cheeks flushed, eyes bright. Drunk. "Our East House spy."

"Sweet saboteur!" Jack crooned.

I eyed Mint, nodding at his whiskey. "The Phi Delt brothers sure love you."

He shrugged, but couldn't contain his grin. "They love all of us. You're probably a lock for Chi O, by the way. After today."

What a stark contrast. Yesterday, I'd been old Jessica Miller. Today, I was the girl in the expensive dress, one-seventh a star, a future Chi O pledge. I thought of Duquette's promise: *We will change you, body and soul.* Maybe it was happening.

Heather spotted Jack and stopped spinning, her eyes focusing like he was the only person in the room. She walked to him and stretched out her hand. Jack looked uncertain for a second, then took a deep breath and walked toward her, reaching out.

"The whiskey," she said. He froze, nearly fumbling the bottle as he snapped his hand back and replaced it with the whiskey. Even the darkness of the room couldn't hide the high color on his cheeks.

Heather took a swig from the bottle, then held it out again. She was smiling her cat-and-canary smile. "For courage," she said.

What was she up to? The perennial question.

Jack made for the bottle, but she grabbed his hand and pulled him in. Right in the middle of the dance floor, with all of us watching, Heather kissed him, whiskey bottle in one hand, Jack's face cupped in the other.

"*Finally*," I groaned, and Frankie whistled so loud I was sure Jack would wrench away and bolt. Mint turned to me, grinning, and opened his mouth to say something, but just then the music hit a crescendo, the bass vibrating through the floor, and Frankie yelled, "This is my favorite part!"

Instead of speaking, Mint grabbed my hand and spun me, the black dress fanning out in a perfect circle. Out of the corner of my eye, I could see Caro laughing with Frankie; Jack and Heather finally pulling apart, their heads still close.

"Where's Coop?" I yelled, against the rising music.

Mint turned and pointed to the back door, which led off the dance floor to a courtyard. "Where else?"

I looked. Sure enough, there stood Coop, in the corner of the courtyard with two other guys. He was deep in conversation, listening to one of them talk. Absently, he pushed a hand through his hair, tucking it behind his ear. I watched a strand curl up rebelliously, but he didn't seem to notice. Only me.

Here I was, in the middle of a crowded party, in a private room of my own.

But my looking pulled at him, and he turned.

"Coop!" yelled Caro, jumping in time to the music, even as it sped. "Come *dance* with us!"

"Don't be a loser!" Heather yelled.

Jack lifted his bottle. "We have whiskey!"

"I'll get naked again," Frankie boomed. "If you ask nice."

Coop laughed and shook his head, turning back to his conversation. I took a deep breath and yelled, "Come on, *Coop.*"

He turned and raised his brows. I raised mine. A challenge. Suddenly he was slapping one of the guys' hands, passing something between them, and walking in the door, cutting across the dance floor. Caro and Frankie whooped; Jack grinned with the whiskey bottle outstretched. And inside me was a feeling I barely recognized, one I didn't have words for. The closest might have been *Look what I can do* or *Oh, what have I done*.

But Coop didn't come to me. He walked straight to Caro, pushed past Frankie to grab her hand and spin her, making her laugh. The feeling inside me turned into an arrow—

Mint seized me just as a boy burst from the foyer onto the dance floor, wearing our banner over his shoulders like a cape, and everyone jumped back, clapping. The song was climbing toward its climax, toward the top of the hill, and we were laughing, the seven of us, jumping, arms brushing. I could see their faces, shining in the dark. And I think I knew, even then, that it would never get better than this. I think some part of me could sense—even here in our triumph, in our wild, perfect beginning—the small seeds of our destruction.

CHAPTER 6
JANUARY, FRESHMAN YEAR

Terror and anticipation: the world's most potent chemical cocktail. Before Bid Day, I'd never witnessed so many girls about to expire from it in my life. The basketball court in the gym was packed, wall to wall, with squirming, shaking freshmen, some talking a mile a minute, others deathly quiet. Caro and I represented both camps: she couldn't shut up, and I couldn't manage a word.

"Do you think it's true what they say, that the frats line up on their porches and yell at us as we run? Do you think it's true they throw things? What if absolutely no one wants us and we fall straight to the bottom, land in AOD or something? What if we don't get Chi O?" Caro closed her eyes, breathing deeply. "It'll be okay. Everything will be okay."

What if I didn't get Chi O? That was the fear haunting me. But I *would* get in; I had to. Getting in would be like getting my forehead stamped with the words *beautiful, popular, best,* so everywhere I walked, people would know.

Our Panhellenic leader handed Caro an envelope, then me.

Heather scooted closer. "Excited?"

"Uh-huh," said Caro unconvincingly. I nodded, throat dry.

"This is our social destiny, right here in our hands!" Heather tossed her envelope and laughed, as if it wasn't weighted with a thousand pounds of expectations. Because of course. I was learning there wasn't a second of her life Heather didn't feel supremely confident. It was intoxicating, normally. Now, I felt a stab of envy.

"All right, ladies," the Panhellenic president called over the microphone. "The time is here. Open your envelopes; then you're free to race to your new home on campus, where your sisters await you!"

Across the gym, squeals and the sounds of tearing. I pulled at my envelope, but it resisted me.

Next to me, Caro shrieked. "*I got Kappa!* Oh my God, Jess. I know it's not Chi O, but I'm still excited!"

I didn't have time to console her. Screams and sobs echoed through the gym. I pulled harder, finally tearing the envelope in half, clutching the beautiful engraved card inside.

Jessica Miller, we are excited to have you as a member of Kappa Kappa Gamma's 2006 pledge class!

Kappa? Though I was sitting, the ground beneath me spun. A sob tried to escape, but I held it back. I couldn't cry here. I wouldn't. I needed to get out before what was building inside me exploded.

A shriek of happiness drew my attention to where Heather and Courtney jumped up and down together, their bridges long-since mended from Homecoming. "We're roommates *and* Chi Os!" Heather crowed.

They'd gotten in and I hadn't. Heather and Courtney. The room tilted.

"Jess, what'd you get?" Caro smiled, but her eyes were worried.

I thrust the card at her.

"This is perfect!" She threw her arms wide. "We're in it together! Jess, this is great. Now we can do it side by side!"

I scrambled to my feet, ignoring her arms, and took off across the gym, dodging clusters of girls, some jumping with joy, others openly crying.

I burst free of the gym and broke into a run, going as fast as my legs would take me, ignoring the cold January air, the strange looks, the guy who yelled, "Wrong way to frat row, freshman!"

By the time I got to East House, I could barely see through the blur of tears. *I'd failed.* I was vaguely aware of passing Frankie and Jack in the quad, the two of them drinking beer and laughing in front of a suspiciously endowed snowman. But I didn't dare stop, just darted inside and up the staircase—running smack into something solid. Arms reached out and grabbed me before I could topple back.

"Jess?"

I rubbed my eyes. It was Coop in his leather motorcycle jacket, probably on his way to wherever he always went and refused to tell us.

His hands were on my shoulders, warm even through my peacoat. He studied me. "What's wrong?"

I shook my head. I really wanted to go to my room. Even if Rachel was there, I didn't care. I would let myself cry anyway, and she would have to deal.

He rubbed my shoulders, and I couldn't help leaning into him. "Seriously, you can tell me."

"I didn't get into Chi O," I blurted out, unable to keep it inside any longer. "I preffed them but they turned me down, and now I'm a Kappa. I can't believe I didn't get it. What's wrong with me?"

"This is about sororities?" Coop dropped his hands from my shoulders and stuffed them in his pockets. "You know that's elitist bullshit, right? Why would you want to be part of that? It's literally designed to make you hate yourself—that's the juice the whole system runs on."

That was the final straw. I burst into tears.

"Oh shit. You're really upset. Okay, we can fix this." Coop put his arm around my shoulders and opened the door to the third-floor hall. "Come on, let's talk. You can tell me the mean things the Chi Os did, and then we'll egg their house or something."

"No," I said, even as I let him pull me down the hall to his and Mint's room. "I don't want to bother you."

He opened the door and ushered me in. I couldn't help the ghost of a smile, even now, in their room. It was the perfect representation of how different Mint and Coop were: one side was masculine brown and blue, expensive sheets, swimming trophies, everything neat. The other was band posters and bright-pink sheets, crap strewn everywhere.

"Trust me"—Coop planted me on his bed—"you're far from bothering me."

He dropped his keys on his desk and walked to the door. "Stay right there. I'm going to get us root beer and Red Vines so we can get some sugar in your system. Those are your favorites, right? You're always eating Red Vines when you study."

I nodded, trying to keep the tears inside.

"Okay, be right back. Seriously, don't move." Coop slipped out and shut the door behind him.

Alone, I let myself cry. I didn't understand what I'd done wrong. During rush I'd tried to tell myself not to get my hopes up, tried to hedge my bets, but it didn't matter: I'd wanted Chi O with my whole heart. I'd pictured walking around campus with those letters on my chest, letting everyone know where I stood. Imagined telling my dad I'd gotten into the top sorority on campus. Presenting him with the irrefutable evidence: *Look who I am. So good. Other people saw it and gave me this as proof.*

The door swung open and I jerked in surprise. But instead of Coop, Mint stood in the doorway, staring. I scrubbed the tears from my cheeks, fingers coming away black with mascara. *Oh, god.* The day was only getting worse.

"Sorry," I said, jumping to my feet. "I was hanging with Coop. I'll go."

"Hold on." Mint swung his backpack to the floor, dropping his coat on his desk. "You're crying." He peered closer. "It's sorority Bid Day, right?"

Of course Mint knew about Bid Day. He, Jack, and Frankie started pledging Phi Delt next week. It was a relief he understood the significance of what I was going through, but also an embarrassment, because he hadn't had any problems shooting straight to the top.

"Come on." Mint sat on his perfectly made bed and patted the spot next to him. I walked across the room and sat, looking at him out of the corner of my eye.

"I didn't get into Chi O," I admitted, the words painful. "I really wanted it."

"Of course you did. What'd you get?"

"Kappa."

Mint knocked my knee with his. "Kappa's a good one."

I looked at him. How was it possible that even here, midday in a dingy dorm room, his eyes were so impossibly blue?

"You don't have to lie to me. We both know Chi O's the best. Courtney and Heather both got in."

"Heather?"

I swung to face him. "I know, right? I don't mean to be rude, but..." I stopped. It was eating at me, chewing a hole in my heart. I wanted to say it out loud, but I wasn't sure how Mint would react. What if he told me to leave, then told Heather? I took a breath, then took the plunge. "Why *her*?"

Courtney, I understood—of course she got Chi O, she was born for it. But Heather? Heather was barely pretty. Her forehead was too big. She was short. It's not like she had stellar grades or was so much more popular. Being part of the East House Seven gave Heather and me equal standing, or so I'd thought. She came from money—was that it? Or was it the power of her loud voice, her confidence, her outsized personality?

It was a terrible way to think. I *loved* Heather. She made me feel brave, like there was nothing we couldn't do when we were together. But I just couldn't stop picturing her jumping with Courtney, laughing and waving the card that should have been mine. What if our spots had gotten mixed up? What if I went to the Panhellenic president and opened an inquiry, and they realized their mistake? I envisioned the president taking Heather's card from her and handing it to me, the rightful owner.

No. Obviously, I couldn't do that. But I felt so helpless. I wanted to do something to take control, take away the pain. The vision of Heather's happy face cut at me.

"Look," Mint said, putting a hand on my leg. "Chi O made a mistake by not choosing you. Show them that."

"How?" Where we touched, my skin tingled.

"Kappa is number two, right? All you have to do is take the number-one spot from Chi O. Rush harder. Beat them at their own game. I'll help you."

"You will?"

He turned and faced me, cross-legged. I couldn't help it—I pictured the scene in *Sixteen Candles* when Jake Ryan sits across the table from Molly Ringwald's character, birthday cake between them, and tells her to make a wish. He was Jake Ryan, but in gold.

"Of course. Whatever I can do."

I almost asked why, but didn't want to ruin the moment. "Tell me something," I said instead. "Something embarrassing."

"What?" Mint looked taken aback.

"I just told you how I failed," I said, "and now I'm sitting here feeling ashamed. Tell me something to level the playing field."

Mint's cheeks actually turned pink—was I witnessing him blush? I marveled at my power.

"Something you've never told anyone else," I added, emboldened.

He studied me. I must have looked pitiful, because he blew out a breath. "Okay. I'll tell you something I'm ashamed of, if you swear never to repeat it."

"I swear." The words were a binding oath. I could feel a string snap taut between us.

"My mom…" His voice caught, and he took another deep breath. I got goose bumps—he really was going to tell me something important, I could feel it.

"Last year, I found out my mom cheated on my dad."

I gasped sympathetically.

"It was humiliating. She'd been cheating on him a long time, it turned out, with one of the members of the board of my parents' company. Everyone found out. But she refused to stop seeing the guy. I expected my dad to end things, divorce her—hell, punch the asshole in the face. I was preparing myself to be a latchkey kid. But he totally folded."

"What do you mean?"

"He was so weak. He didn't even fight it. He let her walk all over him, let this other guy emasculate him. He cried for days and begged her not to divorce him, said she could keep seeing the guy, anything she wanted. Everyone found out about that, too, and now everywhere we go, people whisper about how my mom's getting it from some other guy, and my dad's a fucking cuckold."

Mint's voice had grown harder and sharper as he spoke. When he said *cuckold*, that strange, old-fashioned word, it was like jagged glass. I leaned back. "My dad's the biggest coward. I hate him. Everyone at home talks about me behind my back, and it's all his fault. At a dinner party my mom threw before I left for Duquette, he came late from work and I locked him out of the house. People were laughing and pointing at him through the windows. And you know what? Instead of feeling bad for him, I felt good. *Really* good. *He* was the loser, not me."

"Mint, that's terrible," I said, unable to help it.

"Yeah, well. Now you know a shameful secret. Feel better?"

We sat in silence while I processed the fact that the perfect Mark Minter had such a messed-up family. I swallowed. "I think I hate my father, too."

Mint had been studying his comforter; now, he looked up at me. "Really?"

"I think so."

"Well, will you look at us. Two jerks who hate their dads."

I laughed with relief, because of course Mint wasn't a jerk, and if I was grouped with him, I was going to be okay.

"I can't believe you told me something so personal," I said.

"You asked me to."

"Yeah, but…I didn't think you'd actually do it."

"Jess." Mint blinked. "I like you."

For the second time that day, the world tilted on its axis. Mark Minter liked *me*? Me, Jessica Miller? It was the most improbable of victories, like winning the lottery, or finding a golden ticket in your chocolate bar.

He swallowed, looking unbearably nervous, and I realized I hadn't yet responded, lost in wonder. "I don't believe you," I said.

He cracked a smile, bright as the sun, and he was back to being the golden boy, shameful confession far behind him. "Why not?"

"Because you're…*Mint.*"

He put his hands on either side of my face. "I like the way you think of me."

I took a deep breath, smelling his cologne, orange and spices, and then he was pulling me toward him, kissing me with that beautiful mouth. It was slow and gentle at first until I scooted closer, rising onto my knees, and he deepened the kiss, tangling his hands in my hair. I pulled away, breathless. *The most perfect boy in the world.*

"I like you, too," I said, the understatement of the century, and kissed him again.

A heavy thud made us wrench apart. I twisted to the doorway, heart racing. Coop stood there staring, Red Vines in his hand, two bottles of root beer rolling at his feet.

CHAPTER 7
NOW

If there was a hell on earth, it was this moment.

"Kill your father, then you're free? Quoting Freud at a college party is too clichéd for you, darling." In slow motion, Caro walked past me to where Coop stood, leaning in to kiss him. It was a surreal image, like rewatching a beloved movie, only to find the actors suddenly switched and everything now wrong. I looked away, focusing on the way my stiletto heels stabbed twin holes into the grass.

"I, for one, would be sad if Coop's brand ever changed." Mint raised his glass. "Long may my favorite roommate darken our otherwise idyllic lives."

Courtney's candy-red lips widened into a smile, flashing teeth as white and straight as her husband's. "Actually, since Minty and I couldn't make the engagement party, let's cheers to Caro and Coop."

The engagement party. Memories surfaced, too fast for me to push back, edges blurred by alcohol but still clear enough to be damning. I refocused, realizing everyone else had lifted their glasses. I hastily added my own, though it was empty.

"To Caroline Rodriguez," Coop toasted, "a living saint, who rescued me from depression and poverty after law school. May I eventually be worthy of her."

Caro blushed prettily.

"To Caro and Coop," everyone sang. I echoed, a beat too late.

"Speaking of depression and poverty, guess who I saw?" Courtney raised her brows. "Eric Shelby. Remember him, always creeping around wherever we went? Figures he'd worm his way into our Homecoming party."

Caro's cheeks flushed. "He *works* here. And you should be nicer to him."

"I need a drink," I announced, to no one in particular, then dug my heels out of the dirt and hurried in the direction of the bar.

My plan was unraveling. No one was reacting the way I'd thought. I hadn't anticipated Caro ambushing me so quickly, hadn't expected to be shoved into Courtney and Mint, to feel the claustrophobic pressure of Eric somewhere out there, circling us. I hadn't in a million years expected my own reaction to seeing Coop again.

It changed everything. What chance did I have of showing everyone the newer, truer me—brilliant, beautiful, successful Jessica—if I had to spend all weekend avoiding him? How would I secure my triumph if, at every moment, I had to focus on pushing memories away, acting like I didn't care?

I thought I'd already beaten this, the stirring in my blood, the prickling awareness of real, flesh-and-blood Coop, only yards behind me. My body was so alert, and he'd barely glanced at me.

I had to leave. Put as much distance between us as possible. The bartender filled my glass to the brim with wine, somehow sensing my need. I shoved money into his tip jar and fled out of the tent, heading toward the velvety blackness of the trees. Tonight was ruined, but I'd recover tomorrow. All was not lost. The important thing was staying away from—

"Running away?"

I froze midstep.

"I guess your brand hasn't changed much, either."

I turned slowly, hoping against hope, but there he stood, tall and lit by the glow from the tent, his face half-shadowed.

I straightened. He watched the movement closely, following the way the straps of my dress pulled over my skin. I cleared my throat. "Coming in swinging. That strategy always worked so well for you."

Coop grinned. A rare thing.

"Why are you here?" I asked.

"Why wouldn't I be? I graduated from Duquette, didn't I? No matter how hard those bastards tried to stop me."

I tipped my glass back, letting wine slide down my throat. *Talking to him alone is a bad idea. Walk away, Jessica.*

"Cheers," he said, lifting his glass.

I tried not to look at his eyes, but I couldn't help it; his gaze dragged mine up from the ground. Eyes vivid green, dark-lashed, looking at me like he always did—too intense. Goose bumps crawled across my arms. "If I recall, the old Coop thought Homecoming was stupid."

"Maybe the new Coop is full of school spirit." *The new Coop*—of course. It had been ten years since college. A full year since we'd even talked. Like me, he was different now. It wasn't just that he was a lawyer, which had always seemed so improbable in college. Or that he lived in a new city, wasn't joined at the hip with Jack and Frankie and Mint. He was *engaged* now. He belonged to someone else. To my best friend.

I repeated it to myself, over and over.

"Well," I said, starting to step around him. "I'm glad you came. If you'll excuse me."

He caught my arm. "What... We're not going to talk about it?"

A chill ran the length of my body. His hand was warm, the fall air

71

cold. He was so close. I opened my mouth to speak, but he shook his head.

"Don't you dare say *talk about what.*"

I didn't move. "I don't think there's anything to say. It's been a year."

He clenched his jaw. "Can we have an honest conversation for once in our goddamn lives?"

I laughed—I couldn't help it. "Having an honest conversation is what ruined things in the first place."

A light sparked in his eyes. His fingers flexed on my arm. "I thought you said you were drunk at the engagement party."

A memory: my heart, shattered into pieces. My body, unsure how to function without it. Unable to put one foot in front of the other, swimming in pain. The beautiful brass bar, the bottles of red wine, Caro, resplendent in white. The desperate thought: *I have to tell him.*

We were crossing into dangerous territory. I could feel the ghosts starting to stir. "I was," I said carefully. "Very drunk."

"Well, which was it? Were you being honest, or were you drunk?" The look in his eyes was too serious. *Jesus Christ*, Coop. He always wanted so much.

It all rushed back. Caro and Coop's engagement party. Everyone there—families, all our college friends, except Mint and Courtney, of course, off on some glamorous vacation. At first, the news that Coop was dating Caro had been a slash to my heart. As Caro's friend, I had to hear every excruciating detail about how they'd reconnected. How Caro—who checked in on her old friends, no matter how much time had passed, because she was that kind of person—gave Coop a call one day out of the blue.

And apparently it was perfect timing. Coop, struggling with law school and full-time work, but also haunted by something—Caro had whispered it, like a secret between us, *haunted*. He'd needed a friend, and there she was. I'd acted puzzled, kept my voice light over the phone, even as my heart hammered, even as I wanted to scream that I *knew* what haunted him, and it had its hold on me, too.

I'd borne their relationship silently, because I had to. Waited for the wound to heal, or for them to break up, which I told myself was inevitable.

But then the opposite happened. Caro said she was moving to Greenville to live with him. Then, too quick, the call came, the one where Caro was shrieking, and my knees were buckling. They were engaged. And something inside me crumbled, something important that had been there for years, holding me up, although I'd never realized it. I'd tried all my usual tricks to dull the pain, but the only thing that worked reliably was wine.

"Jess, I need you to be honest." Coop tugged my arm, pulling me closer. "It's been years since I could read you."

Was I being honest, that night at the engagement party? Clutching him in the darkest corner of the bar, begging, *Don't marry her. You're supposed to love me. Love me, love me, love me.* Like an incantation, powerful if said enough times. Grabbing his hand. *Leave with me right now, let's go. Let's run away and never come back.*

His hands on my shoulders. *You're drunk, Jess. You don't mean what you're saying.* His face stony. *I know you don't mean it. Because if you did, it would be the cruelest thing you've ever done.* Stepping away, putting distance between us. *And Caro is your friend.*

Honest, or drunk?

I looked at Coop's hand on my arm, his strong, graceful fingers. I followed the hard curves of his biceps, visible through his sweater, skimming the elegant swoop of his neck to his full lips, long lashes, shock of dark hair. Every inch of him familiar, beautiful, infuriating.

I felt alive in a way I hadn't for a full year, maybe longer, and the feeling made the decision for me. I couldn't let him disappear from my life again. From this moment on, I would play by the rules, take no risks, stick to friends only. Even if all I ever got was a sliver of Coop—a few friendly words, a hand on my arm—I would make do. No matter how much it hurt.

"I was drunk," I whispered, the words like a door closing. "Of course."

He closed his eyes for a moment, then opened them, dark and burning. "Coward."

CHAPTER 8
MARCH, JUNIOR YEAR

No matter what I did, the bills found me. If I avoided my mailbox in the student center, they were delivered to my door. If I buried them under books and papers on my desk, somehow they unearthed themselves, knocked over accidentally by Caro or Heather and scattered across the floor.

The same day I opened the red envelope and discovered, as a college junior, I was ten thousand dollars in debt—bolded words threatening *legal action for continued nonpayment*—Heather's parents surprised her with a brand-new BMW. It was the first day of Parents' Weekend, which always turned campus into a cheery, buttoned-up version of itself. My own parents never came. Surely, they'd received the invitation from the school, gold-foiled and thick-weighted, but they'd never once mentioned it.

When I opened the door to our suite, bill in hand, I found not only Heather and Caro, but Heather's and Caro's parents, squealing and popping champagne in our tiny kitchen. Clinking slender, fizzy glasses, they made a beautiful, if confusing, tableau.

I stopped in the doorway. "What's going on?"

"It's a precelebration for Heather's twenty-first birthday," Dr. Shelby said fondly. Heather's mother was a carbon copy of her, down to the too-big forehead. She was dressed in loose, roomy clothes and heavy jewelry, like the proprietor of a spa in Sedona. It was a style I'd grown familiar with at Duquette and taken to calling Rich Woman Over Fifty.

"They got me a new *car!*" Heather tossed me a set of keys. "No more old Audi. I'm taking Jack and his parents for a ride later if you want to come."

I caught the keys with the hand holding the red envelope, then jerked away quickly, lest they see it. The keys were large and heavy, inset with the blue-and-white BMW logo, that potent talisman of value. I swallowed and set them down. "Ah, regular old keys." I smiled to show I was joking. "Thought they'd be gold-plated or something."

I wondered what they'd do with Heather's Audi, all of five years old.

"Let's pour you a glass," Mr. Shelby said. He was short, balding, and never without a smile. "It's French. The real stuff."

"Actually," I said, clutching the bill, "I forgot I have an art lab."

"*Art* lab?" Caro's mom looked puzzled. "I thought you were an econ major."

"She is," Heather said, waving a hand. "Jess is a total brain. But she doesn't actually like econ. She *loves* painting."

"Econ is a much more practical choice." Caro's dad shot her a warning look, as if he was worried my impracticality was contagious. "Especially in the middle of a recession. Did you hear they're saying the housing market—"

"I like having an artist friend, personally," Heather interrupted. "Not everything in the world has to be about money." She winked at me, raising her champagne glass. "To Jess, our very own Renoir."

"Don't worry," I said to Caro's dad, ignoring Heather's theatrics. "It's just a hobby." I backed away to the door, catching a flash of Caro's confused face as I waved over my shoulder. She memorized my schedule every semester, so she knew I was lying about the art lab. But I had to get out.

I raced through campus, not sure where I was going until I stood in front of Blackwell Tower. I slipped inside and climbed the stairs, tears coming as I moved, circle after winding circle, higher and higher.

Of course I wasn't an art major. I needed a serious degree, one that could lift you up in the world, open doors. At Duquette it was easy to see what power looked like: students with internships at their fathers' hedge funds that seamlessly transfigured into jobs; deans who came to academia from private equity firms after donating huge chunks of money; endowed professors who took a break from teaching to advise the president on trade deals. Power looked like Maseratis parked in the season-ticket-holder spots at football games and familiar names on the baseball stadium. It looked like Dr. John Garvey, celebrity economist.

I'd finally gotten into one of Dr. Garvey's classes this semester, and it was hard not to be mesmerized by his lectures. He had a dry, cutting voice, wore three-piece suits, and name-checked Defense secretaries. He berated any student who dared walk in late, expected us to have read all his books on economic theory.

He'd reminded me of somebody I couldn't quite put my finger on, someone familiar, and it wasn't until last week's class that I'd finally realized, with a kick of shame, who it was. Dr. Garvey reminded me of the man I imagined my father was before he'd become my father—a Harvard econ major with dreams of working in DC, dreams of changing the world. The should-have-been, would-have-been dad.

It was strangely fitting, then, that Dr. Garvey was my best shot at realizing my father's ambitions. If I played my cards right in his class, worked above and beyond to secure his powerful endorsement, I'd have a strong chance of winning the Duquette Post-Graduate Fellowship next year. The fellowship would open doors to Harvard grad school and give me the money to make it a reality.

Not everything in this world has to be about money, Heather had said.

Heather: my staunchest defender, ever since the day she'd stood up for me to Courtney. But Heather was also the girl who got a BMW just for being born—not for getting high grades, or winning any award, or doing anything remotely special. Heather didn't need to worry about practical majors. She got everything she wanted, got to fit in effortlessly with the Chi Os and the Phi Delts, all the rich kids who mattered.

Meanwhile, *I* had to hide where I came from, my family's lack of money, my father's…situation. *I* had to dig myself into a debt-ridden grave just to have one inch of what Heather had, or Courtney, or so many other kids on campus.

Especially Mint. Like Heather, my boyfriend got everything he wanted at the drop of a hat. As much as I loved him, our lives were as different as night and day.

I finally reached the top of Blackwell Tower and burst into the hidden storage room, a secret space known only to upperclassmen. I didn't bother stifling my sobs.

"Jess? What are you doing here?"

Shit. I whirled, frantically wiping my eyes. Save for the stacks of old furniture and cardboard boxes, the room had looked empty through my tears. But there he was, leaning against the wall in the corner, one hand in his pocket.

"Coop." I tried to make my voice light. "Figures. Why do you always seem to find me at my lowest?"

"Actually," Coop said, "you're the one who finds me."

"Sorry. I'll go. I thought I'd be alone."

He dropped something on the floor and ground it out with his foot. He walked closer, both hands in his pockets, eyeing me cautiously. His hair was so mussed he looked a touch feral.

"Should I get Mint? I think he's with his parents at a steak house, but I can find him."

I tried to smile. "No. But thanks." Mint was the last person in the world I could tell about my debt. And the thought of his parents catching wind made me sick to my stomach.

"Okay. I cede the room, then." Coop tucked his hair behind his ears and walked to the door.

"Wait."

He stopped. I swallowed, looking out the large windows at Duquette's campus, in the process of being swallowed by dusk. "Will you stay, actually?"

Coop turned, and we locked eyes. I tried to read his face, but he kept it carefully blank.

"Sure," he said finally. He made his way back, standing awkwardly beside me. "Are you going to make me guess why you're crying?"

I dropped to the floor, drawing my knees to my chin. "It's nothing."

"Liar." He sat, too, keeping a careful distance between us. But it didn't matter; I could still feel him, a humming energy across the empty space.

I clutched my bill tighter on instinct, and the movement caught his eye. Before I could stop him, he lunged and snatched it.

"Coop—*no!*"

He unfolded the paper from the envelope and scanned it. My heart plummeted. This was it. The moment my veneer was shattered, when my ugly truth came out. First, Coop, then surely everyone would know.

He whistled, eyeing me. "Damn, Jess. That's a lot of money. You better pay it fast."

I stared at him, wide-eyed.

He frowned. The magic-hour sunlight played over his face, dappling it with shadows from the trees. "What, you're embarrassed?"

I couldn't move.

"Jess, my dad split when I was five. I was raised by a single mom who worked two jobs my whole life, three for a couple of years. If you think I'm a stranger to the red envelope, you're wrong."

I released a breath. "Really?"

He laughed. "Are you kidding? None of the rest of those spoiled assholes would understand, but I do." He shot me a coy look. "Apologies for slandering your boyfriend. I know how much you adore the golden boy. King of the frat and beloved of professors and all that."

"You sound jealous."

"I am. But not of those things."

I pressed my legs together against the sudden charge in the air.

His eyes dropped to my knees. "So, you're going to pay it off, right?"

"I can't." Saying the words out loud made the tears well again. I dragged my hand over my eyes before he could see. "Neither can my parents. They'd kill me if they knew I opened this credit card. I did it secretly, so I could have the same things as everyone else." I didn't know why I was confessing so much, but here it was, out in the open.

Coop ran a hand through his hair, and it went wild again. It stayed upright even after he dropped his hand to the floor and leaned back to brace himself.

"I'm fucked," I said. "I'm going to get sued."

He studied his legs, stretched over the floor, then took a deep breath. "I'll give you the money."

"That's absurd. How would you get ten thousand dollars?"

"Come on, like you don't know."

"I really don't."

Coop's voice rose a notch. "I sell things. I thought you knew."

Did he mean drugs? Like an actual drug dealer? Somewhere in the back of my mind, the pieces fit—Coop always *had* drugs, he went mysterious places at mysterious times—but it didn't lessen the shock.

"Say something."

"Does Mint buy his molly from you?"

"Everyone does. Pot. Molly. A few other things."

"That's bad, Coop. It's dangerous. People get killed over drugs."

"Yeah, well, my scholarship only goes so far. And there's no way I'm adding to my mom's plate when she can barely make rent. I told myself if I went to college, I'd make sure she never had to worry."

I eyed him sharply. "*You* got a scholarship? What were your SAT scores?" I hadn't made the cut for a scholarship to Duquette, but *Coop* had?

He leaned closer, dark hair falling over his forehead. "Seriously, that's your takeaway? You know I'm prelaw, right?"

I laughed, even though a small voice said it was mean. "A drug-dealing lawyer sounds like a pretty big conflict of interest. What if you get caught?"

"The law is nuanced and complicated, and I like nuanced and complicated. Plus, knowing the law helps me break it better. Didn't you get a scholarship, too? I assumed, you know…"

And just like that, the old wound opened. The ruined remains of my relationship with my mother, dug up from the grave. "No," I admitted. "I'm paying for it all myself."

He looked at me with wide eyes. "Why the fuck would you come here, then? No one who isn't rich as sin could afford this tuition."

I thought back to the night I'd gotten my acceptance from Duquette. The thick envelope, the slice of scissors across the top, the way I went too far, the sharp metal sliding against my finger, the bright spark of pain, but it didn't matter. Because the paper, pressed red with my blood, said *Congratulations*, and then there was the look on my father's face, the one I'd been waiting for my whole life.

"It was the best school I got into."

"No school's worth that…" Coop's voice trailed off.

No school's worth saddling yourself with this kind of debt, Jessica. You don't understand what you're doing. You're burying yourself alive. My mother's words, sharp with anger. But it didn't matter what she said, or how many times she said it, because none of her warnings compelled me. None of her criticisms compared to what Duquette gave me with my dad.

The day my father crashed our car and nearly shattered the windshield, my mother screamed for hours. I'd never heard her yell so much. Even though I locked myself in my bedroom and stuffed sheets in the crack under my door, I could still hear her intermittently, the words *serious problem* and *kill yourself* and *has to end*. I couldn't believe she was finally speaking up. For as long as I could remember, my dad's problem was something she and I had borne silently, addressed only obliquely, even when it was just us.

Although the truth was unspoken, I knew it was the pills my dad swallowed, day and night—such small, innocuous things—that made him the living dead. Gone from the world for hours, or awake but high, so disoriented, walking into walls. Stretches of days where he couldn't take off his bathrobe. Those days used to be occasional, but they'd grown more frequent. Someone from work had called, left a message on our answering machine. He was in danger of losing his accounting job at the steel company, which he hated, which was beneath him, which we needed.

In the days after the crash, he seemed lucid more often, but that only made me terrified to be in the same room with him. What if he looked up from his cereal bowl and noticed me—really took me in for the first time in years—and hated what he found? I tiptoed through the house, trying to be invisible.

Until it was time for college applications. One day I passed him at the kitchen table, wearing his Harvard University alumni shirt, and paused. Heart hammering, I told him I was filling out an application to Harvard.

A light went on inside him. He looked at me—really looked—and asked what my grades were, my SAT scores, my extracurriculars. He started talking feverishly, tapping his leg against the chair. I brought him the application and he pored over it. Getting into the best school in the world was imperative, he said. It would mean *I* was the best, the cream of the crop. When he got into Harvard, his parents told him it was the proudest moment of their lives. I knew he was telling the truth, because my grandparents brought up Harvard at every holiday. In their eyes my father was perfect. Smart, flawless, always one step away from getting his life back on track and becoming something big.

They didn't know about the pills.

My dad became obsessed with college applications. The moment I got home from school each day, I rushed to get them, fourteen in all, safeties and reaches, and we spread them over the kitchen table. Talked about answers to questions, reworked essays. We revised the Harvard application seven times until it was perfect, and then he took off a day from work so we could mail it together, ceremoniously. He kissed the stamp and closed the mailbox and I felt, with every fiber of my being, that my father loved me.

For months we waited, speculating about which dorm I'd get assigned to, where my classes would be. He was so normal, a version of himself I barely remembered but was thrilled to have back. Even my mother couldn't complain. When she wasn't in the room, he talked in a low voice about moving with me to Cambridge. Four whole years of father-daughter time.

Then the letter came in a thin envelope. *We regret to inform you*, it said, and the thing I wanted was gone, closed, ripped away. I wasn't good enough.

I waited for my father to say something—*anything*—but he locked himself in his bedroom and didn't come out for two days. When he did, he wouldn't look at me.

Two weeks later, the envelope came from Duquette. Not Harvard, but the next-best school on my list, number sixteen in the country. When I showed it to him, the light came back, and he broke his silence.

Good job, Jessica.

After that, it didn't matter that I didn't win a scholarship, that Duquette offered me no financial aid. There wasn't a universe in which I would have made a different choice.

I couldn't find the words to describe this to Coop, even if I wanted to. So instead I said, "You wouldn't understand."

He was quiet for a beat, then repeated in a low voice, "I wouldn't understand…"

I looked out the window. Below us was the central thoroughfare, a promenade that ran the entire length of campus—Frankie liked to run it every morning before football practice. Beyond that, a rolling expanse of treetops, broken by the elegant spires of teaching halls and dormitories.

"Jess."

When I turned, I found Coop leaning so close our knees almost touched. I inched back. My heartbeat notched higher. And I realized: *It was just the two of us. In a private room.*

"I understand everything about you. I know you're obsessed with making Kappa the top sorority because the Chi Os rejected you. I know you're obsessed with Mint and the Phi Delts because everyone else is, and it's a status symbol. I know you sneak Adderall to study all night even though econ makes you want to kill yourself. And now I know you charge thousands of dollars to a credit card you can't afford just to fit in."

I jumped to my feet. "Stop it, Coop. Shut up."

He got to his feet, too, taking a step toward me. When I pulled back, he grinned, a glint in his eyes.

"I understand," he said slowly, drawing the words out, "that you'd do anything to win. You're kind of a sociopath."

I froze. "That is the single worst thing anyone has ever said to me."

Slowly, his grin faded. But his eyes held mine, waiting.

What was happening to me? Where was the outpouring of anger, the indignation? Why did I feel not a *blaze of rage* but a sparking warmth, blooming somewhere deep, somewhere intimate and dangerous?

"I don't understand"—my voice was rising, almost yelling—"why I'm not *furious* right now. Why don't I want to hit you?"

"Because," Coop said, "you know I'm right. And you know it means I see you."

As soon as he said it, I knew it was true—not the sociopath part, but him seeing me. He always had. Ever since the first day.

Something wild unleashed inside me. Without pausing to think, I closed the distance between us and dragged Coop's mouth to mine. I kissed him hard, desperate to pull him under with me, wherever I was going. His full lips parted instantly, his fingers pushing through my hair, gripping me tighter. I kissed him hungrily, and he kissed back like a starved man, fisting his hands in my shirt, lifting the hem to press his palms against my stomach, running them over my ribs, his touch rough, as if desperate for each next square inch.

Abruptly he broke away, chest heaving.

"Are you sure?" His voice was husky, taut with worry. Like I held something precious in my hands, something he'd waited for, and there was a chance I'd take it away.

"Yes," I said, barely finishing the word before he was kissing me again, pushing me against the full-length window, my back flush against the cold glass; then the wall, his body a pressure I craved. He pressed his thumbs to the hollows of my cheekbones, fitting his hands against the seams of my face, and tilted my head back. He dragged his lips up my neck to my jaw to my mouth.

I groaned against his lips. I'd never messed up this hard on purpose. I'd never wanted anyone so badly in my life.

"You're my best friend's girlfriend." Coop lowered his head to kiss behind my ear. Delicious heat twisted between my legs. "Mint. The golden boy."

"Stop," I said, tipping my head further, urging him higher.

"I'm not like him."

I shivered, and he captured my mouth. His was warm and tasted faintly herbal. "I'm not an Eagle Scout. I'll do things you hate."

Coop. The boy who always said things that were too close to the truth, the one who made me uncomfortable, who looked at me too long, too closely. "Why are you telling me this?"

"I'm giving you an out." Coop ran his hands down my body, until he reached the place between my legs. He cupped me there, and I arched into the wall.

"I've wanted you since the first day I saw you, walking to class in your pleated skirt. I've spent three years thinking about this. Three years, not allowed to touch you, or breathe a word."

He unzipped my jeans and pushed his hand inside, stroking me through my panties, the heat of his hand too good, too much. I gasped.

"I'm telling you upfront. I need more. I need you over and over. So this is your out. Take it. Otherwise you're mine, the way it should have been."

He dropped to his knees on the wooden floor and slid my panties down. A rush of cool air, goose bumps, and then his mouth was on me, hot and stoking, so good it was damning.

It's just my body, I thought. *Just my body, not me; just a moment, not forever. He can have it.* Coop plunged his tongue. I cried softly and rose on my tiptoes, tangling my fingers in his thick, dark hair.

I didn't take the out.

The next day when I came back from class, I found ten thousand dollars stuffed into two envelopes, resting on my desk.

CHAPTER 9
NOW

I went to the one place Coop couldn't touch me, or press for the truth—back to the party, straight into the circle of our friends. I burst into the tent, feeling him hot on my heels, and sliced through the crowd, heart racing, until I stumbled into Caro.

She spun, smiling brilliantly. "Oh good, Coop brought you back!"

Angling my head, I could see Coop behind me out of the corner of my eye. His sweater brushed my arm. The compressed weight of unspoken words made me swallow thickly. He was so close I could smell him—woodsy, herbal. The same as always.

I dug my nails into my arm, a spark of pain to keep my knees steady.

"I'm glad you're back in time," Caro continued, waving at someone. "Eric was hoping to catch all of us."

I froze, nails still daggering my arm. Someone stepped into the center of the circle.

It couldn't be. The man in front of me was only distantly related to the boy I remembered. His hair was long and lank, his old knobby-kneed skinniness replaced by a thick hardness, stretching the sweater he wore. It was professorial, with elbow patches, and I knew it instantly for a costume. He had dark, haunted circles under his eyes. But still, it was Eric.

Eric Shelby. Heather's brother.

I felt Coop shift, and then he was standing by my side, arms crossed. "What are you doing here? You're not Class of '09."

"*Coop.*" Caro looked aghast. "I told you Eric works here now. Don't be rude." To Caro, rudeness was a cardinal sin.

"He's living the dream." Mint said it good-naturedly, the cool kid graciously making room for someone lesser. But I could see the tightness in his jaw. "He got to graduate but never leave."

"I work in the Alumni Office." Eric smiled, and I sucked in a breath. Gone was the eager, nerdy freshman, wide-eyed and nervous to meet his sister's friends. His smile was a sharp-toothed promise. I could feel it.

He turned, and we locked eyes. "I like being surrounded by memories. Don't you?"

Caro's eyes darted between us. "I was just telling Jess this whole weekend was your doing." Her voice was falsely cheerful. "You're the mastermind behind Homecoming."

"I was thinking," Eric said. "You're all here in one place, celebrating ten years. It's Heather's ten-year anniversary, too, if you think about it. Why not take the opportunity to remember her?"

Frankie shifted uncomfortably and looked to Mint for guidance. Courtney searched past us to where the Chi Os had regrouped, longing in her eyes.

No—this was wrong. The night wasn't supposed to be about Heather; it was supposed to be about us. My evolution. My triumph.

"What did you have in mind?" Coop asked.

"I thought we could go to her memorial and pay our respects." Eric looked at Coop, daring him to say no. "Seeing as she couldn't make it to the party."

Caro winced and stepped closer to Coop, who put his arm around her shoulders.

I looked around, catching my friends' eyes. Frankie. Mint. Even Courtney. No one wanted to go. We all wanted Eric to go away, to stop haunting us, reminding us of the black shroud that hung over our friend group. Finally, Mint swallowed and decided, as usual, to be the leader.

"I guess it's the least we can do," he said.

No, no, no. If things were unraveling before, now they threatened to go down in flames.

"I guess," Frankie echoed.

"Okay, but let's be fast." Courtney ducked her head and whispered to Mint as if the rest of us couldn't hear. "I have other friends, you know."

"I think this is a great idea," Caro said gamely, giving Eric a sympathetic look. She couldn't tell there was something wrong. Why couldn't Caro ever read people, for fuck's sake?

The second I thought it, I flushed with guilt. Caro's ignorance, lest I forget, was the only thing keeping us friends.

Eric gestured with a flourish to the lawn outside the tent. "After you."

In tense silence, we walked as a group, carving a path through the dark trees, away from the light and people. Campus was unusually quiet.

I shivered. "Where is everyone?"

Eric waved. "Oh, you know. They're all at the frats, diving headfirst into vats of swill and making bad decisions. You remember what it's like."

Frankie turned down the path to the right, the one that led to the tree Mr. and Dr. Shelby had planted in Heather's memory. It was right next to East House, her favorite place on campus, where she'd met us: the best friends she'd ever have.

"Wrong way," Eric said, cutting to the left.

"I think I know the way to East House," Frankie scoffed.

"We're not going to East House." Eric smiled that sharp-toothed smile again. "We're going to a place I've come to think of as a more meaningful memorial site."

He started down the path.

What the fuck? I turned to Mint. "*Do* something."

"Like what?" Mint said, at the same time Courtney hissed, "Don't tell him what to do."

I rolled my eyes.

Frankie watched Eric. "I think we have to follow him. He's Heather's brother."

"Frankie's right," Caro said. "Even if he has something weird in mind, we have to put up with it. It's only a small part of the night. We lost a friend, but he lost way more."

Every instinct screamed at me to turn on my heels and race back to the tent, or my hotel. Back to safety. But Caro started trailing after Eric, then Frankie, and Mint and Courtney followed. Finally even Coop left me. I forced the panic down and raced to catch up.

We followed Eric into the heart of Greek row, shooting questioning glances at each other, until we came to a stop in front of the Phi Delt house. The imposing, thick-columned mansion was empty, windows dark. The sight was surreal—it was Homecoming weekend, the biggest party of the year. The Phi Delt house should have been exploding with music and people. It certainly was when Mint was social chair, then president.

Mint spun to Eric. "Why is it empty?"

"The Alumni Office decided the Phi Delts and their dates would be more comfortable spending Homecoming weekend in the Chancellor's Estate. Given their high standing on campus and the exemplary amount of money Phi Delt alumni donate to Duquette every year, it seemed a fitting honor."

"You cleared the frat house," Frankie said, his voice a mix of awe and fear.

"Come on," Eric said. "You don't need an invitation, right? This is your old stomping grounds. Your dominion, your castle. What do the kids say—where the magic happens?"

"Eric, you're three years younger than us," Coop said. "Knock it off."

Eric laughed and practically ran up the porch steps, unlocking the door and pushing it open.

"This is creepy," Courtney muttered.

"What do you think, Jess?" Frankie slung his heavy arm over my shoulders. "Want to go back to the old fratter?"

"I don't think we have a choice," I said. And with that, we stepped into the dark foyer after Eric.

"Almost there," he called. We followed him to the farthest corner of the house, where a dingy door stood. He shouldered it open.

"The basement?" Mint asked, puzzled.

Courtney doubled back. "I don't want to go down there."

"Hey, it's okay." Mint kissed her temple. "We'll just pay our respects to Heather—"

"And Eric," I mumbled. "Guy looks like the walking dead."

"And Eric," Mint repeated, smiling at me over Courtney's head. "Then we'll go right back to the party."

I took a deep breath and went first, following Eric down the flight of stairs.

The Phi Delt basement. It was a legendary place. If the stories were true, this was where secret hazing rituals took place, the ones that had to happen in a windowless room, far from prying eyes. It was also where the inner circle came to drink and escape the masses dancing on the floor above. The number of hours I'd spent in here with Heather, Caro, Courtney, Frankie, and Jack were too many to count. The only person who'd never been allowed in was Coop.

"No way," Coop said as our eyes adjusted to the dim light. The room was spare, only a set of sagging couches pushed up against one wall, an empty keg rolled on its side in the corner. "This isn't the Phi Delt basement. This is a set from *Law & Order SVU*."

"We're all here," Eric said. "Finally, after ten years."

There was old graffiti covering the walls; one wall had a child-sized hole in it. The place really was a shithole. Why had it been so cool to drink here, the invitation so coveted?

"Eric, man, should we, uh, pay our respects?" Mint loosened his collar as he scanned the basement. Was he remembering all the hours we'd spent in here together, the corners we'd kissed in when no one was looking, or everyone was too drunk to care? Losing time, losing everything...

"Ten long years since the Class of 2009 graduated and moved on from Duquette. What in the world have you been up to?" Eric looked at us innocently, and my brain screamed *trap*. "Wait, don't tell me. I already know. You got married, engaged, became professional athletes and business leaders and lawyers. You turned out so successful—everything everyone always expected from you."

"Some of us became social media celebrities," Courtney added, apparently not too scared to plug herself.

"You want to know what *I've* done for the last ten years? After the cops gave up on my sister's case, and let the person who murdered her walk around with the rest of us, free and clear?"

A pall settled over the basement. Eric was like a train barreling full speed in our direction, and none of us could move.

"I've spent every day of the last ten years investigating my sister's murder. Following leads the police didn't have, rumors passed around by students, things no one realized were connected." He looked at us, feverish. "The cops missed so much."

"Eric, man, come on." Frankie shifted from foot to foot. "We're all really sorry about what happened to Heather, but isn't it time to put it behind us? This isn't healthy."

"My sister," Eric whispered, "was stabbed seventeen times when she was sleeping in bed. Who the fuck cares about *healthy*? I care about justice."

We stood in shocked silence. I pushed back the panic, the guilt—the feeling I was on the precipice of something dark and evil, about to topple over.

"You want to know why I call this her real memorial site?" Eric asked. "Because it's the last place Heather was seen alive. I like to come here and picture her happy. Oblivious to what was coming."

I shivered. I hadn't known she'd come here. It made sense, though. The night she was killed was the night of the Sweetheart Ball, and Heather, as Jack's girlfriend, was in the running for Phi Delt Sweetheart...

Caro's voice was small. "I thought the last time she was seen alive, witnesses saw her screaming at Jack in Bishop?"

Eric nodded. "Molly Duvall and Chris Holywell. Both witnessed Heather and Jack in what they described as a knock-down, drag-out fight in the lobby of Bishop Hall." He spoke as if he'd memorized the police report. "At approximately 6:32 p.m. on the night of February 14th. But no, that wasn't the last time she was seen alive. Who am I kidding? Plenty of you know the truth, that Heather was spotted later that night in the Phi Delt house—right here, in this very room. Pregaming the Sweetheart Ball with a group of brothers and one Ms. Courtney Kennedy."

I turned to Courtney in surprise.

"Courtney *Minter*," she corrected.

"Yeah, well, you were Kennedy back then. Witnesses report seeing Heather right here, but at some point before the party started, she left. No one saw her leave or knows why. The next morning, Jack found her body."

The room was deathly quiet. I tried to catch my friends' eyes, but no one would look at me.

"Why are you saying this to us?" Courtney's chest was heaving. "We all know Jack killed her. Heather told me to my face, right here in this room, that things were over between them. They'd had a horrible fight. The weapon was found in *his* room, for Christ's sake, under *his* bed. He tried to look innocent, telling the cops he just *found* her like that. He's a psycho. Look where he came from! All his life in a freaking religious cult, and he finally snapped. It's the police's fault they couldn't nail him. If you're going to put all your energy into something, why don't you fix that?"

"There's only one problem," Eric said. "Jack didn't actually kill her."

My heart seized. Eric didn't think Jack was guilty. There was someone else out there who believed. No, not just someone—*Heather's brother*.

"What do you know?" Coop asked.

"A lot," Eric said. "It's amazing what you can find out when you're a skinny loser who couldn't hurt a fly, whose sister died tragically. People tell you all sorts of things—students, faculty, detectives. I know so much about each of you. Most of all, I know you're not what you pretend to be. The famous East House Seven. God, Heather loved you. Her best friends. And all of you, liars."

This couldn't be happening. My instincts told me to run up the stairs, tear down the walls if I had to. Escape.

"For years, I've traced leads, putting the pieces together, uncovering what you've hidden. Do you want to know what I discovered?"

No, no, no.

"Jack didn't kill Heather. But someone in this room did. One of you is a monster, hiding behind a mask."

CHAPTER 10
FEBRUARY, SENIOR YEAR

It was unseasonably warm for February, which meant all of Duquette was outside, drinking on frat porches, boom boxes blasting music, or lying on picnic blankets on Eliot Lawn, soaking up the sun.

Of course it was warm, because it was the one day I needed the clouds out, dark and cold, keeping campus a ghost town. The only silver lining was that I hadn't frozen on the long walk across Duquette, wearing nothing but shorts and a T-shirt.

I avoided people's eyes as I passed them, keeping my gaze trained on my feet, like I was eight years old again and embarrassed to exist. I told myself the laughter I heard had nothing to do with me, or the oversized gym clothes I wore, and I half believed it. Finally, *finally*, Bishop Hall loomed into view, a sleek, modern dorm for upperclassmen, as different as possible from our old vine-covered home at East House.

Eighteen floors in the elevator, an interminably long time, and then I burst out, down the hall, turning the corner. I was *so close*. I'd hole up in my room and never come out—would never, *ever* think about the disaster of last night again. And then I saw them. A crowd of students, gathered outside the door to our suite.

A dark hole opened inside me. I scanned the crowd and found my friends rushing over. "What's going on?"

Mint looked at me, ashen-faced. "You're okay," he croaked and jerked an arm around me, pulling me hard to his side, his warm turtleneck sweater soft against my cheek.

The hole yawned wider, sucking in light.

Coop gave me a dark look, and I flinched, smoothing my wet hair self-consciously, causing icy drips down the front of my shirt. I squinted at him. His arm was still in the cast he'd worn since November, but he looked freshly beat-up, an angry red scratch down the side of his face. *Strange.*

"It's Heather," Caro whispered, stepping around Mint. Her eyes were unfocused. "I came back this morning, and the cops were here. They wouldn't let me in, but I heard them say Heather's name. I texted every-one to come. Why didn't you answer?"

"Traffic's blocked on Allen," Courtney said in a hollow voice, as if she hadn't heard Caro. A red velour tracksuit hung loose on her, matching her bloodshot eyes. "Cop cars everywhere."

"How'd the cops get in your suite?" Coop asked. "Someone had to have called them. Was it Heather? Maybe she got alcohol poisoning or something."

Caro looked at me, searching. "I have no idea. Do you?"

I was shaking my head when Courtney's vacant stare sharpened. She snapped her head to Caro. "Where were you coming back from, this morning?"

Caro's face flamed. "I...stayed somewhere else last night. After Sweetheart."

"*With* someone else? Who? A Phi Delt?"

"What does it matter?" Coop bit out. "Caro can sleep with whoever she wants. It's not relevant."

"At this point, you know fuck-all what's relevant." Courtney turned to me, her eyes narrowing. I was next.

"Where's Jack?" I cut in. "Someone should call him."

"I tried." Caro gripped the cross at her neck. "He's not picking up. Neither's Frankie."

Mint shifted and looked down at me, confused. "Did you just come from the gym?"

I twisted the shirt in my hands. The fabric was itchy and smelled like a mix of unfamiliar deodorant and laundry detergent. "I—"

"Where were you last night, seriously?" Mint's grip on me tightened until it was almost painful. "I called you a million times. You never came to Sweetheart. I couldn't find you anywhere."

Last night—bruising memories, the edges blurrier and blurrier as the night went on, until they were swallowed up in darkness. Instead of trying to search them, I willed in more darkness to eat the memories whole.

"I was drunk," I said, unable to meet anyone's eyes. "I passed out. I'm sorry."

"Now's not the time to talk about the fucking Sweetheart Ball," Coop snapped. "Something's really wrong—"

A movement down the hall caught everyone's attention. Little Eric Shelby, all one hundred pounds of him, came barreling around the corner. When he saw the crowd staring at him in horror, he froze for a second, cowed, then pressed forward.

"Let me in!" he said, putting his arms up to push through. But the crowd fell back, parting for him. He grabbed the door handle and twisted it open—Caro gasped—but he was blocked by the thick chest of a cop.

"Stand back," the cop barked, and Eric nearly fell backwards. "This is a police investigation."

I took a staggering step back, pulling Mint with me. But instead of slamming the door in our faces, the cop pushed it fully open. Behind him, I could see our living room and kitchen torn asunder, cushions ripped off the couch, every drawer hanging open. A black-clad EMT worker appeared in the doorway to the room I shared with Heather, walking backwards and carrying a stretcher, draped with a white cloth. Another EMT worker clutched the other end, calling soft directions to his partner. The crowd grew hushed as they passed through the front door, into the hall.

I stared down at the white cloth. It couldn't hide the familiar hills and valleys of a human body.

Even through the near-debilitating pain of my hangover, the nausea, the black blurriness of my memories, I knew it. A strange knowing, like déjà vu: *Heather is dead.*

"I need everyone to back up," the cop ordered.

"Is it Heather?" Eric practically tripped over himself as he backed away from the stretcher. "Heather Shelby?"

The sheer desperation in his voice caused tears to spring to my eyes.

The cop squinted. "Who are you?"

"Heather's brother." On the last word—*brother*—Eric crumbled, knees giving out. Mint released me and knelt next to him, resting a steadying hand on his shoulder. But Eric didn't notice. He was staring up at the cop, his whole world narrowed to him and how he would answer.

The cop's glare softened. "Son, I'm going to need you to come with me."

"No," Eric said. He leaned over the floor, and Mint hovered, conflicted. "No, no, no," Eric sobbed. "Not Heather."

The cop looked at Mint. "Help him up when he's ready, okay? I need you to bring him to the station. We've already called his parents."

Mint nodded, accepting the responsibility gravely.

The cop turned to the crowd. "I'm going to need the roommates.

Caroline Rodriguez and Jessica Miller." Hearing my name caused a shock, like I'd been caught at something.

Caro took a cautious step forward. "I'm Caroline."

The eyes of the crowd swung to me.

"Me." I cleared my throat. "Jessica."

The cop nodded curtly. "Come with me to answer some questions."

Panic swelled. With every footstep, the weight of the crowd's eyes felt like a crown of thorns, sinking deeper into my skull.

It'll be okay, I whispered to myself. *You'll tell the truth. Just not all of it.*

CHAPTER 11
NOW

Eric's words echoed through the basement: *One of us. A liar. A monster. A killer.*

"You're insane," Courtney said, staggering toward the basement stairs. "All the evidence pointed to Jack. The murder weapon—"

"I know about the evidence," Eric said. "*All* the evidence, not just what they tried to pin on him."

"What do you mean, pin on him?" Frankie asked hotly. "Jack fucking killed Heather. Everyone knows it."

"Oh, everyone, huh?" Eric turned to me, and the heat of his stare felt like an interrogation lamp. I took a step back. "Do you believe Jack's the killer, Jessica? Is that why you've stayed friends with him all these years?"

Every one of my friends' heads snapped in my direction.

"Is that *true*?" Courtney was a shark, sensing blood in the water. "Are you secret besties with Heather's killer?"

"It's not what you think," I said, panicked by the carefully blank expression on Coop's face, which I knew was his look of betrayal. "I don't believe Jack did it. And it's not fair to punish him for something he didn't do." My voice rose. "He was our *friend*."

"Sounds exactly like what we thought," Mint said dryly. "That's really low, Jess. Here you are paying your respects to Heather like you haven't been betraying her memory since she died."

"You never told me," Caro said accusingly. "All these years."

"He's innocent," I sputtered.

"How do you know?" Coop's voice was measured, distant. I found his eyes. Vivid green, so full of flecks of color they were like miniature universes, caught and suspended in his face.

"I just do. It's an instinct."

"Great," Frankie said. "An instinct totally trumps finding Caro's bloody scissors under Jack's bed."

Caro flinched at Frankie's words, looking at Eric. But the shy, skinny freshman had grown into a solid block of a man, one who could withstand mention of his sister's murder weapon without a change in expression.

What her death must have done to him. His whole life—the person he'd been growing into—reshaped around his sister's death. Like a vase at a potter's wheel, smoothed and molded around the dark, hollow space of her absence.

Eric faced Frankie. "Like I said. The cops didn't tell the public everything. You want to know the truth? They couldn't pin the murder on Jack because the evidence didn't add up. And I mean *all* the evidence, not just what you've heard. For instance"—He took a step forward, somehow looming over Frankie's linebacker build—"I know *your* secret."

The blood drained from Frankie's face. Eric knew Frankie's secret? The one he'd kept for all these years. But what did that have to do with—

"I know where the cops found you the night she died." Eric spun to face the rest of us. "Do you know? How close are you all, really?"

"Eric." My voice was unsure. "Don't..." I met Frankie's eyes. They were filled with fear.

"Ten years you've gotten a reprieve, but now your time is up." His voice rose an octave. "Hours after Heather was killed, the cops pulled young Mr. Francis Kekoa here off the top of Brooksman Bridge."

I sucked in a breath, thrown off-kilter. Frankie had been on Brooksman the night of Heather's murder? Why? I remembered now: he'd been absent from the crowd outside our suite that terrible morning. Jack had been gone, too, but everyone knew Jack had been in an interrogation room, the police's top suspect in the stabbing.

"What did you confess to the cops, Frankie?"

Frankie's face paled.

"Hey, listen, Shelby," Mint said, trying to rise to Frankie's defense, but Eric plowed on.

"You said you were so racked with guilt that you were going to kill yourself, didn't you? You were going to jump off that bridge, but you wouldn't tell the cops why. Tell us now, Frankie. What did you do that made you feel so guilty?"

Courtney gasped, like a light bulb had gone off. "I know!"

How?

"Courtney," I gritted out, "I swear to god, shut your mouth." But my warning only made it worse. She gave me a look of pure pleasure. Oh, she hated me all right. She hated that I'd had Mint first, that when everyone remembered college, they thought of *Mint and Jessica.*

"Remember how Frankie always joked about wanting to steal Heather away from Jack?"

"That was harmless, right, Frank?" Mint stepped in front of his friend, as if he could physically shield him.

"Heather went home with Frankie," Courtney said. "The night of the Sweetheart Ball, he took her home. I never told the police because they were so sure Jack did it. But if Frankie was the last person to see her, and then he was trying to off himself..."

It was so far from what I'd expected to hear that the breath left my lungs all at once.

"Is that true?" Coop took a step forward. Apparently, domestic life—lawyerly life—hadn't bled the tough out of him yet.

Instead of rising to Coop's challenge like the old Frankie would have, he screwed up his face. A tear ran down his cheek. Right there in front of us, in the middle of the Phi Delt basement, Francis Kekoa cried.

"I did it," he sobbed. "I hurt her."

CHAPTER 12
MAY, JUNIOR YEAR

It was late, even for us. We were drunk and tired, but still high off the sheer absurdity of everyone's costumes for the Nineties party. Frankie was carrying Heather down from the second floor of Phi Delt—the only one of us strong enough, as usual, after we'd all had too many tequila shots, and Jack walked beside him, monitoring. Caro and I led the pack down the stairs in coordinating Cher and Dionne miniskirts. We couldn't stop looking back at Coop and laughing.

"I will never be able to look at you the same way again," Caro wheezed, clutching the banister. "Seriously, this is the picture of you in my mind, forever."

Coop grinned and fingered the glittery butterfly clips holding his hair back. He wore a pink baby-doll dress that I couldn't believe he'd found in his size, with knee-high white stockings and black Mary Janes.

"You know, if I'm being honest," he said, "there's probably always been a twelve-year-old girl inside me, waiting to get out."

"Please don't talk about coaxing out twelve-year-old girls when you're in the Phi Delt house, Coop, or I'll reinstate your ban." Jack, in Kurt Cobain flannel, watched Heather over Frankie's shoulder. She blinked sleepily.

It was strange to want Coop when he looked like a mirror image of myself in middle school, but here I was. I caught his eye, and he grinned.

"Uh, guys?" Caro's voice shifted as we came to the bottom of the stairs. "What's going on here?"

In the foyer, a group of brothers a year older than us huddled over the large composite pictures lining the walls. I stepped closer and realized what they were doing: drawing thick, vicious X's over Danny Grier's face.

Danny Grier, the Phi Delt brother who'd just come out. The one frat guy I knew in all the years I'd been at Duquette to come out—which only meant he was the brave one. Anger welled inside me, but before I could speak, Jack was stepping forward.

"What are you doing?"

I felt a moment of fear for him—Jack was a junior and well liked, but these were seniors, popular Phi Delt brothers. They had power, and there were more of them than us. But Jack stood his ground, head held high.

"What does it look like?" one of them asked. He was tall, and I remembered having a crush on him when I was a freshman—a crush I now clawed back in my head. "Cleaning up the composites."

"It's 2008," I said. "How are you this backwards?"

"Yeah, that's some retrograde bullshit," Coop said. "No wonder I never wanted to join your stupid cult."

"Frankie, come on." One of the other brothers, who hadn't stopped drawing on Danny's face when we walked in, raised an eyebrow. "Set your friends straight." He turned to Jack. "Frankie gets it."

We turned to Frankie. The conversation had woken Heather, and now she stood on her own two feet, shaking her head groggily. Frankie looked like he was staring down the barrel of a gun. I tensed, waiting for him to tell his brothers to go to hell.

"They're right," Frankie said instead, voice thick. "Danny doesn't belong here. You can't be that way and be a Phi Delt. It doesn't work like that."

His words punched me in the chest. Next to me, Caro rocked back in surprise.

"Wow, Frankie." Jack drew his arms over his chest. "You sound just like your dad. Congratulations."

Frankie glared back at Jack, anger and embarrassment warring on his face.

Coop lifted his phone and snapped a picture of the Phi Delts. As one, they jumped back from the composites, cursing and tossing their Sharpies.

"Why don't you fuck off," Coop suggested pleasantly, "or I'll send this to the chancellor?"

"Look, no harm, no foul," said the tall one, lifting his hands. "Just a few guys playing a prank. No need to go nuclear."

They skulked off. After a few minutes searching, we found cleaning supplies and started scrubbing the glass. It was hard, nail-splitting work, and no one talked, the shock of Frankie's words still with us.

After the composites were finished, Caro and I decided Heather needed to go home, so we walked her to our suite, only a short distance away. I waited until both Heather's and Caro's lights clicked off, then snuck back to the frat, hoping I'd been fast enough and Coop was still there.

The foyer was empty, the cleaning supplies gone. I crept upstairs to the second floor, thinking he might be huddled over some end-of-the-night drinks, but found all the doors locked. Just to be thorough, I opened the basement door and jogged down the steps.

Near the bottom, I froze. In the corner of the room stood Frankie and Jack. Jack's arms were braced against Frankie's shoulders. He leaned in close. Frankie's eyes were red.

"You don't have to come out to anyone," Jack said, rubbing Frankie's shoulders. "I'm not trying to pressure you. Obviously, I'm the last person to talk. But you can't do *that*. You can't gay-bash, Frankie, even if it feels like protection. It's wrong, and it makes me worry you secretly hate yourself."

"I don't. I just—" Frankie's voice was strained, so low I could barely hear it. "What I said is true, isn't it?" He squeezed his eyes shut. "I can't have both. You see anyone out in the NFL? No, and *I have to get there.* That's what it's been about my whole life. Training, working my ass off, eating healthy. No drugs. Total discipline. All so I could be what the NFL wants, do what my dad couldn't. You don't understand. He'd kill me if I messed up. He'd *kill* me."

"Whoa," Jack said, touching Frankie's jaw until he opened his eyes. "First of all, I do understand. Have you *met* my parents? Second, please don't talk like that. I get what you're dealing with, but it doesn't have to be all doom and gloom, the end of the world. I need you to have a bigger imagination."

Frankie eyed him skeptically. "What, like you, me, and my parents, one big, happy family? Going to mass together? Tossing around a football on the beach?"

Jack shrugged, drawing Frankie closer. "Sure, bud. If that's your version of dreaming big, let's do it."

Frankie sighed and rolled his eyes to the ceiling. But after a second, his eyes fell back down to Jack's face. They were tender. "You know...I think shit like that's possible when I'm with you."

I'd never seen a look like that on my friend's face. My heart swelled with affection.

Jack leaned in, and Frankie closed his eyes. That was when it slapped me in the face, overdue and obvious: *I don't belong here.* I turned to leave, but suddenly my foot slipped, and I gasped, clutching the banister to stop myself from tumbling down the stairs.

Jack and Frankie whirled to face me.

CHAPTER 13
NOW

Frankie hurt Heather?

There was a moment of shocked silence, and then everything happened at once. Caro gasped, Courtney shrilled, "*You asshole*," Coop shoved Frankie onto a radiator, and Mint let him. Eric walked in a half-moon around Frankie, hands behind his back.

"Explain," Eric said, with a strange measure of calm.

Courtney pointed at Frankie. "He just confessed. Call the police!"

"I didn't kill Heather," Frankie said, hanging his head. "But I...did something terrible. That night."

"What'd you do, man?" Coop ran both hands through his hair, making it stand up straight. "Tell the truth; set yourself free."

"If we're going to talk about this, we should call the cops." Caro looked at Frankie. "He should have a lawyer."

Frankie shook his head. "I've kept this secret for too long." He looked up at Eric. "I'm so sorry."

"For what?" Eric paced slowly in front of Frankie, watching him.

"The night of the Sweetheart Ball, Heather got really, *really* drunk. Like, blackout. Courtney told me she needed to go home, so I took her."

All the heads in the room swung to Courtney.

"Um, *no*, do not look at me like that. Heather was really upset at Jack. She said she wanted to forget her whole night. I'm not about to deny a girl her therapy." Courtney tossed her hair over her shoulder. "Besides, how was I supposed to know to worry about Frankie? He was one of you stupid East House Seven."

"Nice, Courtney," I said. "Way to take her home yourself like a good friend."

"Shut up. You weren't even around. She kept thinking you were going to show at Sweetheart, but you never did."

I jerked back like she'd hit me, but it was the truth.

"What happened when you took her home?" Eric pressed.

Frankie's eyes darkened. "I got her to her suite, no problem. But when we got inside, she didn't want to go to bed. She wanted to talk." Frankie's voice cracked. "She was going on and on about how Jack betrayed her. That night, he'd told her he'd been cheating on her, and she was devastated. She always thought she was going to marry him. I really didn't want to talk about it, especially when she was drunk."

He looked at Eric, pain in his eyes. "I tried to put her to bed, but she didn't want to lie down. I finally got her in Jess's bed, since it was the closest, but we kind of wrestled for a second, and then...she fell and hit her head. I didn't think it was bad at the time, you have to believe me, but after...after I found out what happened, I kept worrying—what if I gave her a concussion and it kept her from fighting back when the murderer came?"

So that's why Heather was found in my bed. I'd always wondered, assumed she'd simply been too drunk to tell the difference.

"That's why you climbed to the top of the bridge?" Eric's voice was made of steel. "Because Heather hit her head and you felt responsible?"

"No," Frankie said miserably. "It was the other thing she told me." He looked up at me from his seat on the radiator, and I knew what was coming. "That night Jack didn't just confess he was cheating on her. He told her he was bi."

I caught Caro's eyes, and she raised a brow. The news about Jack wasn't a surprise—he'd come out after he'd been cleared by the police, saying he wanted us to know the whole him, no reservations. But the fact that Jack had told Heather the night she died was new information.

"I don't know why she told me," Frankie continued. "Other than she was drunk. What Heather didn't realize was that I already knew. Because I was the one Jack was cheating with."

A moment of incredulous silence.

He did it. Frankie had actually uttered the words out loud. Years of keeping the secret because I loved them, of covering because it was the right thing to do, bubbled over inside me.

"You and...Jack?" Courtney looked like she'd been presented with the world's most bewildering math problem. "*Together?*"

Coop shook his head. "So let me get this straight. You were going to literally jump off a bridge because you were into Jack? I don't mean to minimize what you were going through or anything, 'cause I definitely remember what your dad was like, but that's a little Lifetime movie, don't you think? I mean, Jack was handsome. Who wasn't attracted to him?"

Frankie shook his head. "It wasn't that. I mean, yes, I was carrying a lot of shame back then. I would've done anything to keep people from finding out. And then Heather, of *all* people—my friend who I felt so guilty about, because of Jack—wanted to talk about it. *Really* talk about it. And even though it was about Jack and not me, I couldn't stand it. I just wanted her to stop talking. I was trying to pull the covers over her, and she was resisting, and then she fell." He looked at the floor with wet eyes. "I hurt Heather because she made me so uncomfortable, I couldn't stand to be in the room with her one more minute. That's what horrified me. It wasn't the kind of person I wanted to be."

"I kept thinking, over and over, that I'd hurt Heather because I was trying so hard to hide, while Jack had the guts to be himself. I always used to talk about my dad, how he'd hate me if he knew, but Jack's parents were just as bad. And he still did it. I went to the bridge that night because I kept imagining my life, and I couldn't see a way I would be happy if I couldn't be myself. But I also couldn't imagine ever being brave enough to give up on the NFL, on everything I'd worked for. Jack used to say I didn't have a very big imagination, and he was right." I could hear the traces of something close to love in Frankie's voice—*still*, after all these years—until he cleared his throat. "That was before I knew what Jack did."

The affection I'd felt listening to Frankie talk about Jack disappeared like smoke in the wind. "Wait… You actually think he killed Heather? Even though you know what kind of person he is?"

Frankie met my eyes. He looked exhausted. "I think he could've changed his mind, gotten scared. I can even understand it."

The words hung in the room until Frankie continued. "Jack had to have done it. Because if he didn't, I lost him for no reason."

Mint kicked off the wall and strode toward him.

"All that time," he said, "you and Jack were together behind my back."

Frankie watched him anxiously. Mint was his idol. What he said meant everything.

"Have you told your dad?" Mint asked. "Your teammates?"

Frankie shook his head. "Not yet. Michael Sam's the only NFL player who ever came out before he retired, and look what happened to him. People protested. His career was over in the blink of an eye. I keep picturing that happening to me, and I…can't bring myself to risk it."

Mint said nothing, only turned and walked away.

"In case you were wondering, the autopsy showed Heather had

three major bruises on her head, five minor." Eric tapped his foot on the concrete floor, stealing Frankie's attention. "But none of them caused a concussion."

Frankie closed his eyes and nodded, looking like he was trying very hard not to weep.

"You heard, obviously, that Heather didn't put up the kind of fight you'd expect from anyone, let alone my sister. There was no skin under her nails, no blood from her attacker. Combined with the fact that there were dozens of people's DNA everywhere in that room—including all of yours, and mine—the cops thought forensic evidence was a dead end."

We'd all heard about the lack of usable DNA. It was one of the things that surfaced after Jack's charges were dropped, when the whole campus was up in arms over him being let go, with no new suspects to take his place.

"What wasn't public is that a toxicology report revealed the reason Heather barely fought back," Eric said. "Her system was flooded with a drug cops couldn't identify. It would have dulled her senses, slowed her reactions."

A drug? Caro and I shot each other surprised looks. That didn't make sense. We were Heather's roommates. We would've known if she had a drug problem.

"The closest thing the cops could compare it to was this drug that was giving them a lot of trouble back then. A street drug called tweak."

Tweak. I heard the glass shattering, the crunch of footsteps, the deep, terrible scream of pain. The dangerous people—violence in their eyes, darkness pulsing beneath their skin.

I didn't have to lift my head to know who was staring at me from across the room. Like always, the pull of his gaze was magnetic.

I found him against my will, in time to watch a terrible knowing dawn in his eyes.

"*That. Is. It!*" Courtney shrieked, taking everyone by surprise. She picked up a discarded beer bottle and threw it against the wall, where it shattered into sharp rain. "I'm not going to stand here one second longer and listen to Heather's creepy little brother, *who used to stare at my breasts when he thought I wasn't looking*, try to frame us for her murder."

"Court—" Mint started, an amazed look on his face.

She whirled on him. "No! I'm not playing this game. What's next? Busting out a Ouija board? Taking lie-detector tests? Digging up Heather's grave? I'm going back to the party, and so are you." She turned to the rest of us. "You assholes can do whatever you want."

A slow, satisfied smile crept over Eric's face. He raised his hands and clapped. "Brava. Truly, a stirring performance."

CHAPTER 14
JANUARY, SOPHOMORE YEAR

Over time, I'd learned there were other girls like me—Kappas who were unhappy being second-best. No girl ever said it out loud, but still, we found each other. Our first opportunity to dethrone Chi Omega came rush, sophomore year. We poured our hearts and souls into it—hours of researching freshman girls on Facebook, buying them alcohol, holding secret rush parties in our dorms, slipping into forbidden conversations in line for frat bathrooms. We did everything we weren't supposed to do.

I'd also learned that sometimes, the space between what you were and weren't supposed to do was one of those messy gray areas. Like senior year of high school, when I was neck and neck with Madison Davies for salutatorian. Madison, with her perfect, corkscrew curls and hottest-girl status, was also smart, much to my dismay. The class ranking came down to winter finals. Whatever position we held at the end of fall semester was what we'd report to colleges. What I'd send off to Harvard.

It was the last exam on the last day before winter break. We were in the library, which had been cordoned off for senior tests. Over the course of ninety minutes, the other students had sighed, packed their pencils, and turned in their tests. Madison and I were the only two left, using every last minute. Finally, she stood up, shuffled her pages, and gave me a smile—not a full smirk, but a knowing look, like a smirk in church clothes.

In her cloud of self-satisfaction, she didn't notice the test page that slipped out of her pile and onto the floor, sliding under the proctor's desk. Instead of stooping to collect it, she handed her test to the proctor and flounced out the door.

I bubbled my last circle and gathered my papers carefully, rising and walking to the proctor, who reached out to accept my test. I hesitated. She raised an eyebrow.

I glanced down at the corner of Madison's missing test page, the small triangle of white sticking out from under the desk like a flag of surrender.

Then I smiled and handed the proctor my test.

She wished me a good winter break, settled my papers in her bag, and hummed on her way out. I tracked her silently down the hall until she disappeared.

I became salutatorian.

It was so easy—that's what I thought when I looked back. It couldn't have been simpler: spot the paper. Give the proctor that wide, ingratiating smile, like everything was normal. And then *do nothing*. Stay quiet. So little effort, such maximum effect. Doing nothing was comfortable, like slipping into an old, warm robe.

The other thing I thought when I looked back: how pathetic that I had to fight for second place.

But the competition with Chi O wasn't for second. It was for first. *Best.* And, if I was being honest, it was for revenge.

Caro teased me about how intensely I rushed sophomore year.

I suspected she was jealous of the time I spent with other girls, the ones who cared as much as I did. Caro was like that—always trying to stay glued at the hip, resenting any time we spent with people outside the East House Seven. I'd noticed she'd do anything—really, *anything*, even go watch Frankie's football practice—to keep from being alone. Sometimes, when I stopped to think about it, I felt bad for dating Mint and leaving Caro behind, just like Heather did with Jack.

But other times I needed space. Sophomore rush was one of them.

The holy grail of freshman girls was Amber Van Swann. She was rich, beautiful, perfectly dressed, and dating a senior Phi Delt. The number one recruit on campus. I wanted her so bad I could taste it, and I knew—because I was friends with Heather—that the Chi Os were hungry for her, too. Heather had instituted a no-talking-about-rush rule to keep things friendly, but *still*. I knew.

Then the night before Bid Day came—the night we got our list of pledges. And despite how hard we'd tried, Amber Van Swann wasn't on it. She'd chosen Chi O. Standing in Kappa's front lawn on Bid Day, my friends and I watched her run to the Chi O porch and get swallowed up by screaming, hugging girls. In the center of the mayhem were Courtney and Heather, wearing matching gold foil crowns and pink boas.

Stop punching down.

I stood there and imagined ripping the crowns from their heads, my hand arcing through the air, seizing the pointed tips, jerking their blond hair out, collateral damage. I shivered and blinked the picture away, turning to my friend Kristin, who hated second place as much as I did.

She looked at me and said, in a voice with zero inflection, "Amber Van Swann made a sex tape."

I stared, but only for a beat. "Show me."

That night, three of us sat in Kristin's dorm room, gathered around her desktop computer—me, Kristin, and Caro, who'd insisted on following me. Kristin pulled up a video, grainy at first, then very, very clear. Amber Van Swann and her Phi Delt boyfriend, going at it. Loudly.

"How did you get this?" Caro asked, once the video ended and she'd uncovered her eyes.

Kristin shrugged. "Amber sent it to her boyfriend, and he sent it to a Phi Delt I hooked up with last weekend. He showed me as a joke, and I asked for it. Simple."

"That's terrible," Caro said.

"It really is," I agreed. "You have to be so careful what you film nowadays. What are you thinking, Kristin?"

"It's pretty obvious," Kristin said. "We send it anonymously to JuicyCampus."

"What?" Caro sputtered. "Isn't that illegal?"

"Good question." I squinted at Kristin. "She's eighteen, so it's not child porn, but are there any other laws?"

"In some states. But not North Carolina."

"Hmm." I tapped my chin.

Caro looked back and forth between Kristin and me, her eyebrows lifting higher than I'd ever seen them go. "For the love of all that is holy, do not tell me you're actually considering this. What we should do is track down every copy of the video and delete them. That's girl code."

"Oh yeah?" I asked. "Was it girl code for Amber to string me along so I'd buy her tickets to the Nelly Furtado concert and a whole semester's worth of alcohol?" *On a credit card I couldn't afford*, I added silently. "Is it girl code for Courtney to throw herself at Mint every time she thinks I'm not looking?"

Caro turned pink. So she'd noticed.

"Or, sorry—you know I love her—but for Heather to keep *casually* mentioning that the last five Phi Delt Sweethearts have been Chi Os, when she knows we all want it? Is that girl code?"

Kristin snorted. "Or what about Courtney telling Emma Davis she needs to lose weight to get a boyfriend, when Emma has a thyroid problem and Courtney's only skinny 'cause she takes secret diet pills her mom buys from China?"

"*None* of those things are good," Caro cried. "Especially Courtney's pills. Those things are basically speed and they make her crazy and way too thin. It's sad her mom buys them for her. But releasing some poor freshman's sex tape to get back at the Chi Os is worse." She turned the full force of the Caroline Rodriguez guilt stare on me. "Please tell me you recognize that. You're going all Lady Macbeth, and it's freaking me out."

Outside Kristin's window, the sun began to break through the steel-gray sky, warming the half inch of snow on the ground. A lone bird trilled.

I sighed. "Caro's right. It's wrong. And we could get caught. Sorry, K."

Kristin only shrugged.

"*Thank God*," Caro said, dropping her head in her hands.

She and I went back to our dorm room, made popcorn, and watched *Felicity*. Two days later, Amber Van Swann's sex tape was sent from an anonymous number to a handful of fraternity brothers, who passed it to their friends, who passed it to theirs, and within a week the whole school had it.

Amber was destroyed. She wouldn't leave her room. Her parents threatened to sue the school, but there was nothing the administration could really do, and Amber refused to let her parents go after her boyfriend, the likeliest source of the leak. She transferred out of Duquette before the semester was up, and for months—several glorious months—the whole campus called Chi Os *the sex-tape girls*. Heather was furious. Courtney refused to say Amber's name out loud.

A light dimmed in Caro. For a while, she didn't want to go out, didn't want to binge nineties shows, studied alone at the library. But for all her talk about right and wrong, she never once insisted we go to the chancellor with what we knew.

I was horrified, obviously. But the day it leaked, my first thought—I couldn't help it—was that sometimes, you really didn't have to lift a finger to get exactly what you wanted. Sometimes, all you had to do was sit back and do nothing, and it was just that easy.

Of course, I banished the thought.

CHAPTER 15
NOW

We practically ran, all of us fleeing the haunted Phi Delt house, desperate to get back to the white tent with its lights and music and safety. We didn't talk—that was for later, when the image of Eric—damaged brother, deranged detective—wasn't so vivid. For now, we moved, hearts beating fast, breathing labored.

Just as the tent loomed into sight, Frankie jerked to a stop. "I'm not going in."

Caro braked so hard she nearly stumbled. "What… Why?"

"That, back there, with Eric? I wasn't expecting…" Frankie blew out a breath. "I wanted it to be different, when I told you. Not tied up with Heather and those accusations. And now…I don't know. I can't go back in the party and pretend it didn't happen."

"We care about you, Frankie," I said quietly. "We support you. Who you love changes nothing. We're the East House—" My voice caught. We weren't the East House Seven. Not without Heather, or Jack. Not with the way we'd started looking at each other, ever since Eric said the word *secrets*.

Caro hurtled herself at Frankie, catching him in a fierce hug.

"Whoa," he said, rocking back.

"We love you." Caro's words were muffled against his jacket. "Don't leave."

"She's right," Coop said. "Even if you are a meathead."

Something was wrong—Coop was trying to be lighthearted, but his face was drawn. Haunted. Eric had stirred bad memories, sure, but this seemed deeper...

Frankie scanned our faces, his own brightening until he got to Mint, whose eyes were locked determinedly on the sidewalk. Frankie's smile deflated. "Yeah, well... It's probably best if I go to bed anyway. I've got the parade tomorrow."

Caro gripped him by the shoulders. "Frankie Kekoa, grand marshal of the Homecoming parade. Making us proud."

He shrugged her off. "I'm just the first Duquette player to go pro. But thanks. See you tomorrow." He couldn't resist one last look at Mint, who still wouldn't make eye contact, before turning and escaping into the shadows.

"God, if you're out there, please grant me the power of seven vodka tonics to forget this miserable detour ever happened." Courtney turned on her slender heels and stalked away, kicking up grass with every step. "I don't hear you following," she called.

With one last look in Frankie's direction, we did.

Either we'd been in the quiet, creepy basement of the fraternity house for too long or the Class of 2009 had gotten drunker while we were gone. Either way, the chatter inside the tent was dialed up to eleven. Now back in the safety of the party, Eric behind us, I remembered my plan, the reason I was here. I could still do this. Everyone was gathered, ready to experience Jessica Miller 2.0. I could turn it around.

Courtney fled into the circle of Chi Os—but to my surprise, Mint didn't. Instead, he turned to me. "Is it still red wine?"

I blinked. "It is."

"Be right back." He strode in the direction of the bar.

Was Mint actually getting me a drink instead of joining his wife? I looked around, searching for witnesses. Caro and Coop stood in a corner, having a heated conversation. Well, Caro was heated; Coop looked like he was a million miles away. My stomach clenched.

I was starting to wonder if I should walk over when Mint reappeared, handing me a glass.

"Are you sure you won't be missed?" I nodded toward Courtney.

"She's all spun up—I guess because of Eric. I've seen it before. I've got at least five minutes before she realizes I'm gone." Mint took a sip of his drink. "Besides, I wanted to talk to you. I miss talking."

I almost spit out my wine but caught myself just in time, making a graceful gagging sound.

The corners of Mint's blue eyes crinkled as he smiled. "I feel bad that's such a surprise."

What was happening? I was looking at the old Mint—kind, smart Mint, the brave leader. It was like traveling back in time and getting another chance to talk to someone I'd lost and grieved. I had so many things I wanted to say, so many questions. *Do you regret it? Do you really love her? What did I do to make you leave me?*

But I didn't know how long I had with the old Mint. The window could be closing, even now.

"I…miss it, too." I swallowed, then cleared my throat. "I can't shake how messed up Eric is. We graduated and then never checked on him. We kind of abandoned him here, where she died." I shook my head. "I feel like a bad older sister or something. Is that weird?"

"It's not weird. But Jess, Eric is nuts. I don't know if grief turned him crazy or if it was in there all along, but that man in the basement was unhinged. Playing some sort of cat-and-mouse game."

"One of us should reach out to his parents, see if they know. Hey—" I slapped his arm. "Also, what the hell with you and Frankie?"

Mint's eyes darkened. "What?"

"Don't pull that on me. You were icing him out, punishing him. How can you do that? Are you really so bothered by"—I lowered my voice, obviously not wanting to out Frankie without his permission—"Frankie being gay?"

"No, of course not." Mint took a rough sip of his whiskey and wiped his mouth with the back of his hand. "I don't give a fuck who Frankie dates. But he *lied* to me. For *years*." Mint's voice rose. I glanced around, but no one was looking. "We were supposed to be best friends, and all that time he and Jack were going behind my back. Do you know what that makes me? A chump. A loser without real friends. You can't let people do that to you, or next thing, you're a walking joke."

Jesus. "You're not your dad, Mint. And Frankie isn't your mom. No one is betraying or emasculating you. It's not even *about* you."

His eyes flashed, color flooding his cheeks. "Not about me, huh? Well, you didn't look too surprised when Frankie told us. And if you already knew, that means Frankie chose not to tell me specifically."

"Oh, I *wonder why*."

In a flash, Mint's anger cooled into a calm mask. But his eyes were his tell—they turned hard and cold as flint. "I forgot you knew that story about my dad."

"Yeah, well, we used to be friends." I sighed. "I'm sorry about him, by the way. I should have told you that last year."

Mint's gaze focused over my shoulder. "He hadn't been the same for years, anyway. It was a blessing when he finally died. Miserable and alone, like he deserved."

Mint's dad, a fallen giant, a hero laid low. There was so much anger in Mint's face, in the clench of his jaw, the barbed wire of his voice, it bordered on fury.

I reached out, laying a hand on his shoulder. Cool silk, sharply cut lines.

He looked at me. "We used to be so much more than friends."

My breath caught.

"Mint?" Appearing out of thin air, Courtney glared at my wrist until I dropped it from Mint's shoulder.

Maybe it was the disappointment of getting so close to the old Mint, only to have him ripped away, but the words came out before I could check them. "Oh, good. Everyone's favorite person."

She stumbled a little in the grass, but caught herself. "You know what, Jessica? You lost, fair and square." She raised her voice, sounding drunker than ever. "Do you hear me? Get over it."

The words were like blades in my chest. I heard a giggle from somewhere close, and looked around, expecting to see mocking eyes looking back at me. People were staring—but not at me. At Courtney. Our classmates were whispering as she wobbled. To my surprise, the looks on their faces weren't kind.

They weren't rooting for her.

I straightened my shoulders. "Me, get over it? My college boyfriend cheated on me with you, married you, and ten years later, you're crowing about it. I feel sorry for you, Court. How little has happened in your life that you're still obsessed with this?"

The whispers grew louder; I thought I heard someone laugh softly. Courtney's eyes widened. Her hands trembled at her sides, and she clutched them to keep them still. Was she just drunk? Mint's words came back. *She's all spun up—I guess because of Eric.* No—something else was going on, I could tell. This wasn't a fair fight. But I was so hungry to beat her for once on my own that I kept going.

"Someone once told me that underneath the designer clothes and bitchiness, you were just an insecure little girl who desperately wanted to be liked. I think I finally see it. It's okay, Courtney. We get it. You can stop lashing out."

No one was trying to hide their laughter anymore, or bothering to whisper. I heard my name pass through the crowd.

Her face turned as crimson as her dress. Instead of replying, she ducked her head and pushed through the crowd, forcing it to part for her. Mint followed, leaving me alone, but it didn't matter, because after a beat of fraught silence, someone who looked vaguely familiar—Brittany Lowell, Pi Phi, maybe?—raised her glass to me, and I raised mine back. And then I was flooded with people, laughing and commiserating. *Jessica Miller, that was hilarious. Jessica Miller, you're so brave. Courtney has been awful for ages; that's exactly what she deserved.*

It was a scene lifted straight from my Homecoming fantasies, so close to what I'd dreamed that it felt surreal to actually live it.

To my surprise, Mint broke back through the crowd, and everyone stepped aside, responding unconsciously to the power of his presence. He put a hand on my waist, drawing me close, his mouth brushing my ear as he leaned in and whispered. I closed my eyes. *This was a dream.*

"I'm sorry about that. Courtney needs to be alone." He lifted his head, catching my eyes, and my body burst into a thousand sparks, leaking into the night like fireflies. This was the old magic. The pull and draw of him, the gravitational force. "Come talk to me?"

Motion over Mint's shoulder caught my eye. It was Coop, stalking alone out of the tent, Caro nowhere in sight. Where was he going? Foreboding snuffed the fireflies.

I looked back at Mint. His face so close—achingly beautiful, like a prince I would have conjured when I was fourteen. The golden boy, the first boy I'd ever loved. I'd wanted this moment so badly, played it in my mind so many times. It felt like redemption, like a litany whispered in my ear: *You were right. You were right. You were right.*

Then I looked at Coop, disappearing into the line of trees, his shoulders hunched high with tension. Promising nothing good.

Mint, or Coop?

CHAPTER 16
ONE YEAR AFTER COLLEGE

Mint was going to propose. I could feel it in my bones. This whole year after graduation I'd struggled to reinvent myself, to move on from the paths I thought I'd get to take, the ones that had closed so abruptly senior year. I'd had to find a new career—right when job opportunities shriveled for everyone in the whole country—adjust to the hollow new shape of my family, grapple with the ruins of the East House Seven. For a year, Mint had been the only good thing.

Starting with the day he'd shown up on my doorstep, a week after Heather died. He'd fallen on his knees, raw and grieving and so grateful I was alive when Heather wasn't—and so awash in guilt for the thought. My own guilty heart had melted. I'd buried my betrayals, and our relationship grew stronger than ever. While the rest of our friends drifted apart, we clung to each other, inseparable.

Heather's death had been a dark chasm ripped through our lives, breeding misery. I wanted things to be normal again, good and upright. I wanted to live in the sunlight.

Mint was the sun itself. We'd moved to New York City, Mint to start law school, me to take an entry-level job at Coldwell, the most prestigious option available to me, now that my other choices were gone. It had been a hard year, but we'd just survived our first Homecoming back at Duquette, proving the good memories outweighed the bad, reforging friendships. Life seemed hopeful again, and now here we were, out for dinner at my favorite restaurant, the one so expensive I felt grateful when Mint picked up the tab. There was nothing to celebrate, no real reason we were here. Which meant…

Mint sat across from me in his high-backed chair. The restaurant's dim lighting turned his face into an oil painting, all warm skin, luxurious lines, and soft shadows. He held my hand.

"I want to tell you something. It's important."

My heart swelled, and I squeezed his fingers. I'd been eyeing his jacket all night, wondering where he'd hidden the ring.

"Jess, you know I love you. I have since freshman year."

"I love you, too," I said, not even caring how breathy my voice sounded.

"And this year in the city has been good. Better than I expected."

I nodded.

He took a deep breath. "But the thing is, I don't think this is working."

I stared at him, confused.

"I'll always be grateful for what we had, but…I think I've been trying to keep something alive that should've died a long time ago."

It was finally sinking in. "What?" I whispered.

He ran a hand through his hair. "I have to confess something." He swallowed hard. "I cheated on you, Jess. At Homecoming. You know Saturday night, when I didn't come back and told you I slept in Frankie's hotel?"

I didn't move a muscle. As if refusing to participate could stop the whole thing from barreling forward.

"The truth is, I got wasted. I went to Wendy's with a bunch of people after the bars, and—I'm not proud of this, obviously—but I hooked up with Courtney. In the bathroom. And then we went back to her hotel."

Not Courtney. Anyone but Courtney.

"I think I've liked her for a while," Mint continued, twisting the knife deeper. "In college, I think I had a crush on her but just never acted on it, obviously, because we were together. But I want to act on it now."

My fingers let go of my fork, and it clattered against the plate. "What are you saying?"

His eyes actually filled with tears. I'd only seen him teary a few times, so rarely I could count them on one hand. The sight broke through the fog of my shock, made the moment real. "I'm so sorry, Jess. I won't ever be able to apologize enough to you, not for this, or anything. I'm so full of guilt, I can't…" He took a shaky breath. "But I need to break up. It's for the best."

Panic—cold, gripping, tearing my heart. "No," I said, my own eyes filling with tears. "Don't do this. Don't break up with me."

"But I cheated on you," Mint said, lowering his voice, now that mine was rising. "With Courtney."

Everything became crystal clear in that moment. Exactly what the score was, exactly what I needed to do, what I could and couldn't live without. I couldn't lose Mint, the person who'd looked at me and smiled freshman year and *turned me into somebody.*

"I forgive you," I said. "It doesn't matter. We'll move on like it didn't happen. I swear, I'll never hold it against you. Please don't leave me."

I was low, I was scraping the floorboards, I was a puddle of muddy water you stepped over to get to the sidewalk, but I didn't care. Desperation buzzed through me, electric and dangerous. I would scream; I would turn the table over. I would do anything to stop this.

Mint could read it in my eyes. He shoved back from the table. "Jessica, you're acting crazy." He glanced around the restaurant, at the heads bobbing in our direction. "I thought it would be easier here, but it's not. Come on." He tried to wrench me up, but I planted myself in my chair, jerking my hands back.

"Jessica," he hissed, eyes widening. "Why are you acting like this? It's pathetic. Get up. Let's go."

No, no, no. If we left, I felt sure it was over. I would lose Mint and myself. I'd already lost so much. I couldn't lose anything more.

So I did a horrifying thing. I slid out of my chair to my knees and clasped my hands together. The diners around us hushed, their attention turned to the spectacle of the begging girl.

"Please," I cried, my voice thick with tears. "Please take me back. Please don't leave me. Please love me. I'll do anything."

Down, down, down, I went.

I would never, for the rest of my life, forget the horror, the depth of disgust in Mint's eyes, when he finally saw me for who I really was.

CHAPTER 17
NOW

I plunged into the trees after Coop, heels slashing the grass. I knew in my bones something was wrong, so I'd ignored Mint's incredulous face, brushing past him out of the tent. I forced myself not to think about what I was doing—leaving behind my dream moment, right when everything had fallen into place.

Away from the light of the party, into the dark heart of campus. I could feel it happening now, the old Duquette promise: *We will change you, body and soul.* The metamorphosis was supercharged, unfolding as I ran. My feet twisted in my heels, bruised and sliced; my heart pounded, turning inside out. Ten years of armor cracked and fell off with each footstep.

"Coop!" I called, voice echoing.

He stopped and spun. I kept running toward him, trying to push away unhelpful thoughts—like how long I'd wanted to do exactly this, how much it would be like a movie, running and throwing myself into his arms. Despite my best efforts, my heart still flooded with warmth.

He waited for me but was unable to stay still, pacing back and forth. "What are you doing here?"

"*Me?* What are you doing?" I tried to steady my breath, but this close to him, there was no chance. Whatever layers of armor had lifted off me had taken my reserve, too. Now I found it almost impossible not to touch him. I lifted a hand as he watched.

Fuck it. I laid my hand over his chest, his soft black sweater, and he let out a deep breath.

"Where are you going, Coop?"

His heart raced under my palm. I curled my fingers.

There was no escape for me. No matter how hard I'd tried—both in college and after—I couldn't resist him. Not for long.

His look stilled me. His eyes were desperate, and sad. "I'm going to find Eric. I have to tell him about the tweak."

I shook my head, inching closer. "Heather having drugs in her system must have been a coincidence. You never sold tweak, anyway. You stopped dealing senior year."

The truth was plain on his face.

"Coop," I said, unsure. "You said you were getting out. That there were some things you wouldn't do."

"I know." He reached for me, cupping his hands around my shoulders. "Listen. I was getting out for you. I don't know if I ever said that, because I was an idiot, but it's the truth."

"I knew." I met his eyes. He was handsome ten years ago—dangerously so—but he made me ache now. I wanted to kiss him. Hit him. I was at war with myself.

His gaze lowered. "You remember right before Thanksgiving, at my place."

It wasn't a question, because neither of us would ever forget.

"When I told them no, they said they'd come after me and the people I loved."

I searched his face for a clue. "Where are you going with this?"

"Jess." Coop took a deep breath and pulled me in so close I could barely focus on what he said next. "They came after me again, on campus, after break. I never told you because you were already so scared, already pushing me away. I panicked and ran to Bishop Hall. I thought they wouldn't follow me inside a dorm."

He barked a laugh. "But they were fucking crazy. They kept coming, and I led them right to your suite. I used your passcode to get inside and slammed the door on them, but they kept banging. They said they were going to kill my people, starting with you."

I drew a sharp breath.

"I led them straight to you, don't you see? I made a terrible mistake. I was so horrified, I told them I'd do anything. Sell tweak."

"You did not." I gave in to my desire and shoved him back an inch. But he didn't let go of my shoulders, didn't look away.

"It's worse. Jess, I was supposed to start selling *that* night—the night of Sweetheart. But I got cold feet. They were calling, looking for me. That's why I didn't meet you out like I was supposed to, remember?"

I didn't, because I didn't remember that night at all past a certain point. I knew the memories were buried somewhere, but from the moment I'd woken the next day—an unreasonably warm February 15th—I'd done everything in my power to forget.

"What I'm trying to say"—Coop's breath came faster now, his heart back to pounding under my palm—"is that they knew your dorm, and they'd threatened your life, and Heather's system was flooded with a drug just like tweak."

I finally saw where he was going and shook my head, pulling away from him.

"What if they did it? You know what they were capable of."

The memory of a terrible scream—Coop's—echoed back, and goose bumps prickled my arms. "What if they broke into the dorm, looking for you, and found Heather instead?"

"That's insane," I said. "The cops never said someone broke in."

"What if they just *knocked on the door*? You don't think Heather, of all people, would answer without thinking? She thought she was impervious."

"They wouldn't kill someone just to teach you a lesson. Do you know what kind of heat that would bring them? They weren't stupid—they were smart, which is why they were scary."

"But the pieces fit together," Coop insisted. "Especially the tweak. It's basically a smoking gun. All this time, I've been sitting on information that could've helped the cops find Heather's killer."

There was resolve in his face, and suddenly I saw exactly how this would go: Coop, the rebel, the outcast, the drug dealer. The poor one from the single-parent family. The unlikeliest of heroes, yet always rising when it was time, only to get cut down in the end. Always.

I'd even done it to him myself.

"Please," I begged. "Don't go to Eric with this. He's looking for a villain. He'll crucify you."

Instead of looking at me—my desperation—with disgust, Coop's face softened. It was a look I knew well. I used to think of it as one of his private faces, an expression he reserved just for me, a secret code for a secret feeling. I'd learned, too late, that it had always been bigger than that.

"I have to, Jess. If I'm right, Heather died because of me. I have to tell Eric, because it's the right thing to do. And after that, I'm turning myself in to the police."

CHAPTER 18
NOVEMBER, SENIOR YEAR

I lined the vegetables in a neat row on the cutting board—mushrooms, green peppers, olives, all of Coop's favorites—and placed his knife next to them. I took a step back and surveyed. Picture-perfect.

The door to the bedroom swung open and Coop stepped out, running a towel through his hair, wet and curled from the shower. His chest was bare, basketball shorts low on his hips. He looked up and jerked back, eyes wide.

"Holy *shit*, Jess." He put a hand to his chest. "What are you doing here?"

I held out my arms like Vanna White. "Dinner. I brought pizza ingredients. Remember, you said you'd teach me?"

His face broke into a warm smile as he tossed his towel on the bathroom floor. I rolled my eyes at his insufferable sloppiness, which only made him grin wider.

"My girl comes bearing food." He sauntered across his tiny studio and, ignoring my squeal of surprise, lifted me into his arms. "This is a good day."

"You're dirtying the counter," I protested as he leaned me up against the countertop and pressed close between my legs.

"Come here," he said, tilting my face and kissing me. Somewhere along the way, Coop's kisses had changed from heated and urgent to tender. Weighty.

I pushed my hands into his hair, winding the wet curls around my fingers and opening my mouth so he could press inside. When it came to Coop, there was no such thing as too much.

I was addicted. Like father, like daughter.

"How long do I have you?" he whispered.

"All weekend." I grinned against his mouth.

"All *weekend*?"

"Mint went to the Georgia game. Last-minute decision."

Coop spun me in a circle. "A whole weekend." He set me down. "This is perfect. I got you something."

"You didn't have to do that."

Coop produced a bottle of red wine from his pantry with a flourish. "Your favorite."

"You remembered." I'd discovered red wine this year, and it was like my entire palate changed overnight. Now, it was the only thing I wanted to drink. It left my lips and teeth stained crimson, like a vampire's, but I didn't care. Red wine was classy, sophisticated. A sign I was growing up.

Good wine was also expensive.

"You didn't have to buy it," I said as he twisted the cork with a small pop. I hated when Coop spent money on me, because I knew where it came from.

"I wanted to talk to you." The wine, dark as blood, snaked out of the bottle and down the side of the glass. "About something important."

My heartbeat picked up. This couldn't be good.

"Here," he said, handing me the glass. "Cheers."

I clinked and downed half the wine, feeling it coat my lips. "So. Something important."

Coop took a step closer. It took everything in me to keep my shoulders straight, not lean into him, bury my face in his chest. He smelled like things that came from the earth—wood and citrus and grass.

Panic gripped me, sudden and fierce. I didn't want this to be over.

"Come on," he said gruffly, picking me up again.

"Hey!" My feet kicked uselessly. "You're so manhandley tonight."

"Grab the bottle."

I rolled my eyes but snagged the wine.

"And—set—it—down—right—there," Coop took a few exaggerated steps to his bed and lowered me over his bedside table. The instant I placed the bottle down, he tossed me.

"Jesus, Coop!" I bounced high on his bed, but he reached for me, pulling me over so I lay against his chest, our legs tangled.

He rested his head on his hand. "Come home with me for Thanksgiving. Meet my mom."

I drew back. "What?"

"Hear me out." He raised a finger. "One. My mom really wants to meet you. Two. You could see my teenage bedroom, *including* all my emo band posters from high school. The blackmail material writes itself. Three. We'd get a whole week together without anyone else. Just you and me in the exotic town of Greenville, South Carolina. And four—I know you don't want to go home."

I didn't. My dad's latest stint in recovery had ended in flames when he got high and drove his car straight through the parking lot and into his office lobby. That made three unsuccessful admissions to rehab in three years. Three pointless family days, sitting in a little circle, waiting for my dad to do something—*anything*—different. Maybe look my mom full in the face without cutting his eyes away; maybe say something to me that wasn't about school; maybe talk about those times when I was young and he reshaped me with his cruelty. Maybe he could admit to being sad, or lonely, or depressed. Or even mildly disappointed.

Yeah, yeah, we asked for so much.

The first stint in rehab, my mom and I had expected the impossible—waited for him to say something that let us know he recognized the pain underneath the fog of the pills. But he didn't, of course, and after that we'd stopped expecting it.

And now this. He was finally unemployed, and spiraling. No one knew what to do next.

"What about Mint?" I asked, pushing thoughts of home aside. "He's going to think it's weird if I go home with you."

"I was thinking," Coop said slowly, studying my face. "What if you ended things?"

My mouth opened, but no sound came out.

"We could tell him together. I mean, I'll do it if you want. We could come clean, and then after a little while…we could be together. For real. In public."

My brain was having trouble processing. Coop, scorner of all things traditional, earnest, wanted to be my boyfriend?

"You want to date?" I asked dubiously.

He took my face in his hands and looked me in the eyes. How terrifying, to be truly *looked at*.

"Coop—" I started, wanting him to turn that gaze away, unsure where this was going. There was a charge building in the air, a feeling: *Today, something starts that will never end.*

"Jessica Marie Miller. You have to know by now I love you."

I made a sound of surprise.

He smiled. "I feel like I've worn it on my sleeve since the day I met you."

"The fortune," I said, three years too late.

"Of course. The first week of class, you and I left East House at the same time. You didn't notice me, but I watched you the entire time we were walking. You were so beautiful. But the thing that really fascinated me was that I could read everything you were thinking."

"What do you mean?"

"It was so easy to tell what you were feeling. It was right there on your face for everyone to see. Longing when you passed other students, happiness when you saw Blackwell Tower, worry when you got close to Perkins Hall, where your class was. I remember thinking how innocent that was, or brave, how much I wanted to know you."

Coop leaned down and kissed my nose. "Now I can never tell what you're thinking."

"I—"

"I wanted to ask you out, freshman year," he said in a rush. "You taped the fortune on your door, and I thought there was hope. But then Bid Day, when I walked into my room and you and Mint were on the bed... Mint was my roommate. And you obviously liked him. So I told myself to forget you. But I never could."

"You could have," I said quietly. "You could've been with anyone. They all wonder why you don't date."

He shook his head. "Tell them I've been out of my mind for you since we were eighteen. There's no one else for me. I thought I could handle being with you in secret, because at least I'd get part of you. I told you when we started that I wanted more—"

I could still hear those words: *I'm telling you upfront. I need more. I need you over and over.* Even remembering them brought heat to my face.

"But more's not enough."

"What do you want, then?" My heart was pounding so hard I could feel it rattling my rib cage.

He looked at me, green eyes serious. "I want everything."

The words were like a spell. The weight of what I'd been holding back for a year hit me—meeting in secret, stealing time, wanting him so badly I ached with it, alone in my bed, trying not to think about what it meant that all I thought about was *Coop, Coop, Coop*. The truth was there, yet I hadn't let myself look until now. Because I was afraid.

I knew what could happen if you loved someone with your whole heart.

"But Mint—" I started.

"You don't love Mint," Coop answered, so confident I would've laughed if I hadn't been scared. Coop didn't understand what it felt like to walk across campus with Mint, arrive at parties holding his hand. The way people looked at me: appraising, envious, wistful. The rush of being valuable. What it meant to me. I did love it.

"The drugs," I said instead. It was my ace card, the only thing we ever fought about. Coop insisted it was low-level dealing, mostly pot and molly to college students, just to keep a cheap roof over his head and shield his mom from debt. He refused to sell the hard stuff, which nowadays meant tweak, sometimes heroin. He'd never sell that, he insisted, no matter how pissed it made the people above him. He wouldn't mess with real addicts.

I'd never told him about my father.

"I quit," Coop said, and waited for my reaction.

"*What*—when?"

"Yesterday. I told them I was out. It's senior year, so I'll be gone by May anyway, and I've saved up enough money. It's time."

I kissed the corner of his mouth. "I'm really happy to hear that."

Coop turned his head, finding my lips, and kissed me hungrily. Still as urgent as the first day, a starved man.

"Jess," he said roughly.

"What?" It was hard to talk, or breathe, when all I wanted was to kiss him.

"Say it." He wrapped his arms around me and crushed me to him, pushing a leg between mine. Warmth bloomed where his leg rubbed me, and spread. I arched into the bed and he kissed me harder, pushing hands through my hair, lowering his body over mine. I ran my fingers over his shoulders, the hard planes of his back, feeling the dip at his waist, pressing him against me, wanting to feel his weight.

He tilted my head back. "Tell me you love me."

There was a sharp *crack* behind us, and the glass shattered on the French doors leading to Coop's backyard.

I screamed, scrambling to sit up, and Coop rolled quickly to his bedside table, groping for something.

A hand snaked through the broken pane on the door and untwisted the lock, swinging the door open.

"Fuck," Coop hissed, tearing open his bedside drawer.

Two men walked into the apartment, glass crunching under their shoes. Though my instincts screamed not to, I couldn't help it—I looked at their faces.

They were both tall. The one with long hair had a scar running diagonally across his pale face, so deep it changed the shape of his mouth. The one with a buzzed scalp had eyes so dark the pupils were drowned.

I froze, heart thundering. These were not good men. I could see the evil in their faces.

"Cooper," said the one with the scar. "Bad time for company."

Coop reached an arm across me like a shield, his other hand still rooting in his drawer.

The one with the buzzed scalp stalked to him and wrenched his hand from the drawer. He reached in himself and pulled out a long knife—a machete. "Nice try."

Coop had a machete? Next to his bed, this whole time? That meant he knew he was in danger, no matter how much he insisted he wasn't.

The man with the buzzed scalp pointed the tip of the knife at Coop. "I told you you'd regret trying to leave."

"Fuck off," Coop said. "I have neighbors. Cops are probably already on their way."

The man with the scar smiled a jagged smile. "In this neighborhood? Nah. I'm sure we have plenty of time."

My attention had narrowed to one place: The machete in the man's hand. My body was so tense, so still, it was like I was dead already, suffering rigor mortis, head to foot.

"I'm not changing my mind," Coop said, brave and stupid as ever.

The man with the scar walked closer, shaking his head. "Not only are you changing your mind, but you're going to level up. From now on, weed's for high schoolers. You're on tweak, making us some real money."

"I don't know what I have to say to get this through your thick skulls—"

The man with the scar seized me, and I screamed, the rigor mortis broken. I scrambled in the bedsheets, trying to wrench my arm from his grasp.

He pulled a gun out of his jacket with his free arm and flipped the safety. He held it to my head, and my entire existence became a ring of cold metal pressed against my temple.

"Watch your mouth, or I'll put something through her skull."

Coop lunged at him, moving so fast I didn't have time to react, knocking the gun out of his hand and shoving him to the floor.

"Coop!" My scream was gutteral. But Coop wasn't listening to me; he was punching the man, over and over, blood flying.

The man with the buzzed scalp shoved Coop off his partner and thrust the machete under his chin. "Don't move." His voice was ice. His eyes dilated, making him look mad, and his veins twisted like dark tree branches under his pale skin.

Coop froze. The man with the scar scrambled to his feet and wiped the blood from his face with the back of his hand. "You're going to regret that."

I leapt from the bed to the kitchen, where I'd left my phone.

"Hey!" barked the man with the machete. "Move one more inch and I slit his throat."

I stopped and turned.

The man with the scar seized Coop's wrist. "You're not quitting. You're coming back and you're recommitting."

"Go to hell," insisted Coop.

The man grinned and pulled Coop's arm straight. For a second, I was confused, because it looked like a dance move. Then the man struck like a viper, snapping Coop's arm at the joint.

For a split second, it was the worst sound I'd ever heard—bone shattering, ligaments tearing—until Coop's bloodcurdling scream.

He dropped to his knees. I rushed forward, barely able to see past my tears, knowing I had to protect him. But the man with the machete pointed it at me, and I halted before I ran into the blade.

"Coop," I sobbed.

"If you don't come back," said the man with the scar, "we will hunt you down." His eyes shifted to me. "We'll hunt *her* down. And we'll kill you both."

"You don't get to walk away," the man with the knife said. "Remember that."

Waiting in the emergency room that night, alone and shaking, all I could see was Coop's face when the glass door first shattered, his lack of surprise. The way he reached automatically for the machete in his bedside table—the movement quick and fluid. Practiced.

I'd known, but I'd forgotten: Coop was dark, wrong, the opposite of perfect. What was I playing at?

It would never be right between us. Not after this.

He may not be able to walk away, but *I*—I still could.

CHAPTER 19
NOW

The *police*. Years of being an outlaw, of skirting the cops, and now Coop was handing himself over. Tying himself to the stake. Going up in flames.

"I won't let you." I moved ahead of him and crossed my arms.

"You don't get a vote. For about a thousand reasons."

"Does Caro know?" I hated to bring her up, but I needed any ally I could get.

A rustling noise made Coop look past me into the trees. "I came clean about dealing. Told her all of it—the pot, the molly, the tweak. The whole thing." His eyes found mine. "Well, I left you out. She doesn't want me to go to Eric or the cops, either."

"That's because it's an insane plan. The cops are not the answer."

Just like that, we were twenty-two again, arguing a decade-old argument. My voice echoed back: *Just go to the cops, Coop, and turn them in. They're dangerous, and they're going to hurt you. I bet you'll get immunity or something.* His voice: *I can't do that. I'd torpedo law school and kill my mom. It's hypocritical, anyway. I'm not innocent.*

How ironic that we'd now switched sides: Coop, running to the cops. Me, urging him not to.

Time, making fools of us all.

He schooled his face into a blank expression. "Jess, if you don't agree with me, just walk away. It should feel pretty familiar by now."

Like a knife to the heart. "I don't want to."

Coop moved around me. "Let me guess: you just want everything to go back to normal. You want to go back to the party and parade yourself in front of everyone, show the whole school how successful and glamorous you turned out. You want Mint to follow you around like a lovesick puppy. You want to pretend everything's perfect and none of us are fucked up. Same old, same old."

I seized him before he could walk away. "You're wrong. I don't want anything to stay the same. Don't you see? I hate how things used to be. I hate it so much I want to scream."

"Then scream, Jessica. Christ, be honest."

When I moved, it was both surprising and inevitable. Like a gun going off in a movie you've already seen. I saw my hands move to Coop's face, pull him down with a familiar roughness. Twenty-two or thirty-two, it didn't matter: it was always going to happen like this. The movement echoed backward and forward through time, too quick for Coop to be anything but surprised. I kissed him and drowned in it.

If we were being self-destructive tonight, Coop had nothing on me.

There was a moment of perfect—his stubble rough against my fingers, his hair as soft as I remembered, his mouth moving against mine, breathing me in, my heart, untethered, lifting—and then he broke away with a sharp intake of breath.

Coop looked at me with such wonder that I knew, for all his provocations, he'd never expected me to do this. Then the wonder turned to hunger—that old, private look, like he was a man starving for me, and no amount would ever be enough.

"I've got to admit, I didn't see this coming."

I wrenched myself out of Coop's arms.

Eric. He stepped out of the dark trees, where there wasn't even a path.

"It's not…" I fumbled the words. "We were just…"

Coop moved in front of me. "I have something to tell you."

Still cloaked in shadow, away from the circle of light cast by one of the old-fashioned lamps, Eric crossed his arms. "It would seem so."

"Don't—" Before I could finish, there was a slapping sound—footsteps on the stone path.

Oh god. My heart seized. Caro ran toward us, Mint and Courtney close behind.

Ground, swallow me whole. This was it. Eric would tell them.

"Coop, I told you no!" Caro's perfectly curled dark hair was now loose and stringy over her shoulders, a sheen to her face. Her eyes were red-rimmed. She looked terrible.

Caro, who didn't deserve any of it. Caro, who would hate me if she knew.

"Will someone please explain what's going on?" Mint clutched his chest. "And why Caro made us run out of the party?"

Courtney swayed on her feet. "You took us back to *him*."

"It's past time this came out," Coop said. He looked at Caro apologetically, and I hated myself for feeling wounded by it. "Eric, I know why the toxicology report showed tweak in Heather's system."

The shadow that was Eric didn't move.

"I sold pot and molly in college. Party drugs. I needed fast money, and I've never thought those kinds of drugs should be illegal in the first place. I'm not proud of it now, because of everything that happened, but I swear, until senior year, I wasn't hurting anybody."

I thought of my father, bent over the steering wheel of his smoking car, the office lobby in shambles around him.

"Yeah, we all know," Mint said. "Everyone bought from you."

"*I* didn't know," Caro said.

"Neither did Eric," Coop said. "He was too young. I didn't fully real-ize until I tried to stop selling, but the guys I worked for were territorial and violent. I brought in a lot of money selling on campus, and they didn't want to lose it. After I quit, they broke into my apartment and broke my arm as a warning."

The terrible scream. The machete, the gun, the evil pulsing underneath their skin. Those dark eyes.

"Wait, *that's* how you broke your arm?" Mint looked stunned. "Not playing basketball?"

"I lied," Coop said. "In reality, a hulking man snapped it while I watched."

"I can't..." Caro shivered.

"They told me if I refused to sell—and if I refused to sell tweak, specifically, which was hot back then, profitable but dangerous—they'd kill me. And..." Coop looked at me, then looked away quickly. "My friends. To teach me a lesson."

"It was *you*," Courtney breathed, a strange look on her face. "Are the rest of you hearing this? It was *his* fault."

"Shut up, Courtney," Caro snapped, to everyone's surprise.

Coop turned to face Eric. "No, Courtney's right. It is my fault. The guys tracked me on campus, and I led them right to Heather's suite. I was trying to hide and I wasn't thinking straight. I told them I'd sell tweak just to get them off my back, and the day Heather died, I was supposed to start. But I didn't want to. They went searching for me. They knew what my friends looked like. I think there's a strong chance they went back to the suite looking to hurt someone close to me and found Heather. And then they..." His voice faltered, but he straightened his shoulders and drew a breath. "Killed her. Making me responsible."

"You're not," I said quickly.

"I can't believe you kept this secret for ten years." Coop's news seemed to act like a splash of cold water to Courtney. She was no longer wobbling, her face now lucid. "You're a bigger liar than Frankie."

Caro whirled on Courtney. "I have been nothing but nice to you since college, defended you despite everything you've done, and you have the nerve—"

"No one broke into the suite," Eric said. "And it wasn't tweak."

Everyone turned to stare.

"What?" Coop asked.

Eric finally stepped out of the shadow, into the light. "The cops found no evidence of a break-in. They suspect whoever killed Heather knew the code to the suite."

Someone close to her.

"And you're forgetting what I said. I told you the cops found a drug *like* tweak in Heather's system. It looked like the street drug, but it wasn't tweak itself. The cops checked."

Coop blinked. "What was it, then?"

"It was a weight-loss drug," Eric said, his eyes leaving Coop to travel over the rest of us. "Illegal in the States because it was basically speed. Ridiculous, toxic side effects. It baffled the cops, because we told them Heather didn't take things like that. You could only buy the drug in China, and the cops could never find the purchase transactions in any students' or professors' accounts."

My stomach dropped. Coop had been right—the drug in Heather's system was a smoking gun, a virtual fingerprint, but it didn't point to him.

I spun, but Caro beat me to it.

"You!" she yelled, pointing at Courtney. "*You* did it!"

Courtney looked like a deer caught in headlights. All of a sudden she turned to bolt, but Caro—tiny Caro—sprang and knocked her to the ground.

"Caro, *Jesus*!" Mint knelt and pulled Caro off his wife.

Caro thrust her finger in Courtney's face. "She's guilty."

"Give her a chance to defend herself." Mint looked at his wife. "Babe?"

Courtney blinked at him, then turned to look around the circle of faces, searching for an ally, a single measure of sympathy. That day freshman year echoed back—the one where she'd tried to humiliate me but Heather had stepped in to stop it. Heather wasn't here anymore.

Courtney's eyes found mine. Her stare was murderous. A chill crept up my neck.

"*Fine,*" she said, taking me by surprise. "I drugged Heather. Are you happy?"

CHAPTER 20
FEBRUARY, SENIOR YEAR

Courtney

If ever someone was born to wear a crown, it was Courtney Kennedy. She of the glossy blond hair, regal face, and astounding proportions. And she knew it, which was important, because other people wasted so much time demurring. Every Valentine's Day since freshman year, she'd watched girls get crowned Phi Delt Sweetheart—always a Chi O, always a senior—and she knew, with unshakable certainty, that one day it would be hers.

That day was today.

The Phi Delt basement was packed with brothers. They'd dragged in a keg and were doing keg stands, following with shots of whiskey. Tonight was no regular night. The Sweetheart Ball was a famous party, and this year was going to be bigger than ever, because Mint was president, and Mint and his real estate money did everything bigger and better than anyone else.

Courtney watched Mint from across the room, ignoring the small crowd of guys who'd gathered around her, trying to get her attention, trying to get in her pants. There was never a shortage of boys, and tonight—well, tonight she was extraordinary. A skintight red dress, red lips, the perfect amount of tasteful cleavage. A look that screamed *I am your Sweetheart, your college queen.*

It didn't matter how many boys surrounded her, because to Courtney there was only one who mattered. Mark Minter. If there was ever a boy born to be with Courtney, it was him. Gorgeous, heir to a fortune, practically Duquette royalty. She would never understand why he'd dated Jessica Miller, that absolute *nonperson*, since freshman year. That was the frustrating thing about life: sometimes the losers won, for absolutely no discernible reason.

Sometimes people met freshman year and banded together into stupid groups like the East House Seven, and cut you out of the deal right before they rode to campus glory. Just because of some stupid comment she'd made to Jessica—as if no one else in the history of the world ever teased each other—they'd forged this thing without her, even though she lived in the same dorm, *in the same room* as one of them, and was Courtney Kennedy to boot.

Mint was talking to Frankie, that giant oaf, when he looked over and caught her staring. Courtney smiled her best smile, and he smiled back. She lifted her Solo cup to say cheers, and he echoed her, taking a sip. Even after Courtney looked away, then slid her eyes back, his gaze lingered. He was going to be hers one day; she could feel it.

Maybe that day was today.

She was about to walk over, leaving the circle of boys—who were still talking, maybe even asking her questions—when Heather stumbled down the stairs, practically tripping into Courtney's arms.

"Christ, Heather." Courtney shooed the boys away and righted her friend. "What's your damage?"

Heather hiccupped, which was not a good sign. In fact, now that Courtney could get a good look at her, something was definitely wrong.

Heather was never going to win any beauty pageants, let's be honest, but the girl had a zero-limit credit card, thanks to her doctor mom, and could usually pull herself together. But now, even though Heather's pink chiffon dress was cute and obviously designer, her mascara was smeared and her nose red, like she'd been crying. Courtney felt a reflexive kick of worry and glanced around, trying to see who'd noticed Heather in this state.

Heather followed her eyes around the basement, clocking Mint and Frankie, and pulled Courtney into a corner. "It's Jack," she said, her voice low and thick with feeling. "He just broke up with me, and I'm freaking out."

"What?" Now *this* was news. Jack and Heather were like Mint and Jessica—permanent fixtures, practically Duquette institutions, despite being totally mismatched. Courtney had always been able to see it, even if no one else could. It sounded like Jack was finally coming to his senses.

Heather nodded, tears welling in her eyes. "He told me—" Her voice dropped to a whisper. "He's been cheating on me. We got into a huge fight, and I didn't know where else to go. I figured everyone would be here."

Well, would you look at that. Courtney wasn't surprised at all. It seemed perfectly believable that Jack would find someone prettier than Heather. It had to be another Chi O. She wondered who...

"Where's Jess?" Heather's eyes scanned the crowd. "I need to talk to her."

Courtney bristled. "You don't need Jessica. I'm your best friend. You can talk to me."

Heather shook her head vehemently. "Jack told me...a lot. Shocking things. And Jess knew about it for an entire year. I can't believe she kept this from me. I have to find her."

Aha. Courtney seized her opportunity. "That doesn't surprise me. Jessica's never been a very good friend."

Tears spilled down Heather's face, taking her mascara with it. "God, this was supposed to be the best night. A celebration. And now I feel like my entire life is falling apart. I thought Jack and I were going to get married."

The sight of Heather openly crying tugged at Courtney's heart. "Hey," she said sternly. "Don't waste your time crying over someone who didn't respect you enough to keep his dick in his pants. He's the one who lost you. So don't get sad—get over it. Hell, get even."

Courtney patted Heather on the shoulder, proud of herself for such a good speech. "Now go clean yourself up in the bathroom. You've got mascara everywhere. It's ridiculous. Your face looks like a Jackson Pollock painting."

Heather wiped her eyes. "Thanks," she whispered and left for the stairs.

With Heather gone, Courtney stepped back into the center of the room. She eyed Mint near the keg and strode over, fanning her hair over her shoulder. Just as she was about to reach him, a big chest stepped in front of her.

"Was that Heather?" Frankie asked. "She's not leaving the party, is she?"

God. The insufferableness of the East House Seven. Like a damn cult, all of them so wrapped up in each other they were practically in love.

"Calm down," Courtney said, rolling her eyes. "She's just going to the bathroom. She'll be back in a minute." *Pathetic.*

"Good," Frankie said, straightening the lapel of his suit jacket. He grinned at her. "Tonight's going to be a big night for her." He glanced around and lowered his voice. "Don't tell anyone, because I'm not supposed to say, but Heather won Sweetheart. I'm really glad. She deserves it."

The floor dropped out. She grabbed Frankie's shoulder to steady herself. "*Heather?*"

153

"Yeah, great, right?" Frankie frowned. "Am I missing something?"

Courtney swallowed hard, feeling like she was going to throw up. "Who was…runner-up?" If Frankie said Jessica, she was going to light this frat house on fire.

"*Oh*," Frankie said, looking suddenly guilty. "You were. Sorry. That was a dick move to tell you Heather won like that. I never think before I say things."

She was runner-up. Close, but no crown. It was almost like it had been ripped right off her head. Courtney forced herself to smile. "Don't be ridiculous. It's just a stupid tradition. Who cares?"

She left Frankie staring at her guiltily and grabbed a Solo cup, pumping the keg to give herself time to think. *Heather?* How had Heather beaten her? Put the two of them side by side and there was no comparison. Heather was lucky to even be a Chi O. She'd probably only gotten in because she was Courtney's roommate. She'd been lucky to date Jack, and look, she couldn't even keep him loyal.

How had this happened? And how could she fix it, turn it around, make the night go the way it was supposed to?

An idea came to her. It was wrong, of course, but no more so than Heather winning Sweetheart instead of her.

Courtney pulled the pills out of her purse and found the darkest corner of the basement, where there was a stumpy radiator, and no one was watching. She poured the pills onto the radiator and, glancing around just in case, crushed them with her phone. Swept them into the beer, mixed it with her finger. She stared at the cup for a second, then dumped two more pills, ground them, and brushed them in. There. That would do.

You couldn't crown a passed-out Sweetheart.

It made sense, in a funny way, that her pills would help her with this. Courtney would never forget her mother standing beside her in the full-length mirror the night before her first day of high school, closing Courtney's hand around a single white pill. She'd pinched the baby fat poking over the waist of Courtney's jeans and said, "This little thing is going to save you." Their eyes had met in the mirror, and Courtney's mom smiled a conspiratorial smile. And she'd felt in that moment like she was being let into some secret club, some tight circle where she and her mom would be closer than ever, not just mother-daughter, but two *women*. Her mom had winked. "It'll get you every-thing you want. Trust me."

And look at it now, doing just that. The secret club she'd hoped for with her mom had never materialized, and neither had the special closeness, but at least this part was turning out exactly like her mother promised.

Across the basement, Heather descended the staircase once more, her mascara back in place, nose no longer red. Courtney, resenting the regal bearing of Heather's shoulders, made her way over. But before she could say anything, Heather gave her a triumphant look—the kind a villain in a movie wore when they'd hatched an evil plan.

"I thought about what you said, and you're right," Heather said. "I'm going to get even with Jack, and I know just how. Hooking up with someone else won't hurt him. So I'm going to talk to his parents. Next weekend."

Courtney blinked, taken aback. "Parents' Weekend?"

"Yes," Heather said fiercely. "I'm going to tell them everything. His parents love me, and they're so religious they'll never forgive him. He's always cared what they think, no matter how much he denies it. We'll see how he likes having *his* life ruined." She looked around the room. "I need a drink. I have several hours of my life to forget." Heather turned, gripping her. "Before I get drunk… Don't let me talk to Frankie, okay? I can't tell you why, but promise me."

Courtney was opening her mouth to ask Heather why anyway—or, frankly, to tell her that no matter *what* Jack had done, nothing justified getting his parents involved—when she realized Heather had given her the perfect opening.

"Here," she said instead, thrusting her cup at her. "I got you this. Bottom's up."

"Thank god," Heather said, taking the beer and chugging it. She wiped her mouth. "You're a lifesaver."

CHAPTER 21
NOW

I'd always thought the sight of Courtney Minter cowering on the ground, confessing her sins to an angry mob, would make me feel better than it did. Now that it was happening, she looked so small and pathetic, her twig-legs drawn up under her, perfect face in her bony hands, that it was hard to see the traces of my legendary nemesis.

Instead, watching her, one thing was crystal-clear: Courtney Minter was not a happy person—or, a healthy one. Yes, she'd done something terrible. But for all the days of her life, Courtney was going to have to live with herself, locked in the cage of her body with nothing to keep her company but her own brain. And that was a severe punishment if I'd ever heard one.

Caro did not share my sympathy.

"You drugged your *best friend* to get her out of the way so you could be queen of a *fraternity party*?" Caro's face was so red you could see it, even in the dim light from the lamps.

Looking at Courtney, I felt an uneasy stirring in the pit of my stomach. If I hadn't been so consumed with winning a prize greater than Sweetheart, it could've been me that night, stewing in the shadows, gutted by Heather's first-place win, Courtney's runner-up status. The insidious voice whispering, *Jessica Miller, the Phi Delt president's girlfriend—and not even second in line for the crown.*

I recognized myself in her.

"I know you're mad, Caro, but keep your voice down." Mint looked around. "We don't want to attract unwelcome attention."

"Oh, no. Like from *the cops*?" Caro threw her arms out. For a second—it could have been the lighting—she looked like a gold cross, burning bright against the night. "Jail's exactly where we should send her. Courtney, you're the reason Heather couldn't defend herself that night. You might not have stabbed her, but you basically tied her hands behind her back. And you were willing to let Coop take the fall. How do you live with yourself?"

"It was supposed to make her go to sleep, that's all. How could I have *known*?"

Courtney's hands trembled in a way that was deeply familiar. "After she died, I was broken. I didn't eat for a week. And the only way I could get out of bed was to think...well, she would have been killed anyway. Someone wanted to stab her. It was only a coincidence both things happened the same night. I told myself it didn't matter and made myself forget." Her voice dropped to a painful, throaty whisper. "I should have won Sweetheart in the first place. It was meant to be mine."

"'Uneasy lies the head that wears a crown,'" Eric said, his voice ice.

I made myself forget. The black hole at my center stirred. A flash of memory: *Two hands, covered in dried blood.*

No. I shoved the image away.

On the ground, Courtney's hands started shaking so bad she could barely hold them in place. She reached for her purse, but before she could get there, Eric snatched the bag, and she gave a cry of protest.

No one moved to stop him.

He yanked open her purse, rummaged, and pulled out a sleek orange cylinder with Chinese letters.

"You're *still* taking the pills?" Coop shook his head. "Goddamn, Courtney." He looked dazed, as if he couldn't believe the turn the night had taken.

"Lucky for us," Eric said, turning the bottle to look at it. "Now we have evidence."

Mint sat down at his wife's side and gave Eric an evil look. "She doesn't say another word. We're getting a lawyer."

Courtney burst into tears. "I don't care about a lawyer," she cried. "Please, just give them back. *Please.*"

A memory of my father, begging: *Please, Jessica. Please, sweetheart, just to take the edge off. You don't understand how much it hurts.*

I grabbed the pills from Eric's hand, taking him by surprise, and twisted the lid off.

"What are you *doing*?" Caro asked.

"She's addicted." I dumped the pills in my hand, leaving one in the bottom of the bottle. "You can still have your evidence. You don't need all of them."

I handed the bottle back to Eric, who took it with a raised brow. Then I crouched by Courtney. She looked at me with cautious hope, and I realized, with a sinking feeling, that we'd been bad to her, too. Not the same kind of bad she'd been to us, but we'd known about her problem, in the back of our minds, and done nothing. Brushed it off all four years of college. Worse—in some ways, we'd even celebrated it. Courtney, the most perfect girl in school, had a humiliating vice. A fatal flaw. We'd all sighed in relief.

I pressed the pills into her hand and closed her blood-red fingernails around them. She nodded, embarrassed but grateful. I stood, catching Coop's eye. He gave me a puzzled look.

"You all need to sign an NDA," Mint said, wrapping a protective arm around Courtney's shoulders.

"Are you kidding me?" Caro screeched.

"Not about her drugging Heather," Mint said hurriedly. "Just about the diet pills. She's a fitness influencer. It would ruin her career."

Coop shook his head. "She's lying on the ground shaking, dude. Her career is the least of her worries."

"For the record"—twisted the pill bottle in his hand, watching it catch the lamplight—"I wasn't staring at your breasts in college." His gaze moved from the bottle to Courtney's face. "I was staring at your ribs. You were a walking skeleton, and I couldn't believe no one said anything. Not even Heather. She used to brush it off when I asked." He pocketed the bottle. "I always had a feeling the drug in Heather's system was yours."

Something about Courtney's story was still bugging me. I turned to her. "After Heather got blackout at Phi Delt, and you asked Frankie to take her home, what did you tell him?"

Courtney blinked, rubbing mascara-streaked cheeks. "I don't know," she said shakily. "I guess I told him Jack had broken up with her. And she was drowning her sorrows, planning her revenge."

Her voice became firmer, surer. "I definitely did. I told Frankie that Jack had confessed some terrible secret, and Heather was planning to tell Jack's parents at Parents' Weekend to get back at him, ruin his life. I remember I told Frankie *specifically* because I thought it was messed up of Heather, and I was hoping he'd talk her out of it. She was more likely to listen to him than me, anyway." Courtney laughed, a small, bitter sound. "He was one of you East House Seven, after all."

"Frankie didn't tell us that part." Coop shot me a worried look.

Caro frowned. "Why wouldn't he mention Heather was planning to tell Jack's parents? That's huge."

"You guys," I said, "Frankie's parents always came for Parents'

Weekend. His dad practically lived for it. If Heather was going to spill the beans, make some spectacle, there's a strong chance Frankie's parents would have found out, too."

"But Heather didn't know Frankie was the guy Jack was cheating with," Eric pointed out.

"Maybe she did." Mint ran a tired hand over his face, mussing his golden hair. "Heather asked Courtney to make sure she didn't get drunk and talk to Frankie. Maybe that's why."

We were all silent for a stretch, until finally Caro spoke. "He's guilty, isn't he? Heather was scared to talk to him that night, and at *best*, Frankie lied by omission earlier. We all remember what his dad is like. Frankie said himself he would have done anything to keep his dad from finding out. He has to be guilty."

"I don't know," Eric said, scratching his jaw. He looked unsure for the first time all night, and for a second, I caught a glimpse of the soft boy I remembered, before his face hardened. "It doesn't satisfy all the other evidence, but it's worth checking out."

"What other evidence—" Mint started, but Caro interrupted.

"We know where Frankie's going to be tomorrow. He's grand marshal of the Homecoming parade. There will be tons of people around. If we confront him, he can't run."

Coop whistled. "You want to accuse Frankie of murdering Heather in front of hundreds of people?"

"What other choice do we have?" I asked. "This could be our only opportunity to solve Heather's murder."

Eric eyed me. "Since when do you care about solving her murder?"

The words were a knife through my heart. But only because I knew— in the deepest, darkest part of me—that I deserved them.

I deserved so much worse.

"Since always," I said quietly. "Since now."

"Well"—Eric patted the pill bottle in his pocket—"whoever else cares,

I'll see you at noon tomorrow by the basketball stadium, at the start of the parade route. We'll demand an explanation from the grand marshal."

With that, Eric slipped back into the trees, where there wasn't even a path, and dissolved among the shadows.

"Fucking Ghost of Christmas Past," Mint muttered. "Back to punish us for our sins."

Everyone went back to their hotels. Tomorrow we were confronting Frankie, and there was nothing left to say.

Except for me. I stood in the middle of the now-empty white tent, watching the bartenders pack bottles. The party was over. My perfect plan, ground to dust, ruined by Eric Shelby. But as I stood there, a new plan slowly formed, more ambitious than the first. If I could pull it off, I wouldn't just be proving myself—I could settle every debt, right every wrong. Quiet the insidious whisper. Unmake the black hole.

Eric was right: for ten years, I'd lived a lie. I'd pretended I was fine, pretended I'd moved on, but the truth was, the past was still open inside me, like a half-cracked door, because it was a raw, unhealed wound.

Showing off for my classmates was only a Band-Aid. I would step inside that door. Dive into the past. I would find Heather's killer and be healed.

"You really don't want to go home, do you?"

I spun to find Coop.

"What are you doing here? I thought you left with Caro."

He put a finger to his lips and walked backwards to the bar. While the bartenders' backs were turned, Coop grabbed a bottle of whiskey and slid it under his sweater. He waved at me to follow and sauntered, as if nothing was amiss, out of the tent.

I drew a deep breath and followed.

He led me through the dark, eerie campus. I remained behind, eyes on his back, walking in silence. Halfway, I knew where we were going, so I wasn't surprised to see the ivy-covered walls of East House rise in front of us.

He walked past it into the quad, over to our picnic table, the one beside the oak tree Heather's parents had planted ten years ago, a memorial in her favorite place. The tree had grown to twenty feet now. Looking at it was like looking at the passage of time, made solid and tangible. The branches reached toward East House like imploring arms. It looked uncannily like a person, as if Heather herself was frozen and trapped, begging for help.

I pushed away the thought. We'd been happy here.

Coop ignored the picnic bench and sat right on the table. He twisted the cap off the stolen whiskey, took a long pull, then held it out to me.

I couldn't help the ghost of a smile. "In the middle of the *quad*? Out in the open? You rebel."

Coop didn't smile back. "Who do you know with an addiction?"

I took the whiskey and sat down next to him. Slugged a mouthful. I had to force it down, trying not to gag. "My dad. OxyContin, at first. Then whatever he could find."

Coop nodded, looking across the quad at East House. A slight breeze picked up a tendril of his hair and brushed it over his forehead. "All those years, you never told me."

"Yeah, well, it was the last thing I wanted people to know."

A few of the windows were still lit in the dorm. Students, up late. I searched for the window on the fourth floor, in the corner. My old room. But it was dark, the curtains drawn.

Coop ran his hands through his hair and held them there. "I feel like I know you so well, and then I discover something like this. I wish you trusted me."

I scooted the whiskey bottle toward him. "I don't trust anyone."

"That sounds lonely. You have to let people in. Let them love you for who you are, the good and the ugly. Then you know it's real."

Coop had grown into a good man, or maybe he'd always been one. Either way, he didn't understand that there were some truths too ugly to see the light of day. Some that would ruin love, if they were uncovered.

The memory came back, this time more vivid. Waking up, disoriented, my head pounding. The sunlight too bright, streaming through vaguely familiar windows. Bracing my hands against the floor to push myself up, only to feel my hands stick to the wood. Looking down. Breath catching. My hands, splayed on the floor, rust-red from fingernails to elbows, covered in flaking blood. Crimson splattered across my pink dress like ink on a Rorschach test. The horrible question: *What had I done?*

Nothing, I answered fiercely. I'd done nothing. I had to rebury the memory alongside the others. There was nothing to be had from it but ruin and rot.

I turned away from Coop, not wanting him to see my face.

"In the spirit of openness," he said, "there's something I wanted to show—"

"Coop." I swallowed the lump in my throat. "Why was it so good here?"

"What?"

I wiped my eyes and looked around the quad, at the ivy-covered dorm pulled from a fairy tale, the ring of trees, standing sentinel. Here, in the grass, I'd been reborn, committed myself to a new religion, a strong magic. That magic was still buried in the soil of this place.

It was my home.

My hair fell like a curtain in front of my face. When I spoke, the words were barely discernible. "Why was it so good here, and so bad? It didn't matter—whatever I was feeling, it was dialed up so high. Why can't I make myself feel that way again? Everything these last ten years has paled compared to it. I'm scared college was the last time I was really alive, the way you're supposed to be, and I'll never get it back."

"Of course college felt extreme," Coop said. "You had infinite freedom and almost no responsibility. Nothing was fixed—you had your whole life ahead of you, and it could go anywhere. You had best friends you spent every minute with, so you were never alone. And you were in love. *Real* love."

"Yeah, well, Mint turned into Courtney's Stepford husband, so look where that got me."

Coop brushed my hair back from my face. "I wasn't talking about him."

CHAPTER 22
MAY, SENIOR YEAR

I thought I was ready to let go, until graduation day. I sat in the sweltering heat, lined up with the other Millers, watching students in crimson robes inch across the stage, and panic set in. If I walked up those stairs to shake the chancellor's hand—if I allowed this day to come and go, packed my things into my mother's car and drove back to Norfolk—it would all be over.

After Heather died, after Mint and I recommitted to our relationship, driven by a gutting guilt neither one of us wanted to talk about, after I started avoiding Coop, I couldn't wait for the semester to be over. I thought I wanted to move on. But now that the day was here, red-and-white-balloon arches and Eliot Lawn crammed with families in folding chairs, I realized: there was no more time to change things. This was how it was going to end. How the story would be written.

It would go like this: I'd officially failed to beat Chi O and take their first-place rush record. The East House Seven were officially drifting apart. I'd officially fallen out with Coop, both of us going our separate ways, no reason to run into each other again. I'd officially lost the chance to follow in my father's footsteps—failed him for the last time—and now I had no idea what I'd do with my life once I walked off this lawn.

I'd officially made it to the end without Heather.

I hadn't realized at the time, because going to school after Heather's death was painful, but being a student at Duquette at least kept things alive, the ink still wet. There had still been time for anything to happen, and now it was over.

A line from the poem came back—the one Caro had given me, shoving it in my hands with a tear-stained face: *What is it you plan to do with your one wild and precious life?*

I had no idea.

I glanced behind me into the rows of families, scanning until I found her. My mother, dressed in black despite the heat, straight-backed, eyes on the stage, waiting. And, because she didn't realize I was looking, everything she felt was written clear across her face: a current of raw emotion, passing like clouds across the sky. Even as it hurt me to watch, I couldn't help thinking how alike we were, as much as we'd always tried not to be.

At the very least, we'd both made it here, to this day. My father hadn't. I'd started this whole thing for him, but she—*she*, who'd never wanted it in the first place—was the only one left to finish.

The graduation concert was a Duquette tradition. The Alumni Office sponsored it, hired some big act every year, and as if to mark our transition from students to real adults, the Duquette administration let its hair down and served wine and beer to everyone. This year, the party was bigger and better than ever, because Mint had graduated, and the Minters—despite the real estate crash—did things bigger and better than anyone else, including showy donations.

They'd built a memorial for Heather. A wall, covered in pictures of her, notes, teddy bears, and bouquets of cheap flowers she would have hated. I couldn't look at it—couldn't stand to see her face, over and over. Heather at Homecoming senior year, red and white ribbons in her hair; Heather in a Chi Omega shirt, gold crown, and pink boa on Bid Day; Heather's baby face, wearing her confident grin, outside East House freshman year. And my face, staring back from so many of the pictures; my eyes seemed to follow when I passed, like a haunted painting, trying to communicate something was wrong though my mouth was locked in a permanent grin, frozen forever on film.

Heather's family came—Mr. and Dr. Shelby, and Eric—but they'd left shortly after Eric walked stiffly across the stage, accepting Heather's honorary diploma.

I breathed easier once they left.

Now my mom sat at a table with the impossibly glamorous Mrs. Minter and her paramour, the board member, a tall, gruff man with a handlebar mustache. Mint's dad was mysteriously out of the picture. It was excruciatingly uncomfortable. Lately, every time I tried to ask Mint about his dad, or about how his parents' company was surviving the crash, he shook his head, refusing to say a word. Sometimes, if I pushed, he left me for the night, and I wouldn't see him until the next day, when he was apologetic but no more forthcoming.

The Minters, as I'd realized long ago, were a fucked-up family.

But at least they were in good company with my mom, who sat still and quiet as a statue, radiating sadness.

"Mint," I whispered, turning to him. He wore a splendid navy suit with glossy buttons, every inch the graduating prince. "Let's get out of here."

He gave me a grateful look. "I thought you'd never ask."

We got champagne and strode to the edge of the crowd gathered around the stage, where some rock band was trying its hardest to turn the party into a night at Madison Square Garden. If our story had unfolded the way it was supposed to, without Heather dying, Jack would have been right there in the front row, our resident music geek, with Frankie beside him, ready to throw his body around with wild abandon. Caro would have been squished between them, dodging elbows but happy to stick close, and Heather would have spun through the crowd, talking to everyone.

I blinked away the what-if. In the real world, Heather and Jack were missing entirely, and Frankie and Caro were sitting on the outskirts of the lawn with their families, quiet and somber.

Maybe Mint saw it, too, the ghost of the *should-have-been*, because he waved me away from the stage.

"Too loud," he yelled.

"I don't mind," I answered, once we were far enough away to hear each other. "The ride home with my mom is going to be four and a half hours of silence. I've got to soak up sound while I can so I don't forget what it's like."

He eyed me, and I could tell he was wrestling with something, at war with himself. Finally, he forced it out. "What if you didn't go home? What if you came with me to New York?"

I looked at him in surprise. I'd been so focused on getting through each day that I hadn't spent a lot of time thinking about what would happen next between Mint and me. "And do what?"

"Anything you want. We can get an apartment together on the Upper East Side. I'll go to law school, and you can find a job. There has to be something. Maybe consulting. That's prestigious, and they're probably one of the few places still hiring. You could make lots of money." Mint's brow was furrowed, his gaze focused on my shoulder. The way he spoke—pushing the words out—was like he was forcing himself to do it.

"It's no Harvard," I said, unable to help myself.

His face flashed with anger—then, just as quickly, smoothed into a calm mask. "Yeah, well, you didn't get that fellowship, did you?" His voice was cold. "Even though you went above and beyond."

I blinked at him.

"I'm sorry." Mint shook his head. "I'm just really stressed with my mom here. And *him*."

"It's okay. I'll think about New York," I promised.

Mint nodded, looking off into the distance. I could still see the anger, alive in his eyes, see him struggling to kill it. "I'm going to take a walk," he announced.

I looked around. It was the last moment of twilight, right before night fell. The sky was purple; the lights of the stage turning on, one by one.

"Okay," I said, and he walked away.

I stood there by myself and tried to picture Mint, New York, consulting. A prestigious job—a good life. But instead, the shadow thoughts bubbled up, as they always did: My dad. Heather. The pull of memories, trying to tug me under.

"Jess."

It was spoken too loudly. A little slurred.

I turned to find Coop walking toward me, the sleeves of his dress shirt rolled to his elbows, hem untucked. His hair was sticking up wild, as if he'd run his fingers through it a million times. But nothing was as wild as his eyes, rimmed with red.

I backed away. "I have to go. Back to my mom."

"Stop running," he said. "Why won't you talk to me? Ever since you showed up at my door that night, you've refused—"

"Coop, I'm with Mint. I need to do it right this time. I have to be a good person." I started to walk away.

"If you leave like this, we'll never see each other again."

I froze. The thought had plagued me all day. I turned slowly, afraid of what I'd find when I stopped—real, magnetic, flesh-and-blood Coop, and the short distance between us. But I was unable to resist.

"You're drunk," I said as soon as I got a close look at him.

"Yeah, well, my heart is broken."

Goddammit, Coop. He always asked so much. But he didn't know the truth, and what would he say if he did? Desire and fear warred inside me.

My voice dropped. "You were right about me, what you said that day in Blackwell Tower. I'm a bad person. But I don't want to be. I want to be good."

Coop closed the distance between us. "Fuck it. I don't care if you're good or bad. I love you, and you love me. Say it."

"Coop, *listen* to me."

He dropped to his knees in the grass and clutched my hands. My heart beat wildly; I searched around, looking for prying eyes. But we were at the edge of the concert, and no one was paying attention.

"Get up," I insisted.

"Tell me. Just once."

I wanted to throw my arms around him. Kiss him, tell him, dissolve. But I couldn't. I'd messed up too much already. I needed to make the right choice. Everything pointed to Mint, the boy from the right family who had the whole world at his feet, the one who could make me into someone valuable, someone important.

I shook my head and spoke words that would slide softly between his ribs, like a sharp knife. "I love Mint."

Coop's head jerked like he'd been slapped. He focused on the grass, biting his lip. I watched him struggle.

Then he turned back to me, letting me see the rawness of his face, his glittering eyes, wet lashes. "No, you don't." Coop gripped my hands, his voice fierce. "Jess, come with me to law school. Marry me. You can paint, be an artist, do everything you love. I'll make you happy, I swear."

Give up everything I'd worked for? Even though nothing was turning out the way it was supposed to, I couldn't do that. I had to find a way to *fix* it, not blow it all up.

"Jess, do something radical. Choose happiness."

Happiness? That was a luxury I'd never been able to afford. Besides, Coop didn't know that I didn't deserve to be happy, even if I'd wanted it.

I saw Mint far off in the distance, walking back to Eliot Lawn from wherever he'd gone. It flashed before my eyes, a whole life: Mint. New York. Consulting. Becoming someone valuable, someone my father would've been proud of, even if the details looked different.

I looked down at Coop, on his knees. Just like the first time we'd kissed, at the top of Blackwell Tower, when he'd warned me he needed more, that I had to choose all or nothing. He was always asking me to make radical choices.

But I never could. And so, one year later—and far, *far* too late—I finally took the out.

CHAPTER 23
NOW

The knock on the door sounded like a gavel striking wood: once, twice, three times. It wrenched me awake. I came to in the dark hotel room, lying on my side, breathing hard.

The pounding came faster, and I stumbled across the room, barely conscious but desperate to make it stop. I flung open the door and shrunk against the blaze of light from the hallway.

Caro, dressed in wrinkled pajamas. For a second, she blinked at me with red-rimmed eyes. Then they filled with tears and she pushed past me into the room.

I froze, gripping the doorway. Caro had figured it out: Me and Coop, ten years ago. One year ago. *Tonight.* And now she was here to tell me I'd stabbed her in the back. To burn me alive. Why else would she burst into my hotel room in the middle of the night?

I shut the door softly, slowly, feeling as though I was locking myself in a prison of my own making.

Behind me, the mattress springs squeaked. When I turned around,

Caro looked at me from my bed: a small, sad face and halo of dark hair against a sea of white linen.

"Jess," she choked.

My heart seized. This wasn't the way it was supposed to go. With my back against the wall, I slid to the floor, unable to take my eyes from her, waiting for the strike.

"I have to tell you something." Her voice was urgent. "I can't keep it a secret any longer."

It took me a second. "What?"

She hid her face in her hands and shook her head, as if the action could ward something off. "It's really bad."

I could do nothing but watch her, tensed, a lump in my throat.

The room was dark, save for silvery light from the cracks in the blinds that told me we were nearing morning. Coop must have slipped back into his hotel room only hours ago, and now Caro had slipped out of it, like two ships in the night. The sight of her sitting on my unmade bed, the sheets still warm with the heat of my body—her lashes wet, her hair catching silver, her face wide open—was surreal. After everything I'd done to keep her at arm's length, here she was, so close.

Just the two of us, watching each other.

I spoke carefully. "Caro, I don't think you're capable of anything bad."

It was the wrong thing to say. A tear dropped down her cheek. "I was so tired of being left out. Afraid of losing everyone. Especially you."

"I don't understand."

She squeezed her eyes shut. "It's the real reason I think it's him."

I thought about walking across the room and brushing her hair from her forehead, then felt a stabbing guilt.

"Him who?" I asked instead.

Caro opened her eyes, and even in the dark I could see the shame.

"Frankie. It's why I think he killed Heather. She was going to ruin his football career."

"Caro, we already know about Parents' Weekend and Heather's plan."

"No, not that. Something else. Something I'm not supposed to know about."

I sat up straighter. "Tell me."

It was a long moment before she spoke. When she did, she watched me warily, like she was waiting for me to grab her, shake her, push her away in disgust. "Frankie started using steroids in college. He said it was a temporary thing, just to take him over the finish line. Get him into the NFL."

"There's no way," I said. "He'd never."

"Jack helped him. Whenever Frankie had to take a drug test, Jack would pee in a cup."

Jack? Rule-abiding, church-boy Jack? He wouldn't dream of it. Unless...unless he'd really loved Frankie. Enough to risk not just scandal but expulsion.

Caro's voice turned soft, her gaze drifting to the wall above me, like she was looking through a porthole into the past. "Senior year, Heather found out. You remember what she was like. Everyone always had to do the right thing. Or whatever she thought that was. She told them they had to stop. Frankie begged for a little more time, just one more test. But she told them they had to quit, or she was going to tell Frankie's coach. She was so mad at Jack. I'll never forget the look on her face."

I started to speak, to ask about Heather, but then the strangeness of her words caught me. *I'll never forget the look on her face.* A frost spread over my body, my hands turning cold, as if the blood was slowly draining from them. "Wait...Caro. How did *you* find out?"

She paused, those dark eyes and that silvery hair making her a surreal creature—Caro, but uncanny. Close to the person I remembered, but just a hair off. And I knew in that moment that whatever came next was the real secret, the truth that had launched her across the night, from her hotel room to my doorstep.

"Sometimes I used to watch you," she said. "When you didn't know I was there."

CHAPTER 24
DECEMBER, SENIOR YEAR

Caro

Here was the truth, no matter how much Caro hated it: even within the East House Seven, among supposed equals, there were hierarchies. Mint was at the top, of course, and then Heather and Jack, well known and liked by everyone. Frankie, a little less high, but he had the shine of an athlete. Jess, squarely in the middle. She was Caro's best friend, but also Mint's girlfriend, so she was caught in between, always on the verge of plunging or ascending. There was Coop, who didn't care about things like hierarchies. And then, at the bottom, there was Caro.

It didn't used to be that way. Freshman year, when she'd suggested they build their dorm's Homecoming float together, each and every one of them had thrown themselves into it, working day and night, rallying around *her* idea, even after Courtney complained about it being a stupid arts-and-crafts contest. And look what happened—the East House Seven was born as a direct result. Secretly, she'd always believed it was her doing and felt a certain possessiveness: by right, they were hers.

If she was being truly honest, sometimes it felt like the lonely girl she'd once been had dreamed them into being: Mint and Frankie, the perfect brothers; Heather, preternaturally confident, just like the girls she used to stare at in high school; Jess, the sister she could tell secrets; Coop, the one who gave them all an edge; and Jack, the one who understood, whose upbringing seemed so painfully close to hers.

In the beginning, the novelty of having these friends—the sheer relief of it—was enough to sustain her. After so long watching from the sidelines while other kids, then other teenagers, had sleepovers, trick-or-treated, went to prom—things her parents didn't approve of—it was a wonder to finally belong. Especially to the East House Seven, which was the loudest kind of belonging, almost showy.

But over the years, the precious tightness of their circle had loosened, stretching to accommodate other friends, other interests, the occasional spring break with other people. Maybe it was only natural—inevitable— but Caro hated it. Everything felt so precarious, like one gentle nudge was all it would take to send it shattering.

Charles Smith had been the one secret she'd kept from the rest of them since freshman year—since the night she'd gone to Chapman Hall to steal his float keys, then spent the night, surprising herself, then never stopped, surprising them both. All the time Charles wanted her to go on trips, be his formal date, meet his parents. But what he didn't understand was that ever since the East House Seven was born, since the float debacle freshman year, in Caro's mind it was *us* versus *them*, with them being everyone else, and especially Chapman kids like Charles.

Charles was nice, Charles was handsome, Charles was funny and athletic. But he was still, in some fundamental way, the enemy. She would never choose him when she could choose them.

The problem was, her friends didn't feel the same way.

She could feel them pulling away, and feared, as the person at the bottom, that she didn't have the power to draw them back. What would she have if she no longer had them? The anxiety notched, forming a pit of dread in her stomach. She was certain, on her worst nights, that she would lose them and be alone again. She wanted assurances. She wanted to be close. She wanted to know where they went and what they did all those times they didn't invite her.

And so, sometimes—rarely, but *sometimes*—she watched, and followed, and listened. Just to *know*. And in some small way, be a part of it.

Because of the December chill—beanies pulled low, masking students' faces, and a sea of identical dark peacoats bundled against the wind—Caro almost didn't spot them walking across campus. She was turning from the coffee cart, warm cup in her hands, exhaling a crystal cloud of breath, when out of the corner of her eye, she recognized a familiar parting of the crowd.

She'd always wondered if they knew what they looked like. All of them, even Jess, even Coop, even Frankie, with his muscled shoulders and stiff gait. When they were together, they moved like a flock of birds, in perfect sync, legs extending, arms swinging in unison. It had an effect. Other people moved out of their way, allowing them to glide through spaces with a buffer, move as freely through campus as if they owned it. Caro always paid attention to the cadence of her steps when she walked with them, but try as she might, she could never hold the beat for long.

Today they carved like a knife through the winter hats and coats: Heather, Jack, and Frankie. But something was off. Heather strode ahead, the point of the triangle, her face grim, eyes locked forward; Jack and Frankie behind, forming the base, eyeing each other every few steps, their shoulders hunched.

What was going on? Where were they going? Caro hadn't received any calls or texts about meeting up.

She hitched her backpack higher and set after them.

After a minute, it was easy to predict where they were going: Heather was beelining straight for Bishop Hall. Caro wondered if she was taking

Frankie and Jack to their suite, where Caro couldn't follow without being obvious. But to her relief, and surprise, Heather marched across the Bishop lobby, past the groups studying for finals, and straight into a meeting room in the administrative wing. It was one of those all-purpose rooms the college reserved for less popular student groups that didn't warrant their own dedicated space: the student jugglers, improv actors, *The Simpsons* trivia group. Caro had been there once, just to try the Society of Christian Feminists, but she'd never gone back again.

With her breath held, she slipped inside after Heather, Jack, and Frankie. It was dark as she crept along the back wall, so she heard them before she saw them.

"You're lucky we're not having this conversation in the middle of football practice!" Heather said, her voice heated. "Or out in the lobby, where everyone can hear."

Jack's voice was soothing. "Calm down. Let's talk this out."

Caro crouched behind a nearby chair, peeking carefully around the side. In the middle of the room, there was an empty space with chairs encircling it, meaning improv had to have been here last. In that space stood Heather, arms crossed and jaw locked. It was a bulldog scowl Caro recognized—the one Heather wore when she wasn't going to let go of an argument. Jack faced her, arms reaching out, but Heather leaned away. Frankie was slumped in one of the chairs, head in his hands.

"Talking sounds *great*," Heather said viciously. "Talk about this, then." She reached into her bag and pulled out a Ziploc, waving it at Jack. Caro had to squint to see, but through the plastic she could make out one of those cups doctors gave you at annual checkups. She was confused until Heather spoke again, voice rising. "Why did I find a urine test with Frankie's name on it hidden away in *your* bathroom? And before you say it, Frankie, don't even *try* to tell me you decided to walk all the way across campus to pee in a cup in Jack's bathroom instead of your own, because I'm not an idiot."

Jack's eyes fell to the floor. Frankie didn't move his head out of his hands.

"Why is Jack taking your drug test? I know for a fact you've been a puritan about not smoking pot for four years, because it's been really annoying. What exactly are you doing that's so bad you need Jack to cover for you?"

Jack looked at Frankie, so Caro did, too. All of Frankie's muscles were tense, arms flexed tight as he bent over. He'd worn his dark hair buzzed ever since they were freshmen, but this year, he'd let it grow a little longer. Trying out new things, he'd said, and Caro remembered the absurd flicker of sadness she'd felt when he said it, the desire to tell him nothing needed to change.

Frankie finally lifted his head, meeting Jack's gaze. Something passed wordlessly between them, leaving Frankie wincing. He took a deep breath. "I only use sometimes, before really big games. When I *have* to be better than everyone else. It's not permanent, I swear. I'm going to stop after this season."

Use what?

"Bullshit," Heather spat.

"You have no idea how much pressure he's under," Jack insisted. "And other people do it. It's practically an open secret in college ball. If he didn't, he'd be at a disadvantage."

"I can't believe you." Heather's eyes widened at Jack. "Defending Frankie's steroid use. Your parents would be so proud."

Caro nearly lost her grip on the chair. Frankie couldn't be using steroids. He was on posters around campus. He was so important he had lunch sometimes with the chancellor. There was a real chance he was going to make the NFL, especially if Duquette won a Bowl game. Caro owned his jersey and went to his practices religiously, just to cheer him on.

She felt a stabbing pain, deep in her heart. He'd been keeping a secret.

"That's a low blow," Jack said, anger creeping into his voice.

"It's *cheating*, Jack. You used to be better than this. What's happening to you? You're like a different person this year."

Was he? For all her careful attention, Caro hadn't noticed anything different about Jack. She was seized again by the certainty that she was failing, that her friendships were going to dissolve, leaving her alone. The pain in her heart sharpened, and her palms started to sweat. *Calm down. Don't panic.*

Frankie stood. "Leave Jack alone. All he's guilty of is being a good friend. Your issue is with me."

But Heather was not intimidated. "Damn straight it is. What are you thinking? If you and Jack get caught, you're both going to get kicked out. I know you don't want that, but Jack"—she waved a hand at her boyfriend—"he *can't* get kicked out. Do you understand? He can't go home; he'll get trapped there. His insane pastor barely let him come to Duquette in the first place. Can you imagine what his parents would do if he was involved in a scandal? He'd never see the light of day again." She turned to Jack. "I don't want to lose you." Back to Frankie: "How can you be so selfish?"

Frankie's face flushed red. "If I get caught with drugs in my system, then I get kicked out *and* my career is over. My whole fucking life is over. I'll be a public disgrace."

"Then why take them in the first place?"

"Because I have to," Frankie shouted, and Caro's blood pumped faster, hotter, until she could feel sweat gathering at the nape of her neck under her jacket. "You have no idea what kind of pressure it is. From the school, from all of you, from my dad. I *have* to play better than anyone else, I *have* to get drafted. There's no other option."

The hard expression on Heather's face melted, her brown eyes softening. "But the side effects—what if it permanently messes you up? Are you even thinking about that?"

"It's worth it," he said gruffly. "I'd pay any price."

Silence stretched around Frankie's confession. *Any price.* The anxiety was making it hard for Caro to breathe quietly. She wanted to tear off her jacket, take a big gulp of air, scream at the top of her lungs. But they couldn't know she was here. So she only squeezed her eyes shut and crouched lower.

"I can't let you do this," Heather said. "Not to yourself, and especially not to Jack. Come clean with your coach, Frankie. He'll help you. It's in his best interest to keep it quiet, anyway."

"I can't." Frankie sounded desperate. "I just need to pass this last test with Jack's help, get us to a Bowl game. And then I'll stop. I just need this last time."

"I'm sorry." Heather's words had a ring of finality. "That's not good enough. If you try to use Jack to cover for you, I'm going to tell your coach."

Jack was astonished. "What's wrong with you? Normally you couldn't care less about following the rules. What's this really about?"

She turned to him. Even in the dim light, Caro could see her eyes were clear and resolute. "It's about right and wrong. It's that simple."

No. Anger seized Caro. What Frankie was doing was wrong, yes, but Heather would destroy his life if she told his coach, get him expelled. Which meant she would destroy the East House Seven.

Abruptly, Heather shoved the Ziploc with the cup back in her bag and spun away, moving fast, straight toward Caro. She barely had time to crawl deeper into the chairs, away from Heather's line of sight, before the girl swept past.

"Heather, *please*," Frankie begged.

"You'll *ruin* him," Jack said, his voice thick.

"Not if you do the right thing," Heather said and flung the door open and burst out of it.

"I can't," Frankie said to Jack. Caro couldn't see them anymore, hidden as she was, but the fear in his voice made her panic spike. She tried to concentrate on breathing: *In, out. In, out.*

"I know," Jack said simply. "Come on, let's get out of here. This room feels wrong for some reason. Almost sentient. It's creepy."

In, out; in, out. Caro matched her breathing to the patter of feet as they walked past. Jack's eyes roved, searching for the source of the wrongness, but mercifully they didn't light on her. Finally, the door swung behind them, leaving Caro squatting in the thicket of chairs.

Breathing heavily, she tore at her jacket with clumsy fingers, ripping it off, then unbuttoned her shirt, desperate for cool air. She used to blame this kind of anxiety on the fact that she'd been so sheltered her whole life, but she was going on four years of college and it hadn't changed. She didn't know what was wrong with her, but she did know that Heather was going to ruin Frankie's future. How could one member of the East House Seven do that to another? Heather would destroy the only friends Caro had ever belonged to. Send her right back to the sidelines.

Her panic kept rising until a single thought interrupted. It gripped her, ice-cold and powerful enough to slow her galloping heart, cool her burning skin, fill her with a sense of conviction so strong it felt almost like faith. Heather wouldn't take away anything. Alone in the dark, she brought a hand to the cross at her throat, feeling the metal ends stab her fingertips, the pain like a promise. Caro wouldn't let her.

CHAPTER 25
NOW

We didn't plan to stow away on Frankie's float, the six of us. But it was a madhouse outside the stadium, the Homecoming crowd an ocean, tides pulling, impossible to navigate. And though we looked like everyone else, dressed head to toe in crimson and white, we were a world apart, skittish with anxiety, with the weight of our questions for Frankie.

I couldn't shake the feeling that I was missing something; couldn't stop looking at Caro every time she turned her back, thinking of her raw face in the morning light of my hotel room. Imagining her ten years ago, watching us from across campus. Determined to know us better than we'd let her, terrified of being left behind.

Where had she followed *me*?

Everyone had things they were ashamed of. Caro was still the same person. But as we pushed through the crowd, she turned, catching me staring. And I could feel her confession like an electric charge between us, buzzing my skin.

So when we got to Frankie's float—the football float, where the grand marshal rode, first in line—I didn't think before I leapt onto it, propelled by the discomfort of being around her. Everyone followed, Eric included, and we huddled behind a six-foot replica of Blackwell Tower, agreeing to grab Frankie once we spotted him among the swarm of football players, tug him off the float to talk. But then there was a giant thrust, a roar from the crowd, and suddenly we were moving.

"Oh god," Caro said, face paling. "It's starting."

I looked over the railing. Waving, cheering fans, young and old, a sea of crimson and white. I felt nauseous. "We have to get off."

"Don't be crazy," Mint said. "Everyone will see us. Let's just stay here and hide, and confront Frankie once the parade's over. It'll be fine."

"*Mint?*" A big voice—Frankie's—boomed from the other side of the tower. "What are you doing here?" Resplendent in the grand marshal's blood-red cape and scepter, his mouth agape, Frankie looked like a very startled king of Duquette.

"Uhh—" Caro looked desperately at Eric, waiting for him to take over the questioning, but he just arched an eyebrow, as if to say, *This was your idea.*

"You came to cheer me on," Frankie said, with unexpected emotion. He looked at us, searching our faces, lingering on Mint's. "This is even better than I pictured. Come up front with me." He tugged Mint with him; the rest of us followed, looking at each other uncertainly.

At the front of the float, Frankie turned to me. "Just like freshman year, huh?"

Jack banished. Heather dead. And your friends ambushing you to ask if you killed her. Yes, Frankie, exactly the same.

I cleared my throat. So many people in the crowd were waving to him, shouting his name. One man even wore his Saints jersey.

"They love you," I said. "You really are a star."

Was Frankie still using? What would all these people think if they knew?

"Let's hope so," Frankie said. "Because I stayed up all night thinking. And I have a plan."

"We're here to ask you something," Eric cut in, voice rising to be heard over the cheering. "About Heather."

Frankie looked around at us, the first hints of understanding—and betrayal—dawning on his face. "Wait. You're here to interrogate me?"

"You knew Heather was planning to out Jack during Parents' Weekend," Coop said. "And your parents would likely hear the news right beside them. Your *dad* would hear. Why didn't you tell us that part?"

"It's a pretty big motivation to kill Heather," Mint said, pulling no punches. "Killing her would keep her from telling your dad about Jack, maybe making him suspicious, making him ask you questions."

Frankie's mouth dropped open. All around us, people kept shouting his name.

"I can't believe you guys. I didn't tell you about Heather's plan to out Jack because I didn't want to say something so ugly about her." Frankie scrubbed his face with his hands and paused. "She wouldn't have gone through with it."

"How do you know?" Caro leaned against the rail, dark hair fluttering in the wind.

"Because she regretted even telling me Jack came out to her. She cried and said she was too drunk, and wasn't supposed to say anything, especially not to me, because she thought I'd hate him. Try to kick him out of Phi Delt. She remembered what I'd said about Danny Grier the night guys were drawing on his picture in the frat house. She thought I was a homophobe. She *died* thinking I was a homophobe."

I thought of how Caro had described Heather reaming out Frankie for dragging Jack into his steroid cover-up. "She was trying to protect Jack," I said. "Like always."

Frankie nodded. "That's why I know she wouldn't have told his parents. I know it in my bones. What she said to Courtney—she was just hurting and letting off steam."

Suddenly, I couldn't take it anymore. I had to know, even though Caro was going to kill me.

"Did you stop taking steroids? Senior year of college, when Heather confronted you and Jack, did you come clean like she asked, or did you have Jack cover for you? Are you still using them?"

Caro gasped, but everyone else grew deadly quiet.

"Are you suggesting Heather had *more* dirt on Frankie?" Eric asked, eyes narrowing to slivers. "Career-ending dirt?"

Frankie stared at me, too surprised to do anything but gape. "Heather told you?"

I could feel Caro's eyes burning my face. "It's not important. Answer the question."

"There's no way Frankie—" Mint glanced at the crowd and the other football players waving near the back of the float. It was too loud for anyone to hear us, but still, he lowered his voice. "Cheated."

To my surprise, Frankie shook his head. "It's true. I was an idiot. I messed around with that stuff back then. Jack helped me pass the drug tests, and the last time, senior year, Heather caught us. She threatened to tell my coach. Jack and I did it anyway, and I kept expecting the sky to fall. But nothing. I guess Heather changed her mind." He looked at Eric. "So I had no reason to be pissed at her. And I stopped using, anyway. She scared the hell out of me, and that was what it took."

Why hadn't Heather told Frankie's coach, like she'd sworn to? I tried to find Caro's eyes, but she wouldn't look at me. A puzzle piece was missing.

"So all that talent," Mint said, "that was the drugs, not you? Not the *pride of Oahu*?"

"I swear, my NFL career has been all me," Frankie said.

"No one's perfect," Coop said. "People in glass houses, right?"

"No, Mint's right." Frankie looked across the sea of people. "I'm tired of pretending to be someone I'm not. I've done so many things because I didn't think who I am was good enough. It's time to stop being afraid. I'm going to have a bigger imagination."

Before anyone could say anything, or ask any more questions, Frankie grabbed the microphone from the stand in the corner and closed his eyes—briefly, only for a second—then opened them and shouted into the mic with a giant smile: "Happy *Homecoming*, Duquette!"

His voice boomed through campus like the voice of God. The crowd roared back. I clutched the railing.

"My name is Frankie Kekoa, class of '09. For those who don't know, I led the Crimson football team to four division championships while I was here."

Everyone shook their pom-poms and whooped.

"And then I was drafted by the Saints."

The stomping and shouting grew louder.

"And you won a Super Bowl!" someone screamed, followed by a ripple of laughter.

"And I won a Super Bowl," Frankie agreed, laughing. "Maybe two. Who knows? This year's looking pretty good."

The crowd ate it up. Frankie was a natural; he always had been. A huge personality. So much like Heather.

"But let me tell you some things you don't know about me."

My heart raced. I resisted the urge to throw my arms around Frankie, shield him.

"In addition to being the highest-scoring player to ever grace Crimson stadium, and the only Duquette alum to play in the NFL, I, Frankie Kekoa, love the color blue."

Everyone laughed at the feint.

"I love a good steak," Frankie continued. "I think Easter is the most underrated holiday. And—I am a proud gay man. So now you know a few things about me."

It was amazing to watch hundreds of people in the throes of cheering suddenly freeze.

Oh god. Somehow, Frankie had found a way to get even more naked atop a Homecoming float. He stood stalwart, his shoulders held high, gazing defiantly at the crowd.

I shot Coop a desperate look over Caro's head. *We have to do something.*

Coop nodded, a wild look in his eyes. "Hey, I'm going to take off all my clothes and streak across campus. Right now."

"*What?*" Caro hissed.

"Fast," I whispered.

But a strange thunder had started in the distance. It took a second, but then I realized: it was cheering. Shouting, coming from all around us, all four directions, building and building like a tidal wave: *Frankie. Frankie. Frankie.* The people closest to us on the sidewalks almost toppled the barriers, shaking their pom-poms. Someone screamed, "*We love you, Frankie!*"

The parade had turned into mayhem.

We were rushed by the members of the Duquette football team as they poured in from the back of the float, surrounding Frankie, slapping his arms and squeezing him until they lifted him, despite his protests, high in the air. Frankie Kekoa, dressed like the king of Duquette, laughed and bounced on their shoulders.

He'd done it. Frankie, always so careful, so anxious, had reimagined what his life could look like. I tried to picture what Jack would say if he could see Frankie now.

In the midst of the chaos, one hand clapped to his ear against the noise, Eric pointed to the now-empty back of the float. I didn't want to go, wanted to stay here and soak up Frankie's triumph, but the look on Eric's face brooked no argument. The rest of us followed, gathering around him in a tight circle, pressed shoulder to shoulder.

"I don't think Frankie did it," Caro yelled. "I believe him."

"Me too," I said, casting an eye at the crowd, which was still going crazy, not paying the slightest attention to us. What Frankie told us hadn't exactly cleared him. He could be lying, after all; maybe Heather had still planned on telling his coach and he'd done it to stop her. But I felt certain of Frankie's innocence. Another one of my instincts.

"Now what?" Coop asked. "Where do we go from here?"

"I told you the Frankie theory didn't match all the evidence," Eric said. "It's time to look at everything. Connect all the dots."

He slipped a hand inside his jacket and pulled out three pieces of white construction paper, enclosed in sheet protectors. Mounted on each was a carefully reconstructed photograph. Three different pictures of the East House Seven. One from freshman year, outside East House. The second from sophomore-year spring break, our trip to Myrtle Beach, all of us sunburned and in bathing suits.

The last was from the final day of junior year. Coop and I stood close together in the back; I could still remember how he'd slipped his hand inside of mine at the last minute, right before the shot. How I'd jerked in surprise, but the next moment, I'd slipped on my mask. The camera had caught that instant—that millisecond—when you could see the conflicting emotions plain as day on my face.

Each photo had been torn into jagged scraps, then pieced back together, like a puzzle. In each, Heather's head was violently scratched out in pen, so hard the strokes had cut into the photograph—manic swirling circles, knifelike X's. In the last picture, the pen strokes had been so intense that half of Heather's face was missing, a gaping maw where her smile should have been.

The world narrowed to those hateful marks, stabbed in ink. The noise of the crowd retreated, the float's jerky movements falling away. My stomach plummeted. *It couldn't be.*

Eric held up the photos, turning so we could all get a look. "I started investigating Heather's case two days after you graduated. I wasn't very good at it back then, but I was trying."

I remembered Eric, stiff and alone, walking across the graduation stage to accept Heather's diploma, the sound of his shoes scuffing the wood the only noise against a suddenly silent crowd.

"I sat in her room at home and forced myself to unpack her boxes, because my parents couldn't bring themselves to do it. I knew if I didn't, she would just sit there, alone and untouched. I remember that it felt like all I had of her was in those boxes—like she was in there, somehow, and needed me to take care of her. So I took them apart. There was a strange mix of stuff. The police had dumped things quickly, after they'd finished searching her room."

I remembered that too, the dark-clad men rifling through my things.

"I found these strange little scraps of photographs tucked into Heather's papers from her desk. It took me an hour to find all the pieces. But when I put the first together, lo and behold—" He tapped one of the pictures, right where Heather's face was slashed by black X-marks. "New evidence. Clues the police missed. That's the exact moment I knew they'd gotten it wrong, and it was going to be up to me to find my sister's killer."

The black hole inside me was spinning, memories spilling out, faster than I could push them down. I'd told myself I would look for Heather's killer, but I hadn't expected the path would lead to this.

Eric scanned the circle. "I've waited ten years, imagined all the possibilities. I know it's one of you. So confess."

"No one here is that much of a freak," Courtney said, shaking her head. "Those pictures are straight-up stalker material. *Sociopath* material."

From across the circle, I felt Coop's eyes burning into my face. He wanted me to look up, reassure him, tell him unequivocally with my eyes that there was no way I was responsible, despite what he'd said all those years ago. I kept my gaze locked on my feet and heard his sharp intake of breath.

It was enough. The black hole burst, and the memories cracked open.

CHAPTER 26
DECEMBER, SENIOR YEAR

Memories are powerful things.

But—and this is important, my therapist said—so are the dark spaces. The things you choose, consciously or not, to repress. Always, they're the things you need protection from. The *too much*: too terrifying, too shameful, too devastating. The things that, if allowed, would threaten the very core of who you're supposed to be.

It turns out the real you is a quilt, made up of the light and the dark. The life you've lived in sunshine and your shadow life, stretching underneath the surface of your mind like a deep underwater world, exerting invisible power. You are a living, breathing story made up of the moments in time you cherish, all strung together, and those you hide. The moments that seem lost.

Until the day they're not.

The day before Christmas, senior year, the morning my father overdosed, I woke from a terrible dream that I was trapped, held with a gun to my head. The gun kept going off, over and over, and the last thing I saw each time was a pair of eyes so dark the pupils drowned in them. When I jerked awake, heart hammering, I lost the thread of the dream, but gained a memory. It rushed back, all at once: I was eight years old, a dreamer. A naive kid with her head in the clouds. More than anything, I loved to write and draw stories. And I loved my parents—worshipped them. My angelic mother, always there when I needed her. My handsome father, an important man, someone everyone looked at with a shining admiration.

They said he was better than the steel company where he worked, a temporary job to make ends meet. He was a Harvard man with promise, after all, and eventually he'd find his way to where he belonged. Even his friends whispered it, even my mom—he'd go to Washington like he'd planned, work among the important dealmakers, use the economics degree he'd worked hard for. It was his destiny. He was so smart, so valuable. Any day now, he'd do it. Any day.

The thing about my father was—he was getting sick. At eight years old, I noticed it, even when no one else did, even as they kept whispering about where he'd go (*up, up, up*) and when (*any day now*). He'd started spending hours alone, turning the lights off in the living room and staring at the ceiling, arms hanging off the sides of the recliner like deadweight. Sometimes he nodded off, but a lot of nights, he just stared and stared at nothing.

Finally came the day when everyone else noticed. My dad arrived home first, red-faced, beelining to his bedroom and slamming the door. My mother followed minutes later, eyes bloodshot, held by her best friend—back when she had a friend, the wife of a man my father worked with. No one said anything to me, as if I didn't exist. So when my mom went into the kitchen, I hovered at the door like a ghost, listening.

I couldn't understand what they were saying—*He betrayed me*, from my mother. *Threw himself at the boss, no one can believe it*, from my mother's best friend. *Told her he was better than this, that he belonged at the top, with her. Everyone's talking about it.* I didn't know what it all meant, but I knew my mother was crying, and it had something to do with my dad. Suddenly, I realized what it had to be: they'd discovered his sickness.

I knew what to do. I'd been thinking about it for a while. Whenever my mother was sick, I drew her pictures and told her a story, and it always made her feel better. I went to my room and took out my pencils—precious things I'd gotten for my birthday, the kind real artists used—and drew for an hour until I had the perfect thing. I gathered my drawings and slipped into my parents' room.

My dad lay slumped on the bed in the dark, an arm hanging limp. I climbed up and perched next to him, sitting close to his face so he could see better. Then I took a deep breath and shook his shoulder.

He woke with a gasp. Immediately, my stomach clenched, instincts whispering, *bad idea.* His eyes were cloudy as he struggled to focus, his dark hair sweaty, breath shallow, rapid, like he'd just run a race. For a second, the face that stared back at me was a stranger's.

"Dad?"

His voice was garbled. "Who are you?"

My heart squeezed painfully. "Jessica," I whispered.

His gaze listed to his nightstand. He extended a clumsy hand, groping for an orange bottle just out of reach. It fell to the floor, top popping off, white pills scattering.

"*Goddammit.*"

"I'll clean it, I promise." I held up the drawings. "I drew you a story." I peered around the paper. "Once upon a time, there was a king, see—" I pointed to the picture. "He had a beautiful wife who was the queen and a daughter who was the princess." I pointed out the drawings of my mom and me, which I was proud of, as I'd done very good noses. "One day"—I switched to the next piece of paper—"an evil witch cast a spell on the king, and he fell into a deep sleep. It was up to the princess to break the curse. She—"

"Get off." My dad's voice grew sharper. "I need to rest."

I moved closer to him, lifting the drawings. "Dad, see? It's you and me, and Mom, in the story. I made us into kings and queens. Your wife and daughter—"

"I don't have a wife or daughter." He rose abruptly and I lost my balance, tipping off the bed to land, sharp, on my knees and elbows. My father stumbled from the bed and dropped beside me, sweeping the spilled pills into a pile with shaking hands.

My eyes filled with hot tears, knees and elbows burning. But I didn't let myself cry. I watched him, his trembling fingers.

"I'm young," my dad said out of nowhere. "I have my whole life ahead of me. I'm going to get out of this shithole town and go to DC. Use my damn degree and stop wasting my potential."

Hunched over in the darkness, arms spread over the floor, my dad looked nothing like the king I'd drawn. I was frozen and afraid; I wanted the ground to swallow me whole. For time to race backward and deposit me, safe, back in my room.

My drawings were scattered, but I was too scared to pick them up. Instead, I crouched, watching my dad put the pills back in the bottle. Then he slumped against the dresser and looked at me. Really looked.

"I hate it here," he whispered. He squinted at the light over my shoulder, which came from the door I'd left cracked open. His pupils turned to slits, like a cat's. "I really do."

"No," I said, feeling my chest cleave.

As he dropped his gaze from the light, his pupils dilated, the blackness pooling in each eye. I watched the change with horror.

"Why do you insist on *dragging me down*?" he whispered.

I scrambled back, head hitting the wall.

"It's supposed to be better than this." His eyes were now twin black holes, pupils drowning the white. And I knew, with sudden clarity, that I didn't hold the cure. I was the thing making him sick.

My mother flung open the door, and light flooded the room. My father shrank back, and they stared at each other for one horrible, frozen moment. And then they started screaming.

Hours later, I let my mother hug me, apologize, cry. She brought my drawings back, and I let her put them next to me in bed, waited until she left the room before I tore them to pieces and stuffed them in the trash. For days afterward, I told her I was okay. For a year, I stayed quiet, especially after we moved from Bedford to Norfolk, so my dad could transfer to a different branch of the steel company.

I pushed the memory of his sickness, and its cause, so far down it formed a tiny rupture in the center of me, a small black hole of my very own. And no matter how many years passed, I never looked inside.

Until senior year of college. Home for Christmas, when I woke from that nightmare gasping, still feeling the cold gun pressed against my forehead, still seeing the drowning pupils of the drug dealer, and the dream terror was replaced, by sinister sleight of hand, with the sudden rush of memory, unburied after fourteen years.

Only hours later, we got the call: my father had been found in a motel room, arms splayed over the side of the bed, dead of an overdose.

No one came to his funeral. When my grandparents arrived at the burial plot and saw it was just me, my mom, and the priest, my grandmother burst into sobs so violent my grandpa had to hold her to keep her from crumbling. Instead of hugging us, patting my shoulder like she did when I was young, my grandmother pointed a trembling finger.

"It's your fault," she said, eyes blazing at my mother. "You trapped him with your pregnancy. You made him miserable. You *killed* him. And look!" She flung her arms at the empty grounds. "No one even cares he's gone. *He was supposed to be somebody.*"

My mother took two steps forward and slapped my grandmother

hard across the cheek. She staggered back, mouth open, and my mother strode from the burial plot, out of the cemetery, never looking back.

So in the end, it was just the three of us. My grandparents and I stood silent as the priest read the burial rites and my father's coffin lowered into the ground. It was a freezing winter day, and I'd left my coat in the car, but the strange thing was, I could barely feel a thing. There was this snowy fuzz, a blanket of white noise, both inside my skin and out. As the dirt fell, shovelful after shovelful, two voices echoed in my head, on a loop timed with the soft patter of earth hitting the coffin. My father's voice, pulled from the recovered memory: *I'm supposed to be better than this.* And my grandmother's: *No one even cares he's gone.*

I did, of course. But perhaps I didn't count.

When the holiday break was over and I returned to Duquette, I avoided everyone, sleeping during the day, walking around campus at night, when Heather and Caro were asleep. Sometimes I had clipped conversations with my mom. Strangely, she'd started calling me, which she'd never done before.

Then one night I got back to my dorm and Caro was waiting on my bed, tears in her eyes. Somehow, though I hadn't told her, she knew what had happened. She wanted to hug and talk, to be my best friend, but I pushed her aside, told her I wasn't ready. She'd just nodded and thrust a sheet of paper at me before leaving.

I dropped to my bed, looking at the paper without interest. It was a poem by Mary Oliver. I scanned until I came to the last line, a question: *Tell me, what is it you plan to do with your one wild and precious life?*

I sat up with a surge of anger. Why should I be satisfied with one wild and precious life? A vision of my father's grave flashed, three small figures huddled around it. It wasn't fair. People deserved more than that, more than a small, brief existence, only to fade away in the end.

Tears stung my eyes. I tore the poem and stuffed it in the trash. One life, full of mistakes, and not enough time—not enough chances—to do it right. It wasn't enough. Who was this Mary Oliver, encouraging people to accept smallness, while in the meantime she was famous? While in the meantime, she knew her life would be infinite—her thoughts and words repeated for hundreds of years. I wanted *that*. I wanted to become big enough, important enough, to never really die. Then I would never get trapped in a hole in the ground like my dad, with no one around to care.

I knew exactly what to do. I sat at my desk and booted up my computer, tapping impatiently as I waited for it to start. If my grandmother was right and my dad's life had ground to a halt because of me, I had to show him I was worth it, make him proud, and live for both of us: Harvard for grad school, then Washington, with the important dealmakers. I'd go *up, up, up,* and I would take him with me. He wouldn't have to end like this. I would give him one more wild and precious shot.

I waited until the last student left the lecture hall before I approached him. Dr. John Garvey, Duquette's campus celebrity, its shining star economist. Double Harvard: Harvard undergrad, Harvard PhD. Economic advisor to two presidents, and the school's pride and joy. His classes were nearly impossible to get into unless you'd declared an econ major, with the exception of Heather, who had gotten into his class last semester even though she was an English major, because that was the kind of luck she had.

Dr. Garvey was tall, with thick, dark hair that was starting to gray. He'd probably been handsome, in a professorial sort of way, when he was young. No student had ever seen him outside a well-pressed suit, bow tie knotted expertly around his neck.

He was gathering his papers, picking up his briefcase, preparing to leave. It was now or never. I clutched the application so hard I nearly bent it. The Duquette Post-Graduate Fellowship, informally known as the Duquette Fulbright. The fellowship awarded one senior per year a full ride to the graduate school of their choosing. And it nearly guaranteed, with that honor on your résumé, that you'd be accepted anywhere you applied. Even to an Ivy League school.

I wanted this more than I'd ever wanted anything. This was our last shot, my father's and mine. I needed to wow the fellowship committee, and nothing would do that better than a recommendation letter from Dr. Garvey.

"You're hovering," he said, stuffing his papers in his briefcase.

I cleared my throat. "Um, Dr. Garvey, I wanted to ask you something."

"So? Spit it out."

Butterflies soared in my stomach. Timidly, I held out the application. "I'm applying for Duquette's Post-Grad Fellowship, and I was hoping… since we've had four classes together and I've gotten A's in all of them, and you wrote on my last paper that I had very sophisticated thinking… Well, I was hoping you would write me a recommendation letter."

There. It was out.

He stopped packing his briefcase and looked up. Scanned me, head to toe. I forced myself to remain still, shoulders high.

"Remind me of your name."

"Jessica Miller," I managed to say, though my throat ached all of a sudden. "Jessica M."

Dr. Garvey stood looking at me in silence for so long that I began to grow deeply uncomfortable. Sweat gathered at my neck. He was going to say no. Of course he was. It was humiliating. Crushing.

"Have dinner with me," Dr. Garvey said, and the fact that he'd finally spoken was enough of a shock that it took me a second to process what he'd said.

"Dinner?" I repeated.

"If you want a recommendation, I'd like to get to know you better."
Dr. Garvey snapped his briefcase shut. "I'll take you to dinner Friday
night, and we'll talk." He walked to the door and adjusted his bow tie.
Then he turned to look at me over his shoulder.

"Well, what do you say, Ms. Miller? How bad do you want it?"

CHAPTER 27
NOW

I'd wanted so badly to come home to Duquette, to feel the magic that was in the soil. But standing here, staring at the pieced-together photographs in Eric's hands, felt more like returning to the scene of a crime. I inched toward the edge of the float. Eric's eyes swung around the circle, looking for fissures in somebody's mask.

"It was one of Heather's roommates," he said. "That's what makes the most sense."

The dread was like an anchor, rooting my feet.

The cheering was finally dying down. Eric's voice cut through the remaining din, loud and recognizable. Frankie, still surrounded by a throng of football players, turned in our direction.

But Eric only had eyes for Caro. "Was it you? Little Caroline Rodriguez? Always the good girl, the loyal friend. But how did it feel, being the odd one out? You tagged along for years with Mint and Jessica, Heather and Jack. Were you jealous? Heather was a Chi O. She was popular, the Phi Delt Sweetheart. She had a boyfriend and a plan for the future. What did you have? No boyfriend, no plans. I saw your file—a film major, and you barely scraped by with a 2.0. In the height of the recession, no less. You were unemployed for a year after graduation. An overqualified temp. The only one who didn't soar."

Caro had never told me that. The surprise was enough to make me halt my slow retreat. Her cheeks flamed.

"I didn't—" she started.

"And now you're an elementary school teacher." Eric's voice was acid. "Life took a pretty hard turn, didn't it?"

"Teaching's not what I originally planned." Caro's hands clenched into fists. "But it's a noble profession."

"You know what I always wondered?" Eric circled her like a shark. "Why you were so obsessed with your friends. That's why you never paid attention to your grades, right? It was always about the East House Seven." Caro cast a furtive look at where Coop and Mint were standing. "Oh, I know all about it," Eric added. "You used to memorize their schedules, sign up for their classes, call and text day and night, try to follow them home on breaks. You know what Heather used to say about you?"

"Knock it off, man. Caro had nothing to do with this." Coop's voice was gruff.

"She used to say you were her own personal stalker." Eric thrust the cut-up photographs at Caro. "It's like Courtney said—this looks like something a stalker would do. Did you? You stopped wearing your cross after Heather died. What made you lose your faith, Caroline? Did you do something that made you unworthy of wearing it?"

Tears sprang to Caro's eyes. Instinctively, she reached for her necklace, fingers skimming her collarbone.

"Right before Heather died, you confronted her," Eric accused. "She told me she was angry at you, that you'd threatened her. Why?"

"Caro, threatening?" Mint's voice was doubtful.

I tried to avoid looking at the torn-up photographs. "Caro would never—"

"She was going to get Frankie *expelled*," she burst out, hands flying to her face. "She knew he was still cheating on his drug test, and she was actually going to tell his coach. I couldn't let her."

"What the hell?" Courtney asked. "Did Heather tell *everyone* about Frankie's drug scandal except for me?"

"She didn't tell me." Caro's voice cracked. "I knew because I was spying on her when she confronted Frankie and Jack. Okay? I'm sorry."

She was confessing? Oh no, Caro, bad idea—

"What do you mean, *spying*?" Coop looked at Caro like he was seeing her for the first time.

She winced, then took a deep breath and forced the words out. "I used to eavesdrop. On all of you. It was a bad habit." She looked at Coop, pleading. "One I grew out of."

"Oh my god," Courtney breathed. "You literally *were* Heather's stalker."

"Did you stalk me?" Mint asked, horrified.

"I didn't stalk anyone!" Caro grabbed at her hair. "I just needed you all more than you needed me, and I was ashamed of it. Growing up, I was the freak kid, the one with super-religious parents. And then I came to college, and all of a sudden, I had you guys, and I was part of something. But no matter how hard I tried, you always left me out. I was always at the bottom. Just like Eric said. It drove me *crazy*."

"Caro," I started. "You don't have to say all this—"

"No—I want to know." A tear rolled down her cheek. "Why not me?"

No one said anything. I tried to remember times we'd left Caro out, or times she'd seemed unhappy, but I couldn't. She'd just been…there. Reliable, dependable, good-natured Caro. Someone I took for granted.

I was supposed to be her best friend.

"You can't even think of a reason, can you?" Caro looked around at us, dark eyes rimmed with red. "That's how little you thought of me, when you were all I ever thought about."

"I think about you," Coop said softly.

Caro glared at him. "Not then."

"You're *very* good at playing the victim, I'll give you that." Eric stepped forward, clutching the photographs. "Poor, pitiful Caro. None of her friends loved her enough. Why don't you get to the part where you threatened my sister a week before she died?"

Caro darted glances at the rest of us, waiting for something—to be defended, maybe. For protests that *Caro couldn't possibly*. But when none came, she swallowed hard. "I found out Heather scheduled a meeting with Frankie's coach." Her eyes flicked away, ashamed, and we all knew then how she'd uncovered it. "So I confronted her. I said if she did, I'd tell everyone she leaked Amber Van Swann's sex tape sophomore year because she was jealous Amber was getting all the attention."

Oh god. What had we done to Caro in the space of two years to turn her from the girl who'd refused to leak Amber's tape to the one who used it for blackmail?

"*Heather* leaked it?" Courtney screeched. "She leaked the tape of *my* Amber, the girl who was supposed to be my little sis?"

Caro closed her eyes. "No. But I told her I had access to the original file, and I could make it look like she did. It was a bluff. A halfway bluff. But she believed me. I told her if she went to Frankie's coach and ruined his life, I'd ruin hers back."

"Damn," Mint breathed. "Ice cold."

Caro opened her eyes and found mine, her hand drifting to her bare neck. But what was missing was bigger than a necklace. It was the laughing girl I'd met when we were eighteen, in the East House quad. It was the girl the rest of us had killed slowly, over the course of years.

"So it *was* you," Eric said, growing calm again, now that he had Caro in his crosshairs. "Heather must've stepped out of line, and you were following up on your threat." He shook the photographs at her. "Was this supposed to be a message?"

"No!" she shouted. I could see heads in the crowd turn to look at us, a strange tableau: the crying woman on the football float, a group of people gathered around her in a tense circle.

"I didn't touch those pictures," Caro insisted. "I never would've cut up our memories. I just wanted to scare her with the threat. And it worked. She never told. I had no reason to hurt her."

"It wasn't Caro," Coop said, his menacing voice back. "She's not perfect—none of us are—but it wasn't her."

"Well, in that case"—Eric jerked his head in my direction and grinned, like everything was going exactly according to plan—"we have one other possibility."

My back hit the railing and I gripped it, tight.

Eric held up the photographs. His eyes glinted. "Tell me, Jessica. What did Heather do to make you want to kill her?"

CHAPTER 28
JANUARY, SENIOR YEAR

Dr. Garvey didn't take me out of town. He didn't try to hide it. We sat in the middle of a crowded restaurant across the street from campus—the nice steakhouse, the one Mint's parents took him to every Parents' Weekend. I wondered if Dr. Garvey knew somehow that no one would catch us—like he'd struck a deal with the restaurant—or if he simply didn't care.

The professor insisted I call him John. He tipped the wine bottle and filled my glass, over and over, speaking at length about the new book he was writing, which was sure to make a splash, earn him yet another offer from the White House. He never once asked me a question. Didn't inquire about the fellowship, why I wanted it, or where I would go if I won. I knew within five minutes of sitting down that Dr. Garvey didn't care about getting to know me.

But I was glad he didn't stop talking, because I couldn't have managed a word. I was an automaton, moving in the ways I was supposed to, doing things I could see other people doing in my peripheral vision: unfolding my white napkin, laying it across my lap. Taking sips of water. Allowing the waiter to scoot my chair close to the table, cage me. I ordered fish by pointing blindly at the menu, then ate two bites.

What was I doing? I wanted to be somewhere safe. I thought of Coop's apartment on instinct, before remembering the two men shattering the glass, the hand untwisting the lock. Maybe there was nowhere safe. Still, every instinct screamed at me to leave as fast as I could.

But I had to have the recommendation.

My phone buzzed on the table, Mint's name flashing across the screen. I stared at it a second, then clicked it dark.

I had to have it.

Besides, I didn't know how this would end. Maybe Dr. Garvey would take his last sip of wine, sign the bill, and shake my hand with a thank-you for the company and a promise to have the letter on Monday. Maybe he was just lonely. Maybe it was innocent.

But when the check came, he looked at me and cleared his throat, loosening his navy bow tie. "Back to mine for a nightcap?"

No. I shook my head. "I really have to go home."

He smiled. "Don't you want your letter? It's sitting on my desk, in my office. Come back with me, have a drink, and you can have it."

I blinked in confusion. He'd already written it? What was the point of this dinner, then?

"I can pick it up on Monday," I said, picking the napkin off my lap and folding it on the table.

"Ah," he said regretfully. "I'm out of town for the next few weeks. Off to Europe for a mini-sabbatical. The fellowship deadline's before then, isn't it?"

It was in a week. *A week, a week, a week.* I had to have the letter. I had to win. There was only one more chance for us. The door was closing.

My throat constricted. I clutched my chest, trying to pull in air, fighting the feeling that I was trapped. The couple at the table next to us turned to stare.

Dr. Garvey simply raised an eyebrow. "Is that a yes?"

I stepped outside myself.

Watched, from a distance, as Dr. Garvey unlocked the door to his enormous house, led me inside, down the hallway, and into the study. His home was beautiful, dimly lit, masculine colors. He had shelf after shelf of books. I studied them, pausing over the titles I recognized, repeating the words under my breath. They were familiar. Comforting. Everything would be okay.

And then I saw them, hanging on his wall: Two Harvard diplomas. One, a twin to my father's. The undergrad degree. The second—the PhD—was huge. Larger than life, just like I'd imagined.

He'd been the same major as my father, of course. Economics. They'd been equal, once. Then Dr. Garvey had gone back a second time. And then to work at Duquette, and in Washington. In the thick of things. So important, so much to be proud of. He was living the life my father always wanted.

Dr. Garvey poured whiskey from a cut-crystal decanter and handed me a glass.

I had to have the letter.

I took a sip, and Dr. Garvey slipped a hand down my arm.

He led me down the hall to the bedroom.

One night when I was sixteen, I walked home by myself from a classmate's party. Halfway there, I caught a man out of the corner of my eye, his pale face stark against the night. He was a few feet behind me, tracking my steps. When I sped up, he sped up. When I turned, he turned. A wild, terrible knowing seized me then, a charge under my skin, the kind of tension a girl learns to read without anyone teaching her.

Terrified, I ran. I could remember that moment so vividly: using every ounce of my strength, running so hard I eventually couldn't feel my legs. Running for a mile, all the way home, to escape the danger in the dark, right behind me.

Walking into Dr. Garvey's room, the wild, terrible knowing seized me again. But this time, I didn't run. This time, my legs moved slowly, one after the other, toward the bed. My arms remained by my side, clenched, as he unwound his bow tie. My face a mask, set in flat lines.

There was still the sixteen-year-old girl inside me who wanted to be free and safe. Untouched. I could feel her heart thumping with terror, nowhere to go. She was running, she was screaming, she was banging on my rib cage to get out.

But I locked her inside. I knelt on the bed. This time, I let the danger catch me.

I drowned her in the dark.

And when I walked home that night, clutching my letter, there was no one left inside to be afraid.

CHAPTER 29
NOW

It was so close to my Homecoming fantasy—every eye on me, rapt, waiting to see what I'd do next, just like it used to be with Heather—that for a moment, I felt an absurd flash of joy. Of gratefulness. *Jessica Miller, star of the show.*

But of course, now that it was finally happening, it was all wrong. They weren't gathered around me to applaud, set a crown on my head. They were waiting for me to confess.

It was getting hard to breathe.

"Well?" Eric asked. "You're awfully quiet."

"I didn't kill her." My voice cracked. "I'm not hiding anything."

Liar.

"That night, someone took the scissors from Caro's desk and used them to cut up three photographs." Eric stepped closer. "Someone who was very angry. And then those very same scissors—do you remember what happened next?"

Don't say it.

"Someone used them to kill Heather. Stabbed her seventeen times."

One, two, three cuts.

"A crime of passion, the cops said." Eric took another step, and there was nowhere else to go. The railing bit into my back. "They thought it had to be Jack, the boyfriend. On the surface, it made sense. But Jack wasn't so passionate about Heather, was he? Oh, he loved her, don't get me wrong, but he wasn't so angry that he could do *that* to her, like the cops thought. He was already moving on. No, someone else hated her."

Four, five, six.

Eric pointed the photographs at me. "It was either you"—he turned to Caro—"or her."

Coop shouldered his way past Eric and stood in front of me, arms out like a shield. "*Enough.* We played your games. We confessed our sins. There's nothing left to say."

"Coop?" Caro looked at him, standing boldly in front of me like a knight before a dragon, then at the empty space in front of her. She frowned.

"Coop's right," Mint said. "We've practically given you our entire Homecoming. Because you're Heather's brother, and we feel bad. Really, we do. You're clearly hurting. But sometimes, as terrible as it sounds, mysteries go unsolved. Cases remain cold." Mint gestured at the line of floats behind us. "Why don't you go and use this day to mourn your sister?"

Eric's calm mask shattered. His eyes flashed. "I'm not going anywhere until her killer is brought to justice. I promised her." His eyes found mine over Coop's shoulder.

"I didn't do it," I said, my voice hollow.

Seven, eight, nine cuts.

"If no one will confess to killing her," Eric said, "maybe you'll confess to the other crimes."

"What other crimes?" Courtney asked warily.

Caro was still looking at Coop, measuring the distance between him and me.

"The night of Heather's murder, two other crimes were committed, but of course, neither got as much attention. The second crime the cops investigated but, like Heather's case, never solved. The first was never even reported. It was considered minor, only a campus issue. That crime was my most important clue. It took me years to find it. Took joining the Alumni Office, making friends with the one person who was on staff back then, who remembered the night Heather died. And what they found the next morning."

My heart, pounding and pounding.

Ten, eleven, twelve.

"Jesus Christ, Eric," Coop started, but Eric cut him off.

"Do you remember a professor by the name of John Garvey?"

I stepped outside myself. I was not here. I was a million miles away.

Coop clenched his fists in front of me. He was going to hit Eric. I could see it happening already, unfolding like a foregone conclusion. Even Mint went rigid as a board, feeding off Coop's tension.

Caro squinted. "The economics professor? The big shot who went to work for the president after we graduated?"

"That's the one. Amazingly tight-lipped, Professor Garvey. Didn't want to talk at all about his years teaching at Duquette. Even less excited to be asked about the night Heather was killed, the night someone—"

Coop took a threatening step forward. "I swear to god, Shelby, *not here.* You're dealing with people's lives."

"I'm dealing with *her life*," Eric growled. "That's the only life I care about."

"Let him talk," Mint said in a flat voice.

"That same night," Eric said, looking at Coop defiantly, "someone broke into Professor Garvey's house. Smashed it up. Glass shattered, paintings ripped from the walls, shelves turned over. The damage was

214

nearly a hundred thousand dollars' worth. But you want to know the most interesting part? Whoever broke in wrote the word 'rapist' in every room of his house."

What? The shock filtered through me. I searched myself, combing through memories, but I couldn't find the break-in. There was a point in the night when the reel went black—utterly, utterly dark—so it was possible. It was possible, but it didn't feel right.

No, it didn't feel right. Not like *thirteen, fourteen, fifteen.*

"If you say one more word, I'll shut you up myself," Coop said. "You don't have the right to bring this up. It's not yours to talk about."

Caro looked at me with the strangest expression.

Rapist. Someone had written it, over and over. An accusation, a punishment. Who even knew, besides me? Were there other girls? The thought made me dizzy.

"It *is* mine to talk about. Because Professor Garvey was connected to Heather. He wrote her a letter—the recommendation that landed her the Duquette Post-Grad Fellowship. Ring any bells?"

"That's right," Courtney said, a faraway look in her eyes. "That award she won. She found out the day she died. I remember she was excited. She told me she'd applied on a lark."

A lark. The words brought the pain back, as fresh and vivid as it was ten years ago. A knife straight through the heart.

Sixteen.

"February 14th, 5:03 p.m. Heather called our mom to tell her she'd won the fellowship. The Duquette version of a Fulbright, the highest honor any graduating senior could receive. My mom told her she was proud. It was the last time anyone in our family spoke to her."

Coop couldn't seem to help it. He turned over his shoulder, searching my face for a clue. His own was a mask of uncertainty.

"The people Heather beat for the fellowship must have been livid," Courtney said, tapping her chin. "She wasn't even an econ major and

Garvey wrote for her." She gave a puff of laughter. "She kept going on and on about how she didn't even care, then she goes and wins it."

"Funny you say that." Eric smiled at me, and I knew what was coming. Mint and Coop turned, following the direction of Eric's smile, and suddenly, all eyes were back on me.

"It turns out Professor Garvey wrote one other recommendation letter for the fellowship. But it took me nearly a decade to find out, because the evidence went missing from campus the night Heather died."

"The first crime," Mint said softly. "The one they said was only a campus issue."

Eric nodded.

Lucky number seventeen.

"Who?" Courtney breathed.

She didn't remember, of course, but the rest of them did. There had only ever been one econ major among us.

Caro turned to me, her eyes wide and frightened. "Oh my god. *What did you do?*"

CHAPTER 30
FEBRUARY, SENIOR YEAR

February 14: Valentine's Day. I used to know that, used to dream about red roses, the Phi Delt Sweetheart Ball, a golden crown lowered onto my head. But this year, the day meant only one thing: the winner of the Duquette fellowship would finally be announced.

I sat in my pink dress for Sweetheart, refreshing the fellowship website over and over. I was intensely grateful that it was a Saturday, and I didn't have to suffer through classes, hadn't told any of my friends, keeping it clutched close like a treasure. Because what if I lost? *No*, my brain whispered, *impossible*. Still, it was better this way. This was a private dream, a private moment between me and my dad.

Four fifty-nine—one minute to go. I was so close, just a sliver of time away. With my high grades, thanks to Adderall and constant all-nighters, my essay, revised seven times until it was perfect, like my dad taught me, *and* my recommendation letter from Dr. Garvey, I had to win. It had to be me, for once.

Five o'clock. I took a deep breath and pressed the refresh button, closing my eyes. The butterflies in my stomach were on speed, banging around everywhere. I opened my eyes and blinked at the screen. The announcement was up.

We are pleased to congratulate this year's winner of the Duquette Post-Graduate Fellowship: Ms. Heather Shelby.

Heather Shelby? I closed my eyes, rubbing them vigorously. Reality had blipped, gone sideways for a second, but all would be fine.

I opened my eyes and squinted.

Ms. Heather Shelby. It was still there, in black and white pixels. Like someone had dug into my nightmares and pulled out the worst possible scenario, the one that stabbed the deepest. It didn't make any sense. Heather hadn't applied for the fellowship. Had she? She hadn't said a word about it. How was her name on the screen?

It hit me, sudden and fierce: *I didn't win.*

I tried to step outside myself, to look from a distance, but the pain was too much. It kept me tethered to my body. I felt the loss like someone had cracked open my rib cage, thrust a hand inside, and squeezed my heart.

I'd failed again. Now my father would be nothing more than a body buried in a hole in that shithole town he hated. Forever a small, unimportant man. He'd fade away into nothing.

Everything I'd done to get here—none of it mattered. Dr. Garvey, his arms encircling me, pulling me down—

The door to the suite burst open. "Jess, you home?"

It was Heather. I sat frozen, the walls of the room closing in.

"There you are!" She practically bounced into our room, wearing a sparkly red sweater printed with Sweetheart candies, her idea of a cocky joke. But maybe she would get crowned Sweetheart tonight. Maybe she'd get everything. "Jess, I have the craziest news!"

Her presence in the room felt threatening. Like a gun pressed to my temple. *No wrong moves.*

I snapped the laptop shut. "What?"

When she spoke, I had a sense of déjà vu. Like I'd been here before, a thousand times, and knew exactly how it would go.

"I won that fake-Fulbright thing. I just found out. Can you believe it?"

When I didn't say anything, too choked with emotion, she rolled her eyes. "I know, I know, it's super-nerdy. Honestly, much more up your alley than mine. I totally applied on a whim, because I was like, why not? We're in the middle of a freaking recession, and there are no jobs, anyway. Everyone's going to grad school to wait it out."

"How?" I whispered. How had she done it? How had she managed to steal the thing I wanted most? Her grades were average. She wasn't a virtuoso writer. *How, how, how?*

Heather flopped on her bed and shot me a look. "I'm going to choose to not be offended by that. I am smart, you know. I wouldn't have even known about the fellowship if that professor hadn't sought me out."

I twisted in my chair. "What professor?"

"That famous one. You know, the one you love." Heather snapped her fingers. "Garvey. He just came up to me after class and said I was totally gifted and should consider applying for the fellowship. He even wrote me a recommendation."

Dr. Garvey? Suddenly it was clear. He could only have had one motivation.

I recoiled. "You went to dinner?"

Heather frowned. "What dinner?"

"With Dr. Garvey," I said. He'd done it to both of us. I couldn't believe it.

"Ew," she said. "Why would I have dinner with him? He's old. And, like, a professor."

I froze. Dr. Garvey hadn't made Heather have dinner with him? Hadn't made her go back to his house, kneel on his bed?

She wasn't looking at me anymore. She was texting on her bed, legs propped up on the wall.

Dr. Garvey had simply written her a letter because he thought she was good.

I didn't know what was keeping me alive, now that my heart was outside my body.

"Anyway, it's silly, I know," Heather said, swinging her legs off her bed. "But my mom was happy, and it gives me something to do for a few years. And I needed some good news. This has been a surprisingly shitty semester. Speaking of which, Caro didn't find a date for Sweetheart, did she? Because she is the absolute last person I want to see tonight."

I should have asked *why*, or *what's going on between you guys*. She paused, waiting for me to do it. But I couldn't make my mouth move.

Heather waved her hand, as if casting away the negativity. "So the deal with this fellowship is you're pretty much guaranteed a spot at whatever school you want. Maybe I'll go to *Haaa-vard*." She pantomimed pulling a monocle away from her eye. "With all the supersmart uptight people. I know that's your vote—you've always been obsessed. Or maybe Oxford, and then I can go to the theater in London whenever I want." She clapped. "Okay, well, I'm off to get a blow out for Sweetheart. Mom said I can do whatever I want as a reward. You want to come?"

She doesn't know, I reminded myself. Somehow, I managed to shake my head.

"Boo. Fine. I'm sure you have some very important studying to do or whatever. Pregame in the basement tonight, don't forget. You better be there."

All of a sudden, Heather reached down and hugged me. I stiffened in her arms, but she didn't seem to notice. She pulled back, squeezed my shoulders, and smiled. "I don't know why you're being weird, but tonight's going to be the best night ever. We're going to celebrate, okay? And look, I know we're Sweetheart rivals, so—" She winked, flashing her impish smile. "May the best woman win."

When she slammed the door, I picked up my laptop and threw it against the wall. It hit the floor hard, screen tearing free of the keyboard. Looking at it—the laptop I'd bought with a credit card I couldn't afford—I sank to my knees and sobbed, each breath like dragging glass up my throat.

Everything had been ripped away in a single moment. Heather had beaten me, and she'd barely even tried. Like always, she'd come out on top, and I was second-best. I needed to get rid of this pain—it was going to destroy me, burn me from the inside out.

I scrambled through my desk drawer until I found the Adderall, opened the plastic bag, and shook the pills into my mouth. I chased them with the handle of whiskey Heather kept in her closet.

It wasn't enough. I needed to really escape.

I tore through Heather's dresser, looking for whatever else she had that could take these feelings away. In the bottom drawer, I found an orange bottle with Chinese writing that I recognized as Courtney's diet pills. Heather was always stealing them from her, saying, *we have to save her from herself.* But it was pointless—Courtney's mom just overnighted her more whenever they went missing. *Evil woman,* Heather would say. *The depths some parents will sink to.* But what did Heather know about bad parents, or the weight of expectations, or what it felt like to want more for someone, want to *be* more for someone? Heather's parents did nothing but dote on her. What did she know about anything?

I popped the top off and poured the little white pills into my palm, then froze, and thought of my father. The number of times I'd witnessed him doing exactly this. Where it had led him.

Then I thought of Dr. Garvey and the life my father should have had. I swallowed the pills and chased them with whiskey.

After time, my vision blurred, and I wobbled, catching myself on Heather's desk chair. The cocktail was kicking in, doing what it was supposed to: carving away the sadness, the horror—but instead of soothing numbness, the hollow space in my chest filled with anger.

Not anger. *Rage.*

Dr. Garvey had used me. Taken advantage of how much the fellowship meant to me, flexed his power and authority, dangling the letter over my head, all to get what he wanted.

My pulsed raced. And *Heather.* It had all worked out for her. Of course it had. She'd been approached by Dr. Garvey out of the blue, the kind of opportunity people like me only dreamed about. He'd treated her like he should have, like a student, using his power and authority to help, not hurt. The world had worked the way it was supposed to for Heather Shelby. Why her and not me?

Four years of Heather getting everything. Chi Omega. A BMW on her birthday. Beautiful dresses. Heather was never afraid of the future, never afraid to speak up, never afraid she wasn't worth listening to. Heather had two loving parents and a bright future. Heather had the fellowship. Heather had *Harvard.*

A seething rage rose inside me, tall as a tidal wave. You were supposed to win if you were the best, but Heather somehow tricked the system, threw the scales out of whack. *She* was the one who deserved to have everything ripped from her. *She* was the one who deserved to be left with nothing. Not me.

My thoughts blurred into a single desire: I wanted to claw it back from her. I wanted to punish her, erase everything unfair that had happened. All the way back to the first day, freshman year.

I looked at the pictures pinned on the corkboard above Heather's desk. The seven of us, smiling. Sophomore year, Myrtle Beach, waves behind us. Junior year, Coop's and my hands clasped, our secret. Freshman year, seven round faces outside East House.

In all of them, the light seemed to shine special on Heather. She was in the center of the group. The center of attention, with her high theatrics, breezy confidence.

I tore the photos from the wall and stabbed a pen down hard into

Heather's face, scratching her out, erasing her, clawing back the spotlight she'd gotten unfairly. I scratched, X-ing her out, and it felt *so good*.

I stabbed harder, the pen piercing the photograph, marring the desk underneath. Without Heather, I could've had so much—Chi Omega, Amber Van Swann, the fellowship, Harvard. Moving to DC, becoming an important person, the kind my father wanted to be himself.

I hated her. It was the truth, pulled from my shadow life, a feeling that had been simmering underneath my conscious mind for four years, growing and growing.

I stared at the pictures, at Heather's face, destroyed with vicious hex marks.

It wasn't enough.

Everything was kicking in now. I could feel the dizziness circling, trying to tug me under. I stumbled into Caro's room, running into the doorframe, then pulled myself straight. I grabbed for her desk drawer, missed, and tried again. Yanked it open, searched clumsily for her scissors.

The silver pair, nearly large as my forearm, twin points as sharp as blades. For scrapbooking, of course, because it was Caro, who did that sort of thing.

I made it back to my room and took the ruined photographs to Heather's desk. I slid the scissors in and cut, again and again, carving Heather into pieces.

I hated her.

I wanted her gone.

I wanted her to die.

The dark thought twisted in my mind. If she was dead, the world would be balanced. I could finally have what I wanted. I could be *best, first place, winner.*

I cut until she was nothing more than scraps littering her desk.

But it still wasn't enough.

A new idea was dawning. One that could restore the balance, right the wrongs—take back what Heather had stolen from me. It was terrible, and cruel, but as the rage seethed inside me, I knew I'd do it. To punish her, and Dr. Garvey. Everyone.

I dropped Caro's scissors onto Heather's desk and swept the scraps of photographs into her desk drawer.

Then I walked out the door and into the night. And for the first time in a long time, I was in control.

CHAPTER 31
NOW

That's where the record stopped, every time. Where it went utterly dark. That's what Eric didn't understand. *Out the door, into the night, in control. Out the door, into the night, into the night.* The next thing I knew, I was waking up on the floor, sunshine streaming through the windows, my hands and dress covered in blood. Dried in iron-scented rivulets. A record of pain written across my body like a warning in some dark language I didn't understand.

What had I done?

The answer was buried in the black hole. For ten years, I'd known I'd blacked out something important that night, destroyed my memories with whiskey and drugs, truly my father's daughter. And for ten years, I'd refused to look, been desperate not to touch the wound, still as raw now as it was then.

Except for once.

A year after we graduated, right after Mint dumped me and I'd transformed into the worst version of myself in the middle of a restaurant, I'd wondered: What, exactly, was I capable of? Who was I, really, underneath all the layers, when no one was watching? Where were my limits?

I went to a therapist. A fancy New York therapist, with the dark couch and the soothing, neutral-colored walls. *Who was I, really?* She said the answer was waiting in the dark spaces. She wanted to explore them, the moments when time fast-forwarded. I was a quilt made up of light and dark, she said. She told me to trust her.

It was a mistake. I told her about the night Heather died, what I'd done to the photographs, what I'd wanted to happen. I could see her careful mask slipping as she listened, could see the suspicion, mixed with intrigue, as her pencil scratched the surface of her notepad. She told me my blackout was like the black hole, a way to repress. She wanted to know what was inside it. But I couldn't remember, hard as I tried. The dark was impenetrable.

So she hypnotized me. Like Orpheus bringing Eurydice out of the underworld, I followed the sound of her voice back to my dorm room on Valentine's night. Saw the broken laptop, felt my pink dress hugging my hips, burned and burned with rage. But still, the memories wouldn't surface. Still, the picture ended at *out the door, into the night, in control.*

We failed to uncover anything. I quit seeing her.

Then a week after our last session, I woke from a dream and *knew* I'd gone back, that I'd *remembered*; but now, awake, I'd lost the thread. The only thing that remained was a single conviction, dredged out of the dark: I'd done something unforgivable. Something wicked, to Heather. Something my mind was desperate to keep locked away.

So I did. Dedicated myself all over again, with renewed fervor, to being perfect Jessica Miller, a wild success, every surface calm and beautiful. A woman who was unassailable. I needed everyone at Homecoming, all my classmates, to reflect that truth back to me, their eyes and words like mirrors showing the right picture. It was the most important thing, more important than whatever happened with Mint or Coop or Caro. It was life or death.

And here, in my most important moment, I was faltering.

"Jess." Caro's eyes were full of betrayal, suspicion—*fear*. "What did you do?"

Behold Caroline Rodriguez, finally reading someone right. Finally willing to believe the worst, and of her best friend, to boot. What extraordinarily bad timing.

Her voice was so loud that the football players stopped celebrating, turned, and stared. The crowd closest to us went quiet. We were suddenly, and inescapably, on display.

Frankie wrestled away from the players and strode to the back of the float. "What are you guys doing? You're making a scene."

"Jessica was about to explain how she's a psycho freak who killed Heather," Courtney said smugly. *Oh, how the tables had turned.*

Frankie spun to me. "What's she talking about?"

"Did you cut up the pictures, Jessica, yes or no?" Eric watched me with a steady, unblinking gaze. Like everything he'd worked for had been leading to this moment.

"Yes."

Caro sucked in a breath.

"Stop," Coop begged. "You don't owe them anything."

"What are you talking about?" Mint turned to Coop with narrowed eyes. "What do you know about her that I don't?"

I couldn't take this. I had to get out. I looked over the railing at the crowd, who stared back at me, watching the terrible scene unfold like so many voyeurs.

"Did you apply for the Duquette fellowship?" Eric pressed.

There was no point denying it. "Yes."

"Jess—" Coop hissed.

"Did Professor John Garvey write you a recommendation letter, like Heather's?"

"Not like Heather's."

"But a letter?"

"A letter," I agreed.

This time Eric's voice boomed, his question ringing out over the sea of red and white, no microphone needed. Everywhere, faces turned to us. What a spectacle, what a show, like all my fondest dreams. The star of Homecoming.

"Did you kill my sister?"

Except in real life, I was the villain, not the hero.

The whole crowd tensed in anticipation.

I met Coop's eyes, begging me. Mint's eyes, hard and cold. Caro's, full of horror.

It was buried in the black hole, spinning at the center of me, a darkness growing, eating the light: something unforgivable, something wicked.

Did I kill Heather?

I couldn't look. And so I did the one thing my instincts had been screaming at me to do since the moment I'd spotted Eric at the party.

I vaulted over the railing, landing hard on the street, and pushed into the crowd.

People sprung back, as if my touch was poison.

From far away, someone shouted "*Stop her!*"

I ran for my life.

CHAPTER 32
FEBRUARY, SENIOR YEAR

I woke to sunshine, warm and gentle. I could tell, even with my eyes closed, that the world was full of light. I felt it on my face, sensed the glow through my closed eyelids. The sunlight reached inside me, into my rib cage, and filled me with peace. It felt like waking up on a Saturday morning when I was a child, bedroom full of sunshine, no cares in the world, nothing to do but play. Sometimes I wished I could dial back time, be a child again, stay forever in the *before*.

I opened my eyes.

Tall windows looked back at me. Outside those windows, tree branches, leafless but lit by the sun. It looked almost like a summer day, and for a dizzying moment I thought I *had* traveled in time.

But I knew those windows. And beneath them, the rows of easels. Worktables, and paint tubes, brushes half washed by lazy college students. This was the art studio, and I was lying on the floor. As soon as I recognized it, my muscles started aching.

What was I doing here?

I pressed my hands against the floor to push myself up and froze. *My hands.* They were covered with something dry, something sticking ever so slightly to the wood. I held them in front of my face and choked on a scream.

They were covered in blood, like I'd dipped them in paint, the red drying as it snaked down to my elbows, leaving track marks. My palms and fingers stung with pain.

I looked down at my dress—pink, for Sweetheart. Blood everywhere. I looked at my thighs, my knees. Covered in thick, dried blood. Wherever I looked, the pain started—burning, stinging pain.

What the hell had I done last night?

I sat up, clutching my head, vision swimming. All of a sudden, the sunlight through the windows wasn't peaceful but oppressive. It came back like a punch to the gut: Heather had won the fellowship. She'd gotten a letter from Dr. Garvey. I would never go to Harvard.

Oh god. I remembered taking the Adderall, and the diet pills, chasing both with whiskey. *What was I thinking?* I felt a flash of panic—I'd cut up those photographs. I had to go back, clean up the pieces, before Heather opened her drawer and found what I'd done.

But what exactly *had* I done? I'd blacked out after leaving the dorm, no doubt because of the pill-and-whiskey cocktail. I couldn't remember anything. I looked down at myself. Why did I look like I'd survived a serial killer? And why was I in the art studio—had I been too angry at Heather to sleep in the same room? Had I even made it to the Sweetheart Ball? My stomach clenched thinking about what I could have said, while blacked out, to Mint and Frankie, to Heather and Jack. I was holding on to too many secrets to get this drunk. It was like playing Russian roulette with everyone's lives.

Something caught my eye—a manila folder on the ground, covered in red fingerprints. A terrible suspicion dawned. I reached for it, ripping it open.

Inside was my application to the Duquette Post-Grad Fellowship.

Alongside it, the committee's ranking of candidates, on official Duquette letterhead. In case the winner declined, or something happened to her, god forbid, they'd chosen students for second and third place. I stared at the three names. I could see where I'd traced my fingers over the letters, brushing them with blood.

First place: Ms. Heather Shelby. Second place: Mr. George Simmons. Third place: Ms. Katelyn Cornwall.

Like déjà vu, the jolt of discovery.

I wasn't even on the list. Heather hadn't edged me out. I'd never been close, not even with Dr. Garvey's letter and my impeccable grades, not with all the years of working so hard. No matter what I did, it never changed. I wasn't good enough.

I sat numbly while time passed, letting my powerlessness wash through me—the smallness of my life, all the times I'd tried in vain. For some reason, the rage I'd felt toward Heather—the anger that had driven me to stab and cut her pictures—had mysteriously vanished. Maybe it was because now I knew she hadn't stolen my dream right out of my hands. In reality, it had never been within reach.

This was what it felt like to fail utterly.

My spine straightened, survival instincts flooding back. I was covered in blood in the middle of the art studio. Holding my fellowship application and the committee's confidential papers, which I clearly wasn't supposed to have, and I couldn't remember how I'd gotten them. If anyone walked in—if anyone caught me—I would be in a world of trouble.

I'd done something wrong last night. I knew it, felt the conviction simmering inside. I had to get out of here, had to get rid of these blood-stained clothes.

I tore the papers and manila folder into the smallest pieces I could manage, then opened the kiln and placed the scraps in the far corner, where no one would notice before firing. I snuck, heart hammering, out of the art studio and into the sunlight.

It was far too warm for February. The weather felt like a mockery of everything that had happened to me, a reminder that the world would keep turning, no matter how ruined my life was. I snuck quickly, arms covering my dress, jumping every time I heard a noise, desperate to avoid running into anyone. What could I do? It was a sunny Sunday, which meant everyone would be outside. I was all the way on the other side of campus from my dorm.

It came to me in a flash of inspiration: *the gym*. It was right next door.

I walked inside as quickly as I could, eyes locked on the floor, beelining for the girls' locker room. Just one person, changing in the corner. I darted to the showers and peeled the blood-splattered dress off, turning the water to scalding. Red water spiraled down the drain. The water burned everywhere it touched.

Ripping open the plastic shell around one of those flimsy bars of complimentary soap, I scrubbed my hands, my face, my knees and thighs. Red bubbles slid across the tiles. With the blood gone, I could see the cuts across my palms and thighs.

What in the world?

It didn't matter. I just had to fix this, and then I would never think about last night again. I'd never do anything wrong for as long as I lived, to make up for all the things I couldn't remember.

When I was done, I grabbed a towel and wrapped it around my body, took another and scrubbed my hair, trying to squeeze out all the water. I opened the towel. The faintest red stains marked the white.

In a flash, a vision: *torn blond hair, sticky and red, matted against white sheets*.

No—where had that come from? It was painful—terrifying—and I shoved it away.

Movement caught my eye. In the row of lockers, a tall, athletic girl laid her gym clothes on the bench and disappeared into a bathroom. I darted over, glanced around, and snatched her clothes, pulling on the too-large shirt and baggy shorts as fast as I could, smelling the mix of unfamiliar laundry detergent and deodorant. I shoved my bloody dress and towels to the bottom of the trash can, and then I fled, out the gym and down a block, trying not to think about the people staring. Finally, I forced myself to slow. It was a long walk across campus to Bishop Hall, and I couldn't run the whole way, as much as I wanted to. It would look too strange. I had to act normal.

I steadied my breathing. *Everything was going to be okay.* I was covered in cuts, so that was clearly how I'd come to be awash in blood. How I'd gotten those cuts, I had no idea, but I wouldn't think about it now. I'd bury the night, and whatever bad choices I'd made. *Everything was going to be okay.* I said it to myself over and over, like a spell, true if repeated enough times.

I'd get back to my suite, tell Heather and Caro I was going to sleep, and then I'd really do it, even if they whined about the Sweetheart Ball and all the gossip they wanted to dissect, or if Heather brought up the fellowship, wanting to talk more about where she'd go next year. I'd close the door to our room and hide under the covers and sleep until it all disappeared, no matter how long that took—a week, a month, ten years.

Everything was going to be okay.

CHAPTER 33
NOW

I ran, streaking across campus, legs pumping hard and fast. All the crimson-clad people—students and alumni—stared in shock at the girl sprinting, but I didn't care. All I cared about was getting somewhere safe, outpacing the angry mob that was surely only steps behind me.

It was all so clear now, so terrifyingly obvious. I was the villain; I always had been. It explained everything—why I'd never gotten what I wanted, no matter how hard I'd tried. It wasn't because life was unfair, or not working the way it should. I'd had it backwards my whole life: I wasn't the princess, set upon by misfortune; I was the *witch*. And life had unfolded the way it was supposed to, giving me what I deserved.

I ran with all my strength past the people and into the trees, the famous Duquette forest, carving a path where there wasn't one.

Did you kill my sister?

The truth I'd resisted for ten years now rang through my head.

I could have.

It was possible. That night I'd hated Heather so fiercely, so violently.

And, if I was finally being honest, I'd hated her long before then, since freshman year, when I first saw that everything came so easily to her, when she got Chi O and I had to watch her celebrate with Courtney in the gym.

Branches whipped my cheeks, but I pressed faster, faster, looking for somewhere safe.

Tears rolled down my cheeks, though they were too late. I'd tried so hard to be good, to use the love I had for her to stifle the hate I sometimes felt. But it had always simmered underneath. It had simmered until the night it boiled over, the night she stole the *one thing* that was most important, the *one thing* that should have been impossible for her to take.

I'd probably killed her. That's what the blackout was hiding. Blackout, black hole, two defense mechanisms. Like the memory of my father telling me he hated his life when I was eight that my mind kept safely tucked away for fourteen years—even if the poison had seeped out over time, slowly shaping me.

It all made sense. The cuts and blood all over me the next morning. The strange certainty I'd done something unforgivable. Well, here it was, the truth finally exhumed out of the dark.

I'd killed her.

It became clear where I needed to go. I'd run through campus, desperate and blinded by tears, once before: Junior year, Parents' Weekend, the day Heather got her BMW and I got my red envelope.

Blackwell Tower rose before me, its black spire piercing the sky. I ran until I reached the massive double doors, swung them open, and found the winding staircase, climbing as fast as I could.

Up, up, up. To the top of the tower. Like the villain, hiding from a pitchforked mob.

I burst into the hidden storage room, where students used to smoke pot and have sex—all the forbidden things that once felt so wicked—and jerked to a stop. The room was filled, wall to wall, with leftover furniture, cardboard boxes, stacks of old newspapers. There were classroom chairs, desks stacked on their side, outdated couches from dorm lobbies. No longer a place for rebellion, but a dump. Nothing at Duquette was the same, not even this.

I didn't care. I scrambled through the maze, tumbling over a couch, until I landed on my hands and knees on the floor before the wall of windows.

I was alone and safe, finally. With the thought, I started to shake, every muscle on fire from running. I pressed my knees to my chest, rocking back and forth, trying to soothe myself.

I didn't remember stabbing Heather, but I *could have*. I had to have done it, and I was just too terrified to let myself remember, to pull back the curtain and look at my true face.

One of you is a monster, hiding behind a mask.

I stopped rocking and stared out the window. I was so high up I could see most of campus. The parade was winding closer. That meant...

I laughed out loud when I remembered: Blackwell Tower was where the parade route ended, where the chancellor gave his speech. All the eyes of the crowd—the photographers and the video cameras—would be pointed right here. At me.

It was almost like I *wanted* to get caught.

I watched the parade inch nearer and considered it. I'd thought I was obsessed with Homecoming because it was the perfect second act, and I wanted to be admired and envied for once in my life. But what if it was more than that? What if all along there'd been another plot, orchestrated by my shadow self, the subterranean Jessica Miller, who was capable of things I couldn't imagine?

The last thing my therapist said to me was a warning: "Listen to me, Jessica. The real you—whoever she is—will get what she wants in the end. Whether you realize it or not. It's what the subconscious always does. Wouldn't you rather know? Don't you want to see it coming? You have to reconcile yourself."

She'd been right. Maybe this is what the real Jessica—the one who came out when I was too drunk, the one who existed in the moments I shoved away—wanted all along. To get caught. To be punished. And now, finally, we were reconciled, all her crimes my own.

I couldn't breathe. The air in the room was too thick, heavy with dust, and I couldn't force it into my chest. I had to do something.

I looked at the chairs stacked in the corner, then at the window, and lunged, hauling a chair to the window. With all my strength, I lifted it and smashed it into the glass.

Nothing. I swung the chair again, almost doubling over with the lack of air. Again and again, I struck the window until my arms ached, and finally there was a *crack*, unspindling like a thread across the glass.

I held the chair aloft and brought it down, hard, over the crack. The window splintered. I smashed the pieces of glass, fighting the strangest sense of déjà vu. It felt like every move was a move I'd made before.

A chill wind whipped into the room. I took a deep breath, cold air filling my chest, inflating my lungs. There, that was better. Now I could breathe.

I stepped to the edge of the window, glass crunching under my shoes, and looked down at Crimson Campus. My heart swelled, hair flying like a flag behind me—no longer the mouse-brown of college but blond, like Mint's and Courtney's, Jack's and Heather's. I stretched out my arms. A strange calmness filled me that made me think of Eric. A calmness that came with having nothing left to lose.

I'd loved this place so dearly. It had been an escape, an open world of possibilities. I'd screwed it all up, of course, but I wouldn't think of that now. I would think only of how right it felt to be back where it began, where the magic of my old happiness still pulsed in the soil.

I inched both feet onto the windowsill. The sky was so blue. I could swear I smelled the magnolias—heady and sweet—luring me toward them.

I'd really loved it. I swear I'd loved *them*, my friends, even when I hadn't. But I'd made every wrong decision, I knew that now. Since the day East House first loomed into view, and probably long before then. The wrong boy. The wrong major, wrong career, wrong obsessions, wrong allegiances. Valentine's Day, I'd made the worst possible choice, done something there was no coming back from.

I was so sorry. I hoped they'd know.

"*What the hell—*"

CHAPTER 34
APRIL, SOPHOMORE YEAR

"—*are you kids doing*?" The gas-station owner, a silver-haired man in coveralls, stepped out of the doorway, waving a red kerchief at us.

"Oh shit," Frankie said. "Hurry up, guys. I can't get in trouble—"

"*I'm on the football team*," we all finished, nailing his inflection.

"You know, Frankie," Heather said, carving her last letter, "I'm really starting to get over this whole football thing. Constant practice, never allowed to have fun. You should really find a hobby that suits my lifestyle better."

"Your lifestyle of petty vandalism?"

Heather kissed the blade of her pocketknife, then blew the kiss at Frankie.

"Why does the gas-station owner look like an extra in a 1950s gangster movie?" Caro asked. "Did we slip through a wormhole and travel back in time?"

"One more *Star Trek* reference," I warned her, "and I'm going to start calling you Eustice."

"But Tiny's right." Mint slid his sunglasses over his eyes in full movie-star mode. "We should get out of here, daddy-os. Go burn some rubber before the fuzz shows up."

"Nerds." Jack waved a hand at us. "And everyone at school thinks you're so cool."

"Give me—one more… Okay, done!" Coop rose from the picnic bench and snapped his pocketknife closed. "You asked for immortality? Well, here it is. Feast your eyes."

The seven of us gazed at the tabletop, where Coop had carved a message—with a little help from Heather, who couldn't stand being out of the spotlight. *EH7 was here.*

"It's beautiful," Heather said. "I commend myself."

"Classic," Jack said. "Concise."

"Good craftsmanship," Mint agreed. "I know we're all so surprised Coop knows how to wield a knife."

"Did anyone else realize we just signed our names to a crime?" I asked.

"Uh, guys?" Caro looked over her shoulder. "The owner's coming."

"Oh fuck," Coop said, scrambling. "*Run.*"

Heather squealed, and we took off across the rest stop to where the cars were parked, the boys piling into Mint's Range Rover, the girls into Heather's convertible.

Heather revved her engine and tossed the gas-station owner a kiss.

"You kids are delinquents!" he yelled, waving his kerchief after us.

"We're so sorry!" Caro said as Heather reversed and then roared forward, trailing Mint.

"No, we're not," Heather yelled with a backwards wave. "We improved it!"

We slid onto the highway, which in Myrtle Beach was a two-lane road running parallel to the coast. The sun was setting, casting a softer, golden light. With every break between the houses, I could see the ocean, waves tumbling. The salty wind whipped our hair.

In front of us, Jack leaned out the window of Mint's car and whooped in victory. Heather whooped back.

"You're insane," I told her, spitting hair out of my mouth, where the wind had kicked it.

"It's *spring break*. You know I love you dearly, Miss *Straight-A's-or-Hara-Kiri*, but try loosening up for once in your life."

Caro snorted at Heather's words, turning in the passenger seat to grin at me. Her dark hair flew over her shoulders, streaming into the back seat.

"I'm not uptight," I said. "I'm very loose."

"Ha! That's not what Mint told me."

I glared at the back of Heather's head.

"That's it!" Caro squealed, pointing at the mansion on the corner.

"No way," I breathed. "It's huge."

Heather whistled. "Well, thank *you*, Momma Minter." She turned in her seat and winked at me. "Whatever you do, hold on to that one."

Mint's car slid smoothly into the driveway. Heather followed, sighing dramatically as she hand-cranked her convertible top. "God help me with this car. I need a new one, desperately."

"It's an Audi," I said, popping my door open.

"Yeah, and like, *four* years old."

I caught Caro's eye. We both started laughing.

"What?" Heather asked. "What's funny?"

Coop raced over to us. "Jess, you're going to love this. There's a deck in the back that looks right over the ocean."

Frankie popped Mint's trunk. "Why Jess and not me? I enjoy decks."

"For sunsets," Coop said, as if Frankie was an idiot. "So she can draw then."

Mint swung his bag over his shoulder and raised an eyebrow. "You draw?"

"I don't... It's just a hobby," I said.

Caro practically tripped over her own feet. "Remember she drew our entire float last year? The castle? It was so much work."

"Gross—no one's working on spring break," Heather said. "Even hobbies."

"I call dibs on the master." Jack ran for the front door, then turned back with an impish grin. "Suck it, Mint. Rule of first possession!"

Mint's face paled. "Oh no you do not."

Frankie rolled his eyes. "For sure Jack became a history major so he can cite obscure old laws to get what he wants."

"You can take turns in the master," said Caro, the peace broker.

"*Jack*," Heather admonished. "You know Mint and Jess need privacy. They're sensitive flowers. Let them have it."

My cheeks flamed. *Sensitive, uptight Jessica Miller.*

I looked at the ocean, vast and tumbling behind the house. "You know what? I'm going skinny-dipping."

"You're what?" Jack stopped his mad dash for the front door and turned, wide-eyed.

I yanked off my shirt and tossed it on the ground. "Naked. In the ocean."

Around me, nothing but a circle of shocked faces.

"With the sharks?" Caro blurted.

"With the sharks and the whales and the fish." I sprinted past the house toward the beach. There was no one around but us, so it wasn't the most daring trick in the world, but still, I felt invincible as I ran. Not uptight—strong and brave and unstoppable. The early evening sun was magnificent over the water, creating a shining path that stretched over the waves, all the way to the horizon. I was half-convinced I could walk it, like a bridge.

I tore off my shorts, grinning over my shoulder. "You guys coming?"

Frankie whooped and charged forward. "Way to steal my move, Miller."

"Last one in buys drinks tonight!" Heather yelled, ripping off her top and unhooking her bra.

"Ahhh!" I shrieked, covering my eyes as she ripped off her shorts. As usual, she had to be *the most*. Now, the most naked.

"I know this is an elaborate plan to see me naked again," Frankie said, kicking off his shoes so they flew in opposite directions. "Even though you're probably braced for it, I want to remind you: there is not, in fact, a whale in my pants. It's just me."

"Gross, Frankie!" Caro squealed, tugging on her necklace. She hadn't taken off a stitch of clothing.

"Birthday suit, Rodriguez!" Heather took a running leap into the waves, now one hundred and ten percent naked.

"It's okay—I'm going to skinny-dip in my clothes." To her credit, Caro bounded after Heather into the waves.

Frankie, as naked as Heather, turned to face us with a huge, devilish grin—pausing for a second to wink—then jumped into the ocean back-first, landing with an audible smack.

My mouth dropped open. *Frankie.*

"He wasn't lying!" Jack yelled, jumping in after him. "It's a whale of a tale!"

Still clutching my bare chest, I doubled over, breathless with laughter. And then Coop was beside me at the shoreline, his eyes cast out over the ocean. He turned to me, smiling. There it was, the look that shut out the world. This time, I didn't look away, and something shifted between us. The short distance from his body to mine—the small bit of air and sand—was no longer inert but alive. I was aware of his body, so close to mine, within touching distance. His gaze felt like a physical thing, a finger stroking my arm, raising the fine hairs there.

Coop's bare shoulders sloped with muscle. His Adam's apple bobbed beneath the cut-diamond lines of his jaw. His dark hair lifted in the wind. I reached out to touch it, smooth it on instinct, and he sucked in a breath.

I drew my hand back. "What?"

His eyes, so serious. "I'm memorizing your face in this light."

As I opened my mouth to speak, Mint barreled toward us out of nowhere, scooping me in his arms and lifting me high over his shoulder. I screamed with surprise, heart pumping adrenaline as he rushed to the ocean. The last thing I saw was Coop standing alone on the shore, lit with soft, golden dusk, all sharp eyes and enigmatic smile. The perfect figure drawing.

And then we plunged into the sea.

Under the surface, in the cold, in the salt, swallowed by waves, I pressed my eyes shut, letting myself sink. And in that moment a wild wishing came over me. I wanted to stay here, submerged forever. Above the surface, all the days of my life were waiting like a promise. There was nothing but a blank slate, and *anything goes*, and *what if*. My life could mean anything, I could become anyone, as long as I didn't break surface, as long as I stayed here, suspended, in this beautiful, infinite *now*.

CHAPTER 35
NOW

Coop's voice tugged me back from the window like he had me on a string, my body responding before my mind fully realized it.

"What are you doing here?" I stumbled backwards. "How did you know where I was?"

He stood framed by the doorway, breathing hard, his hair sweaty and disheveled. He looked like he'd sprinted across the entire campus. He'd lost his sweater somehow; I imagined him tearing it off as he ran. Now he wore only a black T-shirt, the sleeves torn, threads hanging over his biceps. He clutched something in his right hand.

"Get away from there." Coop slid over the wall of couches and lunged, pulling me back from the shattered window. He turned me so his back faced the open sky, his chest a shield, fingers gripping my shoulders. His heart drummed. I closed my eyes and memorized the pressure of his body, his scent—woodsy and wild, citrus and earth.

"How did you know?" I repeated.

I felt Coop's chin drop on my head. "This was my place. When things were bad, you always found me."

It was true. Back then, I'd always stumbled into him. A strange coincidence, except it wasn't; it was a gravitational pull. Now, as he held me at the top of Blackwell Tower, it was like we were right back in junior year, back to a normal day. This moment—this precious bubble of time—was a gift, however long it lasted.

Coop pulled away from me, holding me at arm's length. "Please tell me you weren't doing what it looked like."

And the moment was over.

I looked past him, out the window. Even now, at my lowest, I still couldn't say it. Not to him.

His voice sharpened. "How *could* you?"

I jerked to face him, the fear swelling, and the words burst from me. "Because I *killed* her, Coop. I killed Heather."

There—I'd confessed. And to the last damn person I would have chosen, the person who once stood in this very room and called me a sociopath. Well, he'd been right. Now we'd come full circle, and he could see every inch of the ugly truth for himself.

I tensed, waiting for him to shove me away.

Coop took a deep, steadying breath—and, to my surprise, put his hands on either side of my face, cupping my jaw. The tenderness wrenched my heart. "Tell me exactly what happened."

The words spilled free after ten years of waiting. "All I know is I found out Heather won the fellowship and I hated her so much. I lost all sense. I took my Adderall and Courtney's diet pills and chased them with whiskey. I got so messed up that I cut up those photographs. The last thing I remember is I had some plan to take revenge on Heather, make things right. Then I blacked out. And there's nothing until the next morning, when I woke up covered in blood."

Strangely, Coop didn't blink. "That's it?"

I forced the words out. "Coop, I wanted her to die. I remember thinking it. *Picturing* it."

"You don't remember coming to my apartment?"

I took a step back, and his hands fell from my face. "Your apartment?"

He blew out a breath and ran a hand through his hair. Strange—his fingers were covered in dirt. "You showed up at my door that night, wasted and covered in blood, then barreled your way inside. You kept saying you needed a safe place."

My hands flew to my mouth. *The blood. He'd known, all this time.*

"I tried to clean you up, but you wouldn't let me. You wrestled me when I tried to hug you, scratched my face pretty bad. Then you sat in the middle of the kitchen and poured your heart out. You told me all about the fellowship."

I looked at him, disbelieving.

"And the letter," he said softly.

A chill ran over my arms, dragging an army of goose bumps. "What exactly did I say about the letter?"

He clenched his fists. I followed the movement, looking down at what he was holding. "What's that?"

He took a deep breath, then held it up so I could see. It was a diploma, handsomely framed, but covered in dirt, the glass cracked from corner to corner. A diploma from Harvard, the font and scroll unmistakable—it was what I'd memorized, coveted my whole life. The scroll announced the conferral of John Michael Garvey's bachelor of science in economics.

I looked up at Coop in wordless wonder.

His gaze was steady. "I've been keeping this for you."

"How?" I could barely bring my voice above a whisper.

"Jess, you told me what Garvey did to you, and I wanted to kill him. Burn his house down. But you said no, said it didn't matter anymore. I lost it. I wasn't in a good place either, with everything going on with the dealers and the tweak. I think I scared you, 'cause you bolted. I always thought that's why you stopped talking to me after that night."

I'd told Coop about Dr. Garvey. This new information was dizzying. I resisted the urge to grip his arm to stay upright.

Coop's eyes darkened, his lashes dipping as he looked at the diploma. "I had all this rage that had been building for days. When you left my apartment, I went to Garvey's house and smashed everything with a baseball bat. I'm the criminal, Jess. I'm the one who wrote on his walls, caused all the damage."

The enormity of what Coop had done started to sink in. "You could have been kicked out of school and thrown in jail for that. Law school, your mom—everything ruined."

He gave me a fierce look. "Yeah, well, I don't regret it. I wish I'd done more. At least what I did scared Garvey enough to leave Duquette. Good fucking riddance."

I pointed to the diploma. "And you stole that. Why?"

"You told me about Harvard. How your dad went and you felt you could never live up. That he died at Christmas. I wish you'd told me when it happened. I would've come to Virginia to be with you at the funeral. I would have done anything."

I'd told him about my father. The surprise nearly swept me off my feet.

Coop twisted the diploma. "I was in the middle of destroying Garvey's house, and I saw this. I figured you should have it—to burn it, maybe. But after that night, you wouldn't talk to me. So I buried it in the quad outside East House. Under our picnic table. It's been here ever since."

Magic in the soil, I thought dazedly.

Coop stood between me and the window, hair wild, eyes still blazing with hate for Dr. Garvey, like some dark, fucked-up version of a hero.

"So you knew—" I swallowed hard. "About Dr. Garvey, and the fellowship, and my dad—"

"Of course—"

"When you came to me on graduation day and asked me to marry you."

Now it was Coop's turn to look at his feet. *Asked me to marry you.*

The words were so weighty, so forbidden, that I couldn't believe I'd had the nerve to say them out loud. But I had to know.

Almost imperceptibly, he nodded.

"You would've married me, knowing all that."

"I told you. Good or bad, it didn't matter."

We stood for a long moment, looking at each other. Then I reached out, took the diploma, and threw it, as hard as I could, against the wall. It shattered into splintered pieces of wood and glass, raining across the floor. In the end, such a fragile thing.

Coop stepped through the mess, picked up the paper, and held it out to me. I ran my fingers over the beautiful, embossed Harvard sigil, and for a second, the old dream resurfaced, my father's and my own, solid and silky under my fingertips.

But I shook my head. That was dead now.

I tore the diploma into pieces.

Then I stepped to the window, the autumn breeze lifting my hair. I opened my hands, and the pieces fluttered away like butterflies. Something in the wind whispered: *You're gone now, and your story's closed. You are who you are.*

I felt a door inside me shut.

Coop tugged me from the window and turned me so I faced him. He wore his private look, the one I'd discovered, too late, meant something long and deep, not short and secret.

"Thank you," I said, my throat thick, "for what you did."

"Two break-ins, one night," he said softly, tracing my jaw.

"Two?" I pulled back.

Coop looked at me like I'd hit my head. "Of course. I broke into Garvey's. After you broke into the Student Affairs office."

I gripped his arms so I didn't fall backwards. "I did *what*?"

And suddenly, like a key turning in a lock, like a slap to the face, I remembered.

CHAPTER 36
FEBRUARY, SENIOR YEAR

The edges were fuzzy, but here's what I knew: I was a dark goddess, a rageful, vengeful force, slicing through the night. Crossing the streets, away from the Greek houses and toward the administrative offices at the heart of campus. As I strode, I gained a second wind, my steps strong and swift. I passed a group of Chi Os decked out in pink and red, surely on their way to Sweetheart. They laughed and wobbled on slender heels, stopping to take pictures of themselves every ten feet.

I stalked past them and scoffed, loud enough for heads to turn. Imagine thinking the Sweetheart Ball was the most important thing happening. *Tonight*, when only hours before, lives had been torn asunder and scales had been tipped, injustice seeping out like a poison.

But I would fix it. Restore the balance, right the wrongs—take back what Heather and Dr. Garvey had stolen from me. It was simple, really. An idea the whiskey had unlocked, or maybe the pills—either way, I had a plan. I'd take what was mine. Take a page out of Heather's book, or Courtney's, all the powerful girls who got what they wanted.

The Student Affairs office loomed ahead, a small, dark cottage, none-theless imposing. Inside it, a group of strangers had gathered around a table and made a decision that ripped away the dream I'd worked for.

At the front of the cottage stood tall double doors. I wrenched the handles, heels sliding in the grass, but the doors didn't budge.

No bother. I moved along the perimeter, a thief in the night, feeling the prickling needles of bushes catch my legs. There had to be another way in. I finished my circle around the cottage, feeling a trickle of sweat creep down the back of my neck. Either the evening was strangely mild for mid-February or the whiskey was at work, warming me against the cold.

But there was no second door. I couldn't let that stop me. Eyes searching the building, lit faintly by Duquette's old-fashioned lanterns, I spotted my chance.

A single window, low to the ground.

I tried to pry it open, to jiggle and shimmy the panes, but the window was as securely locked as the door. I would have to dispense with politeness.

It's funny how the world reshapes itself according to your desires, if you demand it. The wooden placard in front of the office, announcing *Student Affairs* in scrolling letters, was no longer a sign but a stake, espe-cially once kicked until it snapped. A perfect battering ram.

I took the sign and swung it into the window, relishing the heavy smack it made when it connected with the glass. I laughed as I swung, again and again, almost wishing for an audience, wishing the adminis-trative buildings weren't tucked away in a part of campus students never bothered with.

The window cracked like it was supposed to. The glass made a musi-cal sound as it fell, half into the bushes, half inside the office.

There. I'd made a door.

I heaved myself up, taking care to place my hands away from the glass shards that still poked like jagged teeth out of the windowsill.

Up and over, through the window, landing almost gracefully on a rug inside.

I prowled through the office. So quotidian now that it was dark, the decision-makers gone, leaving behind boring desks and chairs and potted plants. I searched until I found the storage room and, inside, the file cabinet. A drawer labeled—almost comically—*Post-Grad Fellowship*.

Could this plan work? I felt a quiver of doubt. It had seemed so right in my bedroom. But now, standing in front of this file cabinet, in front of this tower of official documents, all this solid, printed proof of the committee's decision, my plan seemed flimsy. Childish, a stupid shot in the dark.

No more doubting. I could fix this. I would pull my father out of that hole in the ground and take him with me, *up, up, up*.

I slid the drawer open. So many files, each labeled with a different student's name. I found *Jessica Miller*, pulled it out. Found *Heather Shelby*, pulled it. Then another caught my eye: *2009 Committee Notes*. I grabbed that too.

I opened Heather's file first and parsed the papers. There it was, on thick Duquette letterhead, from Dr. John Garvey, just like Heather said. In the weak light, I squinted and scanned.

Dear Fellowship Committee, I write in support of an outstanding candidate, Heather Shelby. Heather is not an economics major, and normally I would not write to endorse her, as is my policy. But Heather stands out among my undergraduates. Last semester, she approached me after failing her first exam in my class and asked if I would write her a letter of recommendation for this fellowship if she could prove herself, turn her grade from an F to an A.

This was highly unusual, to say the least. Disarmed by her brazenness—and frankly, expecting her to fail—I said yes.

That semester, she worked harder than any student I've ever witnessed to turn her grade around. And though she ended my class with a B and not an A, I felt that she proved herself to be intellectually capable. But more than that, Heather is dogged in the pursuit of her goals. She goes after what she wants, and she clearly wants to win this fellowship. It is this single-minded attention to achievement, this ability to hold steadfast in the face of obstacles, that will serve her well in graduate school and life after. And that is why I am wholeheartedly recommending her for this award.

I dropped the letter, stunned. Heather had lied to my face. She'd said she applied on a whim, that Dr. Garvey had approached her, but this letter said the opposite—proved she'd been planning her application, had maybe even wiggled her way into Dr. Garvey's class in order to get his all-important recommendation.

A second thought punched me in the gut: If Heather had lied about that, could she have lied about what she'd done to get the letter? Did she go to dinner with Dr. Garvey and then back to his house, just like me? When I'd asked her, heart in my throat, if she had—with all the other questions thrumming underneath: *are we the same, do you understand why I did it, do you lie awake at night and feel his hands on you*—she'd denied it. Had she meant for me to be buried alone under all this shame?

Swallowing nausea, I tore open my own folder, searching until I found twin letterhead, a twin signature slashed across the bottom of the page.

Dear Fellowship Committee, I write to recommend Jessica Miller, whom I have taught in four classes here at Duquette. Jessica is a talented student, as evidenced by her high grades. She has demonstrated sophisticated thinking for an undergraduate, as I have remarked on her papers.

My heart started to sink. I scanned down the letter, the words hitting like fists: *pleasant, important contributions, sure to have a successful career.*

It was so tepid, so perfunctory. So unlike his letter for Heather, full of tangible respect. He could have slipped any name in place of Jessica Miller and gotten the same result.

This was what I'd bought with my soul?

I slumped to the floor, dizziness from the mix of pills and cheap whiskey making my vision swim. I'd thought, for a few stupid, hopeful minutes, that I could steal Heather's file so there was no record of her application, and the fellowship would have to go to me, the runner-up. I'd thought I could scratch her name out and write mine in. Type up a new decision on Duquette letterhead, forge committee signatures, if I had to. Whatever it took.

Now that I was here, the dumb futility of my plan was plain. The righteous rage that had convinced me it was possible was dissipating. Numbly, I flipped open the folder labeled *2009 Committee Notes.* My breath caught.

It was the line-up of winners. First, second, and third places. I should be there, typed in black and white print, under *second place.* But there was no Jessica Miller.

First place: Ms. Heather Shelby. Second place: Mr. George Simmons. Third place: Ms. Katelyn Cornwall.

I wasn't even on the list. I stared at the names, and all of a sudden, out of nowhere, a different kind of truth hit me.

My father was dead, and he was never coming back. I couldn't rewrite him, couldn't turn him into a person who was successful by proxy, who loved me, who was happy. Nothing I could do was going to change the man he'd been. He'd squandered his chances. Hadn't lived up to what anyone expected of him, least of all himself. And that was who he was going to be forever—a man with wasted potential, who died bitter and alone. That was who we were going to be forever, him and me—never close, never forgiven, never redeemed. The ink on the story of my dad and me was dry. The book was shut.

I clutched my chest, heart hammering. Coming here had been a terrible idea. I had to get out.

I shoved Heather's file back in the drawer but couldn't bring myself to put mine back, let them have this record of my failure. I slipped the committee ranking into my folder and slammed the drawer shut, then ran to the window, wanting to be out under the night sky where there was room to breathe.

I threw the file out the window and scrambled after it, thinking only of getting out. But I was clumsy—the window's jagged teeth caught my hands and thighs, tearing at me, trying to keep me pinned. I cried out at the pain, like lines of white-hot heat opening in my skin, felt the slickness of blood on my hands. I used all my strength to keep moving, to tip and tumble out the window.

I landed in the grass, the wind knocked out of me. *Air.* I clutched my chest with bloody palms. *Breathe. Steady. Breathe.*

I had to leave before anyone found me. Had to think of a place to go, somewhere safe. But the truth was—the *truth* was—I wanted more than safety. I wanted…

Oh, how I wanted. I could finally confess that now, couldn't I? Now that I was at my lowest, now that there was no use keeping the mask of indifference on, now that I had so little of myself left to protect. It was my secret shame: I wanted, I wanted, I wanted.

A woman who wanted was an ugly thing. I knew it made me childish and vulnerable. My whole life had taught me that lesson. But *still.* For one moment, laid out on the grass, all my ruined, pointless, pent-up wanting was too great to contain—

I threw open the doors to my heart. The pain flooded in. I'd wanted so many things and lost them all. This was the cost.

I lay on the grass and sobbed. The stars looked on, cold and unblinking.

CHAPTER 37
NOW

I let myself remember. Let my shadow self flood me, the subterranean Jessica Miller who wanted so much, and especially the wrong things. It had been her in my dorm room, ten years ago, cutting up the pictures, swallowing the pills. Her breaking into the Student Affairs office, determined to steal back the fellowship. It had been her running to Coop, bloody and desperate, only to push him away the next day. It had been her, and so it had been me.

"What?" Coop studied my face. "You don't remember?"

"Actually..." I shook my head, catching a glimpse of the floats out the window, the crowd growing close now. "I do. The first crime... It was me."

Coop nodded. "You and me against the world that night."

I *had* hated Heather. I'd hated her so much I'd tried to take away her fellowship, her future, the opportunity she'd carefully plotted and earned. That must be the wicked, unforgivable thing I'd done that had haunted me for a decade. *That* was how I'd gotten bloody, covered in cuts—escaping through the office window. Not stabbing Heather seventeen times.

I didn't kill her. The sheer relief of it hollowed me until I felt as light as air. I almost couldn't process the thought. I'd believed so deeply, and now it didn't feel right to redeem myself.

I looked at Coop, and everything I felt must have been written on my face, because his eyes softened. "You didn't hurt her, Jess. I know you. You're not a murderer."

He was standing so close, his lips, his eyes, the dark shock of hair, all within reach. There was suddenly only one thing I wanted, and it was the same thing I'd wanted for ten years, fourteen probably, ever since Caro pointed to him across the quad that first day and he lifted his head and looked at *me*.

But he loved Caro now. I'd lost my chance.

Coop brushed his hand down my arm, his fingers warm against the chill air from outside the window. His eyes were flecked with color, the patterns like twin constellations. Years ago, Coop had been a boy who'd loved me, who'd always been honest, who'd never wanted anyone else. Now he was a man who kept showing up.

A recklessness seized me. What if I was honest, this time without the alcohol? What if I betrayed Caro, became a different kind of villain… Could I have him? Was there a sliver of a chance?

I took a deep breath, filling my lungs with crisp fall air. "I have to tell you something."

The floor trembled. The sound of approaching footsteps, pounding up the stairs like thunder. Coop pulled away quickly, putting distance between us. I had only a moment to blink at the empty air before Courtney staggered into the room, her eyes lit with victory.

"Murderer!" she shrieked, pointing at me.

Oh god.

The rest of my friends streamed in behind Courtney, sweaty and winded from the spiral staircase, their faces tight with apprehension. All of them were here—Mint, Caro, Eric, even Frankie, still in his grand marshal cape. I took an involuntary step back. It was a tribunal.

"It's not true," Coop insisted. "She didn't do it."

Caro stalked forward, kicking over a stack of old newspapers, as angry as I'd ever seen her. "Coop, what are you doing here?"

"How'd you even know where to find me?" he asked.

This time, Caro didn't look ashamed. "I used to follow you here sometimes. I knew this was your place."

Mint stepped up behind Caro, brushing his hair, dark with sweat, off his forehead. His eyes were the exact shade of the sky outside—except hard and cold as flint. "You both owe us answers."

Mint's eyes—they were his tell. He was measured on the outside, but inside, I knew he was simmering with anger.

Eric wound around Frankie and Mint, stopping next to Caro. He said nothing, but he looked hungry.

I glanced helplessly at Coop, who turned to the shattered remains of the diploma frame laying on the floor. I knew instantly what he was after. Evidence. But I'd cast it out the window.

Coop squared his shoulders anyway. "I was the one who broke into the professor's house ten years ago and trashed it."

"*What?*" Caro gasped. "Why?"

Coop glanced at me. He wouldn't say a word without my permission. He'd stay forever in this purgatory if I asked him.

But I wouldn't.

"Coop did it," I said, steeling my shoulders, "because the night Heather died, I told him Dr. Garvey made me sleep with him in exchange for a recommendation letter. I applied for the fellowship like Heather, and I wanted it more than anything. But I lost, and Heather won. Dr. Garvey wrote her a letter fair and square, but for me, he…" My voice trailed off.

Ten years later, I still couldn't bring myself to say the word Coop had written across every room of Dr. Garvey's house.

No matter—the unspoken message exploded like a bomb.

Caro gasped, hands flying to her mouth.

"I'll *kill* him," Frankie said. "I'll fly straight to DC and kill him right now."

Courtney's outstretched finger, which was still pointed at me, drooped a little as she glanced around, unsure.

But *Mint*.

His eyes were locked on me, so sharp they cut. His face was turning red—bright, painful crimson staining his skin, creeping up his neck. He looked angry, or…humiliated.

I searched his face. He was ashamed of me. Just like I'd feared.

"When Jess told me," Coop said, oblivious to Mint, "I was furious. I broke into Garvey's house and hurt him the only way I could think of." He looked at Caro. "I'm sorry I didn't tell you. But I don't regret it."

Eric crossed his arms, the movement drawing my eyes. *He wasn't surprised.* There was something else in his face—was it a flicker of pity?

"After the break-in," he said slowly, "with that word written all over his house, Duquette administration opened an investigation into Professor Garvey's behavior. One of his TAs—it was a Phi Delt, actually, your year—came forward and said he'd witnessed the professor having inappropriate relationships with roughly half a dozen female students. He was asked to leave, but he got the university to seal the record and stay quiet. And then he skulked off to the White House."

Half a dozen girls? My chest ached.

"I always wondered"—Eric's voice caught, but he pushed forward—"whether Heather was one of the girls. If that's how, with the letter…"

Did I tell him what I suspected? Tell him she'd lied to me about one thing, unwilling to admit the lengths to which she'd gone to get the fellowship, and so she might have lied about this, too? That the truth had died with her, and he would just have to live with the uncertainty?

I looked at Eric. His jaw tensed, waiting for my answer.

"She wasn't one of the girls," I lied. "I promise. He didn't touch her."

He nodded, and there it was—a flicker of gratitude.

"You said Garvey's TA was a Phi Delt?" Frankie scratched his head. "I wonder who. Asshole should've said something way before it got to half a dozen girls."

Eric's voice turned bitter. "Yeah, well, you Phi Delts weren't exactly known for your upstanding behavior, were you?"

A Phi Delt had known about Dr. Garvey. Something about that didn't feel right. There was a connection I couldn't quite grasp.

"You know what I don't understand?" Mint's eyes were cold, but his voice—his *voice* was low and taut, so intense it surprised me.

Fear bloomed in my chest, dampening my palms.

"Why did you go to Coop? I was your boyfriend. If Garvey...took advantage of you...why didn't you come to me?"

Coop and I looked at each other. I could sense the storm in him. What would we say? It was the only secret left, and it was too big, too destructive, to ever speak out loud.

The silence stretched.

"Jess," said Caro finally, her voice shaky. "Answer Mint's question."

I caught her eyes. Dark and beautiful, soft with pain. Caro, my best friend. Caro, who didn't deserve this.

But I needed to do something I should have done years ago. It was much, *much* too late, I knew that—but for once, I was going to make the radical choice.

I took a deep breath. "Because I was in love with Coop. And I still am."

CHAPTER 38
FEBRUARY, SENIOR YEAR

Mint

Mint stared at his laptop, a chill spreading over him. There it was, in black and white, the headline screaming "Housing Crash Claims Real Estate Giant Minter Group." Just like his mother had warned: *It's coming for us like a tidal wave, and we can't stop it. Your father made terrible investment decisions. He failed us. We're going to lose everything.*

But they couldn't. Mint didn't know what kind of life that would be, to go from everything to nothing. The only thing he could think of, the closest comparison, was senior year of high school, when everyone found out his mother had cheated on his father and his father did nothing—just let it happen, let her walk all over him, let the man she cheated with remain on the board of the Minter Group. When rumors spread through school that his father, a man everyone used to envy, had been witnessed staggering up the driveway outside the Blackstones' twenty-fifth anniversary party, begging his wife not to leave him. The way people had whispered about Mint in the hallways, the way they'd laughed in the locker room. The way he'd felt.

Helpless. Worthless. Humiliated. Losing everything would be like that, but worse.

The door to his room flew open with a bang, as if kicked, and Trevor Daly sauntered in. "El Presidente. Just the man I was looking for."

Mint snapped his laptop shut and shoved it away. He forced his voice to come out even. "What's up, Daly?"

Trevor was the last person he wanted to see right now. Not only because he was annoying, one of those teacher's pet types nobody liked but everybody had to put up with because he was a legacy—but because Mint had hated both Trevor and Charles Smith ever since that humiliating vandalism on the East House float freshman year. Even though he couldn't prove it, Mint knew it had been them. They'd always been gunning for him.

Trevor shut the door, which made Mint raise his eyebrows.

"I have something to tell you that's sensitive," Trevor explained, and Mint stifled a groan. Trevor was also a tattletale; this was probably some story about a brother skimming a few bucks off the beer fund, or something equally inane.

He planted himself on Mint's bed and kicked up his feet. Honestly, the nerve.

Mint turned around in his desk chair and glared. "Trevor, spit it out. Sweetheart is two days away, and I have details to iron out."

"Speaking of sweethearts," Trevor said, with a smile Mint didn't trust for a second, "I have some unfortunate news about yours."

He stiffened. "Jess?"

Jess had been distant, though it was hard to pin down exactly how long it had been going on. Maybe a few months, maybe longer. He'd wanted to ask her what was going on, but it was strange, not to mention a little embarrassing, to have to beg your girlfriend to open up to you. The worst part was, she'd stopped touching him. Stopped throwing her arms around him when she saw him, stopped snuggling in bed. She'd even recoiled once when he bent over to kiss her. She'd immediately backpedaled, saying he'd caught her by surprise, but still, it was proof that something was different.

And it was starting to get irritating. Jess had adored him since freshman year—that was what had drawn him to her in the first place, the way she'd looked at him like he was the king of the world. But lately Mint couldn't help thinking of all the girls on campus who threw themselves at him, literally begged him to take them home at the end of frat parties, when Jess had already gone to bed. He couldn't help thinking of Courtney Kennedy, the hottest girl on campus, and the way her gaze lingered, the way her mouth curved in a smile that always felt like an invitation. As puffed-up as it sounded, he was Mark Minter, president of the best fraternity on campus, off to Columbia Law next year, heir to the Minter Group fortune—

Wait, no. No longer heir to a fortune, as of today. What would that mean about law school, about his place on campus, his place in the fraternity? His heart hammered as he thought about what the guys would say when they found out their leader had fallen. He pictured them lining the halls to point and laugh as he passed, just like in high school, but so much worse—

"Yeah, who else? Look, you better appreciate this, because I'm actually taking a big risk with my grades and my future by telling you."

Mint refocused on Trevor. "Say what you came to say."

Trevor made himself comfortable on Mint's bed. "You know I'm a TA for Garvey, right?"

"That big-shot econ professor Jess is obsessed with."

Trevor smirked. "You don't say. Well, something you may not know about Garvey—it's kind of an open secret for those of us in the inner circle, but, anyway—he's a total horndog."

Mint raised his eyebrows. "Why do I care?"

"You care because Garvey likes to hook up with his students."

"Disturbing," Mint said, starting to turn back to his desk. "Why would any college girl do that?"

"I've wondered myself," Trevor said. "I'm sure it comes down to the power. Garvey's been economic advisor to two presidents, probably going to be advisor to another one after his book comes out. He's connected. Hell, why do you think I suck his dick? Figuratively speaking, of course."

"All right," Mint said, waving his hand, hoping Trevor would get the hint and leave.

"Man, for a smart guy, you're really thick." Mint could hear the satisfaction in Trevor's voice. He swung to face him, and sure enough, the jerk was smiling. "Either that, or you're in denial. Dude, your girlfriend is fucking Garvey."

Mint froze. "That's absurd. Get out of here." He rose from his chair to tower over Trevor, but the guy didn't budge.

"Scout's honor. I saw it with my own eyes. Apparently she asked him for a recommendation letter, and Garvey pulled his favorite trick of asking for a dinner in return. I saw them last Friday night at Garvey's usual spot."

The very air seemed to waver around Mint. "Last Friday?"

"Yeah, the night of the Eurovision party. Your girl went to dinner with Garvey, and I hate to say it, but he took her home after."

Mint fell back against the edge of the desk. "I couldn't reach Jess that night." He remembered: dressed in a ridiculous tracksuit, hair in a fauxhawk, dialing and dialing with no pickup. But what Trevor was saying couldn't be true. Even if Jess was distant lately, Mint had specifically chosen her because she worshipped him, and there was no threat she'd cheat or embarrass him. That was the core of her value: she was loyal.

Trevor rose from Mint's bed and started for the door. He clapped his hand on Mint's shoulder as he passed. "Sorry to be the bearer of bad news. Figured you'd want to know you were being two-timed by an old guy, though. Pretty embarrassing."

Embarrassing. From deep within Mint, the panic and fear, rage and indignation, all came together, sparking into a fire. It rose up, dark and terrible, licking over his skin, and he fed it until it grew into an inferno, until he was gripping the desk so hard his knuckles turned from red to white. *Just like your father.*

Mint spotted her from a hundred feet away, walking into Bishop Hall. He'd been waiting for almost an hour, expecting her right after class, but clearly she'd had other plans. The fire burned hot inside him, wanting to get out, but he held it close, jogging after her into the building.

"Jess!"

She froze and turned, face pale. She was the kind of pretty that was safe, that wasn't supposed to give you any trouble, that was *grateful.* And she always had been, had adored him, practically worshipped him ever since they met freshman year.

"Hey." Jess crossed her arms as he approached. She used to open her arms, want to hug him. "What are you doing here?"

"I had a break and wanted to see you." Mint glanced at the other students hanging in the lobby. "Come here." He tugged her to a couch in the corner and she sat, frowning at him.

He took a second to study her. Could she really have done it? Betrayed him in the worst, the most humiliating way? It seemed impossible. Trevor had to be lying.

"What's up?" she asked.

"I wanted to know what color dress you're wearing to Sweetheart so I can get a matching bow tie."

Instead of smiling, she flinched. "Um…pink, I think."

"Got it." He brushed his hair off his forehead. "Hey, by the way, remember the Eurovision party I threw last week? The one everyone said was our best theme yet?"

She nodded, staring at her shoes. "Sorry I couldn't come."

"Remind me where you were again. I forgot."

Jess met his eyes. She looked so innocent, so guileless, that the suspicion washed out of Mint's heart, replaced by guilt.

"I was with Caro. Girls' night. Just wine and popcorn and *Buffy*. You know how she's always going on about spending more time together."

Mint kissed her forehead. "Totally. The usual. Well, I have to run." He hopped up and brushed off his jeans. "But I'll see you Friday, if not before then, yeah? I'll be the one in the pink bow tie."

She smiled, though it didn't quite reach her eyes. "See you there."

"Tiny, wait up!"

Mint pushed through the lunch crowd outside the dining hall, heading for the short, dark-haired girl a few paces ahead.

Caro turned and unwound her scarf from where it was looped around her face. "Minty. What's up? Why you chasing me?"

He threw his arm around her, the height difference so extreme it was almost comical. "Last Friday, girls' night, you and Jess. Hit me with your favorite *Buffy* episode."

"Easy—'Hush.' It's genius." Caro elbowed him. "But last Friday Jess was with you at that Euro party, remember? Must have been a good time if you don't."

Mint stopped walking, causing Caro to snap back to him. "Are you one hundred percent sure?"

Caro rolled her eyes. "Trust me, I'd have to crack open the history books to figure out the last time we had a girls' night. Haven't you noticed Jess and I have barely hung out this semester? And don't even get me started on Heather. Besides, we finished *Buffy* freshman year. I wasn't going to sleep on sexy vampires." She looked thoughtful. "I actually get why my parents forbid that show, in retrospect—"

The fire inside Mint was back, quick and bright and deadly. Jessica had lied. She'd sat across from him, looked him in the face, and fed him bullshit. Which meant Trevor was right. She really had betrayed him. And if Mint knew anything about tattletale Trevor, soon everyone would know.

"I've actually been meaning to talk to you about Jess, and what happened over Christmas break." Caro said the words carefully, as if they were a test. "I assume you know more about her family than I do, but ever since, she's been really—"

Caro wanted to talk about Jessica's *family* right now? "Not now, Caro. Later. I've got to go."

Mint pulled his arm back and rushed away, feeling Caro's shocked eyes tracking him until he slipped around the corner.

He stood in the middle of the Phi Delt foyer, surrounded by brothers, all of them taping red tinsel and Valentine's hearts to the walls, and knew he was seconds away from screaming. First the market crash—Minter Group stock tanking, investors pulling out, his mother and the board in a panic, and his father—the coward—missing in action. Old friends from high school were emailing him to say they were sorry to hear his family was burning out so spectacularly, and he could bum a room, or some money, if he needed.

And now Jessica, sleeping with her professor, going out to dinner where that slimy, loose-lipped Trevor and who knows who else could see. Essentially a public declaration that Mint was a loser, a chump, not worthy of respect. *How dare she.* He wanted to put his hands around her neck.

But this was no time to have a meltdown. He had to hold it together, even the score, undo the damage she'd done to him. Tonight, at the Sweetheart party, he'd confront Jessica, make her confess. Maybe he would do it in front of everyone, so they'd see. Maybe he would make her cry, beg him on her knees. He thought of his father begging to be let into their dinner party, standing just on the other side of the window as Mint and his mother and their friends watched and shook their heads. People had met Mint's eyes after that, letting him be one of them again. No longer the butt of the joke.

He felt a deep satisfaction settle over him as he imagined how he would catch people's eyes tonight and shake his head sadly, looking down at a crying Jessica. The humiliation hers, not his.

He just had to hold it together until then—pull the shreds of his sanity back into a calm mask. He leaned forward and taped a cutout cupid to the wall—not a simpering, cartoon baby but a gray-haired angel, a joke cupid with jaunty wings.

"Yo, Minty. That cupid looks like the old dude your girlfriend's banging."

Mint froze midtape, and the easy chatter in the foyer fell silent. When he turned, he found the brothers wearing hungry, excited expressions. Trevor was planted in the middle of them, trying and failing not to smirk.

Mint's voice turned deadly cold. "Who said that?"

"Dude, chill." Charles, wearing a stupid lacrosse hoodie like always, grinned lazily at him. "Or does getting owned by a sixty-year-old make you a little uptight? Bet it sucks knowing your girl likes old dick better than yours."

Mint dropped the tape dispenser. "Shut up. You don't know what you're talking about."

All the brothers laughed. They were *enjoying* this, enjoying the sight of him laid low. They were wolves circling, eager to see the alpha ripped to shreds.

"I've gotta say, Garvey might have more game than Mint." Trevor's eyes sparkled. "He's actually got a *few* girls on rotation."

"Damn," said Palmer, a fucking *pledge*. "Mint's getting sloppy seconds from a teacher."

Everyone laughed, a few of them so hard they dropped their decorations. Trevor pounded on the wall.

The fire inside Mint burst open, shooting him forward, but then his phone rang. It was his mom. He eyed it. Normally he wouldn't pick up while he was with the guys, but lately every time she called it was some new emergency. And it was probably best to get the fuck out of here anyway.

He spun on his heels and flew out the front door, slamming it behind him, cutting off the sound of their laughter.

"Yeah, Mom," he bit out. "I'm here."

"Mark." Instantly he knew something had happened. His mom's voice was charged. He stopped in his tracks, in the middle of the street outside the frat house.

"What's wrong?"

"Your father." She took a deep breath. "We finally found him and told him about the takeover. He took it hard—"

"What takeover?"

"I'm taking control of the Minter Group. Me and Boone." Boone—not the board member she'd cheated on his father with. There was no way this man would be allowed to take his father's wife and his company. "The board passed a vote of no confidence in your father and ousted him this morning. It's for the best. But—"

"When were you going to tell me?" Mint wasn't proud of the way his voice cracked, but this couldn't be happening.

His mother's voice turned cold. "I'm telling you now, Mark. This is the apocalypse. You want a company to run one day? You want to inherit some goddamn money? Then you need me and Boone in charge. We're the only ones who can fix the royal fuckup your father left us."

"What happened to Dad? You said he took it hard."

It was strange, really, how your entire life could change just like that, from one second to the next. And there was no fireworks show, no dramatic tilting of the world on its axis to signify how everything had suddenly flipped upside down, and nothing would ever be the same.

"I won't sugarcoat it. Your father tried to kill himself last night. He took the coward's way out."

Mint was vaguely aware that he'd dropped to his knees in the street. That a car had swerved to avoid him, honking.

"How?" he whispered.

"An old-fashioned throw-yourself-out-the-window." Her voice was grim. "Like a goddamn investment banker in the Depression. So dramatic. Don't worry, he survived. Couldn't even get that right."

The world, spinning and spinning.

"You're being quiet, Mark. Say something."

He tried to speak but couldn't get words out past the utter destruction, the firestorm of anger collapsing his chest.

"You can visit your father starting a week from now," his mother said. "He's in Mount Sinai. Send my assistant an email if you want to go, and she'll book you a ticket—"

Mint snapped his phone shut and dropped it on the pavement.

He died right there on his knees, in the street in front of Phi Delt. The tidal wave of rage he'd been holding burned him to ashes, from the inside out. And so the person who staggered to his feet, who strode through the front door of the frat house, who grabbed Trevor Daly by the collar and lifted him nearly off the floor, who hit him, over and over, feeling the skin split under his knuckles, the bone snap, who ignored the hands pulling at his shirt, the raised voices, the shrill scream of the freshman pledge—that person was someone else, someone new, a creature born from fire.

CHAPTER 39
NOW

The strike was swift and sure, straight to Caro's heart. I watched her accept the truth of what I'd said in slow motion, time stretching out unbearably, though in reality it must have been seconds: First the shock, her eyes widening, giving way to understanding, an intake of breath. And then the betrayal, the anger, her face hardening. I stood there and watched it unfold, the small tick of time that undid nearly two decades of friendship.

"You and *Coop*?" Mint's jaw dropped, crimson flooding his face.

Caro turned to Coop. "Is it true? In college, you and Jess?"

Coop nodded, jaw tight.

The room was so quiet you could hear the music of the parade, the steady beat of drums, right below us.

Courtney broke the silence with a bubble of laughter. "You have *got* to be kidding me. You were dating Mint *and* cheating with Coop? And you never told Caro, your best friend? I *knew* that East House Seven loyal-friends-forever thing was a crock of shit."

Tears welled in Caro's eyes, which were still locked on Coop. "You never told me because it wasn't over, was it? It wasn't something in the past. Otherwise you wouldn't have cared if I knew."

Caro, too perceptive, too late.

But I knew Coop would deny it. I wanted the floor to swallow me before he did, so I'd never have to hear him say I was in the past, only a college crush, and she was his future.

"Caro, please," Coop said, but then Frankie moved, lunging forward to throw his arm over Mint's chest, seeing something in him the rest of us hadn't been paying attention to.

Mint yanked away from Frankie and took two giant steps toward me. I moved back out of instinct, the chill breeze on my back telling me I was getting too close to the shattered window.

"It wasn't enough, was it?" His face had lost any pretense of control. It was past red, now purple with fury. I'd never seen anything like it, not on Mint, not even on my father in his lowest lows.

"It wasn't enough to fuck the professor, go to dinner with him out in public? You had to screw one of my best friends, too?"

"Mint," Frankie said, giving me an unsure look.

"You were a whore"—Mint laughed—"*the entire time*. Do you know how bad you humiliated me with Garvey? Do you even get what I went through? And that was just the tip of the iceberg, wasn't it? How long were you fucking Coop? And who else? Who else was laughing at me behind my back?"

"Don't call her a whore," Caro said, her best friend auto-programming kicking in despite herself.

Mint was standing close. The short distance between us wasn't inert but alive, threatening, a warning. *A warning, a warning*. A clue.

"How did you know I went to dinner with Garvey?" My voice was taut with dread. "Are you saying you knew about him in college?"

Mint took another step toward me, shoving a couch aside, his blue eyes no longer cold but blazing with anger. My pounding heart screamed, *Move, get away from him*. But it was Mint.

"Of course I knew. That's how it works when your fucking wife cheats on you—everyone finds out."

"Wife? You mean your *girlfriend*, Mint," Frankie said. "And calm down."

"Yeah, Mint, take a step back," Coop said. "You have the right to be mad at us, but you're pushing it."

"No." Mint only had eyes for me, and I couldn't look away, trapped between the cold, open sky at my back and the man who wanted to burn me, the man who was inching closer. "You were going to ruin my life, and you didn't care. You want to know what happened? Garvey's TA told me you fucked him, but he didn't just tell *me*—he spread it to everyone. All the brothers were laughing at me. Just like people did to my father. You made me *weak*."

"Mint," Courtney said, horror dawning on her face, "I don't get what you're talking about. You're not making any sense."

His father. Mint's confession from freshman year came back to me, the first time he'd ever opened up:

Tell me something shameful.

He was so weak. He didn't even fight it. He let her walk all over him.

I hate him. Everyone at home talked behind my back... It's all his fault...

"I didn't mean to make you feel like your father," I said, taking another step back, feeling glass crunch under my feet.

"Mint, back down," Coop said, trying to step between us.

Mint made a choking sound and lunged, not at me but at Coop, shoving him hard. Coop tripped over a chair leg and struck the wall headfirst. Caro screamed.

Frankie darted forward to tackle Mint, but Mint thrust out his hand in warning. "Don't you dare touch me, Frankie."

Frankie—every towering inch of him—went rigid as a board, years of following Mint's lead instinctively taking over.

"Mint," I said, trying to stay calm, "I'm sorry for betraying you, and everything that happened to your dad. But I don't think—"

He spun to me. "My father didn't fight back. He was a coward. But not me."

"You're right." I watched over Mint's shoulder as Caro struggled to pull Coop to his feet. "You're not him."

"You're doing it *again*," Mint spat out, seething. "Emasculating me. Just like senior year. You know I shattered Trevor's face in front of everyone because he disrespected me? Garvey's fucking TA. He couldn't talk for *months*."

Trevor Daly had worked for Dr. Garvey? And Mint hurt him? I'd never heard a whisper of it. It must have been hushed up, muted in the aftermath of Heather's death.

"But you were so much worse than him," Mint said. "I wanted to break your fucking neck."

"But you didn't, did you?" Eric stepped from the back of the room, where he'd been silent and unmoving, watching everything unfold with glittering eyes. He strode to Mint and shoved him by the shoulders, causing Mint to stagger back. "You did it to Heather instead, didn't you? *Didn't you?*"

Mint glared at Eric, his face flaming as he struggled to hold something back. He looked at Coop, then at me, and suddenly the dam broke—the last thing keeping him tethered. As I watched him unravel into another person—a creature of rage, of fire—the surprise I'd felt earlier transformed into something wholly different.

My body knew it first—my limbs went rigid, heart freezing in my chest. Inch by inch, the knowing filtered into my brain.

You recognize this person, a voice whispered.

Danger, it hissed. *Wake up.*

"I thought she was you!" Mint screamed, pointing at me, eyes blazing. "I thought I was hurting *you!*"

CHAPTER 40
FEBRUARY, SENIOR YEAR

Mint

It was better now, with his split knuckles sending a constant thrum of pain through his right hand. With none of the brothers who'd been in the foyer able to look at him, all of them cowering in fear, taking the long route to the keg, sticking to the corners of the Phi Delt basement as everyone pregamed for Sweetheart. Much better with the way Courtney Kennedy was eyeing him, as if she'd like nothing better than to depose Jessica, take her place by his side.

What he'd done to Trevor proved Mint wasn't a coward, wasn't his father, as much as it choked him to even think of his father—his stupid childhood hero, now a broken shell in a hospital bed, too weak for the world. But *Mint* wasn't weak. Mint was back on top, he was king, he was alpha.

No one had mentioned anything about his father or his family's company all day, so either the Phi Delts didn't read the news or his mother's PR team was doing a good job of keeping the disaster out of the press. Of course, it was in everyone's best interest that what his father had done—his mother's voice drifted back, hard and cold, *the coward's way out*—should never see the light of day. Mint himself vowed to never breathe a word of it.

Ever since he'd given it an outlet, the fire inside him was under control. No longer a raging storm but a simmer in the center of him, hungry and waiting, biding its time.

Sweetheart was going to be Mint's crowning glory. Thanks to money his parents had thrown into the party fund—a check cashed before the market crashed, thank Christ—this year's Sweetheart was bigger and better than ever. The best band booked, Party Pics ready to snap their pictures like a crowd of paparazzi, pledges dressed in humiliating cupid costumes, handles of whiskey for every couple. All of it evidence of Mint's generosity, his power as Phi Delt president.

Even better: Jessica would be here soon, all dolled up. She'd be expecting romance—it was Valentine's Day, after all. She'd be soft and pliant, and at the perfect moment, when they were in the very center of the crowd, he'd hit her with it: *he knew*. He'd make her beg to be taken back, make her cry in front of the whole party, and then he'd turn his back and tell her it was over, that she disgusted him. It would be the perfect drama, something to show everyone Mint was strong and unyielding, no chump. No, he was a prize lost at great cost. No one would be able to laugh at him again.

He tugged his pink bow tie, straightening the corners. He would do everything his father should have done, fix his mistakes. The fire inside him rose higher, crackling, eager for it.

Frankie bound down the stairs into the basement and beelined for him. "Hey, we need to talk."

Mint handed a keg beer to Frankie, eyeing the pulled seams of his suit—the same he'd worn since freshman year. "Let me guess. You're finally taking me up on the offer to see my tailor?"

Frankie waved a hand. "Do you see the younger guys giving you weird looks? Like they're about to piss their pants?"

It was true. Where Mint and Frankie stood had become the nexus of the basement, the sun in the center of the party. Everyone orbited them, eyeing them with an assortment of expressions—fear, desire, calculation.

Mint shrugged, taking a sip of his own beer to hide his smile. "I might have asserted myself a little forcefully earlier today."

Frankie's brow furrowed. "A little forcefully? You broke Trevor's cheekbone."

"He was out of line." Mint spoke like he couldn't care less, was already over it. "You know how he gets. It was finally a bridge too far."

Frankie shook his head. "Trevor's a punk, everyone knows that. But what you did is illegal, Mint. Trevor could press charges." He took a deep breath. "And Jack found out. He's really upset. He's going to call an officers' meeting."

Mint thought of his friend—the Phi Delt treasurer, a regular Leave-It-to-Beaver. Always on the brothers' case about completing their philanthropy hours or recycling beer cans. "So what? I'll talk to him."

"You don't get it. Jack doesn't think it would be fair for you to get away with hurting Trevor like that. He says it sets a bad example for the guys, and the frat might be liable, and who's going to pay Trevor's medical bills, and—"

"Since when are you and Jack powwowing about me in secret? And since when is Jack the fucking morality police? I thought you guys were supposed to have my back."

The look Frankie gave him was grave. "I do. That's why I'm telling you. Look, I don't want to ruin your night, but I honestly think Jack might report it to the cops. He's really worked up."

The fire inside Mint flashed white-hot. "Are you kidding?" Jack was supposed to be one of his best friends. And he was going to betray him? Rat him out to the police over *Trevor*? "Tell Jack he can suck my dick."

Frankie choked, dropping his beer.

Mint blew out a breath, watching Frankie scramble, wiping the spilled beer. "Sorry, Frankie. Jack just doesn't get it. Not like you do." Frankie stood, tossing his Solo cup away, and Mint bumped his shoulder. "Sometimes you have to stop taking shit from people and lay down the law. Be a man about it. You know what I mean."

Frankie nodded, but his eyes caught on something across the room. Mint followed his gaze and saw Heather stumbling down the staircase, her face tearstained. Instead of sympathy, the fire inside Mint roared with approval. That was exactly the face he wanted Jessica to wear when he ground her into the dirt in front of everyone.

He put a hand on Frankie's shoulder. "Look, I'll talk to Jack. Sort it out."

"You promise? Because I really don't want you two fighting. I hate it."

Mint squeezed his shoulder. "I swear. I'll make amends." *Fuck Jack, that goody-two-shoes wet blanket.* "But first, we celebrate." He gestured at the row of whiskey bottles. "It's our last Sweetheart ever. You're about to get drafted into the NFL, I'm going to law school"— Mint took a breath, letting the flicker of painful uncertainty pass, and pressed on—"and we only have one semester left to get crazy. It's time to cement our legacy."

Frankie's eyes returned to Heather. She was in the corner, talking to Courtney, and it seemed to satisfy Frankie's concern. He grinned at Mint. "You know I can't say no to that."

"And," Mint added, drawing the baggie out of the inner pocket of his suit jacket, "I picked up a little something from Coop earlier. This'll take us over the edge. Now that the season is over, and you don't have to worry about drug tests, we can do anything."

Frankie groaned. "I have been waiting *four years* for the damn season to be over. You have no idea."

Mint nodded, running a hand through his hair. He was flying high now, his wingman by his side. "No more rules. Time to cut loose."

Frankie handed him a shot glass, then knocked it with his own. "Here's to Mint, in rare form. And to a wild fucking night."

———————————

They'd taken round after round of shots, plus Coop's pill, and Mint was just getting started. He was filled with a nervous energy, keeping one eye on the staircase, waiting for Jess to show, or even Jack, his hands twitching in anticipation.

"Hold up a second," Frankie mumbled, dropping an empty Solo cup on the floor. "I need to talk to Courtney."

Courtney? But Mint only shrugged. "Whatever. Just don't leave me hanging too long."

Frankie strode off and disappeared somewhere, neither Courtney nor Heather in sight. Great. Now he was standing here alone like a loser.

Out of the corner of his eye, Mint sensed movement. He turned to find Charles Smith circling him, walking back and forth in front of the keg. Charles: lacrosse douchebag and Trevor's bulldog. Worst of all: his parents were friends of Mint's, back in the city.

How much did Charles know?

The look in Charles's eyes was clear. He was bruising for a fight, and he thought that would intimidate Mint. But Mint wasn't weak. He was drunk, the concrete wobbling under his feet. But he wasn't soft. He'd show Charles, just like he'd shown Trevor.

Mint cocked his chin and raised his voice. "You got a problem, Smith?"

Charles smiled. It was a look of satisfaction, like he'd been fishing, and Mint had taken the bait. "Actually, now that you mention it, yeah. You sent Trevor to the emergency room. He's eating through a tube tonight. Feel like a big man?"

The people orbiting Mint paused, stopped their conversations, and leaned in instinctively.

"Trevor talked a lot of shit," Mint spat. "So I did everyone a favor and shut him up."

Charles smirked. "Oh, Mark Minter, what a hero. Big man on campus. You know no one actually likes you, right? They kiss your ass because you're rich and you pay for things." His smile stretched wider. "I wonder what would happen if you suddenly lost all your money."

Charles knew. Mint's heart hammered.

Charles reached into his pocket and pulled out a folded piece of paper. "Will you look at this? My dad emailed me earlier. I guess he's a Minter Group stock owner—a pretty pissed stock owner. He says your company's in the trash and your family is dead broke. How many friends do you think you'll have left when everyone finds out?"

The people gathered around them started whispering. *No*—this couldn't be happening, not again.

Charles sensed blood in the water. He moved in, teeth bared. "Rumor is, your dad went AWOL. Let me guess: he ran off to the Caymans with all the money. Taking the coward's way out, eh, Mint?"

It was like pulling a trigger. Mint shot forward, not caring who was watching or what it would mean, knowing only that he needed to smash Charles Smith's face into the floor until it was a pulpy mess, until it could no longer utter a word about his dad.

But a small, dark-haired girl appeared out of nowhere, throwing herself in his path, hands braced. "*Whoa*, Mint! Charles! Stop. *What are you doing?*"

Caro. Dressed in white, with angels' wings and a quiver of arrows over her shoulder. Yet another cupid in the night's menagerie. The whole of them flashed through Mint's mind: the lineup of pledges in their embarrassing cloth diapers; the paper cutout of the old, gray cupid, the one who'd sparked Charles's joke; and now Caro herself, small and beautiful. So many angels.

He gripped his head, trying to clear the thoughts, to see through the red fog that told him, *You are being destroyed; hurt someone else to make it stop.*

Caro took one look at him and spun on Charles. "Chuck, what the hell? He's my friend."

The look Charles gave Caro was confusing to Mint. It was defiant, but also ashamed. Like he was actually worried what Caro thought of him.

"Your friend is an asshole," Charles said bitterly. "Like I've told you a million times."

"Get out of here." Caro made a shooing gesture.

Charles recoiled like she'd slapped him. "You're choosing *him*? But you're my—"

Caro stopped him with a level look. "Walk it off, Chuck."

Charles leaned in. "Fine. Get a girl to save you. Sounds about right."

Mint lunged, but Caro's arms, surprisingly strong, held him back. Charles escaped, swaggering to the back of the room, where a group of guys from the foyer—Trevor's guys—gathered, shooting Mint icy looks.

Charles's words haunted him. *Taking the coward's way out, eh, Mint?* His dad was lying broken in the hospital, and all anyone could say about him was that he'd failed. His dad, who was supposed to be a giant of a man but didn't have the backbone to stand up to his mother. He'd made the wrong investments, all the wrong choices. And then he'd chosen to end his life—to *abandon* Mint—rather than deal with the mess he'd made. If Mint didn't rage, he was going to break. If he didn't hurt someone, he was going to hurt worse than he ever had, and he didn't know if he'd survive.

He spun from Caro. It was so claustrophobic in this basement. The walls were contracting, then retreating, like he was stuck inside a beating heart. He grabbed the whiskey bottle, upended it into his shot glass, took the shot, then again. He needed to feed the fire. The fire wasn't weak.

"Mint, talk to me." Caro rested a tentative hand on his arm, peering around his side to look at his face. "You're scaring me."

"Where's Jessica?" he managed.

Caro frowned, casting an eye around the room. "I don't know where anyone is. No one told me their plans, as usual. I invited Jess to get ready at the Kappa house, but she said she had something to do. I figured I'd find her here. But it's almost time for the party to start. I don't see her. Or Frankie, or Jack. Or Heather, for that matter. Where is everyone?"

"Fucking cowards," Mint slurred. "Can't stand by my side when I need them most."

"*Okay*." Caro pushed him upright against the wall. "Enough cryptic mumbling. What the hell is happening?"

"Is Jessica different to you?" Mint locked onto Caro's face. "Is she a different person than she used to be? Does she still—" His voice cracked, and he hated himself for it, but he pushed forward. "Does she still want to date me?"

Caro would know. Caro was her best friend.

She looked hesitant. "I tried to talk about this earlier. Now's probably not the best time."

"Tell me," he gritted out.

Caro sighed. "Fine. I thought it was ever since Christmas—" She shot him a look, waiting for some reaction, but when Mint didn't deliver, she swallowed and pressed on. "But now that I think about it, it may have been going on longer. Jess is so distant. She sneaks around where I can't… I mean, she's really good at disappearing all the time, and then she acts like nothing's wrong. She won't tell me anything. I'm worried about her." She looked off in the distance. "Maybe she doesn't want to be friends anymore."

Jessica had been sneaking around, even longer than since Christmas.

Caro, the idiot, had all the clues in front of her and couldn't piece them together.

"How long?" he asked, raw as an open wound. "How long has she been like that?"

"It's got to be…I don't know, a year at least." Caro squeezed his arm. "I knew you'd want to help."

His girlfriend had been cheating on him with a professor for an entire year. An entire year of humiliating him. The fire inside him surged.

"Yo, Prez." Harris, the Phi Delt vice president, popped up between him and Caro, eyeing Mint cautiously. He must have heard about Trevor. "It's time to crown the Sweetheart and kick off the party. Crowd's insane upstairs. Probably our biggest year ever."

"You'll help, right, Mint?" Caro looked at him with pleading eyes. "She'll listen to you. The seven of us have to stick together."

That was a cruel joke. "Where would Jessica be, if you had to guess?"

"No idea. Maybe she never left her room? She's been sleeping a lot since her dad…since Christmas."

Harris tugged Mint forward. "Come on, you have to kick off the show. We couldn't find our Sweetheart anywhere, so we're going with the runner-up. It's either that, or no Sweetheart, and I think the crowd would riot. You're crowning Courtney Kennedy, by the way."

Mint let Harris pull him through the crowd and up the stairs, far away from hopeful Caro. He felt the eyes on him, the whispers. But all he could think about was Jessica, what she'd done, this person he'd trusted, this girl who should have been grateful he'd chosen her. Harris led him to the room with the dance floor, where they'd set up a stage for the band. Peeking from behind the stage, Mint could see a mass of people waiting on the other side. Courtney and some other Chi O seniors stood in the middle of the crowd, Courtney's smile wide, her eyes shining bright. The room hummed with anticipation. Did they all know? Not just that his family was ruined, but that Jessica had cheated? In an instant, all the faces in the crowd seemed to flip, and everywhere, they were jeering, pointing, laughing.

No. He shoved his hands over his eyes. Where was Jessica? She was supposed to be here so he could teach her a lesson, punish her and redeem himself. But she was denying him the chance, taking away his control, his only opportunity to be the humilia*tor*, not the humilia*ted*. He couldn't walk out on that stage until he'd done it.

He needed to find her. Mint dropped his hands from his face and squared his shoulders, feeling the blaze of fury fall into a sense of order, purpose.

From the crowd, a camera flashed as someone took his picture.

"All right, time to shine," Harris said, nudging him. "I'll announce you as you walk up."

"No, actually—" Mint forced himself to grin. "Why don't you do the honors?"

Harris blinked. "Why?"

"Well, you know what happened earlier with Trevor. I might not be everyone's favorite person right now."

Harris nodded immediately, as if it was obvious. Mint hated him for it, but he sealed the deal, put the cherry on top.

"Besides, you've earned it. It'll probably be you up there as president next year. Might as well get some practice."

Harris smiled. "Thanks, man."

"I'm just going to run to the bathroom—too much beer. But then I'll be back to watch. Break a leg."

Mint slapped Harris's shoulder, then turned and sprinted away from the stage. But instead of keeping left for the bathroom, he kept going, out the side door, into the night.

He needed and he wanted to hurt her. It consumed him, became an ache deep in his bones. He would take everything that was burning inside him and unleash it on her, put the pain where it belonged.

He strode with purpose across the Bishop Hall lobby—a ghost town on Saturday night—and punched the elevator button. Everything went slightly blurry then, like it was someone else in the driver's seat, and he was just watching what happened.

Up, up, up. He was going to climb the walls of the elevator if it went any slower; he was going to claw his skin off. The ding of arrival, the doors sliding open, and then he was moving, finally gliding down the hallway. Everything grew a little hazier, the walls closing in. He couldn't tell if it was the alcohol or the drugs or the idea of confronting her that was making him slightly delirious.

Punching the code to her suite, twisting open the door. All the lights were off. But even in the dark, he could see the living room was a mess, dark objects laying like booby traps on the floor, the couch cushions ripped up and left sideways. The aftermath of two people struggling, or roughhousing, or—the thought scoured him—*having sex.*

So it was true. He could see it with his own eyes, the traces of where they'd been. It was the final straw that unleashed in Mint something *other*, something animal.

He shoved open the door to her room, panting. So dark inside, the only moonlight coming from a tiny sliver of window uncovered by curtain. He stared at her bed, where he'd spent countless nights by her side before he'd known.

There she was: a dark figure, lying stretched out under the blankets. Asleep, as if she hadn't promised to meet him at the Sweetheart Ball and then stood him up, as if she enjoyed embarrassing him, as if she hadn't a care in the world.

Rage took over, propelling him forward, and then his hands were on her, gripping her by the shoulder and the waist, shaking her.

"*Wake up, Jessica.* Wake the fuck up and face me."

She barely stirred, just made a low groaning noise in her throat.

"I'm not kidding." He rocked her harder. "I know what you did. *Wake up!*"

Her groan grew louder, and she tried, feebly, to shake off his hand. "Go away," she mumbled, her voice barely audible, half-asleep.

"You think you can dismiss me?" His hands were shaking. Even though it was from anger, the sight shamed him, so he shoved Jessica hard, forcing her to roll on her stomach like a naughty child, the better to be spanked. In the movement, her head smacked the headboard. She cried out, her voice catching in her throat.

The sound of her pain sent a tremor of satisfaction, of *rightness*, through him.

"Leave me alone," she garbled into the pillow, the words almost incoherent. She'd clearly been drinking. Her voice was strange and rough. "I told you… I'm done with you. I hate you."

After everything she'd done, *she* hated *him*.

Mint's vision turned red. He grabbed her shoulders and shook her violently, hearing the sound of her head hitting the headboard, again and again, sharp little *thwacks*. "Say you're sorry."

She was making some sort of noise, but it wasn't language. It wasn't an apology. She must think he wasn't someone who counted, someone to be afraid of. Wasn't a man.

Impotence filled him, and the fire exploded.

Mint stumbled back from the bed, hitting the desk, and then he saw them. Massive, sharp-pointed scissors, the blades like knives. And what to do seized him, the rightness of it hitting him as swift as a lightning strike. He swept the scissors off the desk, gripped the handles so hard his fingers hurt, and drove them down like a pike into her back.

She screamed into her pillow, arms flailing. It was like opening a dam, all the rage and pain flowing out of Mint and into her. He wrenched the scissors out and stabbed her again, feeling the solidity of her flesh resist, then accept, the blades. This girl who'd humiliated him, who was trying to ruin him—now *he* was hurting *her*, making *her* weak, making *her* flop like a fish out of water. The tables had turned.

He punished her again and again, taking the apology from her body since she wouldn't give it to him in words. It felt so good that the feeling frenzied him, making his heart smash against his rib cage. He twisted her onto her back, pushing the scissors into her stomach—*the power of it*—and he knew with every fiber of his being that he wasn't his father, that he had a backbone, that no one could laugh at him. She kicked wildly, foot catching the curtains, wrenching them open, and moonlight flooded the room. He looked at her with a thrill of anticipation, wanting to soak in the pain on her face, the horror and regret.

Blond hair, not brown.

His grip loosened on the scissors. They clattered to the floor.

It wasn't Jessica's face that stared back at him, eyes wide in terror, mouth open, fighting for a slow, gurgling breath.

It was Heather.

"Oh god," Mint said. The room spun, fire draining out of him, and he went dizzy, nearly dropped to his knees next to the scissors. What was Heather doing in Jessica's bed? And why hadn't she spoken clearly, said something to identify herself?

What had he done?

Heather's eyes tracked him as he took a step back, and suddenly Mint saw the scene for what it was, in all its terrible truth. He saw the blood everywhere, across the bed and climbing the walls and marring the skin of his hands, the white of his dress shirt under his black suit jacket. He saw the girl who had been his friend, shuddering with pain. He saw *Heather*, not Jessica. *Heather*, rasping and blinking, *Heather*, who he'd stabbed.

He was going to burn for this. He was going to be sent to prison. Everything—whatever was left of his family's fortune, his spot at

Columbia Law, his friends, his family, his future. This time there was no question he would lose it all. His mother would know what he'd done. His father, if he ever woke up. Everyone in the world.

His life was over.

No. Defiance cut through the panic. He'd made a mistake, that's all. He didn't deserve to have his life ruined because of one mistake, provoked by Jessica anyway, and by Trevor Daly, and Charles Smith, and Jack, and his father. It was their fault, not his. But he would fix it. He would save himself.

Mint scrambled to his feet and dashed to the bathroom. Now that the frenzied feeling had worn off, he was viscerally aware of the slickness of his hands, the heavy, coppery smell that clung to him. He scrubbed his hands furiously at the bathroom sink, digging under his nails. Then he saw his face and cursed. Peeling off his clothes, he showered, scrubbing hard, then put the dark suit back on. It was even starting to dry.

Looking one last time in the mirror, he caught it—there, on his neck. A bright-red mark, prelude to a bruise, peaked out from his collar. Heather must have hit him at some point. He pulled his bow-tie higher, hiding it, then closed his jacket over the white shirt so no one could see the blood splatters. He was fine now, covered.

He rushed back to the bedroom. There was no telling how long he had. He grabbed a T-shirt someone had left slung over the door and used it to wipe the handles of the scissors. Then he placed them securely inside his jacket.

A plan was taking shape, guided by survivor's instincts. He wasn't going down for this; there was no way. It came down to a simple choice: him, or someone else. And he knew who he'd choose every time. He just had to be smart.

Mint gave Heather one last glance. And stopped. He couldn't see her chest moving.

She'd died.

While he was in the bathroom scrubbing off her blood, Heather had died alone.

Tears flooded Mint's eyes; he felt like his chest was going to cleave in half. His knees wobbled.

No. No weakness. If he didn't leave now, he'd be as good as dead, too.

He shoved himself out the door and wiped the handle, then strode across the living room, opened the front door with the T-shirt, closed it behind him, wiped again, handle and PIN pad, then stuffed the T-shirt into his suit jacket, buttoned it to the top one final time. He'd burn these clothes as soon as he could, everything he was wearing, and no one would notice because he had a closetful of the same suits, dark and well cut and expensive.

He'd shower, put on another black suit, slip back into the party, act like nothing happened. Complain about drinking too much, having to throw up, if anyone even bothered to ask. Everyone would remember him there, as much as they could remember anything through the black tunnel of whiskey, a bottle for every couple.

From now on, he'd do whatever it took: feign tears and shock. Be a doting boyfriend to Jessica so no one would ever suspect. Fall in line behind his mother and the man she'd cheated with. He'd smooth everything over, wear the veneer of perfection until it was true, until the mask melted and fused to his face. *This* would be the ultimate proof he wasn't his father. He wouldn't give up his life for a single mistake.

He had just one stop to make, one smoking gun to plant. It was poetic, really. One betrayal in exchange for another. Jack Carroll thought he could send Mint to the cops, and now Mint would send the cops to him.

CHAPTER 41
NOW

The whole world ended with Mint's words. Everything I thought I knew gone in the blink of an eye, our past scratched out and written over with the truth, the words dark and terrible. And I was going straight to hell, because the first thought that crossed my mind when Mint unraveled was, *I won.*

Ten years ago, on Valentine's Day, Mint had stormed out of Sweetheart, snuck into my room, and stabbed Heather seventeen times because he thought she was me. Heather was always taking what was mine, and the secret of her murder—the great, intractable mystery of her death—was that she'd simply done it one too many times.

It had been about me this whole time.

Then the shock cleared, and my next thought was, *My body is turning inside out.* I leaned over and threw up everything inside my stomach, acid bitter in my mouth.

The room exploded into noise.

"You *killed* her," Eric screamed, lunging for Mint, but Mint was too fast, twisting away from him to the corner of the room where the shattered window met the wall. He bent and scooped something from the floor, gripping it like a dagger in his right hand. It was a massive, jagged piece of glass. A line of blood snaked down his wrist from where he held it, the same crimson as the Duquette polo he wore.

"Nobody come close," Mint warned.

"Mint, it can't be true," Caro said. "Take it back. You wouldn't do that." She clutched her chest. "You're our friend."

Mint pointed the glass dagger at me. "Where *were* you that night?" He spun to Coop. "With the professor, or *him*?"

My heart was pounding so fast it was going to break through my chest.

Courtney grunted, an unladylike sound, and her eyes rolled back in her head. Caro shrieked, but before she could do anything to stop it, Courtney wobbled, knees bending in unnatural directions, then collapsed on the floor. Caro dropped to her knees and pressed her fingers to Courtney's throat. "Her heart's beating. Oh my god."

"She just fainted, Caro. I've seen it on the field. It's going to be okay." Slowly, Frankie turned from Caro to Mint, his hands spread wide in supplication. "Mint, why don't you put the glass down. This isn't you. Put it down and we'll talk it out." He took a hopeful step forward.

"Stay back!" Mint hissed. His golden hair was disheveled, flipped over his forehead so you could only see one of his eyes, making him look a little mad. Perfect Mint, campus big shot, heir to a real estate empire, king of the East House Seven. A killer.

Eric ignored Mint's warning, stalking toward him. "You planted the scissors in Jack's room." It wasn't a question but a puzzle piece fitting into place. "You framed one of your best friends, threw him to the wolves. Sat back and watched his life go down in flames because of what *you* did. All our lives. And then what, you kept dating the girl you tried to kill, just to keep up appearances?"

That's right. *Oh god.* Mint had come to me after Heather died, drowning in an ocean of emotion he could barely keep contained—guilt and fear and anger. I'd assumed it was survivor's guilt, nothing more than an intense reaction to what had happened to our friend. I could remember now. He hadn't let me touch him for hours, nearly a whole night, even as he'd insisted we recommit to our relationship. And I—awash in my own misery and guilt—had been grateful for the lifeline, the chance to make my life normal again. I was desperate to feel the way Mint used to make me feel—like I was valuable, a somebody.

I grimaced as I remembered the night he'd broken up with me in New York, the way he'd looked at me with revulsion when I'd begged him not to. That had been a glimpse of the true Mint, what he really felt. Everything else had been a lie, carefully calculated by a man who'd actually tried to kill me. My first real boyfriend, who for a few triumphant seconds in the dark thought he really had done it.

My legs went weak. I dropped, unable to hold myself up.

Mint's steel eyes turned to me as I knelt, taking measure of me in that way he had. But this time, instead of wanting to straighten my spine and stand taller, I wanted to cower. To be anywhere other than where he could find me.

"Jack was going to report me to the cops for hurting Trevor," Mint said, his voice cold and detached, almost thoughtful. "I never felt bad about what I did to him. But you—I did feel bad about you. Really. I tried to forgive you for Garvey, to move on in New York. I figured if I could just get rid of my anger, that goddamn fire in my chest, I could wipe the slate clean. But I couldn't. And it turns out I shouldn't have even tried to forgive you, because it wasn't just Garvey. It was *him*, too." He pointed the tip of the glass at Coop, whose gaze was already locked on Mint, eyes narrowed, shoulders tensed.

"For that, I'm going to finish what I started," Mint said. For a second, I thought he was talking to Coop—he was still looking at him. But then he turned to me, his eyes strangely vacant, and I knew the truth. Of course. It was me he hated. Me who'd turned him into his father.

His voice was so measured. "I'm going to do it right this time. You did everything you could to humiliate me, and now you have to pay, for balance. I—"

Eric rushed him in a burst of speed, but Mint reacted quickly, meeting Eric with his foot, kicking him square in the chest. Eric hit the floor hard, hands catching the glass shards. They turned bright with blood.

Coop lunged, trying to take advantage of Mint's distraction, but Mint twisted away and slashed Coop with his jagged glass, making a vicious line across Coop's chest. Caro screamed as Coop staggered, clutching the long gash, his T-shirt gaping open.

I fell backwards to the floor. It was one thing to hear Mint's confession, another to see him strike his friend and draw blood. The surprise must have caught Frankie, too, because he paused his forward momentum, giving Mint the precious seconds he needed to thrust his hand inside Coop's pocket and wrestle out the lighter he'd known Coop would be carrying. He flicked up a flame, as fluid as Coop had taught him to be.

"Don't—" Caro started to get up from where she crouched near Courtney, but Mint leapt past her to the stack of old newspapers and touched the flame to the paper. For one glorious instant it seemed nothing happened, but then the fire spilled from the lighter, racing over the newspaper, and suddenly it was ablaze. The fire caught the arm of a nearby couch, licking across the cushions, until it covered the couch like a blanket.

Mint was setting the room on fire. We'd discovered his secret, and now he was going to kill us.

Eric had rolled to his knees, still struggling to breathe from Mint's kick, and now he and Frankie grabbed Coop's shoulders—ignoring his moan, the hand pressed to his chest—and pulled him back, away from the flames. Caro was trying with every ounce of her strength to pull the deadweight of Courtney's body toward the doorway.

As Mint rose, the fire rose also, as if a cobra, entranced. It was so hot I could feel it on my skin, even across the distance. And it was growing bigger, engulfing the old couches to form a wall between me and my friends. Between me and the door.

Leaving me and Mint on the other side. Alone, together.

He turned to me, dropped the lighter, and smiled.

I scrambled backwards, toward the cool air of the broken window, but Mint closed the distance between us too fast, seizing my leg with his free hand. I was too terrified to scream as he yanked me across the floor, my hands scraping the ground but finding no purchase.

Then I was underneath him, looking up at his face. Even crazed, even in disarray, he was still so beautiful. The best mask in the world. The boy who had everything, who no one would suspect. I breathed faster, coughing as I sucked in smoke. When had Mint become this other person—senior year? Junior? Had this been inside him all along, this dark potential? Should I have known freshman year, the day we sat on his bed, knees touching, and he'd told me what he'd done to his father, how good it had made him feel? Or even further back than that, the day he'd snapped over the drawing on the float?

He had shown me slivers of who he was. And instead of recoiling, I'd leaned toward him. Because he was Mint. The prince of Duquette.

I choked again, and all the while Mint was leaning over me, sinking closer. Why wasn't I fighting? What power did he have over me, what spell had he cast that kept me, even now, in his thrall?

"Why?" I managed to ask, pushing the word out past the ache in my throat.

Mint ignored me, eyes flicking over my neck, my lips, my cheekbones. "You know, my father tried to kill himself. The week of Sweetheart. I never told anyone until now."

Danger, get away. I tried to roll, but he caught me by the throat, his large hand squeezing painfully. I thrashed, gasping, my arms and legs slick with sweat from the fire, but Mint held me fast.

"He failed everyone, so he took the coward's way out. But I'm not like him. I fix my mistakes." Instead of shocking me, Mint's words rang with a painful familiarity. And I realized: our fathers were alike. They'd walked similar paths, and all this time, Mint and I had hidden it from each other. My whispered words from over a decade ago floated back: *I think I hate my father, too.* Maybe we were the same. Mint and Jessica: two sides of the same coin.

Mint squeezed my neck, and I felt my windpipe constrict. Red flooded my vision, the whole world narrowing to a single, desperate need: *air.*

He leaned in, pressing his lips to my ear like a lover, like he'd done a thousand times before. "You're a terrible person," he whispered. "I want you to die knowing that."

Then he plunged the jagged glass into my side.

Pain. It was an electric shock, a strike of lightning, the burning heat of thousands of nerves dying. I wrenched against his hand, the world closing in—the thickening smoke, his unrelenting grip, the pain—*the pain*—worse than I'd ever known.

He pulled back to stab me again and I saw it, like déjà vu: I was going to die like Heather. She'd taken my place ten years ago, giving me a decade-long reprieve, but now fate was back to claim me.

Suddenly Mint toppled sideways, his hand freeing my throat, the jagged glass flying out of his grip. Coop and Frankie were on him, their shirts and pants smoking, their skin a bright, scary red. They'd pushed through the wall of flames. Coop wrapped his arms around Mint's shoulders, twisting him away, and I lurched backwards, screaming when the movement ripped open my side.

I pressed my hand over the wound and made myself keep

moving, even though I couldn't tear my eyes from where Mint wrestled Frankie and Coop, the three of them tumbling over the broken glass.

I gulped air that was mostly smoke, ignoring the pain in my throat. The room was in flames. I could only see the top of Caro's head over the fiery wall of couches, and I couldn't see Courtney at all. Where was Eric? We needed to leave, now.

Sharp movement snapped my attention back to the fight. Mint tried to shove Coop, but Frankie wrestled him to the ground, pinning his arms, both their chests heaving, sweat rolling from their temples. The look on Mint's red face was monstrous. "Get off me!" he screamed, kicking his legs, but Frankie held on.

Mint changed tacks. "Frankie," he begged, "you're my best friend. Let me go—we can talk."

Frankie's face was an open book, his struggle—pain and confusion, love and regret—written across it plainly. Nearly two decades he'd worshipped Mint, been steadfastly devoted. But now he closed his eyes and shook his head, gripping Mint tighter.

Flames crept to my shoe; I yanked my foot back, clutching again at the pain in my side. Coop's head jerked in my direction.

"We have to get out of here," I yelled. "This place is going to burn down."

Coop looked down at Mint, then back at me, nodding. He turned to Frankie. "Pull him up, then let's run. But don't let go, okay?"

Frankie nodded, and together, they yanked Mint to his feet and pushed him forward.

I stood, eyes stinging, blood warm and sticky against my fingers, and followed, trying to track them through the smoke. Over their shoulders, I could finally see Caro, still grunting and tugging Courtney's body toward the door. She was so close.

In front of me, Mint jerked. And I knew instantly what he was thinking: no matter what happened to us, Caro and Courtney, at least, would escape. Caro would tell everyone what happened here, what Mint had confessed. He was a goner.

I opened my mouth to shout a warning, but Mint was too fast. He snapped and twisted out of Frankie's and Coop's grasp, shooting backwards, past me to the corner of the room, where the open window met the wall.

"*Wait*," he screamed as Coop and Frankie doubled back for him. "I'm sorry, okay?" Mint bent over, panting, his eyes two blue dots in a sea of red. He raised his hands in surrender. "I'm sorry for everything I've done. All of it, truly."

Frankie and Coop froze in surprise. In that moment, I could hear shouting from far below. The Homecoming parade—of course. They'd come to the end of the route, and now they were gathered underneath Blackwell Tower. And it was lit with flames, billowing smoke.

Mint looked at me. And to my shock, his eyes filled with tears. "I'm sorry, Jess. There's something wrong with me. I've known it ever since that night. I'll get help."

"Mint—" My voice caught.

"Forgive me, please," he begged. "I'll do anything, I promise. I'll turn myself in. We can salvage this. I'll—"

Out of the wall of fire, a body flew toward Mint. *Eric.* They slammed together, shoulders cracking against shoulders, tumbling until Eric seized control, drawing Mint up onto his hands and his knees. Then— too fast for me to stop it, too fast even for the scream ripping from my throat—Eric pushed Mint out the open window.

I might have only imagined it, like a waking dream, but for a single second, Mint's body floated among the trees, his eyes stark and wide against the sky. And I knew, with all my heart and soul, that I'd loved him, and he'd been good and wicked, and in the dark, secret part of me, we were so much the same.

And then he plunged.

My scream ended only when we heard the terrible, unmistakable crunch of his body hitting pavement. And then everything was drowned in the thunderous noise of hundreds of people shouting and stampeding below us.

Mint's body had fallen from the top of Blackwell Tower in full view of the parade.

Mint was dead. I reeled with it for a second, somehow cold with shock in a burning room. And then something strange happened. Everything clicked into place. I knew exactly what to do.

"Get back!" I shouted to Eric. He turned to me, defiant, but I kept yelling. "Get away from the window. Everyone will see you."

"Jess." Coop rushed toward me, Frankie behind him.

"All of you, *back*," I screamed. The heat from the fire was stinging my skin, making my fingers slippery with sweat. Behind the flames, I could see Caro—her shocked face, wide eyes staring at me from where she stood, paralyzed in the doorway.

"*I* killed Mint," I said, my voice rough. "Do you hear me? *I* pushed him out the window. He killed Heather because he thought she was me, and today he tried to finish the job. You all heard him. He wanted me dead."

"*What?*" Frankie asked.

"If the cops know Mint surrendered and Eric pushed him anyway, Eric will go to prison."

"I don't care," Eric said. "I knew what I was doing."

I looked at him. In that moment, his hard veneer—ten years of doggedness, pursuing justice when no one else would, clear-eyed and coldhearted—wavered. And I could see the skinny freshman boy he'd once been. It was that boy who'd devoted his life to arriving at this moment. That boy who was willing, in the end, to give up his freedom to see his sister's killer dead.

"I promised her justice," he said softly.

I shoved him behind me and stepped to the window. "It was self-defense. See?" I lifted my bloody hand from my side. "He stabbed me, so I pushed him." I looked at Coop and Frankie. "Promise me, right now. Say I did it."

"You did it," Frankie said roughly.

"Coop," I warned. "Say it."

"You did it," he whispered, but his eyes begged me: *Let me pull you from the window, let me save you.*

But it was time I made a different kind of choice.

Sweeping aside glass, I climbed to the edge of the window, making myself visible to the crowd below. It was cooler here, the smoke mixing with crisp air. Below, a ring of people circled Mint's body, ignoring shouts from firefighters who raced up behind them. Some of the Homecoming crowd was running from the parade in fear. But the rest—the majority—gazed up, transfixed by the sight of me. The red-faced, bloody girl, blond hair whipping behind her, standing atop the tower, criminal and defiant.

Gasps spread among the crowd. Arms lifted, fingers pointing. "*She pushed him,*" someone yelled, clear and loud enough to carry up to me.

In front of the whole world: *Jessica Miller, villain.*

Sirens cut through the noise, and I saw, with my bird's-eye view, dazzling red and blue lights. Cop cars speeding toward us, parting the crowd like the Red Sea.

One last moment of freedom. I took a deep breath of cool air, heavy with the scent of magnolias. Looked back at the crowd, and this time I spotted him. Right there at the edge, his face tilted up, mouth set in a hard line. I nearly lost my footing.

Jack.

CHAPTER 42
MAY, SOPHOMORE YEAR

For the first time in a long time, it was just the three of us. Movie night, my favorite, worth suffering through whatever early-aughts film Caro had chosen to see her happy, to see Heather shake her head with secret affection, to lock the door and curl on Caro's bed and leave the rest of the world on the other side.

Tonight, it felt like we'd dialed time back to freshman year. Just me, Heather, and Caro, before everything else had washed in and made life complicated.

The window was open. The night was dark and hushed, not a sound from campus except for the gentle swish of tree branches in the warm breeze. Sprawled at our feet on the twin bed, Caro snored softly, the credits to *Cruel Intentions* still rolling on mute.

I scooted closer to Heather and rested my head on her shoulder. My feet brushed Caro, but she didn't wake. I sighed. "I don't want this year to end. I wish I could stay right here forever."

Heather's cheek rubbed the top of my head. "If you don't want to go home for the summer, come with me to Cleveland. We can do sleepovers every night. We'll swim at the club and get wasted on daiquiris and flirt with the tennis instructors."

I rolled my eyes to cover the fact that she'd zeroed in on exactly what I was dreading. "Do our boyfriends exist in this scenario?"

Heather laughed. "What Jack and Minty don't know won't hurt them. Come on. I want a summer-break buddy. We can call you an intern and my dad can pay you."

I groaned, feeling the weight of everything I'd been ignoring so I could have fun tonight drop back on my shoulders. "I can't. I have to start studying for the GRE."

Heather lay down flat on the bed, rustling Caro, who snored on. She crossed her arms, and I knew what was coming. "Jessica Marie Miller, you are a *sophomore*. That word is synonymous with *zero responsibilities*. I know I say this a lot, but loosen up. You have two whole years to think about your future. I see you studying like crazy every night, freaking out over every test. It looks miserable."

I shook my head. Our arms touched, which made me feel warm and safe, like I could be honest. "I have to go to grad school for econ and work in DC." *Like my dad planned*, I thought to myself, but didn't say out loud.

"You have the most specific, boring dreams," Heather complained.

I shifted onto my side. "Yeah, well, first I have to get perfect grades at Duquette. Then perfect grades in grad school. And then, maybe, I can live a little." I was certain I'd have a shot if I worked hard enough. I tucked that certainty into a warm place in my heart.

"Perfect, perfect, perfect," Heather teased, snuggling closer. "You're obsessed with that word. You know no one is actually perfect, right?"

The unkind thought came quickly: *Easy for her to say*. She somehow managed to get everything she wanted without having to worry about earning it. She was the exception to the rule.

I swallowed the thought and decided to tell her the truth. "I want to make my parents proud." No more *sorry to inform you.* "I want to look back in ten years and know I did everything right." No more *second place,* no more *punching down.*

Heather shifted, staring at the ceiling, eyes tracing the little glow-in-the-dark stars Caro had stuck there. Caro, forever obsessed with what she wasn't allowed to have when she was young.

"In ten years," Heather said slowly, "you're not even going to remember the things that seem important now. You're going to have totally different priorities. I bet you'll look back and laugh at everything that feels so dramatic now."

She yawned and bumped my shoulder. "We'll still be friends, of course, so in ten years, I'll remind you we had this conversation. You're going to laugh. Trust me."

She got excited and turned on her side. "I just had the best idea. Let's do predictions! I'm super good at them. I'll bet you a million dollars that ten years from now, I'm famous."

"How?" I asked, but Heather shrugged. "Don't know. I like my archaeology class. Maybe I'll be the female Indiana Jones. Or Hollywood's hottest plastic surgeon. But most likely reality TV."

"I thought you said you're going to major in English."

"I'll figure it out along the way. Whatever it is, it'll be great." She smirked. "I bet Mint runs his dad's company and Frankie works for him as his secretary."

I thought about Mint, who of course was destined for power, the ley lines running straight through him. Inheriting a real estate empire seemed a surefire way to do it. But then I thought of how Mint felt about his father, the secret shame he'd shared with me.

"There's no way Mint takes over the business. But you're right that whatever Mint does, Frankie will find a way to follow. What about Coop?" I pressed down the little thrill at saying his name, the memory of the way he'd looked at me on the beach over spring break.

Heather snorted. "Coop will either be a lawyer getting people out of jail or locked in jail himself."

I frowned. "Just because he smokes pot doesn't mean he's a criminal."

She patted my head. "Sometimes you're adorable." She glanced down at Caro, curled at our feet. "Caro says she wants to be a film critic. But that's not suited for her. She'll be, like, the president of the Humane Society. Some job where everyone is obligated to love her."

"*Heather*," I hissed, trying to keep my voice low so Caro wouldn't wake and hear.

"Listen, I call it like I see it. Jack, by the way, will end up a minister. At a Southern Baptist church in Georgia. Probably the same crazy one his parents go to."

"Oh, please," I scoffed. "Now you're just being silly."

"Just wait." Heather gave me a knowing look. "College is a vacation for Jack. He gets four years to be free, but he'll have to go back eventually. He's on borrowed time. Besides, he cares way more about his parents' approval than he lets on."

I let the possibility sink in. Was Jack on a temporary reprieve, destined to go backwards after college, rather than forward? He was always so lighthearted when he joked about his evangelical parents, their strict lifestyle, the judgmental church. Was the joking a way of making it light, making himself okay with going back?

I looked at Heather. "And you're fine with that?"

She snorted. "Jack is lucky he met me. I'm what guarantees his life will always be interesting." She twisted on the bed. "But *you*. Jessica Miller, the wildcard. Maybe you'll go work your boring DC job like some wonky nerd. But I have a feeling you'll surprise us."

"Pssh," I said, though I was secretly thrilled. "No way."

"Just wait." Heather lay back down and cuddled close to me. We pressed our heads together and looked out the window at the outline of the trees. "Whatever happens, we're going to be happy, okay? I promise.

So you can stop worrying." She took my hand and squeezed it. "Ten years from now, we're going to be on top of the world together. You and me, looking down on everyone else, laughing and laughing."

CHAPTER 43
NOW

The cops shoved me through the angry crowd, pushing me forward by my shoulders. My arms were wrenched painfully behind my back, hands locked in cold metal cuffs. Someone yelled, "*Murderer!*" and someone else echoed it. Instead of backing away, the crowd pressed closer, their faces hardening against me.

I couldn't help but think of the daydream I'd had just two days ago: becoming the center of attention, the shining Homecoming queen. The star of the show.

Look at me now.

I gritted my teeth and shouldered forward.

"Get back," the cop behind me yelled, and people grudgingly made room for us to pass. Campus had descended into chaos, everyone shouting and running, ambulances and fire trucks wailing. I'd caught the barest glimpse of Caro in the back of an ambulance before they'd slammed the doors and rushed off.

Caro and the others were being taken care of, treated carefully for burns and smoke inhalation. I was a different story. As soon as the fire-men cleared the inferno at the top of the tower, they'd shuffled me down the winding staircase, where I'd been met by a wave of cops. They had seized me, barely adjusting their grips when I screamed I'd been stabbed in the side. They'd asked if I was the one who'd pushed the man from the window, and when I said yes, they'd shoved me down the steps, ignoring my protests, my gasps of pain.

If I'd known what was waiting for me when we emerged out of the doors of Blackwell Tower, I might have refused to ever leave, taken my chances with the burning room.

There was a wall of people, horror and accusation in their eyes. People I'd gone to college with, shock on their faces, tears streaking their cheeks. I'd killed Mint, the golden boy. They didn't know he was a murderer. Only that I was.

I was living a scene from a nightmare. But it was going to be okay, because Caro and Eric and everyone else were being taken care of. *Everything was going to be okay.*

I'd repeated it as they twisted my hands into cuffs, pinching the skin and pulling the cut in my side as the crowd barely shifted to let me through, wanting to see me up close, the murderess, the witch of Blackwell Tower.

Now, as the cops pushed me toward the last remaining ambulance, I caught sight of the Homecoming stage where Frankie should have stood next to the chancellor, giving a speech to rile the crowd. Instead, the stage was empty, balloon arch swaying in the wind. The dumbfounded chancellor stood gaping at the madness around him: Blackwell Tower, the symbol of Duquette, still smoking; Homecoming, the event of the year, descended into mayhem.

The sight of the chancellor shook something loose inside me. I twisted, trying to face the cop who was pushing me forward. "He killed Heather," I said urgently. "Mint, the man on the ground. You have to believe me. He killed Heather Shelby, and he was going to kill me. I pushed him to save my life. It was self-defense."

The cop shoved me harder. "Save the excuses for your lawyer."

It was too late; I faced the ambulance, and the doors swung open, medics rushing out. But before they touched me, a figure darted forward, pushing frantically through the crowd.

"*Jessica,*" Jack yelled.

The medics turned me so the cop could unlock my cuffs. I craned my neck to find Jack's face. "What the hell are you doing here?"

Jack looked like he was about to explode. "What am *I*... What are *you* doing? What happened?"

Suddenly, it hit me. *He didn't know about Heather.* My knees went weak, and the medics grabbed me, holding me upright. "Jack, Mint killed Heather. He's the one."

Jack froze. "*Mint?*"

The medics were cutting off my shirt with scissors to look at the wound in my side, exposing me to everyone. But that was the least of my problems. "He thought she was me. It was me he was after."

"I don't understand." Jack tried to step closer, but a cop forced him back with a forearm across Jack's chest.

Now that they'd found my stab wound, the medics were lifting me into the ambulance. I twisted, finding Jack's eyes.

"I'll explain everything," I promised, raising my voice. "He confessed. Then he tried to kill me again and I pushed him. It was self-defense."

Jack stopped struggling against the cop. He stood stock-still, wonder dawning on his face. "I can't believe it worked," he said, so faint that I almost didn't hear. "The plan actually worked."

"*What?*" The medics strapped me into the gurney, pressing something against my cut to clean it, something that burned like fire, but in that moment I didn't care.

Jack ducked under the cop's arms and ran for the ambulance doors.

"I was going to tell you," he called. "Before you left, at the bar, I was going to warn you. Eric had been writing me letters for months. We'd come up with a plan. He said I couldn't trust anyone, and I—" Jack looked ashamed. "I decided not to chance it. Some part of me thought it could've been you."

Two cops caught up to Jack and wrestled him back, but his eyes stayed on me, desperate with apology.

Jesus. Jack had been in on it the whole time. He and Eric, two of the only people in the world who thought Jack was innocent, plotting to use Homecoming to unmask Heather's true killer. And Jack had almost warned me, excluded me from the suspect list. Then he'd thought better of it.

I tilted my head back and laughed, so loud it stilled the medics. They eyed me warily, but I kept laughing, the sound filling the small space.

"Jack," I called, right before the ambulance doors swung shut. "You have good instincts."

CHAPTER 44
THE SUMMER BEFORE HIGH SCHOOL

I woke to soft Virginia sunshine and the sensation—the finely honed human instinct—that someone was sneaking up on me. I had only enough time to register my brightly lit bedroom ceiling before they pounced.

"Happy birthday," my father yelled, landing next to me in bed.

"*Ah*," I shrieked, rolling away from him.

He laughed. "It's just us."

I lifted my head, heart hammering. Sure enough, there was my dad, stretched out on my bed, grinning, and my mom, standing in the doorway with a cake, candle flames flickering light over her face.

"It was your dad's idea," she said, scooting into the room. "Blame him."

"I wanted to surprise you," he said happily. "Cake for breakfast. It's not every day my princess turns fourteen."

His princess. The words were hollow. I wanted to be his princess too badly for it to be true. That was the way life worked, a lesson he'd taught me himself: *Wanting is dangerous. The less you want, the safer you'll be.* He was better nowadays, on a serious upswing, but the lesson had stuck.

My mother placed the cake in front of me, and I sat up straighter on the bed. "Make a wish," she said.

I looked at her, then my dad, closed my eyes, and blew. All the flames disappeared into tiny swirls of gray smoke, the smell faintly sweet, like burned sugar.

My dad bounced on the bed. "What'd you wish for?"

"You can't ask her that," my mom admonished, setting the cake on my desk. "If she tells you, it won't come true." She turned to me. "I'll cut that up in a second. First…"

Shockingly, my mom jumped on the other side of me, rocking the entire bed.

"Ah!" I shrieked again. My mother *never* played. What kind of alternate universe had I woken up in?

"Torture her until she tells us," my dad suggested and descended on me, tickling my sides. My mom joined him, and then I was gasping, rolling side to side, trying to protect myself but finding no recourse.

"Okay, okay!" I shouted.

They paused midtickle, my dad's hands curled like cartoon claws.

"I didn't wish for anything," I said.

My mom's face fell. "Nothing at all?"

My dad scooped me against his side. "I think that's great."

Alone on her side of the bed, my mom looked at him and raised her brows.

"You, princess, won't need to wish. You're going to *earn*." My dad looked down at me, beaming. "You're off to high school in a month. And you're going to work until you're the best student in the whole damn school. After that, the good things will come to you. 'Cause you'll deserve it."

"Stop it," my mom said softly. She was looking at him with the strang-est expression.

"What? I'm telling her to work hard to achieve things. That's a good lesson. I'm not saying things will get dropped in her lap. I'm saying if she's talented enough, and works hard enough, the world will deliver. It'd better, huh? I'm counting on it." My dad squeezed me tighter, and I let him, let myself think about how nice it felt, even though there was no guarantee he'd do it tomorrow. "Come on, you're going to make me proud."

I wanted to. A fierceness came over me. *I would.* If hard work and being good were what it took, I could do those things. If that could keep us in the sunlight, keep the darkness at bay, I would work at it every day.

"I promise," I said.

My dad laughed and kissed my forehead. And before my mom could say anything, he'd pulled her in, making us a three-person sandwich, me in the middle, my parents hugging me on either side.

Warmth flooded me.

"Just try your best," my mom whispered into my hair. "That's all you can do."

My dad pulled us closer. "My little family," he said. "You two are the best things in my life."

I caught my mother's eyes. She was smiling, telling me it was okay. "It was your dad's idea to surprise you," she said, tucking a strand of my hair.

"This is just the beginning," he said. "We've got a whole day of fun. I remembered a certain *someone* loves the zoo."

My mom rolled her eyes. "When she was eight. She's fourteen now."

He only laughed.

This version of my dad was surreal. I didn't know how to make sense of it, how to square it with the other version. Then a thought struck me: my dad was the angry man in the dark place, true. But maybe he was also this man—this bright and funny father. I'd always thought it was one or the other, fixed and definite. But maybe it was more complicated. Maybe he was both.

He kissed my forehead. "You're going to do great things, I'm telling you."

I buried my face in his shirt, and he put his arms loose around me, like he was making a basket with me in the center. If this upswing ever ended, and the darkness swallowed him again, maybe all hope wasn't lost. Maybe I could find a way to keep this version of my father with me. Then, no matter how bad it got, I could remember how he was now. Maybe that way he could keep being this person, even when he wasn't. Maybe then he could stay mine, stay warm and solid in my arms. Even one day, when he wasn't.

CHAPTER 45
NOW

I woke with wet cheeks to the five of them standing around my hospital bed, watching me. I jerked back, snapping the restraints that kept me bound to the bed, tugging painfully at my newly stitched side.

"Easy," Jack said, holding out his hands like he was placating a scared animal. "Didn't mean to startle you. We need to talk."

I'd spent two days lying in this bed, staring at the white walls, giving one-word answers to a fast-talking lawyer who swore he was a friend of Coop's and would keep me out of jail. Two days of skipping past the local news, first with its nonstop coverage of the Homecoming Queen Killer, the Femme Fatale of Blackwell Tower—my picture flashing, a wildly unflattering photo someone must have pulled from the depths of social media. And then the one-eighty flip to *Breaking News: Shocking Developments in the Heather Shelby Cold Case*, an image of Mint, one of his professional headshots, and then Heather, looking so unbearably young. Two days without my phone, without word from anyone, wondering where the hell they were, what they were doing.

Last night I'd finally given up on seeing them. Fallen asleep with the understanding that I'd made my choices, and now, as a consequence, I was going to be alone for a long time. Maybe forever.

And that's when it happened. Sometime in the night, the final puzzle piece fell into place, and I remembered the whole truth of the night Heather died. But "remembered"—that wasn't right, was it? After this weekend, I knew better.

I'd had the pieces inside all along, a quilt of light and dark, but for years I'd refused to look. When had my body first tried to tell me the truth? Was it the moment in Blackwell when Mint confessed what he'd done, and I felt the heart-quickening pang of sameness? When Eric shoved him out the window, and I was flooded with adrenaline, with the urge to offer myself in Eric's place? Or was it when I jumped off the float and ran through the crowd, legs driven by a guilt I was only just finding words for?

Whatever the answer was, I woke after two days of solitude with the last memory in my head, only to find the five of them staring at me. And my first thought was: *They know.* Every horrible, incriminating detail I'd just dredged out of the black hole, like a bloated corpse from a lake, they knew, and they'd come to see me punished.

"The police aren't going to charge you," Coop said, filling the silence. I could only stare, heart pounding. "It's a solid case of self-defense, and Davis—your lawyer—is working his magic. It should only be a day or two before you're free to go."

Coop's face, like Frankie's and Eric's, was still pink and shiny from the fire. When he spoke, his hand hovered almost unconsciously over the place in his chest where Mint stabbed him. But his expression was neutral—like he was taking pains to be businesslike. I looked closer at each of their faces. No accusatory stares, no *We know what you did* hinted on their faces.

I calmed. They didn't know. But of course not; how could they?

Frankie adjusted his tie. He was wearing a sharply tailored blue suit, dressed like he was headed to the ESPYs. "We all told the cops the same story. You pushed him in self-defense."

There was a moment of heavy silence, and then Jack stepped forward, lowering his voice. "We can talk openly here. The cop guarding you went for a cigarette."

Jack, Eric, Coop, and Frankie studied me grimly. Caro, whose arms were crossed tight over her chest, wouldn't meet my gaze.

I sat up straighter and wiped my eyes. "Where's Courtney?"

"Rehab," Coop said. "Her parents came and shipped her off. Apparently extreme stress didn't mix well with the pills she takes. That's why she fainted in Blackwell. They're trying to hush it up."

"Good luck," Eric muttered. "It won't stay buried forever."

It felt like a warning. I bit my tongue and tasted iron.

"Courtney can follow Mint to hell for all I care," Caro said suddenly. "After what she did, drugging Heather."

The room chilled. The words were harsh, but maybe the harshest part was that they came from Caro. I remembered something I'd said to her once when I was annoyed—maybe sophomore year, maybe junior: *Caro, toughen up or the world is going to chew you.*

Well, she'd toughened. After we'd broken her.

Frankie spoke carefully, eyeing Caro. "It's a good thing Courtney's hiding, anyway, with the media shitstorm over Mint. I gave her mom the number of my PR guy, but there's only so much you can do when you're the wife of a famous murderer."

I looked at him. "Everyone knows Mint killed Heather?"

He nodded. "We told the cops first, but then we talked to the reporters."

"We went to the *Journal*," Jack said, "and found the reporter who'd covered Heather's case ten years ago." His face darkened. "The one who was so convinced I did it. Who smeared me and would never take down those old stories. Boy, was he surprised to see me."

"We didn't come here to chat," Caro snapped. "Let's get on with it."

Jack glanced at her. "Right." His voice lowered. "We're the only people alive who know what happened at Blackwell. We need to swear to each other we'll take the truth to our graves. If the cops ever found out the real story, Eric would go away for a long time. The law's pretty black and white when it comes to killing people, even if they killed your sister first."

What would the law say about me?

"Not to mention," Eric said, "the minute the cops got hold of my laptop, with all my research on it, they'd have a strong case for premeditation."

I studied him. His tone was dry, like this was all vaguely amusing. What was he feeling, now that his sister's death was solved, her killer dead by his hands? Peace, or purposelessness? His face was drawn, like he hadn't slept for days. Was he still haunted?

"Before you ask me, yes, Jack and I have files on you all," Eric continued. He rubbed a hand over his eyes. "And it's not the nicest stuff."

Frankie, Coop, and Caro shifted almost imperceptibly away from him.

"Are you planning to delete those files?" Coop asked.

Eric shrugged at Jack. "His decision. He's the one who supplied most of the real damning stuff. You know, the little tidbits about what made you all tick, what your vices were, who you were jealous of. Helped me put the pieces together."

Quid pro quo, I guess. For ten years we'd blamed Jack and ignored Eric. In return, they'd combed through our faults and orchestrated a plan to extract our confessions.

Jack rested a hand on Eric's shoulder. "We'll delete the files. This is a cease-fire. Nobody wants to see Eric in prison, or any of your secrets leaked."

Our secrets. I looked at my friends. For all our closeness, I'd still missed so much. How well had I ever really known them?

"I swear to let Jessica take all the blame for Mint's death," Caro said curtly. "Can I go now?"

"I swear, too." Coop's eyes slid toward Caro, but she kept her gaze carefully averted.

"I won't say a word," Frankie promised.

"And I vow to take it to my grave," Jack said.

They all looked at me, waiting. "It was me," I whispered. Saying the words was intoxicating. So close to a real confession.

Eric nodded, his mouth set in a grim line. "Thank you."

Caro straightened. "I'm done. From here on out, I want nothing to do with the East House Seven. I never want to see any of you insane, terrible people for the rest of my life." She turned her glare to Coop. "*Any* of you."

She moved to leave, then twisted back to look at me. Her dark eyes burned holes in my face. I became acutely aware that I was an accused criminal, chained to a hospital bed. "You want to know the saddest part?" Her voice wasn't angry anymore. It was speculative. "Even now, to this day, I think you were the love of my life. You were always talking about your dreams, back in college. Harvard this and DC that. Well, you want to know what my dream was? You. A real best friend."

My eyes burned. Caro's voice softened. "I would have done anything for you."

Before I could say a single word of apology, Caro spun and stalked out of the room, leaving all of us staring at her back.

I met Coop's eyes for a second. He drew a sharp breath. "I have to go, too," he said. "Davis will let you know when the police officially clear you."

"Coop, wait—" I sat up, struggling against the restraints, but he ignored me, clutching his hair and following Caro out of the room.

I sat, stunned. I'd risked it and lost them both.

Jack cleared his throat. "Despite what Caro thinks, you should know they think you're a hero."

"What? Who?"

He smiled. "Everyone. The girl who saved herself and avenged her friend's killer."

"I thought I was the 'Femme Fatale of Blackwell Tower.'"

Frankie snorted.

"After the *Journal* published the real story," Jack said, "there was immediate outcry. Some stranger set up a GoFundMe account to raise your bail in case you needed it. Reached the goal in less than twenty-four hours."

"Why would anyone do that?"

He looked at me incredulously. "Because you were almost killed by your ex-boyfriend. The same man who killed one of your best friends. See yourself through their eyes. You did the only thing you could to save your life. You're the victim *and* the hero. No one wants to see you behind bars."

See yourself through their eyes. It was all I'd ever wanted. To see who I was, reflected back at me. *Jessica the victim, Jessica the hero. Exceptional Jessica.* But everyone was wrong. Now I knew that couldn't be further from the truth.

Eric scrubbed his hands over his face and took a deep breath. "My parents said to thank you for getting justice for Heather."

The wrongness of it was searing. If Heather's parents only knew the truth.

"Will you ever tell them you're the one who pushed Mint?"

He turned away. "Maybe. I don't know. Two years ago, they told me to stop investigating her death because it was ruining my life. They were ready to accept we'd never know the truth, but I wasn't. It caused a divide." He sighed. "I thought I'd want the vindication, but now, I'm just tired. It feels like I haven't slept for years." He cleared his throat. "I have to pick them up from the airport. They wanted to be here in person during the Mint investigation. They sounded so…young, on the phone. When I told them the news. Like ten years just fell away. Maybe I should let them have that and not complicate it."

"But what will you do now?"

He gave me a weary look. "Quit the Alumni Office, for one. Get the hell out of North Carolina. After that, I don't know. Heather always wanted to travel…"

He turned to Jack and held out his hand. "Thank you for helping me after everything I did to make your life hell. I owe you."

Jack ignored Eric's hand and wrapped his arms around him. "Thanks for believing me."

Eric nodded at Frankie, and with one last glance down at me—at the restraints, tying me to the bed—he took a deep breath and walked out the door.

I struggled with what to say, how to express my lingering worry about Eric, but before I could, Frankie blurted, "I'm going on the *Today* show."

Jack blinked. "What?"

Frankie's cheeks turned red. "To talk about being out in the NFL. During the parade, I—"

Jack waved a hand. "I saw."

A beat of silence. Frankie took a deep breath, and so did I.

Jack looked at him out of the corner of his eye. "I was proud of you."

A slow smile spread over Frankie's face. "You want to know the best part?"

"Let me guess. Your Twitter following jumped by a hundred thousand people overnight?"

Frankie frowned. "It wasn't a business decision, Jack. Come on."

I felt that overwhelming sense that I shouldn't be here.

"Allow me my cynicism. I've earned it. Especially when it comes to you."

They looked at each other for a long time, something passing between them. Then the ghost of a smile appeared on Jack's face, and he rolled his eyes. "All right, Frank. Tell me. What's the best part?"

"My dad is coming with me to the *Today* show."

"He is?" I blurted.

Frankie nodded, though he was still watching Jack. "Telling him wasn't at all like I thought."

Jack swallowed. "I'm glad."

"Jack, I'm sorry I ever thought—"

Jack shook his head. "Hey, Frankie? Don't."

Frankie looked like he wanted to protest. But after a second, he just nodded. "I understand." His gaze slid to me. "I guess I'll go, then. Hang in there, Jess."

"I'll watch the show," I offered. "Assuming I'm not in jail."

He gave me a weak smile, stole one last glance at Jack, and left, shoulders spanning nearly the width of the doorway before they disappeared.

Jack sank onto my bed and sighed. "Hallelujah. All alone." He nodded at my restraints. "I know how that feels. Just remember, I've got your back."

Jack Carroll, so good, all the way through. Willing to stick by my side through a murder investigation, even though no one had stuck by his.

"Hey," he said, as if he could read my mind. "For a little while you thought I might be capable of murder, and for a little while I thought you might be. That makes us even."

He didn't know the whole truth, so he didn't actually know what I was capable of, but I nodded anyway. "What else are friends for?"

"I've heard they're good for introducing to boyfriends. Will's here. Want to meet him?"

I jerked against the restraints, suppressing a curse. "You *brought* him? What happened to keeping the past separate?"

Jack's eyes searched the wall above my head. "When Eric and I first made this plan, I wasn't optimistic. I was worried Eric wouldn't be able to pull it off, get you guys to talk."

"He was a pretty effective interrogator, actually."

"Well, as much as I didn't want to be let down, I started having this dream that I finally got to come back, like a normal student. Show my boyfriend around campus, cheer on the Crimson, get my old coffee order at the Frothy Monkey. I decided no matter what, I wanted that dream to come true."

"And here you are."

He was silent for a moment. "I still can't believe it was Mint."

"I can. But I don't know how to explain."

Jack eyed me. "Well, you did know him best."

"No. No one knew Mint, it turns out."

We were quiet for a while. Then Jack smiled sadly. "Can you imagine what Heather would say if she was here?"

"She'd tell me I look awful in this hospital gown."

"She'd say it was about damn time we solved her case. And that she'll kill us if we ever forget her."

"I need you to know I loved her," I said, voice thick. "Please tell me you know."

"I know, Jess. Me too."

Jack leaned and placed a hand on my shoulder. "Listen. Before I go, I just want to say that I don't know what's going on between you and Coop—why he's dropping everything to stay here and fight to get your charges dropped—"

"He is?"

"And one day, I'm going to ask you about it." Jack let go of my shoulder and stood. "But today you get a reprieve."

Making peace with Jack was like taking an antidote to the twin poisons of anxiety and guilt. My need for forgiveness was so intense it was nearly physical. So I made a second vow, right there in that moment. A silent one, only to myself: for as long as I lived, I would never tell anyone else the truth of what I'd really done.

A day later, the same cop who'd dragged me burned and bleeding from Blackwell Tower uncuffed me from the hospital bed.

"No charges," he grunted. "Free to go."

I rubbed my wrists. "Thank you."

He squinted. "If it were up to me, you'd be behind bars, and we'd let a jury decide whether you're innocent. But I guess the court of public opinion won this time."

He waved me from the bed. I took a staggering step up, clutching the bed for balance.

"Clothes are on the chair. Get changed in the ladies' down the hall." The cop eyed me. "Wouldn't want to greet your adoring public looking like that."

I frowned as he hustled away, then shrugged and gathered the clothes—purchased by Jack at a Target nearby, bless him—and went to get dressed.

I was free. My hands shook and wouldn't stop as I dressed and washed my face. With nothing left to hold me, I wound through the hospital corridors and stepped out the front door. I took a deep gulp of crisp autumn air.

Then I heard yelling. Across the parking lot, a group of reporters were watching the entrance to the hospital like hawks. They must've been tipped off I was getting released today. I froze as they ran for me, the photographers lifting cameras, each click a bright pop that stung my eyes. The reporters belted questions:

"Jessica! How did it feel to push your college boyfriend to his death? What do you think about the allegations that he murdered Heather Shelby? How do you respond to her parents' statement that you're an avenging angel?"

I spun, looking for a way past them, but they swarmed me, blocking my path. *Oh god*, I'd never get to leave. I'd be trapped here, at the mercy of their prying questions. I stumbled back, clutching my side.

An engine rumbled, cutting off the reporters' questions. Like a mirage, Coop shot through the parking lot on a motorcycle, forcing reporters to jump out of his way. He slid to a stop right in front of me and flicked back the shield on his helmet.

"Get on."

It took only a moment for my brain to unfreeze before I ran and jumped on the back of his bike, clutching the helmet he tossed me. He revved the engine and turned us around. Over the noise I could see, rather than hear, the reporters, openmouthed and shouting as we gunned away.

We took off out of the parking lot in a burst of speed, winding through the streets, passing cafés where I used to study, bar patios where we used to drink buckets of beer, tree-lined streets I'd walked a million times. We passed East House, where it began, then Bishop Hall, where it ended, zooming past the Founder's Arch in a blur. Then we were really off, away from town, the streets growing less busy, wider and more rural. The wind whipped my hair and iced my skin, but I didn't care. We'd escaped.

After ten minutes driving through farmland, Coop slowed the motorcycle and pulled off near a grove of trees. Winston-Salem had started to turn brilliant-hued during the days I'd been in the hospital. The trees Coop parked in front of drooped with russet and burnt-orange-tinged leaves.

He rested the motorcycle on the kickstand, swung a long leg over it, and tugged off his helmet, letting his dark hair spring loose. I did the same, my stomach hollowing. Despite the cool air, sweat gathered at my neckline. What would he say? Where would I start?

Coop dropped his helmet on the ground and walked toward the trees, footsteps crunching. I followed. When he finally stopped, turning to face me, his back against a tree trunk, I felt every inch between us.

He pushed his hair off his face. "No more handcuffs."

"I heard I have you to thank."

"Remember in college when you told me I'd never be a lawyer because I was too much of a criminal? Should we take a few moments to soak in the irony?"

I crossed my arms. "Your humor is impeccably timed, as always."

"I'm partial to it."

"You have a motorcycle again."

He shrugged. "Rented it. I don't know, being back here makes me nostalgic." He looked up when I wasn't expecting it, and I was caught off guard by the brightness of his eyes. "Seriously, though. How are you? I heard Coldwell dropped you."

"I'm okay." I stepped forward and reached for the place on his chest where Mint slashed him, but stopped before I touched him. "You?"

Coop put his hand over mine and pressed them both to his chest. His shirt was cold against my fingers. "Just a scratch."

I withdrew my hand. I had to ask, even if some part of me was afraid of the answer. "What's happening with Caro?"

I knew what was coming: *We made up, and she's back at the hotel, waiting for me to say goodbye.* Or: *I threw myself at her mercy, and she forgave me.* Or: *She's home in Greenville, planning our wedding, and I'm just wrapping up loose ends.*

I closed my eyes.

"You heard her. She wants nothing to do with the East House Seven for the rest of her life. She left for her parents' house straight from the hospital."

I opened my eyes in surprise. "I know she hates us—but you?"

Coop's eyes told me the answer before he pressed his hands to his face. "I really fucked up."

"No, you didn't." I stepped closer. "I'm the one who ruined everything with what I said in Blackwell. I can't tell you how sorry I am. It was self-ish. I'll talk to her, I promise. I'll tell her it's one-sided. You can tell her, too."

Coop dropped his hands. "I did talk to her."

A chill breeze picked up, lifting my hair. I wrapped my arms over my chest. "But then…do you still need me to fix it?"

For some reason, this made Coop angry. He stepped away from the tree, putting distance between us. "You know, just because you were a martyr for Eric doesn't mean I think you're some big hero now."

My mouth dropped open. "I never said that. I'm not."

"You're damn right, you're not." Coop paced, then stopped. He stared me down. "I've known you since we were eighteen years old. Watched you closer than anyone. Do you want to know what I think?"

I was shaking my head, but he kept going.

"You're a narcissist. You've always been vain and petty and ego-driven. You have serious daddy issues and a fucked-up dating history— including, most notably, with me. You always take the safe route because you're scared. Case in point, your lame corporate job. You try so goddamn hard to make everything perfect because you're convinced that's the only way you'll deserve—what? Love? Life, even? And as far as the world is concerned, you pushed my college roommate out a window to his death. You're taking the fall, anyway, for reasons I honestly don't understand."

Maybe it was being back here in Winston-Salem, falling into familiar patterns; maybe it was the stress; or maybe I would always react this way to Coop's uncomfortable truths. Without thinking, I shoved him. He staggered back.

"Congratulations," I said. "You've managed to top your old record. Now *that's* the worst thing anyone's ever said to me. If you hate me so much, what are you—"

Coop seized my shoulders. "Let me finish. I get it. You're hungry. You want things so bad it hurts. You'd do anything to get them."

"Coop—"

"And I fucking love you for it, all right? I always have. One look at you freshman year, and I was doomed. I know it's wrong because of Caro. But it's *always* been wrong, for one reason or another. Never the right time. And Christ, never worse than now. But I can't hide from the truth any longer. Do the wrong thing with me, Jess. I promise, I will make you happy. I will love you for the rest of my life. I'm going to do it anyway; I accepted that a long time ago. But please. Do it with me."

Here it was again, the radical choice: be good or be happy. Thank god I had another chance to do it right.

I kissed him with ten years' worth of longing, pushing my fingers through his hair, the thick shock of it, the hair I'd watched him tuck and smooth and brush away so many times, without being able to touch it. He picked me up and walked me to the tree. I wrapped my legs around his waist and cupped his jaw. This time, I was the hungry one, the one who couldn't get close enough.

I pulled back. "I love you. I loved you at Myrtle Beach and that day I found you in Blackwell and at graduation when I turned you away. I've loved you ever since."

"I know," Coop said and kissed me again. "Come on." He put me back on the ground. "Let's go."

"Where?"

"I don't know. I just want to be free with you in this city. I used to dream about it."

We walked to the bike, and I fit myself on the seat behind him, wrapping my arms around his waist. "I like your dreams better than mine."

The engine roared, and we were off, streaking down the road, nothing but farmland and fiery-topped trees and blue sky ahead of us, a North Carolina beauty that filled me with a sense of home. I looked behind us. Blackwell Tower was still visible far off in the distance. But we were racing away, and it was growing smaller.

I was safe now. All alone with Coop, and he loved me. So I rested my cheek on his back and closed my eyes, allowing myself to remember the final puzzle piece, the last part of the story. Remember it so I could let it go.

I could almost step back to the night, the hour so late after running from Coop's apartment. I was desperate to go home. Still reeling from my confession about my father, and Harvard, and Dr. Garvey; from the way Coop had exploded, yelling at me to *Do something, goddammit, Jessica; he can't get away with it.* All I'd wanted was to stop the night from doing any more damage, to put it to rest.

Bishop Hall had been mercifully empty, everyone out partying for Sweetheart, or because it was Valentine's Day. In the elevator I'd sunk into the corner, letting the walls hold me up, then stumbled out when the doors dinged open, down the hall, and into my suite. It was pitch-black. I tripped over something in the living room, cursing, then pushed open the door to my room and stumbled to my bed. If I was lucky, I wouldn't wake up until a whole century had passed, and I could try my luck with a fresh set of people.

I'd reached for the comforter, then froze. There, in a small ray of moonlight, a surreal vision: torn blond hair, sticky and red, matted against white sheets.

For a second, I'd been dumbfounded. Then, fear made a crack in my heart. I tugged the curtain to let in more light.

And screamed.

Heather. In my bed, blood everywhere.

I staggered back, feeling my legs hit her empty bed. I dropped and stared, still clutching the folder from Student Affairs, the one announcing her victory. Unable to move, my mouth open in a wide O, as if I were silently screaming. I couldn't will a single muscle to move, couldn't process a thought. I sat, and looked, feeling very strangely cold, like my limbs were encased in blocks of ice.

Heather was dead.

As soon as I thought it, she blinked.

I jumped to my feet, another scream lodged in my throat. Her face turned, and she spotted me.

"Jess." Her voice; oh god, her voice was a ruined thing, so raspy and choked I could barely hear it. I could only stare at the gashes across her body, leaking blood, lurid in the moonlight.

Tears sprang to my eyes.

"Help."

I blinked.

"Please...Jess. Help me."

Heather's breath hitched, and—like a slap to the face—I came to.

"*Oh god.* Of course. I'm so sorry, Heather. I'm getting help, I'm going right now."

I spun and dashed for the door, flinging it open, then raced out of the suite. I jammed the elevator button and waited, feeling frantic. I'd go find the administrator on the first floor, the one working the late-night shift. They'd have a phone. They'd call 911.

The elevator doors slid open and I ran inside, pressing the button for the lobby. The elevator started to sink.

I rested my head against the back of the elevator and closed my eyes, seeing my friend laid out bloody in my bed. It was the manifestation of all my darkest thoughts: Heather Shelby, the girl who won everything, who always got what I wanted, begging me for help. Her eyes pleading with me, each breath shallow and gurgling.

The floors ticked back on the elevator screen: *seventeen, sixteen, fifteen.*

Heather, the girl who'd won the fellowship. Who'd stolen my dream. On the edge of dying.

Fourteen, thirteen, twelve.

Everything I'd done to make my father proud, and to redeem him— none of it had ever been good enough.

I'd tried to work hard, do it the right way, but it didn't matter. Either life was unfair, or I was staggeringly unremarkable. Those were the only two options. I couldn't live with either.

Eleven, ten, nine.

And now this insanity. This unexpected horror.

This new twist in the plot.

My insides coiled with rage, grief, and fear. And then I remembered. Amber Van Swann, and the sex tape. Madison, and the test.

Eight, seven, six.

Sometimes, you didn't have to lift a finger. Sometimes, you could do nothing and get exactly what you wanted.

Five, four, three.

Maybe not what you *wanted*. At least not outside your darkest heart of hearts. It wasn't anyone's death you were after—of course not. But the scales evened, the balance restored. The girl who always stole first place, taken off the playing field.

Two.

One.

The elevator dinged, and the doors rolled open.

I walked on hollow legs into the empty lobby and turned toward the administrator's office. It was right there in the corner, door closed, blinds shut, but a light on, visible through the cracks. Then I looked at the front doors. At the dark night waiting outside the glass.

My present self echoed through the memory, calling out a question, soaked in guilt and grief. *What had I done?*

But of course I knew which way my legs had taken me.

I opened my eyes. Coop and I flew down the road, the wind a thousand pinpricks of ice. There it was. The terrible thing I'd done, what I'd spent a decade avoiding and chasing in equal measure. I'd found Heather that night, and I'd left her to die.

I'd been cowardly and selfish, intoxicated and in shock. I knew now that nothing would have saved her by the time I'd found her, but that wasn't the point. The point was, I'd made my choice.

And so finally, the truth had surfaced. The verdict was in. Forget exceptional, or even mediocre. I wasn't close to a good person. Not a murderer, like Mint, but only a few shades better. I could see now that even though I hadn't let myself remember, I'd always been trying to make up for it. Trying to balance the scales.

And maybe I'd actually done it. Look where we were now: Mint, the man who'd killed Heather, who'd betrayed me, dead and exposed to the world. Courtney, the entitled queen, reduced to the wife of a killer, her internet stardom shot to hell, but at least she was getting help. Frankie, who'd stood up to Mint when it counted, a hero, living life with a big imagination. Jack, cleared of all charges, his good name restored. Caro, finally done with us, the people she'd put on a pedestal. I hoped she'd forgive me one day. She was the kind of person who actually might do it. But if she didn't, that was okay, too. In fact, it was probably better.

Coop, the man I loved, finally mine.

In the end, what a Homecoming. What a triumph. For once in my life, everything really had worked out so perfectly.

Coop reached back and squeezed my leg. "I'm just riding," he yelled, "until I run out of gas. Stop me if you see something you like."

I nuzzled closer to him and closed my eyes.

I didn't have a fancy job anymore, or a clean record, or a flawless reputation. I didn't have my dad, or anything close to the dream we'd shared. I'd betrayed my friends, all of them in different ways. But I could let it go.

Because I had someone who loved me, for the good and the bad.

And I had *it* back. I could feel it, building in my chest. The thing I'd been chasing for ten years, the thing that kept pulling me back, time and again, to the past. *Freedom.* Wild, delicious, profound freedom, the whole world uncircumscribed, my whole life ahead of me, newly unfixed. It could be anything.

Coop and I barreled down the road, going nowhere, and there it was, thrumming in my heart, filling my veins, *finally, finally, finally*: the old magic.

I hoped I'd never get what I deserved.

READING GROUP GUIDE

1. Jessica is very determined to prove herself the *most successful* member of the class during Homecoming. Why does she need to prove herself? How do you navigate the dangers of comparing yourself to others, especially people in your graduating class or distant social media friends?

2. Jessica describes Jack as "undeniably *good*" and struggles to think she could ever be good. Do you think there is such thing as a truly good person? Do any of the characters in this book qualify?

3. Jessica's father is not alone in wanting his child to be extraordinary. What are the consequences of placing those kinds of demands on kids? Do you think Jessica is an outlier, or do a lot of otherwise-successful students worry about managing their parents' expectations?

4. Jessica and Coop bond over lacking the privilege their friends all share. Compare their strategies for fitting in without that privilege.

5. The Phi Delta Fraternity of 2008 and the NFL of Frankie's expectations are not supportive places for LGBTQIA+ members. What was your impression of his attempts to navigate those attitudes? What would you do in his position?

6. Jessica and Caro argue about the "girl code" when it comes to leaking the sex tape. How do you feel about the girl code? Do you think they violated it? When?

7. Courtney thinks disdainfully that the East House Seven are all so obsessed with each other that they're practically in love. How does that level of friendship develop throughout the book? Is it healthy?

8. How is the phrase "supposed to be" used as a weapon throughout the book? Whom does it hurt?

9. What consequences would you expect for Dr. Garvey when his affairs came to light? How does tenure work against students in cases like Garvey's?

10. Describe the development of Mint's anger. Was there ever a moment when someone could have intervened? How could he have channeled his anger in a healthier way?

11. Each of the East House Seven carries some form of guilt over Heather's death. Compare the ways they manage that guilt.

Besides the murderer, do you think any of them should be blamed?

12. How did you view Jessica's choice at the end of the book? Where do you see her going?

A CONVERSATION
WITH THE AUTHOR

Jessica's overachieving attitude is so familiar. Do you have any personal strategies for maintaining balance while working toward your goals?

Balance is not something I'm known for, actually. I could probably use some advice from my dear readers on how to reach it. I tend to become consumed by ideas or goals; I expect a lot from myself, and I'm very impatient about next steps, achievements. But I've made peace with this. I am an intense, ambitious woman.

My trick is to allow my obsessions to exist as a hum in the back of my mind, a thing I return to throughout the day when work meetings get dull. It becomes something that pushes me, a fire that fuels me day in and day out, keeping me from burning out. So maybe that means I do have balance, if I've reduced that big, hungry wanting we all feel to a constant hum in my mind? I'm certainly not running around like Jessica, going to wild, destructive lengths to secure the things I want. Even though clearly, I'm capable of imagining those things! I guess my advice is to nurture the flame of your desire, tend to it daily, and become friends with it, so neither of you undermines the other.

Speaking of goals, throughout the book there are many cases of "success" coinciding with "failure." For example, Jessica feels very successful in her consulting career, while knowing that she failed all her specific post-graduate goals. Do you have any examples of failures that ultimately led you to a different kind of success?

I am going to say something bold: I've failed at almost everything I've attempted in my life. At the very least, I've failed to do things the way I expected. In fact, I started writing this book after being crushed by my failure to achieve something I really wanted. This book was born out of failure.

Stewing in grief and anger, I thought to myself, *Why do I feel so frenzied by this disappointment, so desperate?* And what if there was a woman who didn't tamp down those feelings but explored them to their dark ends? And so a villain was born.

The thing about Jessica is, on one hand, she's a privileged woman most people would look at and say, you have so much. You're successful. Part of her recognizes that (and would polish those words like trophies if she heard them). But on the other hand, she's not successful in the ways that are personally meaningful to her. I don't think she's capable of recognizing, at the start of the book, what meaningful success looks like to *her*—not to her dad, or Mint, or the world writ large. It will take her the whole book to do battle with other people's versions of success and discover her own—and by the end, she's done so many terrible things, been so close-minded, that she may not deserve to be successful. I'm leaving the question of what Jessica deserves up to the reader.

If you don't mind me wearing my scholar hat for a moment, one of Jessica's biggest, earliest flaws is that she swallowed the capitalist, patriarchal system wholesale. She's so deeply conditioned by the neoliberal idea of what success means: that she has to be the best at everything; that she has to achieve this uncomplicated, unnuanced version of first place in every aspect of her life in order to be valuable. It's an ugly belief system because it's ultimately about achieving power and dominance over other people; there's no room for give and take. Jessica's fatal flaw is that she saw how bad this belief system treated people like her father and she still subscribed wholeheartedly; in fact, she contorts herself in service of it almost until the end.

Unlike Jessica, I've worked hard to accept that failure is normal, that there's no one right way to be, and that if I tell myself I'm successful, poof! I am. I'm the arbiter of value in my own life. Who else's opinion matters, in the end?

Jessica tries to think of herself and others as "good" or "bad." Do you think people can be just one or the other? Do you think book characters follow the same rules?

I don't think anyone is good or bad—I think we all hold a range of possibilities, and our circumstances tug, seduce, compel, or command certain things out of us. These interactions form patterns of behavior that concretize over time until, often, the way we behave is more a matter of habit.

I think the fact that we can recognize a range of possibilities within ourselves and within one another is the reason we find storytelling so compelling. We want to trace the good in the people we might otherwise call bad, uncover the bad in the people who appear good. We're all hungry to explore our complexities through book characters, so in that way, I do think they follow the same rules (the interesting ones, at least!). The license book characters have is they get to explore the outer limits of our good and bad tendencies, extremes most of us wouldn't be able to get away with. So in that way, reading a book is like watching an experiment unfold: What could happen if I leaned into certain possibilities within myself?

As much fun as it is to watch your characters crumble, you highlight the weight of trauma, insecurity, toxic friendships, and expectations bearing down on them. Do you have any advice for college students, or anyone else, who are trying to manage that weight?

My advice is hard-earned from personal experience, so it might not be right for everyone. With that said, the most important thing I have done is to work on no longer feeling ashamed of myself or anything that's happened to me. That's my advice: let go of shame and guilt. Shame can creep in and manifest as a lot of other things—anxiety, sleeplessness, anger—so take the time to really explore yourself and the weight you're feeling. Look at yourself the way you would a book character, putting together the narrative of your life and thinking about the many events that have shaped you, shaped your desires and your actions, good and bad. See yourself in your complexity, and then give yourself the grace and forgiveness you would give any interesting, complex character.

For anyone struggling with sexual trauma, allow yourself to feel the way you feel. Don't get tamped down or hushed up by the world. Be full of rage, if you are full of rage. Allow yourself time to stop the world if you need to. Know you are loved in the full complexity of who you are and that you are not alone.

The best thing I discovered in college was that I had access to free counseling. (This is true of grad school, too.) What a gift. Talking to someone else about how you're feeling is healing.

When all your characters have secrets, how do you get to know them? Did you have their failures and alibis mapped out before you began writing, or did you figure out their roles as you went?

Ah, people's secrets are the best way to get to know them! That's actually how I dove into each of my characters—I went right for the jugular. I do a ton of character and relationship mapping before writing any book, and especially for this one. I wrote pages about who each character was—not just the surface stuff but, more importantly, how they saw themselves, what they wanted in their heart of hearts, what stood in the way of getting what they wanted, and what, if taken from them, would make their lives crumble. Then I mapped their relationships with each other (Jessica and Mint; Mint and Caro; Frankie and Coop; etc.) and particularly with Heather. I was looking to understand how Heather could threaten each of them in ways that would make them plausible suspects, so she had to be connected to what they most wanted and were most afraid to lose.

Once I feel like I know what makes my characters tick, then I turn to plot. The plot grows logically and usually organically out of characters' worst fears and deepest desires, and how those things interplay. And yes—I keep a very meticulous account of alibis and timelines! I actually overwrite those parts for myself beforehand, so I go into writing each scene knowing more than what's explicitly on the page. Hopefully it contributes to a larger mood and tension.

How did you keep everything—the repressed memories, the motivations, the insecurities—straight once you figured them out?

I devoted a lot of time to imagining who each character was and how they felt about each other and themselves, so I felt like I knew my characters inside out. By the time I started writing *In My Dreams I Hold a Knife*, it was almost like they were friends whose stories I'd absorbed. After my pre-writing, I wrote an extremely meticulous outline, chapter by chapter, where I color-coded the different storylines so I could literally visualize the plots weaving together.

There's a lot of darkness in this book. If you could shield a single character from the secrets and horror, who would it be?

You know, Amber Van Swann didn't deserve an ounce of what happened to her. Neither did Heather, of course, though she wasn't the easiest person to get along with, either. I'd shield those two. Everyone else either bought their trouble or needed a wake-up call.

What draws you to psychological thrillers as a writer? As a reader?

When I pick up a psychological thriller as a reader, I'm asking it for one thing: Tell me who I am—the parts I haven't figured out yet for myself. Of course, I'm reading for all the other things, too: getting hooked by a mystery and feeling that burning desire to uncover the answers, the pleasure of being surprised, the beauty of urgent language and the thrill of swift pacing. But it's that hunger to see characters react to dark, thrilling, high-stakes, emotionally packed events that really draws me. What would I do? What parts of the character resonate or repel me? Even better, what does the book say not just about me as an individual but the larger we?

As a writer, I'm drawn to the genre for a reason that's both simpler and harder to describe: I write psychological thrillers when I have a hunger to tell. When there's something burning inside me and I feel an almost obsessive urgency to get it on the page. To me, it's a genre of confession, and I tend to write hunched over, breathing faster, heart pounding. Writing psychological thrillers is like falling under a spell that won't be broken until I get the truth down on the page.

Do you have a writing routine? How do you get to the page and put together an entire novel?

I'm the queen of routines. I love them. I write in the exact same spot every day, with the exact same rhythms. I am not a spontaneous creature! But I think it helps my productivity. I try to write as much as humanly possible every day, so I fit in writing after pouring my first cup of coffee in the morning and before starting my other work. As soon as the work day is over, I switch back over to my novel, and then the evening hours fly by until it's time for wine (and hopefully my husband is making dinner). Usually I'm able to pull myself out of my fictional world to at least eat, but then it's right back to writing until my eyes glaze over and I drag myself to bed. Luckily, at that point, I usually get a second wind that lets me read in bed—my favorite thing in the world.

What are you reading these days?

This will be a time capsule, because I'm a voracious reader and go through about two to three books a week, across genres. Right now, it's *You Exist Too Much* by Zaina Arafat, *Exciting Times* by Naoise Dolan, *Garden Spells* by Sarah Addison Allen, and *More Than Just a Pretty Face* by Syed Masood. All excellent. But my constants are poetry: on any given week, you can find me re-reading *Crush* by Richard Siken and *American Sonnets for My Past and Future Assassin* by Terrance Hayes. Siken and Hayes slay me.

ACKNOWLEDGMENTS

First, thanks are due to my brilliant editor, Shana Drehs, for connecting with this book and making it better through her insight—and for being such a lovely person and a joy to work with. Thanks also to my talented, gracious Sourcebooks team: Jessica Thelander, Diane Dannenfeldt, Sara B. Walker, Heather VenHuizen, Hannah Strassburger, Ashley Holstrom, and Holli Roach. Molly Waxman and Cristina Arreola, you are the greatest marketing partners an author could have.

To my agent, Melissa Edwards: thank you for being my champion and advocate. You also made this book stronger through your insight, as you do every book. It means the world to have you in my corner.

Thank you to my amazing film/TV agent, Addison Duffy, for seeing potential in this book. I'm excited to do great things together.

Dana Kaye, Julia Borcherts, Hailey Dezort, Nicole Leimbach, and Angela Melamud, I am so grateful for your publicity wizardry. You are amazing partners and wonderful humans.

Thank you to the incredible writers who read early drafts and helped steer me. Ann Fraistat is a joy on top of being a gifted writer and critique partner. Lyssa Smith is human sunshine whose feedback not only made this book stronger but made me feel it was worth believing in. And Maria Dong, who picked me up off the floor and brushed off my shoulders and sent me marching back to work: thank you for helping me think through the idea for this book, for encouraging me to write it, and for being an incredible editor and friend. Ann, Lyssa, and Maria, I can't wait to hold all of your books in my hands.

Thank you so much to Jon Reyes at Tessera Editorial for his keen insight, wonderful editorial eye, and overall graciousness.

Thank you to Pitch Wars for giving me the opportunity to learn from Lindsey Frydman and Katie Beers. Lindsey and Katie, you gave me your time, care, wisdom, and support, and in the process made me a much better writer.

To Lisa Siraganian, my dissertation chair: I can't tell you the impact you've had on my brain. You've made me a better thinker and writer, and you will forever be the person I look up to most. To Katharine Boswell: You are a stunning writer and scholar, and becoming friends with you changed not just my work but me, for the better. All my books are for you.

To Ashley O'Brien, Madeleine Hook, Maggie Winterfeldt Clark, Sarah Parker, and Anastasia Pawlicki, thank you for being my best friends and supporting my writing dreams, even when young me forced you to stop doing cooler things to listen to my terrible short stories. So much of who I am was shaped by you.

Thank you to my brilliant colleagues. The fact that you've always supported my writing is a gift, and I'm grateful to call you friends as well as co-workers: Hannah Sawyer, Helen Spencer, Leila Walsh, Stephanie Getman, David Hebert, Evan Mintz, Rhiannon Collette, Jennifer Sizemore, Jeff Cohen, Jennifer Reyes, Adrienne Faraci, James Cadogan,

Stephanie Akhter, Jeremy Travis, Sebastian Johnson, Julie James, Asheley Van Ness, and Catie Bialick (shout-out, Winsteadies!).

To my amazing siblings: I'm so grateful to have had you as built-in best friends my whole life. Thank you for bearing the brunt of my imagination growing up. Despite my interference, you grew into people I am so proud of. Mallory Winstead, you are my ride-or-die and the artist I admire most. Ryan Winstead, you are a wonderful brother and friend; the moment you told me you liked this book was the moment I thought it could be something. Taylor Winstead, text me back. Just kidding. You have always been the cool one; I cherish the fact that underneath that coolness is a boy who geeked out over fantasy novels with me growing up. I love you all.

To my uncle Russell Graves, who has had such a loving and important influence on my life: You were the first person to tell me I was an artist. Thank you for seeing and loving me. The feeling is mutual.

Melissa and Ron Winstead—Mom and Dad—thank you for a lifetime of love and support. There's not enough space to detail how wonderful it is to belong to you or how lucky I feel. Thank you for being on this journey with me and for being my biggest champions. Also, I did it! So it turns out you were right.

To my grandma Marsha Rodman: I wish you could have read this. I know we could have talked books together. I'll love you forever.

Last, thanks to my husband, Alex Sobey. This book would not exist without you. I would not exist without you, at least the person I am today. You and I grew up together, and our roots are tangled. No matter how many books I'm lucky enough to write, our love story will always be my magnum opus.

ABOUT THE AUTHOR

Ashley Winstead writes about power, ambition, complicity, and love in the modern age. In addition, she's a painter and former academic. She received her BA in English, creative writing, and art history from Vanderbilt University and her PhD in English from Southern Methodist University, where she studied twenty-first century fiction, philosophy of language, and the politics of narrative forms. Her academic essays have been published in *Studies in the Novel* and *Science Fiction Studies*. She currently lives in Houston, Texas, with her husband and two cats. This is her first novel. Find out more at ashleywinstead.com.